Snowflake

by Heide Goody and Iain Grant

Pigeon Park Press

Published by Pigeon Park Press
www.pigeonparkpress.com

Chapter 1

There's a lot of different ways to get dumped.

I've been dumped in person, like when Leo Bickers in year five told me he preferred *Yu-Gi-Oh* cards to kissing girls. I've been dumped by text, too many times: 'It's not you it's me', 'Get a grip and grow up', 'I forgot to tell you I'm married, soz'. (You know, the usual.) And I've been dumped by letter. Gareth, who I thought was going to be my Mr Perfect, wrote me the sweetest letter. I've still got it somewhere.

But I reckon very few people have been dumped by letter, by their parents.

And it had started out as such a lovely day.

Coming home after a trip, there's nothing like it, is there? I'd been travelling since the transfer bus picked us up outside the Akrogiali Resort at five in the morning (that's five in the morning *Greek* time) and my heart lifted when the taxi finally pulled up at home. The streets of suburban England are dark compared to the wide streets and whitewashed buildings of Crete, but I'd really missed the trees. Funny that. You don't realise how many trees there are in Britain, even in the cities, until you go and visit one of the browner bits of the world. Trees lined the streets of home like a guard of honour to greet me.

It takes a fortnight away to make you really appreciate what matters in life: the trees, my own bed, home-cooked food, and someone to pay the taxi for me. I know I should have kept some money back, but I got caught up in the holiday mood. I just had to give the lads at the Ikarus Bar a special tip on my last night. I also gave an extra ten euro note to Bemus, the poor little boy who sat outside the Akrogiali every day. And I had to buy some souvenirs. Had to.

The fine Greek sausage and bottles of raki were in my bag. The pendant I'd bought hung around my neck and Gida the goat sat on my lap in the taxi, just like she did on the plane. Would you believe that a wickerwork goat is just the wrong size to fit inside the overhead locker? Mind you, there was an awful woman sitting next to me on my flight. She complained about me to the cabin crew, saying that Gida was shedding twigs on her skirt and then she said that my bag smelled disgusting. I had to get my sausage out to show her that it was, in fact, a delicacy she was talking about.

"It's called *loukaniko sapio* or something," I told her. "It was the last one in the shop."

"It's off," she had the gall to tell me. "Nothing that smells like a roadie's armpit is fit for human consumption."

I explained to her that some of the world's most sophisticated and sought-after foods are challenging to the immature palate, but halfway through my educational description (I'd read a Buzzfeed article about smelly foods) of how Alaskan stinkheads are prepared by burying salmon heads until they ferment, she ran for the toilets.

Back home now, the taxi driver fetched my bag out of the boot. His expression as he caught a whiff of the sausage reminded me of the woman on the plane. I kept my mouth shut this time and pretended I couldn't smell anything.

"I'll pop my bag inside and pay you in just a minute," I said to him. He sat back down in the driver's seat.

I put my key in the lock but it wouldn't fit. This happens sometimes, particularly since that time I used my key to open a tin of tuna (it was an emergency; the stray cat in the garden looked really hungry). No worries, I'd use the spare key. There's a stone in the front garden that's a different colour to all the rest.

I lifted the stone and groped underneath. No key? There was something in its place though, an envelope.

Lori

It was addressed to me. Well I love post as much as the next person, but I needed to get inside, so I thumped the door as I took out the letter and read it.

Lori,
You know how we always talked about down-sizing and moving off grid once you and Adam were old enough? Well, we've gone and done it. You'll notice that the locks have been changed. We promised Mrs Llewellyn we'd do that when we moved out.

I mouthed those words again, testing their meaning. I tried them out loud. "Moved out?" I stared up at the door. Blue gloss paint with scratches around the lock. It looked the same. I stepped back. The whole house looked the same. I thumped the door again and read on.

We've thought long and hard about this, and done some real soul-searching, and decided that now was the right time both for us and for you.

I'm sure this has come as a bit of a surprise but it's an exciting surprise, isn't it?

We've hardly been able to contain ourselves. This is such an opportunity, as much for you as it is for us. We didn't want to tell you about it at the time because you might have got cold feet (do you remember that time when you refused to go on stage at the ballet recital?). We didn't want you to worry and we didn't want you causing a scene by trying to change our minds.

Look at this as your big chance. We spoke to Adam. As you know, he's away on his lecture tour of the States. He's said you can stay at his flat on Silver Street for a few days while you look for your own place. We've had all your things sent over there. Don't worry. We've not binned anything. The combination to the key safe is Nanna Shap's birthday.

We have provided a little something extra for you though. We had a word with Pat and Dom. They said that the job at the museum really worked out for Melissa —

"Cookie," I said out loud, shaking my head.

"Pardon?" said a man passing by on the pavement.

"I was just saying, 'Cookie'. No one calls her Melissa. Not even her parents."

"She's not in," said the man.

"Cookie?"

"Mrs Llewellyn," said the man, pointing at the house.

He was a handsome if intense looking fellow not much older than me. Having said that, he was wearing corduroy trousers and a

5

tweedy looking jacket so it was sort of like he was an elderly-gent-in-training.

I carried on reading.

— really worked out for Melissa and the application forms are all on-line so we filled one out for you. We couldn't remember if you got a D or an E at GCSE Maths, so we played it safe and put you down as a C. Your interview is at 5 pm on the seventeenth. That is the day you get back, isn't it? The interview is with a Mr Rex McCloud at the big museum and gallery. Wear something nice!

Knock 'em dead, sunbeam

Mom and Dad xxx

There was no address on the letter – not at the top, not at the bottom, not on the back of the envelope. They'd left me and not told me where they'd gone.

"This is terrible," I said.

"Can I help?" said the man. He was still standing there on the pavement.

"I'm looking for my parents," I said.

"They don't live there," he pointed out.

"I *know*," I said, shaking the letter at him. "I *can* read."

He gave me a firm stare. Yes, a very intense looking fellow. It was probably the eyebrows that did it. He had dark hair: a thick comma of it hung over his right eye, nearly down to his eyebrow. Those eyebrows were so thick and dark, I couldn't decide if they were brooding and masculine eyebrows or bushy, don't-trust-me-I'm-a-werewolf eyebrows. Fifty percent James Bond, fifty percent wolfman: secret agent wolfman, in corduroy.

"Ah," he said, suddenly understanding. "You mean the previous occupants. The Belkins."

I didn't like the idea of myself or my parents being referred to as previous occupants. I was still grieving.

"You know my parents?"

"No. I just know they cancelled their papers," he said, which was an odd thing to say. "Have you tried phoning them?"

"Of course, I've tried. Hang on." I pulled out my phone and dialled my mom's mobile number. It made a funny noise. I looked at the screen.

"What does number unobtainable mean?" I said.

"Apart from meaning the number can't be obtained?" he asked. "It might just mean they're somewhere without a signal."

"Oh, God. They've moved to Africa!"

"Or, for example, Wales," he offered. "Anyway, I'm sure you'll get through eventually."

Shaking my head, I turned away and got back into the taxi. My mind was reeling. It was unthinkable that my parents would abandon me. How could they do this after twenty-five years of caring for me?

"Change of plan," I said to the driver. "I need you to take me to my parents please."

I settled back. He seemed to take a long time to get going. I don't know much about driving, but isn't it just check your mirrors and go?

"Where's that then?" he said.

"Sorry?"

"Where do they live?" he asked.

"I don't know where they live, that's why I need you to take me," I said. "You did The Knowledge, right?"

"It doesn't work that way," he said. "I need an address."

I spoke to him soothingly. I could see that he lacked confidence in his abilities. "What's your name?"

"Jed."

"I think you can do it, Jed. Taxi drivers must get requests like this all the time. You're renowned for getting people to the right place. Concentrate, will you? Now my mom, she's about my height, brown hair in a pony tail. She colours it but you can't tell. She likes decoupage, watches *Midsomer Murders,* and does yoga on Wednesdays and Fridays. My dad's a bit taller, but short for a man. He's going thin on top. He wears a lot of outdoorsy stuff, North Face and that sort of thing, but he spends more time reading about the great outdoors than –"

"I can't find your parents without an address. I really can't," said Jed.

I was disappointed in his attitude, but he wasn't budging.

"Well we need to go somewhere," I said. The man wasn't going to get paid without some parental intervention. I'd maxed out my overdraft in Crete and the cash machines weren't paying out to Ms Belkin right now. "Let's go to the paper shop and ask Mr Patel where they are."

"What's the address?" asked Jed.

"Oh, it's just down there, you can see it. Drive slowly though, I need time to think."

Chapter 2

My parents moved house without telling me. Kicked out of my own home at the tender age of twenty-five. I sat back in the taxi and wondered what all this meant. I mean, it's not normal, is it?

That meant they'd been in my room and touched all my things! Isn't there a human right that says they're not allowed to do that? I read this article once that said a landlord has to give you twenty-four hours notice before entering your property. I had rights, didn't I?

I'd never lived anywhere else, and I had no idea what to do next. I thought about my room. What if the new occupant decided to redecorate? She was sure to get rid of the freehand unicorn border that I added. Dad said they looked like pole dancing horses. I was more shocked that he knew what pole dancing was than by his criticism of my art. Dad doesn't always understand my art. He calls it 'doodling'. I don't think he's being deliberately offensive.

My fingers went to the pendant I'd bought in Crete that hung around my neck. It was a heavy red stone – some sort of onyx I think – with a white cameo carving on the top of a man kneeling in adoration before a woman on a pedestal. I hadn't really considered the image properly before; I had just liked the shape and colour of the whole thing and the guy selling it really wanted me to have it. I suppose the woman in the cameo looked a little like me, although her figure would probably be described as statuesque (mine was, at best, thin and shapeless) and her hair fell in bouncing tresses (unlike my wild frizz). Comparing myself to some ancient Greek figure and finding I came up short did little to lift my mood.

I took out my notebook and sketched a little. I drew Florrie, my cartoon alter ego (definitely a thin and shapeless figure with wild frizzy hair) standing in an empty void, homeless and all alone. I added a black cloud above her head. I sketched out another panel of two wicked, sharp-toothed parents, carrying suitcases stuffed with cash and walking towards a waiting jumbo jet.

Jed gave a small cough. We were parked outside the corner shop.

9

I sighed and got out. "Let me talk to Mr Patel, I'll be right back."

"It's still on the meter," he said.

I always feel like a dwarf in Mr Patel's shop. He has this counter that's so high up, you get a crick in your neck when you talk to him. I'm guessing someone once told him that people buy more of the things that are at eye level, so he's made sure that all the sweets, lottery cards and weird natural highs are right in your face.

"I need your help," I said to him.

"Yes?" he said.

"I'm Lori Belkin, Mr Patel. I need to know where you're delivering the papers for my parents now." I gave him my best smile.

He looked down at me from his eyrie. "I am not Mr Patel," he said and tapped a lapel badge that said 'Hi, I'm Norman' above, in a smaller font, 'Small business owners – we do it on your doorstep.'

"Where's Mr Patel?" I asked.

"He went back to Wolverhampton, I think."

"I've only been away two weeks and everything changes."

"The Patels sold this place seven years ago."

Oh. Can I help it if I don't notice things that happen way above my head?

"Right," I said. "Well, where are my parents?"

"It is not a simple matter for me to share information about my customers," he said. "Data Protection Act. Even if the law of the land permitted it, which it does not, I would hesitate, because I have seen so many problems arise from idle tittle-tattle."

"No, it's not idle tittle-tattle, they're my parents," I said.

"It matters not, Miss Belkin. Tittle-tattle ruins lives. Take for example a customer of mine who enjoys the world of model building. I shall not speak his name, but you will know him immediately when I tell you that he walks with such silent purpose that you might imagine he is building a terminator in his lounge. Now, if I were to tell you that as well as *The Modeller* magazine, he also has on order the men's magazine *Razzle*, you might not be shocked. But those other fellows from the model club, perhaps they would be? Friendships ruined and reputations in tatters."

"Yes, I'm not planning on ruining any friendships or whatever. I just need an address."

"Ah," he said, with the sound of a sage old Yoda figure about to dispense some wisdom, "but from little seeds mighty oaks do grow. I give you an address, it's only the thin end of the wedge. Say I was to tell you that a local lady – obviously, I can mention no names, but you'll know her hanging baskets – say I was to mention that her newspaper order has recently been amended." Norman tapped the side of his nose. "She's always had the *BBC Good Food* magazine, as you probably know, but last month, she added *Fine Woodworking* and *Garden News*. You don't need me to tell you what that means! Even the dullest of wits might infer that you-know-who has moved in with her. After that business he had with the fraud squad, I thought we'd seen the last of him."

I was keen to bring him back round to the subject of my parents. "The Evening Mail is all that my parents have delivered," I said, "so can you tell me where you're delivering it now?"

"Client confidentiality is the cornerstone of my profession. I am like a priest, a guardian of secrets and personal privacy."

I was deflated. "You can't help me find them?"

"My lips are sealed."

"But there's been a mix up and I need to find them urgently."

"My sympathies." Norman shook his head in sorrow. "You could always put a card in the window. Though my confidence is a sacred bond, others might be willing to help you."

I looked across at the window where postcards were stuck in uneven rows. I always enjoyed reading them. I knew without looking that there was one trying to sell a boy's bike for seventy pounds (it had been there for months as nobody was ever going to pay that much), one that offered a greenhouse free to anyone who was brave enough to dismantle it and one that offered reiki massage in the comfort of your own home. I had no idea what a reiki was or why it might want massaging.

"Fine, I'll do that. Have you got a pen?"

Norman handed me a pen.

"And have you got a card?"

He looked at me. "People normally provide their own cards. I need to think about my overheads."

"Is that a no then?"

He sighed wearily. "Perhaps you can re-use one of the old ones," he said handing me a pile from the side of the window. I smiled at him and turned one over. I hovered with the pen for a moment while I thought about how I could convey how important this was.

"Have you got any more pens, Norman? Maybe some coloured felt tips?"

"No."

In an effort to do the best job with limited materials, I dug out my sketching pencil from my bag. I drew large, bulbous exclamation marks on the left and right sides of the card. I went over the lines and then shaded them carefully so that they really stood out. In between these two sentinels, I wrote my plea:

Wanted URGENTLY! Information leading to the discovery of local missing persons formerly of Grosvenor Road. Call for details. Small Reward Possible.

I added my phone number and handed the card to Norman.

"It's a pound for the week," he said.

I patted my pockets. "I'll drop that round to you a bit later."

He scowled but he put the card in the window.

A thought crossed my mind. "If I'm going to owe you a pound, could I round it up a bit?"

He turned and looked at me with his eyebrows raised.

"I was thinking we could round it up to, say, fifty. Lend me another forty-nine pounds and I'll get it back to you as soon as I can. I need to pay this taxi driver, you see."

He took a deep breath and stared at the ceiling for a few seconds before replying. "I try to avoid swearing in the presence of ladies, but for you I might make an exception. Get out of here and do not come back unless it is to bring me my pound, do you hear?"

I made my exit and approached Jed who sat in his taxi by the kerb. I braced myself for another challenging conversation.

"Jed, are you someone who is motivated purely by money?" I asked.

He gave the question a moment's thought. "Yeah, pretty much."

I was hoping that he might be slightly more open-minded. "Have you ever thought that there might be more important things?"

"Like what?" he asked.

"Oh, I don't know. The simple enjoyment that comes from being out and about on a lovely day like this?"

Jed looked sceptically at the sky, which was a discouraging shade of pewter.

I tried again. "How about the pleasure of someone's company? I know that I've enjoyed our time together today."

"The bit I always look forward to is the part where you pay me," said Jed, his eyes narrowing with suspicion. "Are you saying that you haven't got the money or something?"

"Well that depends."

"On what?" he asked.

"On whether you mean actual cash. I can offer you payment in some amazing sausage that you can't even buy in this country, how about that? You can't have all of it, obviously, but –"

He started to shout at me then, which was a little unnecessary when I was trying to be reasonable.

"If you mean the stuff that's made my cab smell like tramps' feet then you've got to be out of your mind!" He got out and slammed his door. He kept shouting as he stomped round to the boot. "If a fare doesn't pay, then I'd normally hang onto their bag until they bring me the money, but it's going to take hours before that stink goes. There aren't enough air fresheners in the world to cover up that horrible smell."

"It's not a smell. It's a fragrance. Bold but beautiful."

He opened the boot and took out my bag. He wasn't very careful about how he put it down on the pavement and it popped open. I was slightly mortified by the sight of my unwashed smalls spilling out, but Jed put his arm over his face as a fresh waft of the *loukaniko sapio* sausage smell was unleashed. He hurried round to his door muttering about me being blacklisted and then drove off.

13

He stopped twenty yards down the road. My heart rose. He'd changed his mind; he couldn't leave a fare in distress. It was probably against his cabbie's oath or something.

He got out, opened the back door, took out the wickerwork Gida the goat and hurled it at me before getting back in and squealing away.

I'll say one thing. I didn't know goats were that aerodynamic or that cabbies had such good aim.

Chapter 3

It took me an hour and a half to walk to my brother's flat, four miles from my house – my old house – and in that nice bit near St Paul's, just north of the city centre. I'd used some of my t-shirts to tie the wickerwork goat onto the handle of my case. A nice lady pressed fifty pence into my hand as I went through the underpass at Smallbrook Queensway, but most people gave me a wide berth and unpleasant looks. It might have been because a stone got stuck in the wheel of my case so it made a noise like a pneumatic drill as I wheeled it along. Or perhaps it was the sausage; the heat of the day was really enhancing its presence.

There had been no food on the plane that morning and I was getting kind of hungry. I nipped into a Tesco Express on my marathon walk and, after much shelf scouring to find what fifty pee would buy, purchased a croissant in the reduced section to munch on as I continued my trek.

I found Adam's flat without any trouble, even though I hadn't been round there for ages, (we really haven't seen much of each other since he became Mr International Adventurer and After-Dinner Speaker). The flat was inside a redeveloped factory on Silver Street. Lots of exposed brickwork and interesting old metalwork painted green. I went in through the lobby and up to his flat. The key safe was at the side of the door. There was one of those combination locks on it, with four wheels that needed to be on the right numbers. Nanna Shap's birthday. Did that mean it would be the year of her birth or the month and the day? If it was the month and the day would Adam have put it in the American format? How many goes would I need to get it right and would an alarm sound if I got it wrong? I tried 2604 and, amazingly, the little compartment sprung open, revealing the key. I unlocked the flat and stepped inside.

I kicked off my shoes with an enormous groan of relief and had a look round. I started in his lounge, which was quite large. It was all decorated in mushroomy shades of brown but there was a plush rug that felt really good on my bare feet. I then spotted the most enormous television. It was so big that I thought it was the actual wall. It looked a bit like the ones that they have in shops that you can only really watch from twenty feet away. I was prepared to give it a go though, as the leather sofas looked pretty good for lounging on. I moved over to look at the shelves on the opposite wall. There were books and DVDs on the lower shelves, but I wasn't sure what to make of the pile of rubble on the top shelf. My brother's such a neat freak that it surprised me to see mess like that. I tapped the wall to see if maybe bits of plaster had come loose. I didn't have time to solve that particular mystery right now though, I wanted to check out the kitchen. I was in serious need of something to eat.

The kitchen had only a small window and was in relative gloom. I looked for a light switch but there wasn't one where any sensible person would put one.

"Lights, lights," I muttered to myself as I searched for a switch.

The spotlights over the swanky breakfast bar came on.

"What the hell happened there?" I said.

"Did you not want me to turn on the lights?" said a black cylinder on the kitchen counter. A blue strip on its side lit up as it spoke.

"Are you a robot?" I asked.

"I am Lexi," said the box. "How can I help you?"

"Find me some food."

"There are five local restaurants on your favourites list."

"That's not what I meant," I said as I started opening cupboards looking for food. I really wasn't sure what to make of the weird boxes and packages. I had no idea what tahini was. Or dulse flakes. I picked up a box.

"How do you even pronounce this?" I said.

"This," said Lexi.

"It says 'quinoa'," I said.

"It is pronounced '*keen-wah*,'" said Lexi.

"You sure? You've hardly used any of the actual letters."

I pushed things around, looking for something I recognised. I wondered how a cinnamon stick might taste, but it didn't look all that good once out of the jar. It was more 'stick' than anything else.

Eventually, I found some muesli. I'm more of a Coco Pops girl myself, but at last I'd found something edible, although with a name like *Wild Seeds* I was prepared for it to be heavy on healthy goodness and light on taste. I tipped some into a bowl and then it crossed my mind that there wouldn't be any milk. I really was past caring though, so I added some water from the tap and sat down to enjoy. It was hard going. It had lots and lots of tiny seeds in it that got stuck in my teeth. They were so hard that I was a bit nervous of biting down on them. They were like those silver balls you decorate cakes with but *even harder*. I never knew such a thing was possible. I couldn't ever imagine eating this stuff for pleasure. I began to wonder if my brother had some sort of digestive disorder.

Hunger (and toothache) is a great motivator and, nearing the bottom of the bowl, I had a brainwave.

I poured the rest of the muesli down the sink and went in search of my things. My brainwave? I keep my inking pens in a Celebrations Christmas tub. It was from a couple of Christmases ago, but it still contained all of the miniature Bounties because nobody in our family likes them. That includes me of course, but at this point, I was prepared to overlook the gritty coconut texture and the very thought of chocolate made my mouth water.

I found a pile of boxes in the smallest of the three bedrooms. Each box was labelled: *Lori clothes, Lori desk, Lori shelves* and so on. I stood and stared for a minute. I don't know what I'd been expecting, but as a summary of my life so far it didn't speak of world-conquering success. I realised that I had foolishly been expecting to see the furniture from my old bedroom with my things still inside. My stomach rumbled (was that hunger or *Wild Seeds* making their way through my insides like an army of gritty little stormtroopers?). It crossed my mind that I could have sold my old furniture and bought food with the money. I started to examine my things – perhaps there was something here I could sell? The most obvious candidate was the rocking horse that stood alongside the boxes. I feared that its resale value might have been reduced by the drawings on the side. Guess how they got there? I'd been experimenting with sensory deprivation as a stimulus for creative thought and I just forgot it was there after I put the blindfold on. You live and learn. I pulled some things out of boxes, and realised that this could turn into action-replays of all the classic doofus Lori moments. I sat Gida the goat down next to the rocking horse.

"Check this out, guys! I know you two are going to be the best of friends, but you need to know what you're getting into, now that you're my only family."

I held up a printed certificate. "See this? I won the Gifted and Talented in Art award in year ten at school. You're probably wondering why it's got a rude picture of my art teacher Mrs McGee? Look, you can tell it's her because I've helpfully labelled her 'Mrs McGee', see? Well, it just seemed like a funny idea. We always said that she was half woman, half wildebeest. Nobody told me that we were supposed to pose for photographs showing our certificates afterwards."

I turned it face down with a sigh, remembering my parents' disappointment when I told them why my picture wasn't in the newspaper with the other winners.

"This – ah!" I paused in my reminiscences as I spotted the Celebrations tub. I hauled it out. I counted seven mini Bounties among the pens. I unwrapped one and munched it ravenously. I shuddered at the desiccated coconut (it's like sand and sugar had an unholy baby and some idiot had said, 'people will really enjoy getting this stuff stuck between their teeth.') but swallowed it down anyway.

On with the trip down memory lane: I held up a table tennis bat. "Exhibit two," I said to Gida and the rocking horse. "In my defence, the shape of this bat is a dead ringer for Mutt 'potato head', who ran the youth club. I did it for a dare, and everyone said it looked just like him. See how red the rubber is? Well his face went the exact same shade when he saw what I'd done."

I pulled out some drawings with some early incarnations of Florrie. It gave me a jolt to see how long she'd been with me.

"Say hello to Florrie," I said to the horse and the goat, holding up a picture. "She's the viral internet cartoon hero that the world hasn't quite discovered yet, but trust me, they will."

I paused. One of the Florrie pictures had the Eiffel Tower in the background. I'd been experimenting to see how Florrie liked France. Gareth and I had been a couple for eighteen months when he moved there. He wanted me to go with him. He kept telling me that Angoulême is the French capital city for cartoons. That's all well and good but, did you know, you can't get HP sauce or custard creams in France? They don't even have Greggs. What was he thinking?

I laughed out loud when I turned over the next piece of paper. It was a collage made up from pictures out of magazines. I remembered my mom hitting the roof when she found all the holes in her *Hello* magazine, as she hadn't finished reading it and I'd destroyed Jason Statham's dream kitchen or something. I'd been creating a photofit of the ideal man. My fingers traced Robert Pattinson's eyes and Ashton Kutcher's smile. I'd blended in Channing Tatum's jawline too and, I think, James Franco's ears. I tried to recall what had made me do it, but it's hard to imagine what I was like ten years ago. I've moved on since I was a lovesick teenager, thank goodness.

"What do you think guys?" I asked my audience. "Hot stuff, huh? The question is, does this belong in the portfolio of a serious artist?"

"I will need more information," said the black cylinder on the bedside cabinet.

"Shit!" I exclaimed in surprise. "How did you get in here?"

"I don't understand the question," said the Lexi thing.

"You have legs or something?"

"Let me check. The phrase 'have legs' means that something, such as a news story, will create long-lasting interest. Does that help?"

I just stared at the box and then silently returned my gaze to Gida and the horse. I showed them the picture silently. They gave me a firm though equally silent 'no' so I moved the picture onto the separate pile to throw away. It threatened to slide off the uneven heap of old bus tickets, bounty wrappers and notes, so I popped my Greek pendant on top to hold it in place.

"Off you go, handsome!" He wasn't going to win me round with that cheeky smile, but I pointed and gave him a wink, for old times' sake.

I stood up to stretch my legs and wandered into the bathroom. It was all sparkling glass and slate tiles. There was yet another Lexi thing on the window shelf so I decided to keep my mouth shut. I huffed on the mirror and drew a smiley face just to make the place look a bit less like a showroom. I smiled and remembered a story in the paper where a kid had used the toilet in a fancy shop bathroom display and it took the staff four days to find out where the funny smell was coming from. Four days! I felt sympathy for the kid. This room *looked* like a bathroom, but it somehow didn't look as if I was supposed to use it. Something on the edge of the mirror caught my eye. A little button with the cute puppy logo for Andrex toilet paper. Was it some sort of fancy dispenser? I pressed the button and watched the toilet paper but it didn't move. Maybe Adam had one of those sentient Japanese toilets that washes and dries your backside. I pressed it again and the toilet did nothing. I swivelled the toilet paper holder a little bit in case it was stuck and pressed the button a few more times.

My phone buzzed. It was my brother on video call.

"Hi, bro," I said.

"I see you've arrived," he said.

Jesus! My head swivelled in a panic. Did he have cameras in here? "What? You're watching me?"

"Relax," he laughed. "I can see a spike in the power usage from my smart meter app. You've got all the lights on, haven't you?"

I was already on the back foot. Adam can always make me feel like a nine-year-old who's just put felt-tip lipstick and eye shadow on his action man. I put a hand over the phone and turned to the Lexi box.

"Turn all the lights off," I whispered.

"I didn't quite hear that," said Lexi.

"Turn all the lights off, bitch."

"Is everything all right?" said Adam.

"Perfectly fine," I said, stepping out of the bathroom. "Just getting used to your robot house."

He laughed. He was wearing a suit jacket and a loose shirt. He appeared to be in a hotel lobby or maybe a convention centre. He was lightly tanned. He looked very much at home.

"Lori, you're welcome to use the place as your own for a while," said Adam. "Don't get paranoid that I'm monitoring you or anything."

"Just because you're paranoid doesn't mean they aren't after you," I said.

He laughed again. That's a lot of laughing. He'd probably been in America too long.

"I've installed a few smart home gadgets, that's all," he said. "It will give you a chance to think about your environmental impact."

Distracted, I stumbled into something in the lounge that fell and smashed on the floor.

"What was that?" asked Adam.

"Nothing! I was agreeing about my environmental impact," I said.

"That's just an example, Lori," said Adam. "I guess that this thing with Mom and Dad moving out will give you some thinking time. You've got a chance now to make your own way in the world and understand your part in it."

"I already had a part in the world," I said. "I had the upstairs bedroom at home. Do you know where they've gone?"

If it had just been a regular phone call, he might have got away with saying nothing. But I could see that pursed look on his face.

"You know!" I said. "I've got to find them."

He looked uncomfortable. "Look, Lori, they've done this for a reason. They've done it because they love you. Buckle down and show them that you can sort yourself out. We can see about letting you pop round to visit them if it looks as if you're making progress."

I wanted to howl down the phone and tell him to stop being such a self-righteous prig of an older brother but I somehow bit my tongue, killed the video feed and made a strangled grunt of frustration, which I turned into a light cough. Did that count as 'sorting myself out'? Surely there's some part of being a proper grown-up that involves not shrieking abuse at people that deserve it?

"Oops, lost the picture," said Adam.

"That'll be the poor signal in your flat," I said.

"Oh, that reminds me. You'll want to connect to the Wi-Fi..."

21

While he began to explain how to connect the Wi-Fi – didn't he just write the password on the fridge like everyone else? – I picked up Gida the goat and stomped sullenly through the flat.

Wandering into Adam's bedroom, I spotted another of those weird buttons. On the night stand next to the bed was a button with the Durex logo on it. Surely, he didn't have some sort of condom dispenser? I pressed the button but nothing happened. No condoms appeared. Maybe they descended from the ceiling like inflated party balloons. I tried again.

"What are these buttons?" I asked.

"Buttons?"

"Buttons? Ah, you mean the Amazon Dash buttons. Don't touch those, they're for ordering new stuff like toilet paper and, er, washing powder. Just leave them alone, yeah?"

"I don't suppose there's one for ordering any decent breakfast cereal?" I asked. "Your muesli is the worst thing ever."

"I don't have any muesli, Lori," he said. "You'll need to get some. Now, in terms of supermarkets, I use Ocado but I think –"

"No, the muesli in the cupboard. Maybe you forgot it was there. *Wild Seeds* it's called. Awful stuff."

There was a long pause.

"That's for birds," he said.

"I can't believe the things women do for the sake of their health. It's definitely a step down from Special K."

"No," said Adam in that slow voice he uses when he thinks he's talking to an idiot. "It's for birds. Wild birds. In the garden. You're not a wild bird, Lori."

"Wild? I'm livid, Adam!"

There was silence down the phone. Come on, Adam, that was a good joke. Why could I not make him laugh when I wanted to? I sat on the side of his bed and put the phone up to the side of Gida's head while Adam lectured me some more about reading labels properly and taking responsibility and where the nearest Waitrose was and I don't know what else. The goat nodded along while I pressed the Durex button. When I'd pressed it a hundred times I put the phone back to my ear.

"– and maybe if you hadn't spent that money on a holiday to Crete when they clearly thought it was a business loan –"

"How come everyone's such an expert on how I run my business?" I said.

"I think you have to actually have a business before you can talk about running it. You know I like your cartoons as much as the next person but..."

"But what?"

"Well, just because you're good at something doesn't mean you're going to make any money from it."

"But I'm really very good."

"And you think that makes you entitled to be rewarded."

"I don't think I'm entitled to –"

"Yes, you do!" he said, hotly. "That's exactly it. You think you're entitled to make a living from doodles. You think you're entitled to sponge off Mom and Dad for the rest of forever. It's that kind of entitlement that gives the rest of us millennials a bad name."

I scoffed. "You're not a millennial. You're practically middle-aged."

"I'm thirty, Lori."

"See?"

He sighed bitterly. "You know, while some of us are out there, working, saving for a mortgage and a pension, contributing to society. There are *some people*" – 'some people' was code for 'Lori'; he thinks he's clever but I can read between the lines – "whose world doesn't extend beyond their own social media filter bubble, who are more wrapped up in getting likes for their posts and redefining their identities on a daily basis. One day, they're polyamorous pansexuals and the next they're... they're elfkin or unicorns or something!"

"I met a pansexual unicornkin on holiday," I said conversationally.

"I bet you bloody did! And while we're worrying about your trigger warnings and safe spaces, you're no-platforming anyone who disagrees with you because you bloody snowflakes are all too flipping delicate and special to cope with the teensiest amount of criticism!"

Rant over, he just panted on the line.

"That was a bit harsh," I said eventually.

23

Adam laughed. It wasn't cruel or teasing. Just tired.

"Look, Lori," he said. "Let's just concentrate on the future, shall we?"

"Sure."

"I do care, you know."

"Uh-huh."

"Now, what time's your interview?" he said.

What was it? I looked at the clock on my phone. It was coming up for four. The letter had said five pm.

I hadn't really given much thought to the job interview. I'd rejected it out of hand the moment I read about it. To the uninformed outsider, it might appear that my parents applying for a job on my behalf was a generous act. Of course, it was nothing of the sort; it was a deliberate snub to my business endeavours. They assumed that a young cartoonist couldn't be independently wealthy and would be grateful for a menial position at the university museum.

However, it was a good excuse to get Adam off the phone. I was bored of having everything wrong in my life mansplained to me.

"Ooh, it's quite soon," I said. "Must go and get ready."

"That's the spirit! Best of luck and speak soon. Oh, one more thing."

"Shoot, bro."

"The rocks in the lounge..."

"Yeah, I did wonder."

"Please, do me a favour and just take care of them."

"No problem. See you."

"Bye, Lori."

I blew a loud raspberry at the phone after he'd hung up. Sure, he sounded like he cared but you had to listen to the subtext: Saintly Adam Belkin, so successful that he was touring round lecturing poor unsuspecting Americans on whatever popular science nonsense he was peddling these days, running his life from his smartphone and generally being Shiny Adam with a halo of solid gold.

So, the interview.

Sure, spending the days working alongside one of my best friends had a certain appeal but Cookie was a girl without ambition. As long as she had her weed, her booze and an opportunity to strut her funky stuff on a Saturday night, she was happy. Me, I needed more in my life. I had an independent income from my web-comic, fed by donations from a grateful public. I could live off that and tell the museum to stick its job offer up its boring, dusty bum.

I pulled up the PayPal app on my phone to see how much I'd been paid recently.

"Seventeen pence," I read.

Seventeen pence. In all the time I'd been away.

Okay. Plan B.

I'd need to tap up Adam or Mom and Dad for some money. Mom and Dad would be an easier mark. They might have run off to deepest, darkest Wales but they'd be in touch soon enough. I just had to tell them how I was poor and starving (those Wild Seeds were really doing a number on my empty innards). Of course, they'd ask how the interview went. They might be miffed if I told them I didn't bother going...

I pulled out the letter. I might have to go to this wretched interview after all. If I got the job at least I'd be earning something. If I didn't get it, I could honestly tell the folks that I'd done my best. Either way, if I played along with this grand plan that they'd all cooked up they might cut me some slack. Five o'clock. I had an hour. I went to the *Lori Clothes* box to find something suitable. It didn't take long to pull out all of my potential outfits and spread them out. I like to wear things that reflect my personality, but something told me that I might need to tone things down for an interview. A great many of my tops are hand painted by me. I held up *Florrie Paints the Town Red*. That wouldn't do. How about *Grand Theft Auto - Florrie Edition*? No. My best bet would be *Florrie Does the Funky Chicken*, but it still felt wrong. I went back to Adam's room and looked in his wardrobe. There were shirts and suits hanging on proper wooden hangers and some jeans and polo shirts folded on shelves. The door had a little rack for ties. Everything was sorted by colour. I reached for a shirt. It felt expensive and crisp. Moments later I was wearing it. I smoothed it down. This was going to work. I struggled slightly with the buttons being the wrong way round, but once it was on, and I'd put one of my belts around my waist, it looked pretty good. My figure is on the boyish side, so the fit wasn't a problem. I was tempted to see how a jacket and tie looked as well but I was running short of time. I grabbed my phone and the wickerwork goat (Cookie would love it!) and left the flat.

Chapter 4

It's a short walk over to the University Museum and Art Gallery from Adam's place, through the Warstone Cemetery, along the dual carriageway and past the studenty pubs and clubs on Broomhill Road (where once I spent a night at the worst nightclub *ever*). Seeing it made me realise that the charm of being back in my green and leafy hometown had already worn off and I wished I was walking to the Ikarus Bar in Malia for afternoon cocktails. I crossed the road and went through the ivy-covered university gates.

I'd texted Cookie a summary of my dire situation on the walk over and she was waiting for me by the museum, leaning against the wall around the corner from the grand stone-steps-and-classical-columns entrance. She wore a blue tabard as if she was a cleaner or a dinner lady or something.

She came forward and gave me a hug. I inhaled the faded scent of cannabis that I always associate with her and felt instantly better. Whether that was the reassuring presence of a friend or a second-hand high, I couldn't say. Cookie always hugged for one second too long. I once pointed this out to her and she told me, "Everyone hugs for three seconds. That extra second, that's just for you."

My friend Cookie. What to say about her? We met in the first year of secondary school. I was this gawky stick thing with straw hair. She was a bouncing puppy with afro hair that was even wilder than mine. We definitely weren't the cool girls – not then – but what we lacked in cool, we made up for in shameless joy. Our form tutor in sixth form described us as each other's enablers – this, after the time Cookie fell through a skylight when we tried to break into the school at the weekend – but I wouldn't have called us enablers; we were just each other's personal cheerleaders. And, when it came to trouble, Cookie was less of an enabler and more of a lightning rod. I never had one of those sixteenth birthday house parties where your parents' house gets trashed while they're away for the weekend. Why? Because Cookie had done that very thing two months earlier and I'd seen enough crazy shit to scare me off the idea for life. Taking up smoking, falling off a speeding moped, getting briefly engaged to a Belgian jazz saxophonist twice your age:

27

I'd managed to avoid these excesses because I'd seen Cookie do them first (although I did get some serious snogging action with the saxophonist's trumpeter bandmate). Both our sets of parents approved of our friendship. I was Cookie's moderately well-behaved friend and my parents assumed I was an okay kid if I didn't get into the same messes Cookie did. The fact that my folks held up Cookie's job as a role model for me simply showed how far I'd fallen.

I cherished my extra second of hug-time outside the museum.

"Worst day ever," I told Cookie.

"All experiences are relative," she said. "And all are valid."

"When I get a minute to spare I'm looking to see what the definition of orphan is. Pretty sure I am one."

"I think your parents have to be dead."

"They're not dead," I conceded, "but they've made me homeless. A homeless orphan."

"Mom said you were stopping at your brother's place," she said.

"Well yeah, so I'm a homeless orphan living in a luxury apartment," I said, feeling that she really wasn't appreciating the full extent of my misery. "But I hate it. He's got robots in every room, I'm scared to turn the lights on because he can tell when I'm using electricity and I ate bird food by mistake."

"I did that once."

"Did you?" I asked.

She paused in thought. "No. Not that. But I did try to hatch a coconut once." She steered me up the steps. "After I knock off here I'll come back with you. Help you settle in. Bring some spiritual balance to the festering hovel you're living in."

"You mean drink all my booze."

"You have booze? The gods smile. I just need to call someone about some work first. And – segue! – speaking of work, you need to face the fearsome Rex in his den."

"Is he really fearsome?"

"No, but Rex's sort of old school."

"Old school how?" I asked.

"All the ways you can think of," she said. "Just be really straight with him. You know how you can sometimes talk...?" she made a tumbling motion with her hands.

"Sense?" I suggested.

"Bollocks. You talk bollocks."

"That's rich, coming from you."

"I speak vast truths. Only a fool can't tell the difference. Cut down on the random bollocks. Be straightforward with Rex. He's not really very twenty-first century. If he asks you about your work history, don't say you're a blogger or you'll just have to explain what that means."

"But that's what I do."

"No, tell him you've been building up your home-based art business."

"But that's not what I am."

"Do any of us know who we really are, Baby Belkin? Do we?"

We made our way down a corridor with colourful tiles that covered the floor and went halfway up the walls as well. There were intricate moulded panels and shelves all over the place. I felt sorry for whoever had to keep the place clean.

"Rex will also ask you how you feel about flexibility."

"I can put my foot in my mouth. Literally. Did it for a bet once."

"Not like that. Working extra hours, weekends, that sort of thing. Just agree to everything. He says it to everyone and it never happens. Never."

I nodded.

"Another thing about Rex," said Cookie, as we passed through a door marked *no public access*. "He's a bit strange."

"Strange? Stranger than what?"

Cookie took my elbow and swung me round to face another door.

"In there. See you later, meow-meow."

I knocked on the door and went into a small office that was fifty percent filing cabinets and fifty percent reclaimed secondary school furniture. A large metal cupboard against the wall fizzed and crackled dangerously and white light flashed occasionally at its hinges. A man sat behind a much-marked desk. He had a bushy grey beard, flowing grey hair and a deep Mediterranean tan. This Rex character didn't look old though. He looked like Santa Claus had decided to lose a bit of weight, get some sun and get a job modelling cheap suits.

"Five o'clock," said Rex. He had a commanding voice. He wasn't just relaying the fact it was five o'clock; he was telling time what time it ought to be. "Take a seat, Miss Belkin."

I sat on a chair of metal tubing and ancient canvas.

"You will forgive us," he said. "We are in a transitional period. Ah, which serves to remind... Are you, or is anyone you're related to, involved in the un-retendering programme?"

"I don't think so," I said cautiously.

"Be sure," he said darkly. "For we have to be sure also. There are spies." His eyes darted left and right.

"Um. I am sure. I'm not related to anyone who's part of the untenderi–"

"Un-*re*tendering."

"Un-retendering programme."

"Good," he said with a momentary smile. "So, Miss Belkin, we find it interesting that you have chosen to attend an interview wearing flip-flops and carrying a toy."

Gida. Dammit. I'd only brought the goat to show Cookie. I placed the goat on the floor and smiled at him. "I like to be interesting." I was about to elaborate, but I remembered Cookie's warning and stopped myself.

"Well, you should know that the University Museum and Art Gallery like to run a tight ship here. No room for tomfools, rapscallions and guttersnipes here." He looked down at something that was written on his pad. "Your employment history is not mentioned in the reference that has been provided."

A reference. Written by my parents. How interesting.

"Where have you worked recently?" he asked.

"I have been building up my home-based business," I said. Cookie would be so proud that I had remembered my lines.

"Would it be correct to assume that you mean you've never had a job?" he asked.

"Not a formal job, as such," I said. "I've worked in what you might call a voluntary capacity from time to time."

"Give an example, please," he said, leaning forward.

I hadn't expected that. I thought about how to phrase this. "Well, there was this one time when I put on a tutu and sang *The Locomotion* outside the city train station."

Most people I know would smile when I told them that, but Rex just stared at me as if I was mad.

"And why exactly did you do that?" he asked.

"It was..." my mind raced. I realised that I had stepped straight into the trap that Cookie had warned about. Explaining a flash mob would be up there with explaining a blog. "You know what you said about tomfoolery? Well that's what it was. Voluntary tomfoolery."

He sighed and shook his head. "The position that we're interviewing for is a zero-hours contract where you will actually be employed by a third-party contract company which provides staff for many such facilities services jobs throughout the city. Is that clear?"

I hadn't really heard the bits that came after 'zero-hours'. How did a job work when it had zero hours? It sounded pretty good to me. I grinned at him. "Yep, cool."

"Obviously, given the nasty business with the retendering process and, following the legal challenge by the original contractors, the subsequent un-retendering programme, there has been some confusion, some umbrage taken and some natural wastage. This is where you come in."

I wasn't overly sure what he was talking about and whether I was being accused of being confused, of having taken umbrage or of being a natural waste.

The metal cupboard on the wall crackled and spat, electric light flashed in the gaps.

"Do tell," said Rex, "what you noticed about the museum as you walked through to this office."

I thought for a moment. "Lots of old-fashioned decor."

"Well done!" He seemed pleased by this, as if everyone else got here without noticing where they were. "How would you tackle it?"

31

Ah. I already had thoughts on this. They must know from my parents' application that I had an art degree. They clearly needed someone with an appreciation of style and function.

"I'd probably get rid of a lot of it and replace it with a minimalist decor. Emulsioned walls and a painted concrete floor, that sort of thing. Maybe in white or some simple primary colours."

He looked as if I'd slapped him. His mouth actually dropped open and he stared at me for a long moment.

"You know, like the Dutch *De Stijl* movement," I suggested. "Or, you know, IKEA."

Finally, it was as if he realised he was catching flies and he closed his mouth again.

"Was that a joke?" he said.

"Would you like it to have been a joke?" I asked timidly.

"Well, fortunately for us all, Miss Belkin, you will not be required to redecorate this historic building, merely to clean it."

"Oh."

"One hopes that your keen eye will enable you to spot where your efforts are needed. Do tell though, do you consider a cleaning job to be beneath you?"

I thought about that. It certainly sounded dull. Should I lie to please him? Cookie had urged me to be straightforward, but did she really mean this straightforward? People say honesty is the best policy but people are frequently dumb. Let's see. "Yes. Actually, I'm not all that keen," I said.

He gave me a really stern look. It was like Santa telling you he'd put you on his naughty list. "And yet you are here. Interesting."

"Interesting good or interesting bad?"

"That remains to be seen." He consulted his interview questions. "Conflict in the workplace."

"I'm against it," I said promptly.

"How would you tackle a disagreement between you and a colleague?"

"What sort of disagreement?" I asked.

"Anything you like," said Rex. "Let's say, for example, you overheard them saying something mean about you."

"Mean? Like what?"

"It doesn't matter."

"Not that mean then if it doesn't matter."

"Perhaps they said you're lazy," said Rex.

"I'd be fine with that," I said. "They'd probably be right. I am a bit lazy. My brother thinks it's because I'm a snowflake."

Rex frowned at me again.

"A snowflake?"

"You know, a unique and special snowflake."

Rex shook his head, clearly not understanding. "Conflict. Think about something that would cause conflict. Pretend that they said you'd got an ugly nose."

My hand flew to my face. "What's the matter with my nose? You've been looking at me since I came in. Is it my nose?"

"What? No. Your nose was mentioned as an example. There's nothing wrong with your nose."

"But the rest of me...?"

Could you fail an interview for having an ugly nose? Or being ugly everywhere apart from your nose?

"We are looking at you because you are the subject of an interview," said Rex. He sounded annoyed. Probably not a great sign. "This is a hypothetical question about conflict, Miss Belkin. Now, let's have one last try. Imagine you overhear a colleague saying that you've stolen some money from the museum. It's a hypothetical situation and you are innocent of any wrongdoing. What do you do?"

I sat up and concentrated. "Right." A situation like that would need swift and decisive revenge, preferably that couldn't be traced back to me. I would probably go for the booby-trapped toilet cubicle. A bucket of water balanced across the gap, so that it falls on their head when they open the door. No. That wasn't the answer he was looking for. He wanted something sensible, methodical...

"Police," I said. "SWAT team. Forensics. Criminal psychologist." I'd been counting them off on my fingers and so said, "And Child Line," to round off the handful.

"You report the problem to your line manager," said Rex.

"That too."

"No, just that."

"Oh. Keep it in-house. Sure. Say no more."

Rex shook his head.

33

"Perhaps we should just stop the interview there."

A little part of me was thinking that we were stopping early because I'd already demonstrated my brilliance. But it was only a little part. A big part knew exactly why he had stopped. Oh, well, I could just tell Mom and Dad that I had tried.

"We are desperate for cleaning staff," said Rex, "and despite your level of qualification, your lack of a criminal record and, we should point out, your delightful penmanship, one suspects a cleaning role is not beneath you but utterly beyond you."

I was agog. "I'm *not good enough* to be a cleaner?"

"Frankly, no."

"But... But, you haven't finished the questions. Maybe I'll pull it round with the last question."

"Rest assured, Miss Belkin –"

"Any question. Any! The hardest one you have!"

Rex flicked through his papers.

"Very well. We found this one on the world wide web." He indicated the huge dirty beige monitor on his desk with a flourish of pride before returning to his sheets. "Here. How many piano tuners are there in Seattle?"

I looked at him. Gida the goat looked at him. He looked back at me.

"You just made that up," I said.

"We certainly did not," he replied and pointed to a line on the page.

"But it's ridiculous."

"It's a lateral thinking question. This is not a question you will necessarily know the answer to but we are interested in how you approach it."

"It's like a riddle?"

"I suppose."

How many piano tuners are there in Seattle? Seattle. Seattle. I'd heard of it but I didn't know where it was. I knew *Sleepless in Seattle*. Tom Hanks. Meg Ryan. There was the Seattle sound: Nirvana and all those grunge bands in the nineties. They didn't have any pianos in their bands. Was the answer zero? Rex had got the question off the internet. Ah!

"Got it!" I said.

"You have?"

I pulled out my phone. "Google is your friend." I did a quick search. "Take a look." I held up the map to show him the piano tuners highlighted. "Three pages of results. About fifty? We can count them if you want."

Rex's eyebrows had shot high up his forehead, like a pair of small grey rodents blasting into orbit. "Oh. I didn't know you could do that. No need to count. And so quick. All on that little screen."

"Is it right?" I asked.

"Not an approach I've seen before but it, ah, seems to get results."

He pushed back slightly from the desk and looked at me.

"Right, we can probably draw this interview to a close. In summary, you've admitted to being lazy, told me that your previous employment amounted to *tomfoolery* and declared that a cleaning job is not something you want to do. Have we left anything out?"

I pointed helpfully to the wickerwork goat and he rolled his eyes.

"In spite of all this, we are prepared to offer you a probationary role as a cleaner. You will start at oh six hundred hours and work the morning shift before the museum opens. Normally, we'd do an induction day before you start but, due to the un-retendering debacle, the induction team have a four-month backlog. So, we'll start as we mean to go on and in a few months' time do your introductory training."

I looked at him and beamed. I'd got a job! Boom! A job! I didn't actually want a job but the sense of achievement was real nonetheless.

"Do you have any questions?" he asked.

I pointed at the sparking electrical cupboard on the wall. "Is that thing meant to do that?"

Rex turned slowly to regard it and then looked back again at me. "The fuse box. Like so many things round here, it is old. But it functions perfectly well as long as no one tampers with it. A salutary lesson for all there. Do you have any questions *about the job*?"

I thought. "No. It all sounds great, Rex," I said. "Can I just add a few conditions though?"

"Conditions?"

"I'll want the weekends off. You'll need to provide me with a stepladder so that I can reach the high parts and then I'm going to need some rubber gloves and dusters. If you can sort all of that then we have a deal."

He gave a slow nod. "I don't think we will have an issue with any of that."

I picked up the goat but I was struck with an urgent thought. "Can I have some money now please?"

"No," said Rex, "you'll be paid in arrears."

"I need to get some things," I said. "Food mainly. Think of it as danger money."

"Danger money?"

"Starting work at six in the morning? That's got to be dangerous," I said.

Chapter 5

Maybe I was riding high from getting a job. Number of job interviews attended: one. Number of jobs secured: one. That's a one hundred percent success rate. Maybe I was intellectually abuzz from the stunning answers I gave in the interview. Maybe I was delirious with tiredness and hunger.

Whichever, I had just had an idea.

Adam had said something about maybe 'popping round' to see my parents if things went well. Popping round. That made me wonder if they weren't so far away after all. Norman in the paper shop had refused to tell me anything, but perhaps I could find out another way. The Evening Mail was delivered by an elderly gent who took the papers round in a big tartan shopping trolley. I'd have no problem following him to see where he went. I might spot my parents' new house!

On tired, flip-flopped feet and with Gida the goat under my arm, I headed back across the city in time for the paper round.

The tartan shopping trolley emerged from the corner shop as I approached, although today it was not in the hands of an elderly gent but a much more spritely dark-haired chap in a tweed jacket and cords. It didn't matter who it was, it was the trolley that mattered. If I followed it, it might take me to Mom and Dad's new place.

I hung back as he started off down the road. I'd seen enough cop shows to know how best to follow someone. I practised looking casual and tied my shoelaces. This tested my acting skills to the max as I was wearing flip-flops but I think I carried it off. I looked up and saw he was already some distance off. He walked pretty quickly for a tweed wearer and I realised I had seen this old-guy-in-training before. It was the handsome secret agent wolfman I'd met outside my house – my old house. Ah, so that's how he knew about my parents leaving and Mrs Whatever-her-name-was moving in. He was probably a good source of information. I scampered across some front gardens to catch up, hoping that nobody was looking, then realised that I was the wrong side of a low wall. I got over it, but I left a flip-flop behind and had to go back over for it.

I saw someone twitch the curtain of the house. My cover was blown. I held up Gida to the curtain twitcher and mouthed the words, 'Just looking for my goat' before moving on. Getting through suburbia without being seen is harder than you'd think. There were a couple of times when the paper boy – not that he was a boy but 'paper man' makes it sound like he'd blow away in a stiff breeze – stopped to talk to someone, so I pretended I was studying my phone, perhaps consulting a map. He zig-zagged up and down a series of parallel streets and I was starting to get the hang of things. I'd find the tallest hedge in the street and stealthily make my way to it, so that I could stand and watch unseen while he delivered the papers. When he turned the corner to the next street I'd do it again. I was like a shadow, or maybe a ninja. I moved from street to street with nobody knowing I was there.

I peered out from a huge laurel bush and realised that I couldn't see him. I risked a step forward. I didn't want to blow my cover, but perhaps he was at the end of the street already. I screamed out loud as someone tapped my shoulder.

I whirled around and there he was.

"Is there a problem?" he said. "I couldn't help noticing that you're walking up and down all over the place."

"Yes," I said, wracking my brain for a good alibi.

"Are you lost?" he said. "Oh, we met, didn't we? Still looking for your parents, yes?"

"I might be."

At that moment, my phone started to ring. "This will be them now!" I said for no good reason and walked away as I answered.

"Hello," said the caller. "I understand you need some help finding some missing people? I have extensive experience in this field and I'm sure I can help you."

I knew that voice. "Cookie? Is that you?" I said.

"Lori. What are you doing on this number?"

"It's my number."

"I was answering an ad in the shop window."

"It was my ad."

"The pieces fall into place and the universe reveals its secrets. What's going on?"

"I'll explain everything to you later. I'll meet you at the end of your shift and we'll talk about it at Adam's, yeah?"

Cookie's always looking for work. Her curriculum vitae must read like a directory of mad jobs. I think she made some of them up.

In the time I'd been talking to Cookie, Corduroy had moved on to another street. I forced myself to be even more careful as he'd obviously spotted me before. I began to wonder if the slapping of my flip-flops on the pavement might be louder than I'd first thought. I looked at the houses and had a thought. These were the sort of houses that had a back alley running parallel to the road between the back gardens, with access from the sides and entries between the houses. I could creep along through there and pop out of one of the entries. I tried to gauge where he might have got to and went along the back alley of the next road. About two thirds of the way up there was an entry. I sidled up until I was at the front and then I peered out to the left and then the right.

To the right, Corduroy was standing at the house's front door, talking with a lady inside. They both turned to stare at me. For a long and awkward moment I stared back, and then I did the only thing that I could in the circumstances: I walked up the road until they were out of sight and then I stepped into a hedge. I literally inserted myself into it to hide and to have a rethink.

I heard a car pull up on the road next to the hedge. I peered out. Through prickly branchlets, I could see the blue and luminous yellow stripes along the side of the vehicle. A police car. Ah.

"Come out of the hedge, ma'am," said a no-nonsense voice.

"Me?" I asked.

"Well, unless you've got anyone else in there with you..."

I stepped out as nonchalantly as I could. There were two of them. The nearest one gave me a stern, appraising look. It was the kind of look my part-woman part-wildebeest art teacher Mrs McGee used to give me when she caught me drawing cartoons in her lessons and there was more than a little bit of wildebeest about this woman too.

"Evening, constable," I said.

The police officer pointed at the stripes on her shoulder. "Sergeant. Sergeant Fenton. "Can I ask what you're doing?"

"Doing?" I said.

"We've had three calls about you now."

"About me?"

"A woman with a wicker donkey creeping in and out of people's gardens."

"It's a goat," I said and held up Gida as evidence.

The sergeant's colleague nodded. "It is indeed," he said.

"Thank you for the clarification, Constable Stokes," said Sergeant Fenton.

"I've been trying to find my parents," I said.

"In a hedge?" said Sergeant Fenton.

"No. Not in a hedge."

"So how is this," she gestured at the hedge, "helping you to find your parents?"

"I thought the paper boy might lead me to them if they're still having the Evening Mail," I said.

"So, they're at home? You've not lost them. You've lost your house."

"But they moved," I said.

"Where?"

"That's what I'm trying to find out. They did it while I was in Crete."

"So, your parents didn't tell you where they'd moved to?"

"No."

"And you've tried phoning them?"

"They're not picking up."

Sergeant Fenton gave me a look. It was a complex and rich look that featured impatience, world-weariness and perhaps a desire to go home and sink into a sofa with a large glass of wine. Mrs McGee used to give me those looks too, when I'd pushed the old wildebeest too far.

"You can't engage in stalking and anti-social behaviour to find them," said Sergeant Fenton.

"No," I said.

"Where are you currently staying?"

I gave her my brother's address and she noted it down, with my name.

"Does this mean that you're not treating my parents as missing persons?" I asked as she and her colleague got back in the car.

"No, Miss Belkin. People who want to be left alone are not missing."

Cookie was sitting on the campus green outside the University Museum when I returned. We walked back to Adam's flat and I told her about my awful day. Cookie walks slowly when she's got a joint on the go.

"Rhythms of the universe," she had once explained. "I listen and step to their beat."

But now, having heard my tale of woe, she stopped on the pavement and turned to face me.

"This is epic. You know that, right?" she said.

"No," I scowled.

"There is only ever one story," she said and drew an arc in the air with her arm. "A hero rises. She struggles. She falls."

"That's cheery."

"You've set out on a new path. Your adventure is ahead of you. See how awesome that is?"

I sighed.

"I'm struggling to see the awesomeness, Cookie. My parents have abandoned me. I'm like those two kids in the wood who have to live off gingerbread cottage and kill a witch. And, you know what, I'm kind of angry about that."

"Because you don't have a gingerbread cottage?"

"Well, that, yes, but also that my parents could be so selfish as to bugger off and leave me to fend for myself. Like the boy in *The Jungle Book* left to be raised by wolves and run around in his red undies. And he had a singing bear to help him! No gingerbread cottage. No singing bear. I suspect Mom and Dad don't really love me at all."

"Course they do. Just in a really distant kind of way. This is your moment to shine, meow-meow. And you know it. You're standing at a crossroads," said Cookie. "Mostly we all take the paths we take in our lives and we never know where the important junctions are, but yours is right here in front of you."

"It's not a crossroads, Cookie. It's a roundabout and I've been going round and round it all day with no food and no money. Maybe I'll be able to think about how awesome it all is when I get some of the small stuff sorted out like not starving to death."

She clapped her hands together as we climbed the stairs to Adam's flat. "You're looking at someone who's a black belt at creating a meal from an empty cupboard. I'm your singing bear and I will build you a gingerbread cottage."

"You're the best."

"I am. Also, I've seen you running around in nothing but your red undies. Stirring stuff."

"That was a one-time thing," I said.

"Ah, you say that. Put something on YouTube and it's there forever."

I made her put the joint out and we went inside. She walked into the lounge and tried all the chairs before deciding which was her favourite.

"Check this out," I said. "Lexi."

"How can I help you?" said the cylinder on the table.

"Turn on the lights, please."

The lounge lights came on.

"You've got a ghost butler," said Cookie. "That's neat."

She produced an Aldi carrier bag with two bottles of wine and plonked them onto the coffee table.

"Yo, ghost. Get us some glasses."

Nothing happened. Of course nothing happened.

"It doesn't work like that," I said.

"Fine. Why don't you get us a drink poured and I'll check out the kitchen, see what we can get to eat?"

I found wine glasses and a corkscrew while Cookie made her voyage of discovery through the kitchen cupboards, much as I had done earlier, except that Cookie knows what she's doing. She's been bin-diving behind Sainsbury's for years. And she's been trying to educate the world in the ways of innovative cooking with cheap ingredients for almost as long, but it's yet to take off. The closest she ever got was when a comedy website mentioned her YouTube channel in a feature called *Ten culinary experiences that are worse than eating insects in I'm a Celebrity*, which I thought was a bit harsh.

I passed Cookie a glass of wine and looked at the ingredients that she'd lined up on the counter top. A bag of flour with a picture of a windmill on the front, some lemon juice and something called bicarbonate of soda.

"What is this? I thought you just used this to make model volcanoes," I said.

"It's a raising agent," said Cookie. "It means we can make soda bread. Watch and learn!"

As she found bowls and spoons I leaned against the counter and sipped my wine.

"I'm always learning," I said.

"Course you are. Even in stillness, we move."

"Right. My parents think I haven't moved on since I was a teenager," I said.

"That's not true."

"I drink white wine now," I said, swilling my glass. "And not only when it's the last alcohol in the fridge."

"Same goes for salad," said Cookie.

"It's true. I no longer fear the lettuce. And I've even developed a taste for blue cheese since last Christmas. Ooh! Sausage!"

"You've always had a taste for sausage," said Cookie salaciously.

"Cookie!" I slapped her.

"And penis," she added.

Cookie stirred things together as I dashed off to find my *loukaniko sapio*. I presented it to Cookie with a proud 'ta-dah!' She sniffed.

"That's off, mate," she said.

"No, no. It's Greek. It's piquant and aromatic."

"It stinks of death."

"You don't know what you're talking about."

"Nor do you. You don't even know what piquant means."

"I do," I said. "It means..."

"I bet you can't even spell it."

"P," I said. "Um. E? I don't know. How do you spell piquant?"

"P-I-Q-U-A-N-T," said Lexi from the counter.

"You sure?" I said. "Q? Really? You do know that Q makes a 'kwa' sound?" I picked up the box of quinoa. "How do you pronounce this, Cookie?"

"*Keen-wah*," she said.

"Smart arse."

"And we're going to use it in our bread. That way, we can eke out the flour so you've got enough for another one tomorrow. But either way, that sausage is not coming anywhere near my floury loaf, Baby Belkin."

I put the sausage to one side and smelled my fingers. Okay. It was a *bit* overpowering.

"I'm sure that's not the only Greek sausage you've handled recently," said Cookie. "Do tell, boon companion, has your taste in men moved on? I know you didn't spend all of your time looking at frescoes in churches."

"I had to look at a *couple* of frescoes. It was supposed to be a research trip. You might think that drawing cartoons is simple, but it's important to seek out fresh inspiration."

"Yes. Tell me more about the fresh inspiration."

I toyed with the idea of playing coy and then thought, what's the point?

"There were a couple of lads in Crete."

"A couple? As in two? As in two in two weeks? My, what a jammy tart you are."

"There was this one guy, Vik."

"A Greek waiter?"

"He ran a Jet Ski hire place in Malia. A real man, he was."

"I hear there's been a lot of knock-offs about."

"No, you should have seen him. He had a beard and everything."

"Tell me more," said Cookie. "I'm particularly interested in the 'everything'."

I sighed. "It all fell apart a bit. He took me out for the evening on his scooter. There was a problem with the spark plug and he ended up spending the whole time trying to find the right sort of spanner to take it out. Then he got grease on my dress, so I stormed off."

"Shame. You didn't have another try?"

I shook my head. "I saw him later with another girl. She was carrying a tool box, so I could see there was no competition."

Cookie gave me a look. "Only you, mate. Listen, the bread's going in now. Let's go and put the fire on in the lounge, yeah? Refill our glasses, snuggle down, get some bi-curious tension going."

"Oh, I don't know about that."

"Okay. Scratch the bi-curious tension."

"I mean, Adam's watching what energy we use. If we put the gas fire on he'll be on the phone before you know it telling me that I need to pay attention to my environmental impact."

"Well we need to think outside the box," said Cookie. "He's got a fireplace, right?"

"Yes."

"So, we use it to have a fire in, old style. Have you got anything to burn?"

"Yeah!" I went to find the pile I'd sorted out for throwing away. I lifted off the pendant that was holding the papers down and carried the pile through to the lounge.

"How are we going to do this? There's already a fake fire in here."

Cookie glanced across as she topped up our wine. "Well if it's a fake fire that has flames, then it's going to be fireproof, isn't it? We just make our fire on top."

I cleared aside the weird brass dish ornaments my brother kept in the hearth, knelt down and balled up the old papers, one by one. Cookie passed me her lighter. It flared up in moments.

"Needs something more to keep it going," observed Cookie and she went into the kitchen. She returned moments later with both hands full of wooden spoons and spatulas. "Your brother has got a spatula addiction."

"There are worse addictions."

"Depends what he does with them," said Cookie. "There's got to be at least twenty in there. Nobody needs twenty wooden spatulas."

She threw them down on the fire.

"Nice," I said.

"'N' cosy," said Cookie.

The fire flared up around the wood.

We finished the wine, so I went to find the bag I'd brought back from Crete.

"Drop of raki?" I asked, pulling out a bottle of clear liquid. "It's made with herbs and stuff, for your health."

She knocked back a large shot with a satisfied gasp and grinned. "Rocket fuel with herbs! You can put that in your Jet Ski!"

I wasn't able to knock it back quite as quickly, but I did find that the less time it spent in my mouth the better, so that I didn't suffer too badly from chemical burns.

"Why did you try to hatch a coconut?" I asked.

"Because my cousin told me it was a bear's egg," said Cookie.

"Ah. Makes sense."

I gave a little sniff. "Can you smell something burning?"

"Dur, mate!" laughed Cookie, lolling off her chair in mirth. "We lit a fire, remember?"

"No, but it smells *wrong* burning. Like something plastic maybe," I said.

I realised with horror that something was seeping out of the fireplace, across the floor. It looked as though it was the melted remains of the living flame fire.

"Shit!" I yelled. I grabbed the raki and upended the bottle onto the flames.

I hadn't expected that it would be so very flammable. It went up with an audible *whump*. I leapt aside and, unfortunately, immediately kicked Gida the goat and the small coffee table into the flames. We both spent the next few moments using Adam's cushions and eventually a small and expensive looking rug to put the fire out.

"Your hair!" yelled Cookie.

"What?"

My hair was on fire.

Cookie rugby tackled me to the ground. She rolled me over, beating the flames (and my head) with her hands. We ended up entwined and panting on the floor. Cookie gave me a look that made me crease up.

"You see, a bit of bi-curious tension," she said.

"Do lesbians usually set fire to the living room before wrestling on the floor?"

"I don't know. I cancelled my subscription to *Lesbian Monthly* and fashions move on so quickly."

Extricating myself from Cookie, I realised two things: there was a lot of evil-smelling smoke in the room and we were finding it hard to navigate the tricky terrain of the floor. We were, I concluded, quite drunk.

"We're drunk," I informed the world.

What would a grown-up do? Fresh air was needed so I went over to the sash window and opened it. Immediately the air seemed clearer. I turned and smiled at Cookie, trying to ignore the wreckage of Adam's fireplace and soft furnishings. Before I could speak the phone rang.

It was Adam.

"Hi, bro."

"Hi Lori. I saw from my home security app that you've opened the window."

"Did you?" I said.

"You did open a window, didn't you?"

"Ye-es."

"You know that the whole flat is environmentally controlled with heating and air con that cuts in when needed, don't you?"

I had no idea what he was talking about.

"Oh absolutely, but Cookie and I were just saying that there's nothing like fresh air, is there?"

"Cookie?" Adam's voice took on a stern tone.

"Yeah, she's popped round to bake some bread and..."

"That's a euphemism, right?"

"What?"

"Now I know she's your friend Lori, but I won't tolerate drug use in my flat. She'd better not be smoking weed there."

"I wouldn't let her."

"You can't lie to me. No smoking in the flat, got it?"

I couldn't help turning to look at the charred and melted remains behind me, which still sent up noxious twists of pungent smoke. I turned away and concentrated on sounding like a responsible adult. "No, Adam. No smoking at all."

At that moment, the smoke alarm went off.

Chapter 6

Cookie took the bread out of the oven while I wafted smoke away from the smoke detector in the ceiling. The bread had overcooked a bit while we were putting out the fire, but my stomach still rumbled. The burning smell was unpleasantly sharp and acrid, but it was hard to tell if it was from the bread or the fire in the lounge.

Cookie tapped the base of the loaf. "You can tell when bread is cooked because it will sound hollow when you do this," she said.

It didn't sound hollow, it sounded dead and solid. I took it off her wordlessly and banged it on the counter to see if it made a better sound, but I was a bit worried that we might shatter the granite.

"The road of trials is littered with obstacles," she said with a frown.

"And rock-hard loaves," I said.

"I need to think on this."

Cookie took herself into the lounge. I placed the loaf on a plate, found a long, serrated knife and attempted to cut a slice. Five minutes sawing produced a lot of shard-like crumbs but made virtually no impact on the bread. I tried to break the loaf with my hands, but I just wasn't strong enough. I opened my mouth really wide and tried using my teeth but it was impermeable. Eventually, I set the loaf on the floor and slammed a kitchen chair down on top of it. On the fourth attempt, I managed to break through the crust, and I almost yelped with joy as I stuffed a mouth-sized piece of soda bread into my mouth. Have you ever eaten a gobstopper and wondered for a few panicky minutes if it might actually be impossible to eat and you might have to present yourself at hospital to have it removed from your exhausted jaws? Well it was like that but without the sugary relief. I think I might have burned more calories chewing than it delivered to my exhausted body. I gave up after that first mouthful and dropped the remaining bread on a plate. I should have been more careful, as there was a dull plink of breaking crockery.

Growling with hunger, I turned to the *loukaniko sapio*. I cut into it. It offered no resistance at all. The smell that came pouring out was.... wow. If I had to give a name to it, it would have to be Poorly Dog or Campsite Latrine.

Suddenly, I wasn't hungry anymore.

I went through to the lounge. It turned out that having a think meant passing out on the settee. A joint burned in Cookie's right hand and a glass of raki lolled toward the cushions in her left. I tutted slightly and took them off her, keeping them well apart to avoid igniting the powerful spirits. I took another sip and pondered the life-giving herbal additives touted by the seller in Crete. This stuff seemed more akin to paint thinners than health food.

I looked at Gida the goat. She was still intact, although her head was a charred sleek mess. From the neck up, she now looked more like a racing greyhound than a carefree Cretan goat. I went into the bedroom and put her next to the rocking horse. The boxes in the room, Lori's life in three little boxes, were still mostly unemptied. I rooted through and found my fluffy onesie. I put it on and it felt good.

The day had not been a great success. In the plus column was me getting my first ever proper job. In the minus column was me losing my home, not getting any food or any money, setting fire to my brother's flat, oh, and having to start a proper job in the morning.

I was wondering how many weeks' wages it would take to restore Adam's flat to its former state when I heard a sound. It was a light creak, coming from outside. I crept over to the window and looked out into the rear yard of the building.

It was a naked man.

Definitely a man and definitely naked, his body pale and golden in the streetlights from the next road over. And he was coming up the fire escape.

I went into the kitchen to look out of the window, turning out the lights as I entered to improve my view of what was outside. Was the naked guy returning to one of the other flats? Why was he naked? In the moments that it took me to get to the kitchen window he'd disappeared. He'd either climbed up to the next floor, gone down to the ground, or entered the building. I swallowed hard as I realised that the most likely explanation for him vanishing so quickly was that he'd entered the building somewhere.

The lounge window was open. I had left it open. I had stupidly left the lounge window open. Was he inside the flat? This flat? My flat? I crept back to the door to the lounge and put my ear to it. I could definitely hear some sort of movement. I willed myself not to panic, took out my phone, dialled 999 but didn't yet press the call button. Cookie was asleep in the lounge. If a crazed naked man was in there, she was in danger. It didn't really cross my mind that it might be a sane naked man. I'm not sure there are such things.

I risked opening the door a crack.

Oh, God! He was there! A white and – oh, yeah – definitely naked torso moving slowly across the room.

I hit the call button and backed away.

"I think there's an intruder in my flat," I said, when I got through. "I mean, I know there's an intruder in the flat."

In a voice that suggested they received naked intruder calls all day long, the operator asked me for the address.

"Can you get out?" he asked.

"No, not without going past where they are," I said.

"Try to secure yourself or hide," said the operator.

"But my friend is in the lounge."

"Secure yourself and hide. We'll be there very shortly."

Secure myself and hide? Even if there was somewhere to hide in the kitchen, could I leave Cookie in the clutches of a nude lunatic? Of course not. I crept back to the door and peeked through the gap. The lounge was empty and there was Cookie's foot poking over the edge of the sofa. I had to go and wake her. But I needed protection.

I momentarily considered the bread knife but then the headline 'Local Woman Sentenced to Life for Unprovoked Nude Stabbing' flashed through my mind and I thought better of it. A non-lethal bludgeoning weapon would be much better.

Ten seconds later, armed with a rock-hard loaf of bread, I crept into the lounge. No. No naked men lurking in corners. He must have moved on. My limbs shivering with fear, I took hold of Cookie's knee and tried to shake her awake.

She gave a small grunt and shifted position.

"Wake up, damn you," I hissed.

51

"Nnnh. It's just a little egg," she murmured and rolled over.

"Shit."

There was the sound of something being dropped. The door to the largest bedroom, which opened directly onto the lounge, was open! There! This was an old building with many of the original features, including interior doors with locks and bolts. All I needed to do was to pull the door closed and lock it and the man would be trapped until the police arrived.

"You can do this," I told myself.

I stole quickly across the room and tugged the door shut. It was stiff, so I leaned back to get the catch to engage. The handle rattled from the other side as I turned the key in the lock.

"You're trapped now, mofo!" I shouted and turned away from the door.

And, as I did, I realised I had trapped my onesie in the door. A section of leg material caught in the gap.

The man started to pound on the door from the other side. I'm not normally one for whimpering but I let out a trembling cry.

"Cookie! Cookie, wake up!"

"I'll be your momma bear," she replied, sleepily.

I wasn't being subtle any more, I bellowed at the top of my voice, but she slept on.

The pounding continued, shaking me with each blow. It was a solid door, but I could hear a splintering sound coming from somewhere. I had to get away. There was only one solution and I had no choice. Down came the zip and I wriggled free. I headed across the room, intending to wake Cookie or roll her out of the flat if I had to. I hadn't gone two steps when the door gave way and the man burst through like that man with the axe in that film. You know the one. I turned to him with my only weapon: the remains of the indestructible loaf. I whirled around and summoned my meanest roar. I'd often practised facing down a bear. I like to imagine I'd send a grizzly packing by acting like its mean older brother, so I channelled that skill now. I tried to make myself as big as possible, raising my shoulders and lifting my arms. I let out a primal roar of pure, bear-flattening rage and swung the loaf with all my might at the attacker's head.

The bread connected with his head with deadly, bone-shattering force and he dropped like a stone. My arm even ached from the impact.

Two thoughts collided in my mind: the first was that I'd surely killed him. The second was that he looked familiar. Bizarrely familiar.

The doorbell rang.

His face was one I'd seen in the very recent past.

There was a thump at the door.

"Police! Open up!"

In fact, his face was my own creation. Robert Pattinson's eyes. Ashton Kutcher's smile. Channing Tatum's jawline. He was teen Lori's dream man, so very recently cast into the fire.

"Holy balls of fucking fire!" I exclaimed.

How could this be possible? He was a made-up fantasy picture, and yet he was here, in the flesh. Completely, nakedly, in the flesh, lying unconscious at my feet. Naked. I gawped for a long moment, utterly unable to process what might be going on.

Thump! Thump! "Open up! Police!"

"Coming!" I shouted.

I'd whacked him good across the temple but he wasn't dead. His chest was moving. As were his lips.

"This is the police! Are you okay in there?"

"Just give me a minute!" I yelled back. "Come on," I said to the impossible naked guy. "Look lively. The police are going to drag you off if you can't be a bit less... less naked for one."

Of course, I was naked too. I ran to the smashed bedroom door. He'd come straight through the door, leaving the lock and handle intact. My onesie was still firmly trapped and the door key was gone.

"Open the door immediately!" yelled the police.

"I need clothes!" I hollered back.

I grabbed the small, expensive and fire-damaged rug from the pile of other generally fire-damaged things and fashioned a very primitive dress from it.

"We will break this door down!"

"Two seconds!"

I snatched up one of the brass dish ornaments for the man on the floor who was in the same predicament as me. I looked at the dish and considered what I'd seen. I raised my eyebrows and swapped it for the biggest one.

"Here you are, cover yourself up," I hissed as I rushed past him, thrusting the bowl over him.

I went to the door, carefully arranging the rug dress so that it covered what I needed it to. Movement wasn't easy. I opened the door.

Another familiar face, though this lady-wildebeest one wasn't handsome and it certainly wasn't pleased to see me.

"Miss Belkin," said the sergeant.

"It's Sergeant Fenton, isn't it?" I said. "And Constable..."

"Stokes," he offered.

Sergeant Fenton gave me a long look. "You called to report an intruder?" she said.

"I did, yes," I said. "I thought there was an intruder, but I was mistaken."

Sergeant Fenton exchanged a glance with Stokes.

"You were mistaken?" she said.

"That's right," I said.

"Are you sure?" she said and stepped smoothly past me into the hallway.

"Very sure."

"You're here alone then?"

"I am."

"I'm wearing a bowl on my willy," said a voice from the lounge.

"Alone apart from, you know, the people who are here with me," I said. "It was all a bit of a mix-up, which I would explain, but it's stupid and dull. There's no need for you to stay, to be quite honest." I started to make dismissive flappy motions with my hands, but then I realised that there was a very real danger of my rug dress falling off.

"I think we'd prefer to have a look around," said Sergeant Fenton. "I need to satisfy myself that you're not acting under duress."

The police officers entered the lounge and gazed at the scene. Cookie still lounged in her seat, snoring now. The man from my picture sat opposite, with a mixing bowl covering his groin. He smiled a perfect smile.

"Evening, sir," said Sergeant Fenton, entirely unfazed by the naked hunk. "Has there been a fire in here?" She indicated the charred scatter cushions and general disarray.

"Yes, just a little accident," I said.

"You've burned your hair."

"I can smell cannabis," said Constable Stokes.

"Oh, I don't think so," I said, thinking on my feet. "It'll be the cushions. I always think that burning fabrics smell a bit herbal, don't you?" I picked one up and inhaled deeply. That was a mistake, as it made me cough violently and I momentarily lost my rug. I scrabbled to retrieve it.

"So, what is the perfectly reasonable explanation for all of this then?" asked Sergeant Fenton. "What was it that caused you to call the emergency services to say that there was an intruder?"

"I heard a noise," I said with a shrug. Keep the lie small and real. Would she accept that? Of course, she wouldn't.

"Go on," she said, "were you alone at that time?"

"Well no, Cookie, was here, but she's a very deep sleeper," I said, indicating my snoring friend.

"That'll be the herbal cushions," said Sergeant Fenton with a raised eyebrow. "Go on, what happened next?"

"Well, after I called, I realised that it was simply my boyfriend, who had dropped in unexpectedly to surprise me with some naked cooking!" I laughed. "Isn't he sweet?"

I wasn't sure that 'sweet' was in Sergeant Fenton's vocabulary. I wasn't sure that 'naked cooking' was the sort of activity she acknowledged or approved of either. She gave us all a long hard look. "So, your boyfriend," she said to me. "What's his name?"

Uh-oh. Whatever I said, she might try and check it out, but I had to say something. Robert Pattinson's eyes. Ashton Kutcher's smile.

"Robert," I said.

"Ashton," he said.

We spoke at the same time and it really didn't look good.

I looked at him. He looked at me, all smiles.

The doorbell rang. Stokes went off to answer it.

"Ashbert!" I cried out suddenly.

"What?" said Sergeant Fenton.

"Ashbert. It's a standing joke. Silly nickname. I call him Ashbert because it's cute and dorky."

"Amazon delivery," said Constable Stokes.

"What?"

I went out into the hallway. A delivery guy slid a huge box across the threshold.

"What's that?" I asked.

"There's five more," he said and continued to unload his trolley.

"Mind if I take a look?" asked Sergeant Fenton.

"What?" I said.

"In case it's something... herbal."

I wanted to say no, but a small mewling sound was all that would come from my mouth as it dawned on me what this was. She tore open one of the boxes and pulled out a display pack of condoms. I saw her lips moving as she did some rapid mental arithmetic. Twenty condoms in a pack. Over thirty packs in a box. Five boxes.

"We have a lot of sex," I heard myself say.

Sergeant Fenton gazed once more around the room and pursed her lips.

"I think I've seen enough," she said.

"Yes," I said in emphatic agreement.

"Whatever it is you're doing here," she said. "I don't want any more calls about it."

Chapter 7

An alarm woke me. It wasn't a gentle electronic warbling like my own alarm clock. You see, the problem with sleep is that's it's one of the best things ever but you're never awake to enjoy it. My clock's alarm is lovely; it wakes you up just enough to remind you that you're sleeping and then lets you get on with some serious snoozing.

But not this alarm currently assaulting my ears. It was like one of those old-school ones with bells on the top, designed to give you a heart attack. The worst part of it wasn't the loudness, although it was making my teeth bang together with the vibrations, it was the fact that I just couldn't tell where it was coming from. I jumped out of bed. Ah, yes. The bedroom in my brother's flat. I had just spent the first night in my new prison, my first night in exile. I was in the room with my boxes of belongings, and I briefly wondered if there was an alarm clock in one of them, but no, it was coming from all around me. I ran out of the bedroom and found Cookie still sleeping soundly on the settee.

"Wake up!" I howled and gave her a good shake. "Can't you hear that godawful noise?"

"Mmmf," said the sleeping Cookie. She was sleeping through this! I was a good sleeper but Cookie took it to the next level. If sleeping was an Olympic sport, she'd oversleep and fail to turn up to the event. They'd have to come round to her house to give her the medal.

"I need to turn the alarm off!"

My words were lost in the noise of the alarm, I couldn't even hear them myself, but then, remarkably, the noise stopped.

"Would you like to disable the alarm?" came Lexi's voice.

"Yes! Yes!" I pleaded. After a few moments, I had recovered sufficiently from the trauma to wonder what had just happened. "Lexi, who set that alarm?"

"Last night, you said that you needed to be out to start a shift at the museum at six o'clock. You have forty-five minutes to prepare yourself and the walk is estimated to be fifteen minutes."

While part of my mind did the sums and realised that I was awake at the ungodly hour of five o'clock, the other part was processing what Lexi had just said.

"You listen to everything that we say in this flat and then act on it if you think you can help?"

"Yes, that's my job."

I put a cushion over the nearest sinister black cylinder and wondered how best to keep Lexi's electronic nose out of my conversations. Cookie was stirring now.

"Morning," I said.

"It's a new dawn on a new day," she said and looked around. "Possibly it's even before the new dawn."

"Yeah, Adam's nosy robot set an alarm for us."

"I don't need alarms," she said. "I allow my natural circadian rhythms to wake me."

"Nah, I reckon it was the alarm."

"The body knows what it wants."

"Your body wants you to get up at five in the morning?"

"My body doesn't want to get fired."

Cookie got to her feet. She had slept on a cushion with a heavy brocade and she now had a pattern of flowers and oak leaves imprinted on the entire side of her face.

We might as well get ready and go," she said. First dibs on the bathroom."

"Fine," I said. "Er, before you go, do you remember anything weird about last night at all?"

"God, yeah. That bread recipe has never failed me before. I think your brother's flour might be past its best."

I nodded as she left the room. Surely, I hadn't made up all that mad stuff from last night? But it was mad stuff, wasn't it? We set the living room on fire. Cookie passed out on the sofa. A naked man climbed up the fire escape and into the flat. Not just any naked man, but my dream man – well, my teenage self's dream man. I trapped him in the bedroom. He broke out. We were both naked. I knocked him out with burned bread. The police turned up, the same coppers I'd met earlier that day. I pretended the man was my boyfriend and all was going well until an Amazon delivery guy turned up with three thousand condoms.

58

It had to be a dream. My perfect man in the flat. Both of us naked. And *I* whacked *him* with a big hard phallic loaf. That was some deeply Freudian stuff.

I knocked on the bathroom door.

"Mmm?" said Cookie.

"Have you ever had penis envy?" I called through the door.

"I'd like to be able to write my name in the snow."

"Right."

"But I'd be constantly worried about getting it trapped. You know, in an automatic sliding door or something."

"Does that ever happen?"

"If it did, would a bloke tell you?"

I shook my head. So, was it real or was it a dream? I had brought a man to life. My ideal man had appeared naked in my brother's flat. Whichever way I phrased it, it sounded like a crazy dream. He wasn't here now, but my crazy dream had an answer for that one too: I'd told him I was tired and that he had to leave. He wanted to stay but I flippantly told him to return only if he had a big pile of cash in one hand and a Quattro Formaggi in the other.

I decided to distract myself with a little bit of tidying up. The first thing that needed to be tackled was that sausage. I had to face up to the fact that it wasn't the gourmet delicacy that I'd been looking forward to. It was, in fact, a rotten sausage. I was almost grateful for the fact that no breakfast was available, because eating was going to be out of the question while the smell of it persisted. I could have found it blindfold; the intensity increased as I approached the kitchen. It sat on the counter, with a couple of bluebottles circling around it. Where had they come from? It was tempting to open a window and just throw the sausage outside, but of course Adam would get an alert and phone me up again. I slid it into the kitchen bin instead, making sure I didn't touch it. The smell didn't diminish at all when I closed the lid, but hopefully it would settle down during the course of the day.

Tidying up. Tidying up. What else could I do without breaking into an actual sweat?

I pulled the cushions and the rug away from the mess of the fire. Some of them were seriously singed. I divided them into two neat piles: those that could be put back on the sofa and those that I might have to bin and find replacements for on the internet. I was feeling more than a bit guilty about the mess I'd made in Adam's flat. Well I could do one thing that he'd asked me to do. "Take care of the rocks," he'd said. I'd get them all in a big box and toss them into the rubbish bin outside. I looked around and in the hallway I found five large boxes of condoms.

That bit at least had actually happened.

"Crap." In the living room, I took the cushion off Lexi. "Lexi, how would I know if I was going mad?"

"Do you want to listen to *I'm Going Slightly Mad* or would you like to know *The Top Signs that you Might be Going Mad*?" she asked.

"The second one. Quickly, before Cookie comes out."

"'In this day and age,'" recited Lexi, "'the stresses and strains of modern life cause many of us to worry about our mental health. Dr Julian Mannheim discusses –'"

"Skip the intro, just tell me the symptoms," I said.

"One, confusion," said Lexi.

"Well I can tick that box. I lost my house," I grumbled.

"Two, paranoia."

I kept silent but made a mental note to check with someone *other than* Lexi whether it still counts as paranoia if your every move is being monitored by an absent brother and his houseful of electronic gadgetry.

"Three, conversations with people who aren't there."

I nearly burst with the irony of having that read out to me by a machine pretending to be a person, but then I thought about the conversation I'd had with Ashbert, who was quite clearly a figment of my imagination and gave a soft moan of despair. I nodded along with the others as Lexi read them out. I'd need to be on the lookout for them.

"Four, feeling persecuted. Five, thinking that people are judging you. Six, stress and anxiety. Seven, hallucinations, and eight, being at odds with social norms."

"At odds with social norms? What does that mean?"

"It means behaviour that breaks the rules of society and may cause embarrassment or indignation."

"Well, that doesn't apply," I said and piled the rocks into one of the outer boxes from the Amazon delivery. I also needed to get my thinking cap on about what to do with all those condoms.

Cookie came out of the bathroom, a towel wrapped round her torso and another round her frizzy hair.

"Bathroom's yours."

"Thanks, Cookie."

Cookie sorted through last night's clothes, sniffing them for smoke.

"Cookie," said Lexi, "Lori tells me you have become a lesbian. Would you like to discuss this?"

"Lori!" said Cookie indignantly.

"Lexi! I said no such thing."

"You said she was coming out. Have I misunderstood?"

"Yes," I snapped, stomping into the bathroom. "You are so embarrassing."

"Not cool, ghost butler," said Cookie. "Not cool."

Dressed and ready, and listening to Cookie explain why she would be an excellent lesbian and why I'd be lucky to have her, I carried the box of rocks down to the communal bin area. I flung it in the top of a dumpster and felt pretty pleased that I'd accomplished something with my day while it was still officially night by normal people's standards.

We walked through the city centre while it was silent, which was a strange new experience.

"The quietness," said Cookie, with a wave of her hand.

"Yeah," I said.

"I know what you're thinking."

"Really?" How strange. I was just thinking that this is how things would look after a zombie apocalypse.

"Yeah, that you're at one with nature and your mind can be at peace. Let's not talk, let's *commune*."

We communed all the way to the museum. Cookie gazed up into the branches of the trees that we passed, but I was a bit scared to look up after I thought I saw a big rat scuttling under a bench. We got there in good time – I could tell because Rex was waiting, with only a moderate scowl on his big beardy face, when we walked in.

"Morning Rex!" I smiled, pretending that I was happy at being out of bed at six a.m.

"Good morning. Straight to work now, there's lots to do," he said. He guided me over to a trolley. "Here's your equipment. You should find everything that you need, and we trust that Melissa will accompany you for the first hour or so."

I gazed at the trolley. "All this is for me?" I said. "Cool! Can I pimp my ride?"

Rex gave me the sternest look, and I could see the question forming on his lips before he stopped himself, and turned away. "No," he said. "Tabard."

He passed me a cleaner's tabard. I looked at the name tag.

"Who's Consuela?" I asked.

"Your predecessor. We can't get any new nametags until we've concluded the un-retendering process. You will start in the Greek and Roman gallery. Follow."

We walked through the museum. Past the big bronze statue of the angel with no underpants, past glass cases full of teapots, samurai armour and silverware, round through the galleries of old paintings (featuring such fine art staples as Tired Woman with Jugs, Bored Man in Hat, Ugly Child and Bodybuilder in a Loin Cloth) and to a service lift. This took us up to the first floor where they keep all the history stuff. There was a bunch of stuff from the university's and the city's history, a surprising bunch of Egyptian things – mostly painted death masks and surprised-looking cats (I suppose being mummified would surprise anyone) – and then there was the Greek and Roman stuff.

Well, the exhibits certainly looked old. Most of it was broken plates and the kind of clay models you'd expect a class of six-year-olds to make.

"Right!" said Rex, loudly. "A really thorough job needs to be done in here. You'll see that there is dust on the skirting boards. A white cloth will be used to check them later, so it will soon be obvious if you've skipped any part of them." He swivelled the door and peered behind. "You will observe that there is a paperclip in the gap between the wall and the door. It was placed there as a test three weeks ago, and its continued presence is irrefutable evidence that your predecessor, Consuela, did not clean it up. Do better."

He turned on his heel and left.

Cookie pulled a face at his back and then waved a hand across the broom and the dusters. "You know how to work this complicated equipment, right?" I nodded. "Well you don't need me on your case. Time for the first fag break of the day. Gotta pace myself."

Cookie disappeared and I lifted the broom off the trolley so that I could start sweeping. I picked up the paperclip that Rex had pointed out. Could I sell a paperclip? I was conscious that I still had no money, and I wasn't going to be able to get food without some. Nobody would buy a single paperclip, but who knew, maybe there were more? Had Rex concealed paperclips throughout the gallery spaces to test his cleaners? Finding them would be a mildly diverting game of hide and seek and if I managed to collect fifty or so, maybe I could sell them for a quid? I popped the paperclip into my pocket and ignored the restless growling of my stomach.

I swept the floor and then mopped it. I'd never swept or mopped before but I'd seen it done, usually in musicals. I'm not sure if dancing with the mop and pirouetting were essential but I'm a perfectionist. I stopped a couple of times to scrape chewing gum off the floor. I couldn't recall any dance routines that feature gum-scraping but I did my best.

When I'd finished the floor, I looked across the gallery and gave myself a mental pat on the back. It looked pretty good, all glistening and shiny. I hadn't imagined that I'd get a lot of satisfaction from a cleaning job, so I relished this little nugget. My bubble burst when a man walked straight across the middle, leaving footmarks as he went.

"What do you think you're doing?" I yelled. "I've just cleaned that!"

He glanced up at me. I realised that I'd met this man before. Twice. Those brooding eyebrows like two slightly sexy caterpillars. The old-man-in-training clothing. It was Mr Corduroy, the paper delivery man.

"Oh, it's you. Shouldn't you have a little yellow sign thing?" he said. "Cleaning in progress."

"I've finished cleaning."

"Wet floor then."

"I haven't been given a sign. It's my first day."

"Ah." He nodded. "Found your parents yet?"

"Not yet."

"Keep looking. I'm sure they'll turn up."

He opened a cabinet, nonchalantly, like the world's laziest burglar.

"You can't touch that," I said, approaching the cabinet. I read the label. "It's, er, it's a statue of a man from the second century CE, whatever that means. Anyway, it means that you shouldn't touch it."

He looked up at me then and he rolled his eyes at me. Actually rolled his eyes at me. Lots of people can't do it; it takes practice. "I wrote the sign," he said. "I curate this gallery."

Whether he curated this gallery or the whole tooting museum (not that I was a hundred percent sure what curating was) I wasn't going to have someone roll their eyes at me like I was an idiot. I was determined to bring him down a peg or two. "Well you should take more care," I said, "you've spelled AD wrong. Or maybe BC. It's wrong anyway."

"It stands for Common Era," he said as he altered the position of the little pottery man.

"What? Like when everything got really chavvy?"

"It's the same as AD."

"After Death."

"Anno Domini. The Year of Our Lord."

"Not *my* Lord, sunshine."

"Which is why we use CE and BCE. We like to be inclusive with our signage, although cleaning staff weren't necessarily the demographic we had in mind when we designed it."

"I'm not cleaning staff!"

"You work here, don't you?"

"Yes, but..."

"You clean?"

"Yes."

"Ah." He moved the little pottery man further, unhappy with its positioning. "The name's James."

"That's not a very Roman name."

"Me. Not the statue."

He took a nice-looking SLR camera out of a case and started to photograph the exhibit.

"You don't work here at all," I said. "You deliver newspapers for Mr Patel."

"Who's Mr Patel?"

"I mean Norman."

He looked at my name badge. "For your information, Consuela. I have been delivering newspapers for Norman because my Uncle Phil would normally do it, but he's recovering from a hip operation. So, you can see why I'm very busy. I'm photographing specimens for an academic paper as well as juggling everything else."

"My name's Lori."

"It says Consuela."

"Yes, but that's because we've not been un-retendered yet."

"I see," he said, confused. "So, you were Consuela but once you've been retendered –"

"Un-retendered."

"– then you'll be Lori. Well, I'll hope you'll be happy with whoever you choose to be."

It was said as a farewell, a dismissal. He couldn't have been more dismissive if he'd said "Good day, sir!" and jammed a pipe in his mouth.

I couldn't believe he was talking to me like that. Feeling persecuted was on the list of symptoms that Lexi had reeled off this morning, but I really was being persecuted, wasn't I? By a shameless tweed-wearing mansplainer.

"You're lying," I said.

"Oh?" said James.

"It's After Death. Everyone knows that."

He nodded and packed his camera away again.

"So, it was BC, Before Christ? And then it was After Death, presumably after Jesus's death at the age of thirty-something?"

"Exactly."

He considered this deeply. "And what about the years when Jesus was alive? What do we call them?"

Ooh, that was a stumper. I thought about it while he moved on to another display case.

"They just take a break," I said.

"A break?" said James.

"They'd celebrate New Year and then they'd stick their heads out the window and ask, 'Is that Jesus still alive?' And, if he was, they'd just repeat the year."

"A bit impractical," he suggested.

"It would save money on calendars," I pointed out.

"Bad news for calendar makers."

He finished off fiddling in that case and, without a word of farewell, left. I was happy to have the gallery to myself again, and looked around at all the things I'd need to clean to impress Rex. The glass cabinets had a lot of fingermarks on them, so I gave them all a good polish. I came to a cabinet containing the little pottery man and found that the door was slightly ajar. Presumably I was to clean inside as well, I could clearly see the dust on the plinth. The pottery man was naked and reclined on one arm but, sadly, half of his other arm was missing. I was struck with a sudden thought. I could go above and beyond the call of duty here and really help out. I retrieved the paperclip and the gum that I'd cleaned up and fashioned a replacement arm for the tiny figurine. I even gave him a 'thumbs up'. I attached it to the elbow and stepped back to admire his new look. He had a whole new demeanour – he looked really cheerful.

Buoyed by my success, I looked around at the other exhibits. They all suffered from one main drawback – they were a bit dull. I walked over to look at another statue. It was three women all hugging each other, and their heads were missing. The label blathered on about them being a representation of the Three Graces. I thought for a moment and then got my bag from the bottom of my trolley. I had my pencil case and sketch pad, so I was able to create a better label. It read: *The Kardashians' heads exploded after they all turned up to a party wearing the same dress.* I put the label inside the cabinet and moved on.

There was a large plate on a stand. It had pictures on it and the one at the top was a man sitting on a chair blowing into some pipes. They looked like some sort of ancestor of the recorder except there were two of them in his mouth. I paused for a moment imagining how hellish that must have sounded. I remember being able to empty a room with a single recorder, what on earth would have happened if I'd ever tried to play two? I gave it a label saying *Ancient Greek vaping lounge* and closed the door of the cabinet. The last one that I made a label for a was a model of some sort of mythological creature. It looked to me as if the sculptor had suffered a bad acid trip after looking round a zoo. It had bits of rhino, bits of camel and a face that dared you to look at it wrong. I labelled it: *Hi, I'm a Cameloceros. I'm always horny, but I often get the hump.*

I made improvements throughout the gallery and finished the cleaning and then reported to Rex's office. The big metal electrical cabinet on the wall behind him fizzed and crackled alarmingly but he barely seemed to notice. He ran his fingers through his grey locks and gave me an appraising look.

"All done? Good. The quality of your cleaning will be inspected in due course. One hopes your best efforts have been sufficient but it's taken you much too long. You should be cleaning two galleries in this time. Speed up tomorrow. Take your break now and then report to the tea rooms, they'll want some help clearing dishes."

With that, he returned to his files and papers as though I had suddenly ceased to exist.

I found Cookie looking industrious among mannequins sporting 'clothes through the ages' on one of the lower levels. *Looking* industrious, not really doing anything.

"How am I going to bear being in the tea rooms?" I wailed. "I haven't eaten for nearly two days, and there's going to be food everywhere."

"The universe never closes a door without opening a window."

"Surprised it's never been burgled," I said.

"Your problem is its own solution," she said, strolling through a corridor and spraying a faint trail of furniture polish as she went in lieu of actual cleaning. "You won't believe the things that people don't eat. Trust me."

The tea rooms were in a big hall on the ground floor, all big windows and ironwork balconies and plump leather chairs. It was like an old gentleman's club had moved into a Victorian swimming baths and decided to serve gourmet sandwiches and cream teas. I got my orders from a woman with an unfortunate skin complexion and set off to clear tables from those who had come into the tea rooms for a spot of breakfast.

And Cookie was right. I cleared up some plates from a couple of skinny students, who'd nibbled half a teacake each. I wolfed down the rest on the way to the kitchen. I don't think I'd ever eaten anything so very delicious, I was so hungry! I went back out and looked around to see what else needed clearing. A lecturer type sat reading a newspaper with half a bacon sandwich left on a plate. I licked my lips.

"Can I take the plate for you?" I asked.

"I haven't finished," he smiled.

"We should eat until we're full, not until the plate is empty."

"How do you know I'm full?"

"I'm a good judge of character," I said. I pointed at the paper. "Has it got that news article in it about processed meat knocking five years off your life?" I asked. "Five years! Or maybe it was ten, actually."

"No, I didn't," he said, hesitating as he reached for his plate. He sighed. "Go on, you take the plate, I've had enough."

I made sure I was out of sight before I sank my teeth into the delicious sandwich.

When I came out again I scanned the room. I was in the mood for something sweet now. Yes, beggars can be choosers. A woman sat on her own with a selection of cakes. I plucked a style supplement from the newspaper rack and walked over.

"Can I offer you something to read?" I said.

I walked away and waited for the magazine to work its magic. Stick-thin models, fashion spreads and lifestyle articles create their own toxic blend. Ten minutes looking at that stuff can generate enough self-loathing for a week in my experience. Sure enough, I passed by shortly afterwards and she asked me to take away the remaining cakes. I managed to inhale a millionaire's shortbread, a

Bakewell tart and a cream slice during the short walk to the kitchen.

After dealing with the morning rush in the tea rooms, I cleaned the gallery with the interactive kids' zone in it (clearly the university aimed to get students signed up when they were young). After I'd done the cleaning I pulled out the new, improved wanted posters I'd been working on, depicting my parents more thoroughly. I'd drawn my mom weeding the garden. I thought it might jog people's memories if she was living off the land now. What would my dad be doing? Same as always, spending time in the shed or the garage. He'd almost certainly be working hard on something for their new lifestyle so I'd drawn him creating an irrigation system powered by my old bike. (It hadn't made it to Adam's flat which I thought was significant. Admittedly I haven't ridden it since I was eight.)

I showed the picture to a small girl who was daubing and colouring industriously. "What do you think?" I asked. The girl looked at the picture and then gave me a look of disdain. She pulled the picture towards her and dabbed with a glitter glue pen. She gave my mom a glitter halo, and she added glitter to my dad's handiwork so that his irrigation system looked as if it was powered by fairy dust. All in all, I thought they were improvements so I nodded my thanks and put the pictures away for later.

Cookie and I sat in the sunshine during lunchtime. We were out the back by the bins, so the view wasn't great, but it felt good. I had my sketching pad and quality pens and added final touches to my posters to take my mind off my stomach.

"Feel a bit sick," I complained.

"Did you eat something?" Cookie asked.

"Three plates of chips, two bacon sandwiches, a Cornish pasty, half a chicken pie, a tea cake and six assorted cakes."

"The universe always answers if we learn how to listen," she nodded. "Your stomach will settle."

"The staff in the kitchen kept giving me funny looks. Eventually the old one with a face like a cat litter tray –"

"Trudy."

"Yeah, she asked me if I'd been sorting the trays out properly, as there was nothing in the food waste container. I told her that

69

everyone had been eating up all their food. She gave me this look and then said that they *always* get food waste, the same sort of amount every day. She got this funny smirk on her face and said" – I made sure I replicated Trudy's evil witchy voice – "'tell you what, I'll show you' and then she opened up yesterday's food waste bin. It was horrible! It smelled even worse than that time I tried to toast cheese on the top of an electric heater and it fell in. The smell lasted for weeks, my parents blamed the cat."

"I can see why you're feeling a bit queasy. She's an old bat. Don't take any notice," said Cookie.

"She was judging me," I murmured, thinking about that list of Lexi's.

Chapter 8

By the time I'd finished work at three o'clock – three o'clock! That was nine hours at work! So much for the promise of a zero hours contract! By the time I'd finished work, the feeling of sickness had gone, and I'd started to worry about what I would do for food and money. I wandered about the city centre, on the lookout for dropped change. I ended up down near the markets, and while dropped change was thin on the ground I did find a lemon.

"When life gives you lemons, make lemonade."

All I needed now was some water, sugar, that fizzy gas stuff and a factory to make it in. I didn't find any of those but I did find some other vegetables on the ground that had either rolled away or been cast aside by the stall holders. Some of them were obviously mushy and horrible, but I ended up with a haul of four lemons and a swede. My spirits were high. I was sure to be able to make a meal out of those, although I really wasn't very fond of swede. I decided to walk over to Norman's newsagents to put up the new posters that I'd done. It took a while. The old Belkin family residence (I sniffed nostalgically) and its nearby newsagents was some distance from the city centre but the sun was still out and I wanted to be back among the streets I had known and loved since childhood.

Here, the park with little boating lake Adam and I had played on as kids. Here, the little cut through to Mansfield Gardens where I'd once snogged Leo Bickers and, some years later, thrown up after drinking a whole bottle of Malibu. Here, the garden wall I'd ridden my bike into after convincing myself that I could pop a wheelie off the kerb and jump straight over it. And, here, Mr Patel's newsagent or Norman's newsagent or whatever, a magical world of magazines, confectionery, fags and alcohol. I breathed it in as I entered and the memories flooded back. It seemed like only yesterday I had been here.

Norman scowled at me from his high counter.

"I've brought new versions of the posters," I said. "Can you put them in the window, please?"

"No, I can't."

"I said please."

"You haven't paid me for the last ones yet."

"Aha!" I said. "I can do something about that. How about a nice swede?" I pulled the swede out of my bag and offered it up to him.

"You're mad."

"Or, seven, eight... nine paperclips. And there'd be more where those came from."

"You need to get out of my shop before –"

"Swede *and* the paperclips?"

"What would I...?"

"You could fashion them into a brilliant swede hedgehog. It's a hedgehog. It holds papers. It makes a nutritious soup."

"You're mad."

"She's a bloody menace," said a voice from the back of the shop.

There was a door that led from the back of the shop and in the frame stood Mr James Reynolds. He was pulling his tartan trolley of newspapers with one hand and jabbing an accusing finger at me with the other.

"Did you know he's moonlighting as a museum-thingy person?" I said to Norman. "Reckons he knows about Romans and stuff."

"I do," said Norman, "and he does. He's doing his doctorate. So, you know this woman, James?"

"Yes," said James. "She was in the gallery this morning, messing –"

"I was not messing," I said.

"*Messing* with a load of valuable artefacts. Cleaning staff are *not* permitted to access the exhibits. You have committed vandalism against the university's antiquities!"

"One man's vandalism is another man's art," I said, but he wasn't listening.

"Are you aware of how valuable the exhibits are in the museum."

"What? Some old pots?"

"Old pots as you call it and rare artefacts and a treasure house of painting and sculpture. You know, a very valuable painting went missing from there a couple of years ago. The finger of suspicion ranged far and wide and several people lost their jobs."

"Over a painting?"

"*Zeus wakes on Mount Ida* by Fuseli."

"That's a kind of pasta. You're making it up."

"That's it," he growled. "I'm calling the police."

"Total overreaction! Tell him, Norm."

"Call the police, James," said the newsagent.

Well, that's the last time I support my local small business, I thought.

Now I knew what Lexi meant about stress and anxiety. I clutched my lucky pendant. (I didn't know if it was lucky, but I was willing to give it a go.)

"Don't you think you might be overreacting a teeny bit?" I said.

James gave me a quiet, intense look. "You have no idea what you've done, do you?" he said. It was a genuine question, like he thought I was a moron or something.

How could this be happening? I'd tried to help and it had backfired on me completely. I wondered what I was going to do. I gestured wildly.

"I can fix the things if you want?" I called.

"You'll touch nothing!" he snapped and went outside with his trolley to call the police or whatever.

Norman shook his head sadly and rearranged his sweet display.

Something caught the corner of my eye at that moment. A small movement down by the newspaper rack. Did Norman have a rodent problem? I stooped down to get a better look and really wished I hadn't. A tiny woman glared back at me. It was – I blinked – it was Angela Merkel, the German Chancellor. She was no more than four inches high, and as I goggled at the sight of her, a miniature Vladimir Putin and a diminutive Nigel Farage slid out from within a Times and a Daily Mail respectively. It was like the Borrowers had decided to go all political. Merkel was stabbing at a miniature mobile phone and making small squeaks of annoyance that it wouldn't work.

"Angela, what are you doing?"

And then another Merkel appeared from the pages of the Telegraph. And another and another. Oh, and more Putins and Farages and a few Kim Jong-wossnames and some other world leaders, including that mad one, you know, the one with the hair. The Merkels were trying to corral all the others. The Putins were in deep and secretive discussions with each other. The Farages had started to fight among themselves and one had ripped off his shirt and was wearing his tie as a headband.

I looked up in a panic. Surely Norman must have seen this weird sight too? No, he was rearranging his sweet display. This had to be a hallucination (*another* sign from Lexi's list) but what was I supposed to do about it? I glanced down, but they'd gone.

A weary Kim Jong-wossname, trailing behind the others, vanished through the open shop door. I started after them. Two dozen Barbie-sized politicos stood in front of the telephone box outside. They conferred in a group, and there was lots of finger-wagging and posturing, but I couldn't hear what they said. Hear what they said? It was a hallucination. I might as well try to eavesdrop on a dream.

"Right," I said. "I think it's time you all popped back inside your newspapers before Norman gets really annoyed with me."

Several the figures made some very unstatesmanlike physical gestures and, pushing and shoving as they went, they ran off the pavement and out into the road.

I needed to do something. The tiny figures were running fast and I had no idea how to apprehend them. For all I knew, they might have guns or polonium or something. I should think a good few of them knew nuclear launch codes. That's not the kind of thing I wanted on my conscience.

And that's why I ran out into the road after them and straight into the path of a road-sweeper van.

Chapter 9

I woke up in a bed with one of those old-fashioned blankets draped over me, the sort with holes in it that only come in appalling pastel shades. There was a distinctive smell about the place, too. It was like nail polish with the fruity, fun bits taken out. I realised I could only be in hospital. A lady approached with a tea trolley.

"Care for a drink, bab?" she asked.

Moments later, I was propped up in bed with a cup of tea in my hands. This was nice! I could feel a bump on my head from my earlier adventures, but I had my feet up and someone had brought me a cup of tea. Jobs and hard work had brought me nothing but trouble, but a joyride on a road sweeper ended with my feet up enjoying a cup of tea. Then another.

Two cups of tea later, a doctor came around with a stethoscope and a concerned expression. She took my blood pressure and wrote on the chart at the end of my bed.

"Hi. I'm Jasmin. How are we feeling?" she smiled.

I wondered which answer would be the right one to extend my stay for an evening meal. "Not bad?" I ventured.

"You've had concussion," she said. "No fractures. Do you remember what happened to you?"

I straightened against the pillows. "What kind of a doctor are you?" I asked. "Will you be able to tell if I'm going mad?"

She smiled. She had a nice smile, the kind that could get her a job in a toothpaste commercial. "I'm not a psychiatrist, Lori, but I can certainly help you evaluate the current state of your mental well-being."

"Brilliant!" I said. "Well things have been going wrong for a couple of days. Oh no! I just realised I've ticked another box!"

"What box is that?" she asked.

"I keep getting in trouble with the police. I'm at odds with social norms. It was on a list of signs that you're going mad. It's official, I don't think you need to examine me. I'm definitely mad."

She leaned forward. "Let me be the judge of that. What's been going wrong then?"

"I lost my house and my parents, brought a naked man to life, destroyed my brother's flat, brought some tiny politicians to life and then ran out in front of a road-sweeper and got clonked on the head." My face fell. "Worst thing of all, I got a job."

She didn't laugh at me, just nodded. "There's a heck of list, Lori. Break it down for me, will you? Now you mentioned your family twice in there. What's it like, your family?"

"Oh, pretty much a normal family, I think. Mom, Dad, my brother Adam and me."

"And you all get on well?"

"Yes, mostly," I said. "I mean, my brother is an insufferable overachiever, who never misses an opportunity to remind me that I'm hopeless and my parents sold the family home while I was on holiday, but mostly we get on pretty well."

"You were living there and they sold it while you were away?"

"Yes," I said.

"How did that make you feel?" she asked.

"It was really tough, I had nobody to pay the taxi," I said.

"Interesting. I ask you how you feel and you mention a practical detail," she said. "How did it make you *feel*?"

"Oh." I pushed aside the chaotic scramble for survival I'd endured for the last couple of days and tried to isolate what my feelings really were on my parents' abandonment.

"Like it's not fair," I said finally.

"You feel that your parents have let you down?" she asked.

"Yes! It's their job to look after me!"

"Of course it is," she agreed smoothly. She looked at the chart at the end of the bed.

"How old are you, Lori?"

"Isn't it on my chart?" she said.

"It is," said Dr Jasmin. "I wonder, do you expect to reach an age where it won't be their job?"

What a strange question! I thought about it for a moment. "No."

"Okay."

"I'm not being selfish," I assured her. "Parents live for their children. We're like oxygen to them."

She wrote something on her pad before she looked up and asked me another question. "So, you've been staying with your brother, yes?"

"Not exactly. I'm living in his flat but he's away at the moment."

"So, how's that working out for you?"

"It should be fine except that he has all this creepy spy stuff in his flat, so I'm too scared to put the heating on in case it makes him mad. Looking back, it probably wouldn't make him anywhere near as mad as the fire damage is going to make him."

"There was a fire?"

"A small one yes. It seemed like a great idea to use the fireplace, but it turns out that the plastic parts of a fake fire will melt if you light a fire on top of them. Who knew?"

She made another careful note on her pad and sucked at the end of her pencil for a while. Careful lady, I thought, you might ruin those toothpaste commercial teeth.

"So, you've gone to great lengths to evade the lifestyle that your parents and your brother wish for you. Is that a fair summary?"

"What? No." It sounded like nonsense to me. Surely, she was putting words into my mouth?

"No?" she said. "But your parents seem to think that it's time you took care of yourself?"

"Have you been talking to them? Holy crap!" I scrambled to get out of bed. It suddenly occurred to me that they might be here. "Where are they? I need to speak to them."

It also occurred to me that I was wearing one of those hospital gowns, you know, the ones that are pretty much wide open at the back. I've always thought they were kind of pervy. I mean, who needs quick and easy access to the back of someone?

Dr Jasmin put a hand on my arm and gently ushered me back into bed. "Relax, Lori. I haven't spoken to your parents."

"You sound as if you're in cahoots with them."

"I'm not going to pick sides, Lori. If we all went round judging each other's family lives, we'd never have time for anything else. I'm just trying to picture the dynamic here. For example, did you share the household chores with them when you were all in the same house?"

"Of course. Right, it was always my job to make little cartoons of everyone for Christmas and then put them inside homemade crackers."

"Cartoons?"

"Little comic drawings. I'm a cartoonist, comic strip author and graphic designer. I draw the Florrie comic strip. Have you seen it?"

"Don't think so," she said slowly.

"You can look at it on my blog. Florrie is amazing. And the cracker thing. It took ages. And you know how often Christmas comes around."

"Every year?"

"Exactly?"

"Yes, and did you do any chores when it wasn't Christmas?"

I thought for a moment. "My mom and dad did try to get me to do the cracker thing for a neighbour's silver wedding, but I was worried that I might get taken for granted, you know?"

She gave me a long look – she either thought I was an 'interesting case' or was beginning to fancy me; I couldn't be sure – and she made another note. "So, how about you talk me through some of the unusual things that you mentioned earlier. The naked man, for example."

"Well, I don't know what to tell you. Earlier in the day I'd been looking through a scrapbook from when I was younger. I'd made a collage of a man, from bits I'd ripped out of magazines –"

"– and he was naked?"

"What? No! Where would I get a magazi–? No, don't answer that! Later that evening, a man with the *exact same face* appeared, stark naked outside the flat. He came inside and I panicked. I don't think he meant to hurt me, but he was a bit more *naked* than a stranger ought to be in my view."

"And yet, he wasn't a stranger," Dr Jasmin said thoughtfully. "He was someone you invented?"

"I didn't invent him naked," I said.

"I'm sure Freudian analysts would have a lot to say about how the mind will often use nudity to reflect our inner feelings of anxiety and social embarrassment," she said. "This, they argue, might manifest itself in dreams where you are inexplicably forced to appear naked in public."

"Oh yeah! The riding through Asda on a unicorn dream, I have that one all the time!" I squealed. This woman was good. "Only one problem. I wasn't asleep, I was wide awake."

"I have a question about that," she said. "Was this before or after the fire that you mentioned?"

"After."

"Hmmm. It is very possible that you have experienced some mild poisoning from the fumes. Melting plastic can be very toxic. These hallucinations were perhaps a side effect."

"How long would that last?" I asked.

"Who knows?" he said. "We can run some blood tests to check, but I would imagine that after a day or two you should be fine."

"So, it could be that I was having hallucinations today as well? When I had to chase the tiny politicians?"

She nodded. "I think that's very much possible, Lori."

"Thank God!"

"Whatever issues you might have with your family, and I'd suggest that you might benefit from working with a therapist to resolve those, I'd bet that your hallucinations are unrelated to them. We can discharge you after the blood tests, but you should take things easy for the next day or so. Rest up a little bit."

I beamed at the doctor. This was very good news. Not mad, just suffering from smoke damage, a bit like Adam's flat.

"I'll make sure I mention the smoke hallucination thing when the police come in to chat with you."

"Police?"

"The road-sweeper only hit you in glancing. The driver swerved and mounted the pavement."

"Oh, my God. Was anyone hurt?"

Dr Jasmin smiled. "The only casualty was a tartan shopping trolley, I hear. I think you were all very lucky."

Chapter 10

That evening, I let myself into the flat with a sigh of relief. I had a dressing on my head and a plaster on my arm from where they'd taken the blood. I had my clothes in a carrier bag (they'd had to cut the top off me and the jeans were fairly splattered with my blood). I was wearing a t-shirt and a pair of jogging bottoms that came from some sort of store that they have for emergencies like this. I'd asked if they took them off dead people and they'd told me no, that they were charitable donations, but I'm not so sure about that – these were definitely the sort of things that dead people might wear.

I walked inside, preoccupied with my damaged clothes.

"Lights Lexi," I said.

Sitting on the settee was the man from the previous night, no longer naked, but wearing an assortment of clothes that was almost as bizarre as mine – a Metallica t-shirt and some sort of sarong. He grinned at me. I screamed.

"Hallucination!" I shouted, like it was a protective prayer against the devil.

"I got the things," he said, standing up.

"Not real!"

He held out a pizza box and a very thick pile of bank notes tied up with an elastic band.

"This is just smoke inhalation," I told myself. "My brain's been fried by melted plastic. The doctor said so; it must be true."

His face fell and I felt absurdly guilty.

"You said not to come back until I had a big pile of cash in one hand and a Quattro Formaggi in the other." Now that he was standing up, I could see that his sarong was actually a length of AstroTurf that might once have lined a greengrocer's market stall.

I finally realised what was going on. My mind was constructing the entire thing. It was incredibly convincing, I could even smell the pizza. I inhaled deeply.

"Let's eat then!" I said. It made sense to play the scenario through before it turned into the naked unicorn ride through Asda, and I preferred this one.

His smile returned as I accepted the pizza box. He pushed the cash into my hand as well.

"Where did you get this?" I asked, slightly afraid of the answer.

"I looked around until I found what you asked for," he said, taking a slice of pizza after I'd grabbed one myself. "I had to run quite fast to keep hold of them," he added.

It sounded very much as if he'd managed to find and steal a pizza and a pile of cash, just because I'd asked for them. Nice one, subconscious! Not only was he gorgeous, he was also dedicated to pleasing me.

But was I going to get into trouble for the stolen money? I reasoned it through as I settled down beside him on the settee and grabbed another slice of pizza. Either the money was real or it wasn't. If it wasn't, then there was no problem. If it was, then I couldn't have stolen it because I had been in hospital much of the day. Unless...

I patted the sofa, scrunching my fingers through the fabric of a cushion. I rapped my fingers on the fire-damaged coffee table.

"Is this real life?" I asked.

"Is it just fantasy?" said Ashbert.

"Pinch me. Ow!"

"Why did you want me to pinch you?"

"I was just thinking. Maybe I'm still in hospital, in a coma or something, and all this is an illusion."

"How would you know?" he asked.

"I wouldn't," I said.

"Then it doesn't matter, does it?" he said.

He might be a hallucination but he was chomping down a fair amount of pretend pizza. After we made short work of the pizza I felt good.

"I don't have any wine or beer, I'm afraid," I said to him.

"I can go and get some wine and beer," he said, standing up.

"No, maybe we're better off staying sober," I said, thinking of whatever toxins were coursing through my veins. "Tell you what, have you got any idea how to work a washing machine?"

"No, but I would be happy to try," he said.

We went into the kitchen and took a long hard look at the appliances.

"Why are there two of them?" he asked.

"Well, I guess one's a washer and one's a dryer," I said. "Not sure which one's which though."

I opened both doors and discovered that each machine had a unique smell. One was a bit damp and unpleasant, and the other was very familiar.

"This one's the dryer," I said triumphantly. "It smells like my clothes when my mom gives them back to me."

We turned our attention to the washer. I put my bloody jeans inside the drum as a first step. I looked at the confusing array of buttons and dials. There was a little drawer as well. I pulled it out and looked inside. It had gungy deposits of something soapy.

"Washing powder?" I mused.

Ashbert looked in cupboards and handed me a box of little tablets. I read what it said, but mostly it said things like *3 in 1, XXL* and *non-bio.* It was like another language. I took out a tablet, put it in the compartment that had the right coloured sludge and shut the drawer. I then scanned the buttons for one that looked as though it made things happen. I tried *on/off* but all it did was make a little light come on. I looked again and pressed *start* and this time there was noise and movement.

"Bingo!" I crowed, and high-fived Ashbert. Our eyes met and I wondered why I was wasting this awesome hallucination on such tedious domestic chores. "So, what would you like to do now?" I asked.

He moved closer. "Whatever you'd like to do," he said and took my face tenderly in his hands. I looked up at his face. On paper, he was drop-dead gorgeous. Here in the flesh, looking at me as if I was everything he ever wanted it was almost more than a girl could handle. Almost. His eyes locked onto mine, gentle brown pools but with a breathtaking intensity. Whose eyes had I based this fantasy on? I couldn't remember. I didn't care. All I cared was that his breathing was coming faster now as he leaned in for a kiss. Our lips met and I moved forward to mould my body more closely into his. I trod on his AstroTurf sarong as I did so and it fell away. I wasn't even sorry.

Chapter 11

I woke up early, which saved me from Lexi's nerve-jangling alarm. The memories of the previous night crowded into my mind. I very nearly blushed at what my imagination had conjured for me, but it had been delicious, and I lay in bed replaying the highlights. I rolled over.

"You're still here," I said.

"Do you want me to go?" said Ashbert, who was propped up on one elbow, gazing at me.

"I didn't say that," I said.

Surely, he should have gone by now? The toxic plastic fumes must have worked their way out of my system by now. The flat didn't even smell of the melted fireplace any more. There was a faint, lingering aroma of pizza and the godawful smell of that sausage. I perked up at the thought that if evidence of the pizza was still around then maybe that pile of cash was still here too. The doorbell rang, interrupting thoughts of where I might buy some breakfast.

"Good morning," said the woman at the door. I had only opened the door a crack, so that it wasn't obvious that I was wearing only a pillow.

"Hello," I said.

"Can I speak to Adam?" she said. She was around my mom's age, but where my mom was always smiling, this woman looked as though she could smell something really horrible. I thought of the sausage in the bin and decided that maybe she could.

"Adam's away at the moment," I said.

"Then who are you?"

"I'm his sister."

"I'm Bernadette Brampton, head of the residents' association."

"I didn't know that was a thing."

"I was hoping you could tell me why your rubbish is not being sorted correctly?" said Bernadette Brampton, head of the residents' association. Her eyebrows rose, as if I was supposed to have an answer.

"Eh?"

She indicated a box at her feet. It was the Amazon delivery box that I'd taken downstairs yesterday. Of course, it had Adam's name and address on it. "I found a box of fossils in the household waste," she said.

"Fossils?"

"It's very clear that this is *not* household waste. You need to consult the residents' handbook to ensure that you understand how waste should be sorted."

"Does the handbook mention fossils?"

"They're certainly not household waste."

"I mean, any residents' handbook with a section on fossils is worth reading."

"I'll leave them with you. Some of us have jobs to get to."

She turned and went. I was glad that she didn't stay around to watch as I shuffled backwards with the box of rocks, the edge of the pillow gripped between my teeth to provide some degree of modesty to the outside world. Meanwhile, I'd forgotten about the inside world. A hand caressing my bare bottom was enough to make me drop the pillow in shock. Luckily, I was inside by then. I shut the door and turned to see Ashbert grinning at me. I whacked him with the pillow. "You made me jump! Can't you see that I'm naked and vulnerable?"

He waggled his eyebrows and nodded. "You're not naked, you're wearing a pendant," he said.

My hand went to my neck and I ran my fingers across the stone. "Oh yeah! That's all right then. I wondered yesterday if it was a lucky pendant. I'm beginning to think it might be." I gestured at the box of rocks. "Let's put these somewhere and we can go and see how lucky I can get before I go to work."

He peered at the rocks. "They *are* fossils. That woman was right."

I looked. Those things that look like squished beetles with loads of legs. "Maybe there's a special recycling bin for fossils," I said. "I must look in the residents' handbook at the first opportunity."

"Do you want to do that now?" he asked.

I reached out for the smoothness of his shoulders. "No, not just now."

I caught up with Cookie at break time at work. She took a long draw on her joint and gazed up at the sky. "The sky looks the same as our break yesterday. If nothing changes, can we be sure that time passes?" she asked.

"Blimey, you have no idea how many things have changed since yesterday. I can confirm that time has definitely passed. Hard to believe it's *only* a day," I said.

"You've hurt your head," she said.

Of all the things that had happened, that one seemed relatively insignificant, but I put my hand to the bruise. "Yes, I got run over by a street-sweeper and that wasn't the weirdest part."

Cookie nodded her casual acceptance of this.

"So, a guy from my past appeared over the last couple of days," I said.

I was feeling my way around the subject, trying to find a way to talk to Cookie about the whole Ashbert thing, when I had absolutely zero understanding of it myself.

"Would I know him?" she asked.

"Maybe I showed you a picture I did of him years ago," I said. "I made it out of magazine images, but it's just like him. Exactly like him. *Weirdly* like him."

"Well, you're a great artist, we know this," said Cookie.

I nodded. Was it possible that he really was someone I met, someone I *knew* and then I had made a picture of him? No. I remembered clearly the afternoon I created that picture. I must have been fifteen. I'd been bored and a bit fed up after colouring my hair with a dye called 'Copper Goddess' that should have been called 'Ginger Cake Mix With Weird Orangey Bits'. I can remember poring over Mom's magazines harvesting body parts for the ideal man.

I caught movement from the corner of my eye. Cookie and I were in this quiet corner in a courtyard between the museum and the university chancellor's building. The only access to the courtyard was a tall gate. I could have sworn that someone peeked over the top, but all I caught was a flash of pea green, as if they were wearing a hoodie. I stared for a moment more, but they didn't reappear. I couldn't shake the feeling of being watched though. I was properly on edge! I got back to telling Cookie about Ashbert.

"He appeared after you'd baked that bread, when you were having a nap. He came back again last night."

"Cool!" said Cookie. "You've been spending some quality time with him from the look of your face as well. Your cheeks are quite flushed," she added with a wink.

She knows me too well. I put a hand to my face, imagining that a night (and a morning) of mind-blowing sex was written all over it.

"The thing is," I said, taking the plunge, "I think I made him with the power of my mind or something."

Cookie nodded. "Don't all women recreate men with our wills? Without us they are nothing."

"Yeah," I said slowly. I needed to penetrate the veil of Cookie's world view and make her realise that I was talking literally. "It could be that, but I also animated some people out of the newspaper yesterday. Brought them to life and then chased them."

"Wow. Where are they now?" asked Cookie.

"No idea. I got hit by the street-sweeper while chasing them," I said miserably, realising that I sounded like every kid *ever* who'd failed to do their homework. Lying or mad, take your pick.

Cookie took the joint out of her mouth and stared at it for a long moment. "When I talk to the trees, they sometimes talk back," she said, "and that's cool. I tend to cut back on the weed, though, if it happens a lot."

"The doctor said it could be hallucinations, caused by the melted plastic from the fire we had," I said miserably.

"Could be," she said. "Maybe you could talk to Rex, have a couple of shifts off and rest up."

"God, no," I said. "I'm in enough trouble already. I forgot to tell you about James, the Greek antiquities guy."

"James Reynolds. I know him. He does the gallery stuff here and teaches at the uni as well, I think. Is he a doctor?"

"He's doing his doctorate. He got really mad because I touched some of the exhibits. He was going to call the police."

Cookie laughed. "He won't do that. He's a softy really. He's like one of them, people, whatchacallems? Like Alan Bennett and Stephen Fry."

"Gay?"

"No," she said, flapping a hand at me. "I mean he belongs to a bygone age. All tweedy jackets and tobacco pipes."

"I don't think he smokes a pipe," I said.

"But he looks like he might. No, it's a bluff exterior but he's just a little boy on the inside. Anyway, he left the cases open, yeah?"

"He did," I said.

"QED, Baby Belkin, he's the one who has responsibility for the exhibits, so he'd take the fall, not you. One of the paintings went missing years ago."

"Right. The one of Zeus by somebody Spaghetti or Tagliatelle or something."

"Yeah. The number of people who got in deep doo-doo for that was amazing. Plenty of us, including Rex and myself, only got our jobs because of the people who got fired over that one. James will keep schtum if he values his job. Anyway, I had a family ask me for directions to the Roman and Greek stuff yesterday because they'd heard about the funny speech bubbles. Kudos."

I had been very careful to avoid James, feeling sure that the sight of me would remind him to bring in the SWAT team or whatever, but if Cookie was right then maybe I could breathe easy again.

"Want to hang out this evening?" Cookie asked as she stubbed out her joint and turned to go back inside.

"I can't. Ashbert's planning a romantic meal for two," I said. "He's cooking sausages with onion gravy."

"Is that a romantic meal?" asked Cookie, looking sceptical.

"It's my all-time favourite thing," I explained. "He knew that already, like he could read my mind. It's amazing."

"Well, enjoy your evening of sausage," said Cookie with a rude laugh as we went back inside.

After work, I returned to the flat, wondering if Ashbert would still be there. My hand went to my pocket where I had some of the cash that he'd given to me. It was definitely real, as I'd used some to buy a pasty at lunch time.

I saw a notice taped to the wall at the bottom of the stairs up to Adam's flat. I stopped to read it.

Someone has put something foul and rotten in the food waste. I will be reviewing the CCTV footage to determine who did this. Please respect the fact that you live in a community and take more care with your household hygiene. Yours, Bernadette Brampton (Residents' Association)

Wow, at least I wasn't the only one who'd upset Bernadette with a crime against rubbish. She must be very bored.

As I opened the door, the delicious smell of sausages came to me and it was clear that Ashbert was still in residence. He came out of the kitchen and smiled. From behind his back he produced a small bunch of flowers with a *ta-da*.

"I got you freesias," he grinned.

I was momentarily speechless. How did he know I liked freesias? I can't remember telling anybody that, even Cookie.

"They're lovely!" I said. He kissed me briefly.

"Let me put them in water and check these sausages," he said.

I followed him into the kitchen.

"Lexi, can you play some music?" he said, turning the sausages under the grill.

"Yes, what would you like?" said Lexi.

"Play some McFly, it's Lori's favourite," said Ashbert. He turned to me as the music started and handed me a bottle of cider.

I looked at the label. "Wow, this takes me back, I used to drink this stuff all the time."

"You don't drink it anymore?" he asked.

"I might choose wine *more* of the time now," I said tactfully, "but this is a lovely change. Yum." I sipped the powerful, gassy stuff and wondered how to ask him about this. "How do you know all of these things?"

He shrugged. "I just do. I think you told me, before."

That made no sense at all. I met him for the first time two days ago. I tried a different question.

"Where did you come from? Where were you before you came here, you know, through the window?"

He frowned, taking a swig from his own bottle of cider. "Interesting. It's like if apple juice had an evil twin."

"You must remember something," I said. "How do you know how to cook sausages?"

"Everyone knows how to do that," he laughed.

"I don't," I said. "You must have learned somewhere."

"I guess," he said with a smile. He'd turned the full wattage of his charm onto me now. "I only know what I know, and one thing that I *do* know, is that you're in need of a foot rub after a day's work. I'll turn these sausages down for a few minutes."

A foot rub sounded good. I let him lead me to the comfiest chair. He kneeled in front of me and slipped off my shoes so that my feet were in his lap, and he rubbed them, while he gazed into my eyes. It was a powerful aphrodisiac, and almost made me forget about the sausages, but the smell was so good. I found myself licking my lips, not even sure whether I was experiencing food lust or just regular lust.

Something rustled on the floor in the corner, but I couldn't pull my eyes away from Ashbert's. Let it wait, whatever it was. As long as it wasn't a mini-president or diddy dictator-for-life, I couldn't care less.

Ashbert gave my feet a final caress and stood up. "Let's eat," he said.

"It smells so good," I said. "When I left, the place was stinking of that nasty stuff I brought back from holiday."

"I emptied the bin," he said with a wink.

'I emptied the bin'. Four powerful words and almost – *almost*! – as sexy as a foot rub. Whatever weirdness surrounded his sudden appearance, he was:

a) incredibly hot

b) dedicated to doing whatever would make me happy

c) impossibly knowledgeable about what would make me happy

d) incredibly hot

The sausages were as good as the ones my mom makes, and that is not the sort of comparison that I would make lightly. The gravy was strong and thick, and he'd even scooped the mash into little hillocks on my plate, so that the whole thing looked like a fantasy landscape with the mixed veg forming a rocky coastline. Presentation is important, and he knew just how I liked it. I held back from making the sausages into little towers on the hill tops because sophisticated and mysterious women don't do that. I don't think his eyes left mine for the entire meal. It was so fantastically erotic that it almost took my mind off the food, but he'd bought brown sauce to go with it, which obviously takes any meal to another level. We had bowls of ice cream afterwards, with wafer biscuits. By the time I'd eaten the meal and finished the bottle of high alcohol cider I was stuffed. Ashbert cleared the plates from the table and his lips drifted across the back of my neck as he went past.

"I got us something to read," he said as he came back in.

Reading? Really? I had other things on my mind. He pulled a book out of a bag and handed it to me. I looked at the cover: *Sizzling Sex Positions for Adventurous Lovers.* I smiled up at him, knowing that we were perfectly in tune with each other.

"You choose," he said. "We'll work our way through them all. We can start a new page every night."

I flicked through the images, lingering over the ones that looked as though they might work with a full stomach. This evening was turning out to be more magical than I would have thought possible.

Chapter 12

After I'd been doing the cleaning job for a few days, Rex eased up on his spot checks. Nonetheless, in that time, I had managed to collect thirty-two paperclips, eight pieces of gum, seventy-two pence in loose change and a small plastic dragon. I've no idea how many of them were left by Rex to test me but I collected them diligently all the same. He still made sure that he gave me a little pep talk every time our paths crossed, but he never mentioned anything about me vandalising the exhibits, so I guessed that James hadn't told him. I'd become faster at the cleaning as well, mainly because I'd discovered which cloths and tools were best for each job. It's a skill that will never leave me now, and I felt absurdly proud. I really wanted to tell my parents what I'd learned, but I was no closer to finding them. Cookie and I had spent our lunch hours putting up more of the posters that I'd made, but we'd seen no results.

"Do you think I need to rework the colour scheme?" I asked her, as we walked over to put up a fresh batch.

"You know colour, Lori," she said. "I think this one's as eye-catching as it's going to get. Maybe the people that see it just don't have the answers you seek."

"Yeah, well someone knows," I grumbled.

"Your brother knows," Cookie said. "You could try being nice to him."

I stuck my tongue out at her. It was my standard Adam response, but I guess she had a point. I tried not to think about it. I wasn't ready to suck up to Adam-shiny-superstar. I changed the subject.

"Ashbert's treating me tonight. We're having a 'sensual playtime'."

"I thought you guys were having that, like, every evening?" said Cookie.

"Well we are having a lot of sensual stuff, yeah," I said, "but he's laying on something extra tonight."

"Cool," said Cookie. "You having sausage again?" She waggled her eyebrows suggestively and I rolled my eyes at her.

As I went home later, I pondered the same question. Ashbert was so keen to treat me to all of my favourite things that he'd cooked sausages every night. If I didn't say something soon, I might start oinking.

As I opened the door, McFly's *Five Colours in her Hair* was already playing. Ashbert appeared from the kitchen, wearing an apron. He was wearing nothing else, which was a good look for him. He had a glass of red wine in his hand for me. He'd taken care to move to wine after I'd said that I now prefer it to cider, which was good, but perhaps I ought to say something about not necessarily having it *all the time*. He kissed me, and put an immediate stop to that train of thought. I spent a few happy moments enjoying his attention, but I really needed to go to the toilet, so I moved away towards the bathroom.

"How was your day?" he asked, still not breaking eye contact. The intensity of his gaze, the way he didn't take his eyes off me, was mostly adorable. But right now, it was a bit annoying. I needed the loo.

"Great. Back in a moment," I said, closing the door.

When I opened it again, he was still standing there, the wine glass still raised as he offered it to me. I took it, trying to shake off the mild feeling of irritation at his hanging around. I went through to the kitchen where sausages with onion gravy was making another appearance.

"Your favourite!" he said.

I nodded, trying not to look too lacklustre at the sure knowledge that I'd be awake half the night with indigestion.

I saw that he'd made a neat pile of potato peelings and other things in a small container.

"What's that?" I asked.

"Oh, I read the residents' handbook to make sure we sort the waste correctly. Food waste is collected weekly, and these caddies are provided for our convenience."

"Wow, you've gone to a lot of trouble," I said. "What's all these orangey bits?"

"It's swede," he said. "The mixed vegetables have swede in them and I know you don't like swede so I picked them out."

I'm pretty sure my mouth actually dropped open. I was aghast. "I'm not a massive fan of swede, it's true, but everyone knows that you eat your veggies. It's just a thing you do. It's like life, isn't it? You take the rough with the smooth. You appreciate the carrots and the peas more because you've just had a bit of swede!"

Did that sound like one of Cookie's philosophical ramblings? I wasn't sure, but I realised that it did sound like someone being horrible and ungrateful. Ashbert looked crestfallen. No, he looked more than that. He looked as if I'd taken away his very reason for living.

"Sorry. I know you've gone to a lot of trouble," I said.

He continued to stare at me. I realised with a shock that he'd stared at me for every single moment that we'd been together. It had made our early encounters sizzling hot, but in the context of my minor outburst and his hangdog expression it was kind of creepy and weird. In fact, I realised, it had started to become weird a couple of days ago when I was struggling to pull my knickers on. Most people would look away for a moment, give me time to get my act together, but Ashbert had been staring deep into my eyes throughout, forcing me to turn it into a full-blown clown routine to save face.

I took a deep breath. I'd think about this later, but right now there were sausages to eat and a naked chef who wanted to please me so much that I felt a physical pain at the sadness in his eyes.

"Well I'm starving!" I lied. "Shall we eat?"

I made it through another round of sausages with onion gravy. I was quite proud. I stood up to clear the plates but he put a hand on my arm.

"Wait, there's another surprise. I made heart-shaped chocolate mousse for after. We can feed each other with our spoons!"

I started to protest that I was too full, but the words died on my lips. I just needed to get this over with.

"Lovely!" I said.

He put the dishes down and we each took up a spoonful. We reached across, drawing closer to each other and put the spoons into each other's mouths. I closed my eyes as I ate the mousse. It seemed like a good way to show that I was really enjoying it as well as having a moment's relief from the intensity of his stare. As I opened my eyes, something moved in my peripheral vision.

"Did you see that?" I asked.

"No, what?"

"Something just went under the fridge."

"I only have eyes for you," he said.

Perhaps it was a spider. Never mind. My more immediate worry was that if I ate all of this chocolate mousse, I might explode.

"This is so... hot," I said. "Maybe we should skip the rest and go straight to the bedroom?"

He nodded and we stood. Thank goodness, I could have a lie down, at least! I hurried through so I could get to *Sizzling Sex Positions for Adventurous Lovers* first, and choose something gentle.

"I've bookmarked the ones we haven't done yet!" he called as he followed me. "I thought we should work our way through from the start of the book."

Oh no! I paged through frantically. The first position he'd bookmarked featured the woman doing the splits up the wall. That was never going to happen, even on a good day. I looked at the next one, which was a wheelbarrow, where I had to do a handstand and have him hold me up by my legs. God no! What else was there? The next one wasn't even going to be possible. It featured a horizontal bar where I was supposed to hang upside down from my knees. At least that one wouldn't – oh. I looked up and saw him smiling at me from the doorway, where a horizontal bar was wedged in the frame. The apron had gone by now, and he was clearly excited by the prospect of us swinging in the doorframe.

"Home gym equipment," he said. "Shall we try it out?"

I started to stammer a reply but he held up a hand. "First things first. I've got sensual oil for a lovely massage."

He held out a large bottle of oil and I grinned with relief.

"A massage. That sounds wonderful!" I said.

I spread myself out on the bed and he started to apply oil to my back. He rubbed it in lightly.

"More oil," I said, on the basis that it would make the whole thing last longer if he had to rub in lots of oil. I felt it pooling in the small of my back and he smoothed it into my skin. He'd thoughtfully put towels on the bed so I rolled over after a few minutes to let him baste my front as well. There was so much excess oil that I slathered my hands with it and rubbed some into his chest. In truth, this oil malarkey was a lot of fun. When we swapped positions, I upended the bottle onto his chest and sloshed on more oil. There was hardly any left in the bottle. I ran my hands quickly over his body, spreading the oil so that it didn't *all* run onto the towels.

"You're like a gleaming, shiny goddess," he said, as I leaned over him.

I tried not to let my mind counter him with ill-timed thoughts about me being more like an oven-ready turkey. It was a lovely thing to say.

"Shall we try the bar?" he said, nodding towards the door frame.

"No rush," I said, slowly massaging in some more oil, "let's take it nice and slowly."

"We can take things slowly over there," he said. He seemed very keen on the bar.

"Okay, tiger, hold your horses," I said. "How do we know it's going to take my weight?"

He kissed me. "It will take your weight. I was very careful when I put it up. In fact, I'll prove it. He stood up and walked over to it. The bar was level with his nose. He grasped the bar and swung his legs up and over in a single fluid motion. He hung from his knees and grinned at me, upside down.

"See?" he said. Then I saw his smile falter. I could see that the bar was made of tough, ribbed plastic, but it clearly wasn't a match for the lubricating power of the oil. He slowly lost his grip and slid face-first onto the floor with an almighty thwack.

He grunted in pain and writhed on the floor, clutching his nose.

"Oh, my God. Are you hurt?"

He lifted his hands to look and blood dribbled off his chin.

"Christ. Stay there!" I said, and scrambled off the bed. What I hadn't realised was how much oil was now smeared across the laminate flooring. I managed three steps before my feet skidded from underneath me and I landed heavily beside Ashbert. Right on my coccyx. I was winded for a few long moments, torn between rubbing my aching bum and trying to get my breath. I tried to push myself up, but I couldn't get any purchase.

"There's too much oil!" I complained.

"You said you like the oil!"

"There can be too much of a good thing!" I replied. (And I wasn't just talking about oil, was I?)

Everything was covered in oil. My hands, my feet, the floor. I got my hand flat on the floor, but when I shifted my weight, it skated out from under me. I was completely marooned, and Ashbert wasn't helping at all, as he was doing the same as me, but had managed to mix blood into the oil from his nosebleed. We were like a couple of seals flopping up and down. I tried something different. I wriggled forward on my belly, like a snake.

It worked!

"Follow me, try doing it like this!" I called.

From the wet, slurping noises, I could tell that he too was making his way along the floor. From above we must have resembled an alien invasion of hopeless slugs. An evolutionary dead end if ever there was one. I slithered along the short section of corridor and into the bathroom, Ashbert behind me. The radiator in the bathroom was shaped like a ladder so that you could put towels onto it, and I aimed for it, with a view to hanging on and dragging myself upright. I was almost there when a creature scuttled out from behind the toilet and ran across my hand.

It was an indescribable horror!

That's not true. It was a reasonably describable horror: part crab, part beetle. Kind of like an armadillo that had been forced through a small letterbox. More than anything, it resembled a giant woodlouse with extra legs that rippled weirdly when it moved.

I screamed. I don't mean I shouted. I mean I sodding screamed.

"Holy buggering fucksticks!"

I slithered backwards as fast as I could. Of course, I collided with Ashbert, who had no idea what I was yelling about and simply got a faceful of my arse.

"Giant fucking insect thing!" I screamed. I turned around and part-climbed, part-slid over the top of him as he wasn't moving fast enough for my liking.

"Wow, I wonder what it is?" he said.

"I don't care what it is, it was trying to eat my face!" I said, slowing up, now I was outside the bathroom.

"It doesn't look dangerous," said Ashbert, shortly followed by "Waaaaah!"

The creature appeared, scurrying over his head and down his back. It was heading straight for me again, so I developed a new way of moving. I did a variant of the butterfly swimming stroke – without water of course – flinging my arms out and levering myself along the floor. I'd have bruises to show for it later, but I wasn't hanging around to let the insectoid vampire suck out my eyeballs or whatever it wanted to do. I crashed along the floor into the kitchen where I finally managed to haul myself to my feet. I grabbed a tea towel and tried to wipe some of the oil off me and then I tipped everything out of the pedal bin, so that I could use it to trap the demon insectoid. I didn't want to touch the thing, so I grabbed a sieve as well.

I advanced, a naked warrior with my strange domestic weapons. Ashbert was squealing unhelpfully, going on about how he could feel all its little legs when it ran over him. I closed my mind to everything except the task at hand. The creature was in the corridor. It was butting the wall on either side, maybe looking for a hiding place. I put the bin on its side, hoping that it might look like an attractive cave or something. It would save me a lot of bother if the thing would just run inside, as I really didn't want to get hands-on with it. It ran off in the opposite direction. I cursed lightly and followed it. It ran to a corner and scrabbled ineffectually at the wall. I put the bin down, making sure it was open, advanced with my sieve, and in one smooth movement, I scooped it up and swung it into the bin.

"Yes!" I shouted, jubilant at my skilful manoeuvre.

"Oh no!" shouted Ashbert, who still hadn't managed to stand, but who emerged from the bathroom as quickly as a prone, slithering man could, "there's another one!"

"Balls there is!" I cried in terrified disbelief, but he was right. They were everywhere.

Is this the way the world ends? I thought. Consumed by killer woodlice? That would be a crap apocalypse. I'd rather have the asteroid any day.

In the end, I repeated my patented sieve-to-pedal-bin move another three times. I sank, exhausted, onto the bathroom floor after the last one. There was a lot of cleaning up to do, but right now I was worried about those creatures and where they might have come from. There was something about them that was oddly familiar, but I couldn't quite place it. I checked the whole flat for further intruders, making sure there weren't any more insects that might pop out. When I got over to the front door and looked at the box of fossils that was still there it came to me why those insects looked familiar. They were the same size and shape as the fossils. I turned over one of Adam's rocks and now there was no fossil. It was just a rock. The others were the same. I counted them: four in all. Four fossils that were now rocks and four weird insects in the pedal bin.

"Lexi, can you phone Adam please?" I said.

"Calling Adam."

"Sound only! No video!" I shouted as Lexi put the call through. I *was* still naked after all.

Moments later I heard the sound of Adam's phone ringing out.

"Yes?" came his voice.

"Adam, you know your rocks."

"I think I do," he said. "Igneous, sedimentary and metamorphic. And a good afternoon to you, Lori, or whatever time it is there."

"Your rocks, Adam. The fossils."

"You are taking care of them, aren't you?" he said, suddenly concerned.

"Sure."

"Because there's a really rare enosuchus in one of them."

"Emo sucker? Is that the one with the stripy shell and too many legs?"

"No, the enosuchus was an amphibian. You're thinking of the trilobites."

"Right. Trilobites. Trilobites. And I don't suppose there are many live trilobites around these days...?"

"Live? Lord, no, Lori. They were wiped out in the Great Permian Extinction."

"Of course," I said breezily, as four of them rustled round in the bin.

"In fact, I delivered a lecture in Atlanta about the clathrate gun hypothesis as the main cause of the mass extinction."

"Someone shot them?"

"No, silly. I was going to use those fossils for a similar series of talks when I do the Volga cruises in October. You haven't broken them, have you?"

"No," I said, uncertainly. My mind was whirling with an odd new sense of responsibility. If these were the only trilobites in the world, I couldn't let them die. "What sort of thing did they like to eat?"

"Trilobites? Lori, I'm about to do a piece to camera for a documentary series on Peruvian mummies. What on earth –"

"Lettuce maybe?" I tried. "Might they like to nibble on a carrot?"

"Jesus, Lori, are you high? Trilobites were marine creatures. They would never come across lettuce or carrots." He sighed. "There's arguments about what they would eat, nobody really knows. Those ones of mine lived in the muddy ooze, so it's thought they ate worms."

"Worms, right. Got it," I said.

"Listen, I really need to go now, Lori."

"Sure. Go and do your thing, Adam."

Ashbert emerged from the bathroom, wrapped in a towel. He'd been trying to shower off some of the oil. "Hey, should we get back to *Sizzling Sex Positions for Adventurous Lovers*?" he asked.

"No time, get dressed!" I said. "We need to go and dig up some worms for these little fellas."

"I thought you said something about killing them with fire and flushing them down the toilet?" he said, with a puzzled frown.

"I might have been a bit hasty when I said that," I admitted.

I went into the bathroom and ran an inch of water into the bath. Then I got the pedal bin and tipped it up gently, just over the water. The trilobites splashed into the water and immediately started scooting around all over the place. As far as cockroachy-looking things were able to express pleasure, they looked absolutely over the moon.

"It seems these are trilobites," I said to Ashbert, "and they're the only ones in the world. They should have died out years ago."

"They don't look very dead," said Ashbert, pointing at one that was continually trying and failing to climb up the sloping side of the bath.

"Get down, Dougie," I told it.

"Dougie?" said Ashbert.

"Tom, Danny, Dougie and Harry. McFly."

"And why's that one Dougie?"

"Cos he's the cute one. Anyway, I have a sneaking suspicion that I know how they came to be here, too."

"Time machine?" Ashbert suggested.

"I'm going to try something."

I fetched my sketch pad and sat down on the toilet seat. Ashbert looked at me curiously.

"Are you planning to sketch them?" he asked.

"No. I'm going to draw them some worms," I said.

I drew a simple wiggly worm. Tempted as I was to give it an amusing face or expressive eyes, I resisted because of what I suspected was about to happen. I held my pendant on one hand and stared at the picture.

I stared really hard and waggled my eyebrows a bit like an evil hypnotist.

Nothing happened.

"What's supposed to happen?" said Ashbert.

I sighed and looked at my pendant. The weighty lump of red onyx, the cameo of the woman and her adoring bloke. Huh, kind of like me and Ashbert.

"He hardly charged me anything for it," I said. "I guess they're probably mass-produced in a factory in Athens or China or something. I thought..."

"What?" said Ashbert.

I grinned sheepishly.

"I thought that it was the pendant, that it was magic. And if I..." I pointed at the worm drawing and at once there was a worm resting on my sketch pad. The picture was gone and a real life wriggly earthworm was there.

"You saw that?" I gasped.

"I saw it," said Ashbert.

I tipped the pad over the bath so that the worm fell in. The trilobites all piled on, and used their front mouth parts to dig into the worm. It wasn't long before it was gone completely.

"I'll draw you some more in a minute," I told them.

I looked up at Ashbert. "Well I think this explains where you came from," I said.

"What?"

"I created you in a scrapbook when I was a teenager. The other day when I looked through all my old stuff, I animated you with this pendant. Just hold and point. That's it."

He looked genuinely shocked. "That explains why I have no memories," he said.

"I guess."

"Because I'm not real."

"Oh, you're real all right," I said. "You are the reality that I imagined. You embody everything that I wanted when I was a teenager."

He looked slightly mollified by this. I could see that he was having even more difficulty than me absorbing this news.

"Promise me one thing?" he said in a small voice.

"What's that?" I said, concerned at his tone.

"Please don't feed me to them," he said, pointing at the trilobites.

Chapter 13

It was Sunday and I didn't need to get up early for work. I contemplated my strange new talent for bringing things to life. There were so many questions in my mind. Luckily, my first, and quite possibly my finest creation was lying there with me. I rolled over and gave him an experimental prod between the ribs.

"You're real," I said.

"I am," he replied.

"I mean you're really real."

"I feel real."

He ran his hand down my naked side to make the point. Sure, he felt real. Possibly even flesh and blood like me. I pinched his upper arm to makes sure until he pulled away with a brief 'ow'.

"You're an enigma, Ashbert."

"Is that where they stick a pipe up your –"

"I mean you're a mystery," I said firmly. "What's my favourite colour?"

"You like purple," he said promptly, "but not for nail varnish. You're not an emo."

"An emo? Crisps then. What are my favourite crisps?"

"Salt and vinegar."

"Have I got a favourite television programme?"

"Yes of course, it's *Malcolm in the Middle*," he said. "You think that Francis is cute."

I was coming to a definite conclusion. Years ago, I had been seriously addicted to the show. I had always looked forward to the appearances of the dashing older son, but I'd gone right off him since then and developed a rather disturbing crush on the dad instead (although I hear in a later spin-off series he becomes a meth cook and drug dealer and wears a disturbing hat). It seemed as though Ashbert had a very specific range of knowledge about my likes and dislikes. If he was ever required to go on a quiz show and have a specialised subject, he'd completely ace the *Lori aged fifteen* round.

"I think that some of your information is a bit out of date," I said, as tactfully as I could. "I've grown up since then."

"That's not what your parents say."

I wriggled away from his touch.

"That's not fair! You've not met my parents."

"You said they said it."

"Yes, but…"

I reflected on that statement. Had I grown up or just got older? I slipped out of bed and pulled the cushions away from Lexi.

"Lexi, how do I know if I'm an adult?"

"An adult is a human or other living thing that has reached sexual maturity."

"Not that. I want to know if I'm behaving like an adult."

"Would you like to hear *Seven basic adulting tips for today's generation*?"

"Bingo."

"Number one. Your daily meals don't just appear by magic. Understand where food comes from. How much is a box of eggs? Number two, wash and dry your own towels. As a stretch goal, put them away in the correct place. Number three, make your own dental appointments. Number four, understand your energy bill. Number five, look after someone other than yourself."

"Whoa Lexi! Hold on!" I flopped back onto the bed in exhaustion at the sheer scale of the tasks before me.

"I think we should double check the sexual maturity bit," said Ashbert, reaching for me.

"Really?" I said. "I think we spend enough of our time getting hot and sweaty."

"Nothing better than a bit of a dirty fun and getting hot and sweaty."

"Not now," I said. "Go get a shower."

Ashbert plodded off dutifully and I got up to fetch my sketch pad.

"Right Florrie," I said. "You're coming on this journey with me. We'll have a series, called *Florrie learns adulting*. Now where to start? Lexi, how much are eggs?"

"Free-range or barn-raised?" she asked.

"Free eggs you say?"

"Free-range eggs."

"And are they free?" I asked.

"I cannot find free eggs in the local area. A box of six large free-range eggs is available for the best price of one pound fifty," said Lexi.

I sketched Florrie opening a box of eggs. It was a great picture, if I say so myself, with the eggs having something of the mysterious, pristine appeal of a box of chocolates before you take the first one. Florrie gazed at their speckled brown surface in adoration and quoted the price of them in a speech bubble, before declaring that she might have a delicious egg for her breakfast, safe in the knowledge that she could afford it.

Ashbert had come back, unshowered.

"It might be tricky to use the bathroom," he said. "Those horrible trilobites are still in the bath."

"True," I said and then, "Oh! That's perfect!"

"Is it?"

"Yes. Don't you see?"

He looked puzzled. "If you're thinking they could be like those fish that nibble dead skin off your feet, I think these little guys might be a bit too hard-core."

"No. I mean, as an adult, I need to look after someone other than myself."

"You can look after me if you like." He raised a suggestive eyebrow.

"I can look after the trilobites. If I can make them happy then that will prove I'm adulting properly! You know what I need?"

"A total rethink of your life?"

"No. A vet."

Lexi chipped in at that point. I hadn't put the cushions back in place. She was like having a nosy, super-knowledgeable older sister. "There are five veterinary practices in your area."

"Huh? Really?" I said. "Can I speak to one of them?"

There was a dialling tone and then a female voice came on the line. "Good morning, Furry Friends Veterinary Practice."

"Oh, hi," I said. "I'm after some advice on animal care. Can you help me?"

"I'm sure we can help you. What kind of an animal is it?"

I didn't want to get into specifics. It wouldn't end well. "Let's just say it's a cross between a woodlouse and a guinea pig," I said.

107

"Is it?"

"With a little bit of crocodile thrown in, yes. Likes to eat worms. Would you keep that in a cage or what?"

There was a pause. "I wonder if you'd like to bring your animal in for an examination by a vet?" she asked slowly.

"No, I don't think that's a good idea. There are four of them all together and I think Dougie likes his own company rather than being cooped up with the others."

"It's going to be difficult to offer advice without knowing what kind of animal you're talking about," said the voice. Why was she being so difficult about this?

I tried again. "Well I just need a bit of help. If I put them in a cage, I think they might get out between the bars. They like water and mud so how do I make some sort of house for them?"

There was an exasperated sigh. "I don't think it would be appropriate to offer specific advice without the vet seeing your animals. Or, indeed, if you can't tell me what they are. Some animals need to live in a cage, some in a tank and some in a terrarium."

"Terrari-what?"

"Terrarium. For pets such as terrapins which need a semi-aquatic environment."

"Yes, yes! That's what I need. A semi-aquatic environment. How do I do that?"

"A basic terrarium can be created from a large fish tank. Look I really think you should consider bringing your animals in to see the vet so that you can get some specific advice. We can put you in touch with suppliers for your animals' needs as well. It sounds as if you're new to –"

"No, I'm good now, thanks," I said. "Bye." I didn't want to answer any more difficult questions about what these animals were and how I came to have them in my bath.

Lexi ended the call and I was about to replace the cushions when another thought crossed my mind. "Lexi, what are the other things on the list of adulting tasks?"

"Number six, learn to drive. Number seven, learn basic household maintenance," said Lexi.

I could see that those were for *advanced* adults. I was on a roll though and I knew that I could tackle these if I really put my mind to it. Look how far I'd got in the last ten minutes!

"Driving, huh?" I said. I still had some of the money left from the pile that Ashbert had acquired. "Lexi, how do I learn to drive?"

"There are fourteen driving schools within your area," she replied.

"Cool!" I said with a grin. "Let's book a lesson."

After booking my first driving lesson for tomorrow morning with an instructor called Terence, I was a little shaken at how expensive it was. I either needed to learn incredibly quickly, in three lessons or less, or I would need some more money. I rang Cookie, on my mobile.

"Boredom, food or money?" she said when she picked up.

"Eh?" I wondered briefly if Lexi had texted her.

"It's before twelve on a Sunday," said Cookie. "This is not normal for you, my friend. I'm guessing that an essential strand of your being needs attention. As I say, boredom, food or money?"

"You're a genius," I said, genuinely impressed.

"Just in tune with the vibrational matrix of the multiverse, meow-meow."

"I wanted to ask you about earning some extra money."

"First you had no job. Now you've got one, you want more. The first step on the path to nirvana is recognising that desire is the root of all suffering."

"You've got like a million jobs, Cookie."

"I have one job with a million facets. I am a diamond."

"Sure. Do you ever get any spare jobs? Ones I could do."

"It happens sometimes. You know, when I can't be in two places at once, although I'm working on that. Thought I'd cracked it but the strain was too much, I pulled a muscle in my foo-foo and couldn't sit down for a week."

"Anyway, the jobs..." I said.

"You want me to keep a look out and rope you in?"

Well, let me know what comes up. And it's okay if they got me instead of you?"

"Most people have no idea who I am. They book me and I turn up. If someone else turns up and does the job, why would they care?"

A small part of me thought that perhaps people *would* care, but Cookie's word was good enough for me.

As I ended the call I realised that I had not specified what kind of job I was prepared to do. Cookie invents new jobs every week, so I might find myself being paid to wait in a queue or stand under someone's window singing *Happy Birthday* or *Ave Maria* to them (that one's quite popular, apparently). Not to worry: I could handle any of them, given my bold new foray into adulting.

I had a quick review of my finances. Beardy Rex at the museum had made it clear that I wouldn't be getting any wages until next Friday. I had never heard of a 'week in hand', but apparently it was a thing. I set aside twenty-five pounds for my driving lesson and looked at what was left. Twenty pounds. That wasn't going to buy food *and* a terrarium. I'd have to tighten my belt. Of course, I could reduce the food bill on weekdays when I could eat leftovers in the cafe at work, but what was I going to do for the rest of the weekend? I thought hard and came up with a solution that seemed to have no immediate drawbacks: I could tighten Adam's belt! He was sure to have things around the place that he didn't need any more. I went around the flat collecting things into a carrier bag.

"Going to the shops!" I called to Ashbert and went out.

My first stop was Marks and Spencer. I went to the customer service counter and pulled out three of Adam's jumpers and a thermal vest.

"I'd like to return these please," I said.

"Do you have the receipt?" asked the man, as he looked at the jumpers.

"No," I said.

He handed the vest back to me. "I'm afraid you can't return underwear."

I shrugged and put it back in the bag.

He found labels in each of the jumpers and scanned them. The last one made him frown. "This one hasn't been stocked for the last six years," he said.

I nodded sadly. "No, it's taken me a while to realise that it isn't for me," I said. "It's too big you see. And I seem to have bought a man's jumper by mistake."

I shut my mouth at that point before I made the fatal mistake of talking too much, which is often my downfall.

He pressed buttons on the till and made me fill out a form, but at the end of a few more minutes he handed me some vouchers. "We can only issue vouchers as you no longer have the receipt."

I looked at them and smiled up at him. "Thank you!" I said. This was going very well.

I went to Boots next and passed a pile of razor blades across the counter at customer services. Have you *seen* the price of razor blades? My hopes were high that this could be lucrative. I told the assistant that I wanted to return them. She was one of those women who I reckon dip their faces into honey-coloured plaster every morning, so their face is set in a pristine cast of immovable perfection. She glanced up at me. Her eyebrows were as dark and thick as Cadbury's chocolate fingers and one of them crept up her face by a millimetre. I think this might have been an expression of extreme shock.

"You want to return these? Are they faulty?"

"No," I said, "they're not suitable."

"The pack has been opened," she said, pointing with a crimson talon.

"Just a little bit," I admitted.

"And there are bits of hair stuck between the blades."

I looked. There were. I held her gaze for a few seconds longer. It was like having a staring competition with a cat, there was no possible way of winning. Her face was an impenetrable barrier of Max Factor. I cracked and swept the razor blades back into the carrier bag and made my way out of the shop.

Just outside the door was a man in a pea green hoodie. He was leaning against the wall, but I felt sure that he was watching me. I couldn't see his face because the hood was up, but I felt his gaze tracking me as I went past. The world was judging me for trying to return second-hand razor blades.

That would have to do for returning Adam's things. It wasn't going to buy a fish tank. I needed to do some research on that, so I hopped on a train and went to an out-of-town retail park by the university to look around the DIY superstore. I wandered about and picked up some of those cards that help you select paint colours. If Lexi said I needed to learn basic household maintenance, then maybe I should start by fixing Adam's flat where I'd created those unfortunate scorch marks up the walls and across the ceiling. If I applied my artist's skills to a spot of redecorating then he was sure to forgive me for melting the fire, as I had no clue how to go about fixing that. I took loads of cards as I couldn't decide whether to go with a bright accent colour, or something subtly toning. I knew that Adam wouldn't approve of the bright option, but sometimes you need to drag people out of their comfort zone to help them see what's possible. That's what Cookie says, anyway.

I went over to the pet care section. The fish tanks were quite expensive. It would take me weeks to save up enough to get one of these. I couldn't leave the trilobites in the bath for that long. I went to find an assistant. A gangly youth was restocking shelves with mysterious bits of bent metal.

"I'm looking for something to keep... terrapins in," I said. I'd learned from the experience with the vet. A terrapin was about the same size as a trilobite, I hazarded. "I can't afford a fish tank, can you suggest something cheaper? Much cheaper."

The youth paused wordlessly for a few long moments before turning on his heel and disappearing. He came back with a woman who looked like Marge Simpson. The youth still hadn't spoken a word and he disappeared, clearly relieved to have found someone else to deal with me. If only he had my adulting skills! I made a mental note to come back here and suggest he read my blog, once I'd got a couple of *Florrie Does Adulting* posts up there.

I repeated my request to Marge and she nodded thoughtfully for a moment.

"So, would I be right in assuming that your ideal budget is zero?" she asked.

I nodded.

"But if I sorted you out with something then you'd be happy to put a pound in the collecting tin for deranged cats?"

I nodded again. Deranged cats?

She led me to a massive door that she said I wasn't allowed to come through. She disappeared for a few minutes and then came back towing one of those trucks that holds a pallet. On top of it was a weird looking plastic thing.

"Have a look at this," she said. "It's a walk-in sit-up bath. It's meant for old people who can't get into a regular bath. We got this one in on a special order but the top got broken, see? It's going in the skip, but you can have it if you want."

I peered inside. It was like a luxury apartment designed especially for trilobites. It had a deep bit and a seat, I could see it working perfectly if I put soil in the bottom and then water on top, so that they could climb up and enjoy it like a beach if they felt like it.

"It's perfect!" I breathed. "But how on earth am I going to get it back to my place?"

The woman produced a clipboard. "Put your details on there. I'll get Tony to drop it round when he does the deliveries. I want to see an extra pound go in that tin for deranged cats, mind."

I nodded eagerly. Always happy to help out with the deranged cats.

Tony came round with the trilobite enclosure that afternoon. He'd managed to get it right to the front door of the flat with the help of a wheeled trolley, and he hauled it into the lounge. It looked truly enormous in a domestic setting, but then if you're going to look after a pet, you need to give it plenty of space, so I knew I was doing the right thing.

"Let's put it in Adam's bedroom," I said, and Tony obliged by manoeuvring it expertly through the flat, while Ashbert looked on, slightly confused.

"Tell you what," said Tony, "this was a godsend. We got quotas now. We get penalised for excess waste if we have to scrap too much stuff, and this would have scuppered us for a month or more, size of the thing. Fibre glass, can't be recycled either."

"Happy to help," I said, regretting my earlier generosity towards the collection tin. "If you have any more stuff you need to get rid of, just run it by me!"

"Got five hundred match pots on the van. Past their sell-by date, but they're probably fine."

"Match pots?"

"Yeah, little sample pots of paint. All different colours."

"I'll take them!" I said. There were sure to be some that I could use in my search for the right colour for the decorating.

Adam's room was filling up. There were boxes full of condoms and match pots pushed up against the wall, but in pride of place was the walk-in bath.

"Right," I said to Ashbert, after Tony had left. "We just need to prepare this for the trilobites. Come with me."

We went downstairs and explored the equipment bunker at the back of the flats. I found a couple of spades and a bucket.

"We need some soil for the bottom of their enclosure," I said.

We went out into the carefully cultivated garden. We'd need to tread carefully here. I could already see a face at a window above us.

"I don't think we can take any from here," I hissed at Ashbert, "we'll have the residents' association down on us like a ton of bricks if we mess up the flower beds."

"What about over there?" said Ashbert, pointing across the road. At the edge of the car park was a scrubby bit of waste ground littered with lumps of concrete and beer cans. We went over and poked around experimentally with our spades. It was hard to imagine that there might be soil underneath all of the mess, but we did eventually find some. We filled the mop bucket halfway and lugged it back to the flat. It was nowhere near enough when we got it in there, so we had to make another five journeys, by which time it was dark and we were exhausted, but our hard work paid off in the end. We used the same bucket to add water to the soil, until it lapped gently up onto the beach. There was a glorious deep mud pool and a shallow sloping beach. It couldn't have been more perfect.

"That was fun," I said, wiping sweat and muck from my brow.

"I can think of better things for us to do," said Ashbert.

"What are you talking about?" I said. "Nothing better than a bit of a dirty fun and getting hot and sweaty. Isn't that what you said?"

114

We left the habitat to settle overnight. In the morning, the murky soup had settled down and there was a layer of relatively clear water on top of the silty soil in the lower part. It was time to move our honoured guests into their new home. I told Ashbert that it was our task for the morning and he suggested that perhaps we might just go for a nice walk or something instead. I suggested that the best way to overcome his fears would be to confront them. He pouted and fetched the oven gloves to protect his hands. I could tell it was going to be down to me to do all the work, as he'd have absolutely no dexterity with those things on.

"Should I get the bin?" he asked.

"Hmmm, I think that might be tricky now they're in the bath," I said.

I went into the kitchen to see what might be more suitable. I opened cupboards until I found something that looked as though it would do the job. It was a device for steaming vegetables, I think. It had a base with a wire to plug it in, but the bit that I was interested in was what went on top: a big metal basket with a lid.

"This should do the trick," I said, holding it up. "The water will drain out the bottom and I can pop the lid on to stop them escaping."

Ashbert nodded, looking afraid or cynical – I couldn't tell.

I went to the bathroom and greeted the trilobites by name. Soon they would start to respond to my voice, I was sure of it.

"Morning Dougie! Morning Danny! Tom, you're keen this morning! Harry's only just waking up by the looks of it."

Tom was scrabbling at the side of the bath. I positioned the basket below him and scooped him gently upwards. It worked perfectly. I popped the lid on top, took him through into Adam's bedroom and gently tipped him out into the new habitat.

"Off you go Tom, you can be the first to explore. Doesn't he look at home, Ashbert?"

I repeated the exercise with Harry and Danny without a hitch. I was the trilobite whisperer! I dipped the basket into the water for Dougie, expecting him to scud his way agreeably into scooping range. Instead he shot forward and nipped my hand, just on the fleshy part of my thumb.

"Ow! Jesus, Dougie!" I exclaimed, hurt in more ways than one.

Ashbert whipped open the bathroom cabinet and cleaned my wound with an antiseptic wipe before putting on a plaster. He was an absolute dear but then sort of spoiled it by saying "should have worn the gloves" as he turned away.

I managed to get Dougie into the basket second time around. While they explored their new home, I magically rustled up some worms so they wouldn't go hungry. I couldn't help the feeling that something was missing. Maybe it was because a decent habitat always has something *more* in it. Even the crappiest goldfish bowl has a castle or something for the fish to look at as it swims around. I'd need to get my thinking cap on about that.

I found Ashbert in Adam's room, looking in the boxes.

"You've got a lot of these paint pots," he said. "Dragon's Blood, Flamingo Dream, Regency Decadence. Nice colours."

"They were free. I need to decorate the bits of the lounge I've messed up."

He looked back in the box. "Oh, right. You planning on doing some Jackson Pollock sort of stuff then?"

I goggled at him. "Eh?"

"You know, Jackson Pollock?" he said. "Did drip paintings in lots of colours."

"Yes, *I* know that," I said. "*I* went to art college. But how do *you* know?"

"Maybe you told me?" he ventured.

"Nope. Definitely not, and I went to art college after I made that scrapbook. Which is your favourite of Pollock's pieces?"

"I think his Autumn Rhythm is the most impressive. An almost perfect expression of his work in fractal geometry."

"Wow, it's like you went to art college too," I said.

"I didn't," he said. "I was interested in the arts but studied English at university." He sounded surprised at this news.

I frowned. "You have James Franco's ears, you know."

"Thank you."

116

"No. I mean, literally. I cut them out of a magazine. And he's an artist, I think. Besides doing the acting thing and the general hotness."

"Okay," said Ashbert. "So, what does that mean?"

"If nothing else, it means you can help me paint a background for the trilobites."

I fetched the shower curtain out of the bathroom. It was large and white and would make a perfect canvas. With my paintbrushes and all of this lovely new paint I passed a happy couple of hours painting a backdrop for the habitat that would remind the trilobites of home. I guessed they'd like to see some dinosaurs, so I included a grazing stegosaurus and a pterodactyl flying above a lush rainforest canopy. As a finishing touch I added Florrie, peeking through the undergrowth.

I took a photo and uploaded the picture to my blog. I captioned it *Florrie relaxes after a hard day's adulting.* It was the last of a series. I'd drawn Florrie washing her towels, Florrie making an entry on her calendar for the dentist and the final version of Florrie knowing the price of eggs. I wrote some brief paragraphs about the difficulties that she'd faced, but how she'd mastered the basics of adulting, so now she was kicking back with her friends the dinosaurs.

I uploaded it and then wandered through to the lounge. I contemplated the ruined paintwork and thought about what Ashbert had said. A splashy Jackson Pollock thing might be just the effect to create a striking accent in here. But where to start?

"Reminder," said Lexi. "Your driving lesson begins in ten minutes."

"Damn. I'd forgotten."

I'd done no preparation at all. I checked my watch. Yes, ten minutes. I needed to study a map. Imagine getting lost on your first driving lesson! I called up a map on my phone and it rang while I did.

I put it on speaker so I could look at the map at the same time.

"Hi Cookie," I said.

"Love your new blog, my friend," she said. "Very profound."

"Cool, thanks," I said. The world looked a very different place on a map. I tried to trace the route from here to my parents' old house, but it was just a meaningless set of bends on a diagram. How on earth did people know where to go?

"Listen, I got a job for you, if you still want it."

"Definitely. What and when?"

"What, babysitting. When, tomorrow night."

"Babysitting," I echoed, not especially thrilled at the thought. "A baby, jeez."

"Not a baby. The kid is ten, which is a nice age."

"Boy or girl?"

"Does it matter? Do I detect some nervousness?"

"No!" I said, then in a slightly smaller voice, "Well, yes. Kids. I always think they're going to catch me out."

"Catch you out?" said Cookie.

I cast about for the right words. "It's like they know I'm not properly a grown-up. Adults are mature and wise and know what the right thing to do is and..."

"You think any of us adults know what we're doing?"

"When I said adults, I wasn't necessarily including you in that category, if I'm honest."

"Being an adult is all about image," said Cookie. "It's roleplay."

"Like doctors and nurses?"

"Not the way you play, no. All you need are a few simple rules to establish your position when you get there, show them who's in charge."

"Rules? Great. Tell me," I said, as I looked for shoes and a coat.

Cookie mused noisily. "Kids love ritual. If you can get them to read or recite a long, complicated song or a poem then they won't be any hassle at all."

"I don't know any poems," I said. "I wonder if I could teach him some McFly lyrics or something?"

"That's the spirit," said Cookie. "Another thing is physical exercise. Works well with boys, especially. If they want sweets or to stay up after their bedtime or whatever, make them pay in star jumps or press-ups. It'll help tire them out, and burn off some of the sugar or aspartame or whatever."

"Cool. Where did you learn this stuff? Did you read it?"

"I read the universe, Baby Belkin. It whispers its truths to me."

"Riiight..."

"Also, I got some of it from the Supernanny programme."

I jogged down to street level, almost left without checking if I'd brought my keys with me. I checked. I had.

"Now the final thing you need to know is the power of the Child Catcher," said Cookie.

"The what?"

"Child Catcher."

"Child Catcher?"

"Child Catcher. It doesn't have to the Child Catcher specifically. It can be anything out of the darkest place in your head. Doesn't matter. Put the fear of God in them."

"Fear of God. Check."

I looked along the road. There was a car with a sign on its roof that, bizarrely, said 'DRIVEL' in big red letters.

"Mention the Child Catcher now and again to remind them," said Cookie, "so that if they get out of line you can pretend to call them. Put the number in your phone now, so you're always prepared."

Cookie always had an answer. I did as she suggested, listing her number as The Child Catcher and then noted down the address for my babysitting job. I came off the phone buoyed with my ability to conquer pretty well any field and walked towards my driving instructor.

Chapter 15

"Miss Belkin?"

My driving instructor, Terence, unfolded himself from the driver's seat and got out to shake my hand. The car was very small and he was very tall, and I wondered why he hadn't just bought a bigger car. He patted the roof affectionately. "Meet Arabella, your new best friend. She's a good girl, nice and steady, which is what you want when you're learning."

I tried not to pull a face and hoped that he'd start behaving like a normal person.

"You see, a car has a personality all of its very own, as you're about to discover, as you embark on this journey of yours. I've made quite a study of it, you see. Each car has a personality, and the person who buys each type of car is drawn to it because of their own personality. You can tell everything you need to know about a person from their choice of car."

"What about people who just buy what they can afford after their old car's been declared a death trap?" I asked, fairly certain that my parents had bought all of their cars that way.

"Oh no, there's always a choice," he said firmly.

"And why do you have a car with 'drivel' written on the roof?"

He looked. "It says 'Drive,' Miss Belkin. "And that's an L-plate on the end."

"Which spells 'drivel'."

"It does not. Now, let's get you comfortable."

He guided me into the driver's seat. I wouldn't have called it comfortable with all of the things there. It was pretty distracting to have those pedals and the steering wheel getting in the way. He spent some time showing me how to adjust the seat and how to hold the steering wheel. I could see the minutes ticking away on my lesson and we were wasting time talking about how to hold a steering wheel! I nearly said something, but then he told me we were going to start the engine. There were yet more things to check. I thought driving was about getting from A to B more quickly, but quite honestly, wherever we were going, I could have walked there by now.

When the engine was going, I had to work both my hands and my feet at the same time to make the car move forwards. Terence kept talking about the clutch and waiting for the engine to 'bite' and I didn't have a clue what that meant.

It took a few attempts to coordinate two feet and two arms to do at least three things, because people are *not* designed to work that way. This is why people don't make sandwiches when they are tap dancing or whatever. Our attention needs to be on one or the other. And I don't know why this man thought I could do two things at once because men certainly can't. That's why men never die while they're sleeping.

Anyway, eventually I got the car to pull away and we began to roll along the road. No sooner had I got the hang of that, he wanted me to do something else. Something inside me snapped.

"What's wrong with carrying on like this?" I yelled. I had to yell quite loudly as the car was making quite a high-pitched noise by now.

"We need to change gear to go faster," he said, "otherwise we'll damage the engine. Hear that noise? That's the engine talking to you."

"I thought you said that Arabella was a nice steady girl?" I said.

"She is!"

"She's starting to sound downright *needy* if you ask me!"

Evidently, I am not the first person to panic when asked to perform so many bizarre actions at the same time. The next stage of evolution for humans will surely be to have extra arms and legs, like an octopus. On second thoughts, I can imagine the difficulties it would bring if I had even more limbs to think about. Twenty minutes later I was changing gears and turning around bends and everything, so Terence, the driving instructor, had gone back to his weird theories about drivers and cars.

"See him? In the Prius? Never trust a man in a Prius."

"Why?"

"Do-gooders and dreamers, the lot of them. He'll be too busy snacking on hummus or thinking about his compost heap to pay attention to the road."

"So, what do I do if I don't trust another driver?" I asked, confused as to how I was supposed to use Terence's bizarre insights.

"Give them plenty of room, that's what. Never hurts to give another driver lots of room, does it?"

We were on the dual carriageway now, and there were roadworks up ahead. I was already in the inside lane, so I slowed down as the two lanes became one, leaving plenty of room.

"No! Go faster, don't let that git in!" yelled Terence, as a car came hurtling along beside us to cut in at the last moment.

I hit the accelerator, the car lurched forward and then I saw how fast we were approaching the car in front so I hit the brake extra hard.

"Well done!" said Terence.

"What happened to leaving lots of room?" I asked.

"It's different if someone's trying to cut in your lane. You have to watch out for the sociopaths. They have to be taught the hard way."

"And how do I spot sociopaths?"

"BMW drivers mostly. Mercedes too. Big German saloon equals sociopathic git. Remember that."

I checked the time. I'd booked a two-hour lesson and it was only halfway through. I wondered if my nerves could take much more of this. No wonder drivers swore all the time.

We pulled up at some traffic lights. I knew this one, wait until my light turns green and then I can go. Terence was off again.

"Think of traffic lights as being a bit like horoscopes," he said. "We all pay attention to them, even though they don't really help."

"Surely they stop crashes?" I said, moving forward again. "If everyone here all went forward together it would be a big mess."

"Don't be so sure about that. A good deal of what we see on the roads is not what it seems." He tapped the side of his nose. "Turn left here. You see these speed bumps?" We were on a side street with huge speed bumps all the way down it. I'd have to be blind not to see them, they stretched ahead like a range of very small mountains. "Slow right down for these. The car industry sponsors these."

"Do they?"

"Nobody will ever admit to it of course, but they do. Reduces the lifespan of your average car no end, so they sell more."

I crept over the car-wrecking speed bumps with the feeling that Terence had only brought us down this road so that he could moan about the speed bumps.

By the time we got back to Adam's, I was glad to get out of the car, but I was jubilant that I'd nailed the driving thing, more or less.

"How many more lessons before I can take a test?" I asked. "One or two?"

"About forty is normal," said Terence.

I slammed the door. I might have to find another driving instructor. Even if I could afford forty lessons, I probably couldn't listen to Terence for that length of time.

Chapter 16

Terence had irritated me, put my delicate sense of balance all out of whack – messed with my chakras, Cookie would have said. Creativity was a good way of finding your balance and calming yourself the hell down. So, I decided, now was the right time to start redecorating Adam's flat. Having looked at some of the match pots, I knew that I had a good range of colours to use. The Jackson Pollock approach looked like a winner all round. I went down to the recycling area and found a load of old newspapers to cover everything up. I needed to make sure that I kept Adam's flat from any more damage. I covered the floor and the furniture with newspaper and lined up the match pots. I did a little bit of experimenting to see what method would be best to splatter the paint where I needed it. I flicked it with a paint brush, which was nice for getting an arc across the wall. I found a thing in the kitchen that might have been a turkey baster, which worked well for getting a massive sploosh of colour, but Ashbert came up trumps.

"That's a bicycle pump," I said.

"It is," he replied.

I didn't ask him where he got it from, but we found that it would spray a gorgeous mist of fine droplets, and we could even get it onto the ceiling if we held it over our heads. The artwork was coming on a treat when the doorbell rang. I went over, making a pathway out of newspaper so that I kept the floor clean. It was Bernadette Brampton, head of the residents' association.

"I'm speaking to all of the residents," she said, her face stony. "I'm afraid we've been victims of larceny."

"Someone's set fire to something?"

"Someone has taken the pump from my Pashley Princess Classic. That's my bicycle. Have you, by any chance, seen anyone acting suspiciously?"

I made sure that the door shielded my other arm from view as it currently held a bicycle pump that was dripping with paint.

"No," I said, pretending to think about it for a moment. "We've had a quiet day, not seen anything much."

"I cycle to work every day," she said, as though that was my fault.

"Good for you."

"And what will happen now if I get a puncture between here and the university."

"Oh, you work at the uni too? Cool."

She gave me a suspicious glare. It's the only expression I've seen her use, so I think she uses it on everyone. "You?"

"The museum and gallery," I nodded. "I'm a mover and shaker." Which was true. I moved my trolley and shook my duster here and there.

She humphed as though whatever I did was clearly beneath her and left. When I went back and surveyed our handiwork I had a thought.

"You know what it looks like, going up the chimney breast like that? It looks like a tree. I think I might build on that."

I used my fingers to stipple a bark effect into the trunk and then found all the different shades of green to use for the foliage. I was pleased with the effect, and the parts where it crossed the ceiling looked like a jungle canopy. I enhanced that by throwing a few whole match pots above my head to get some thick coverage. Then I had a brainwave. I fetched a box of condoms from the spare room and poured paint into the bottom of one. I then inflated it, tied it in a knot and slooshed it all around inside. I held it against the wall and popped it with a drawing pin. A lovely explosion of paint surrounded the blast zone, and I cast aside the ruined condom, eager to try it again in a different spot. The effect was something like a vibrant chrysanthemum. Solid paint at the epicentre, with petals peeling away on every side. I filled more condoms with paint and pinned them to the wall, all over.

"Ashbert! Come and help me make art!"

He came through from the kitchen where he was preparing sausages again and I gave him a drawing pin.

"Look! Just burst the condoms and watch the magic happen!"

Together we popped the wall full of condoms and watched the glorious riot of colour enhance the tree. I should perhaps have been a little bit more selective in my colour choices, as it was now looking less like a tree and more like an exploded piñata, but that could be remedied with some basic touching-up, I decided. When it was dry I would hand paint some birds over the top.

I checked the time and decided to finish for the day. As I gathered up the newspaper, I realised with some dismay that paint had soaked through and stained the rug underneath. I took the rug to the bathroom and tried to wash it in the bath but the colour wouldn't budge, and now it was also wet through.

In the end, I got some bin liners and bundled everything up: the newspaper, the rug, even that useless vest of Adam's after I used it to soak up some of the water. I double bagged the lot and tied it round the middle.

"Which recycling bin should this go into?" I asked Ashbert.

"I don't think it can go into any of them. It's not recyclable, so it goes to landfill, but no bag larger than a standard pedal bin is permitted in that bin."

I looked at him.

"I read the handbook," he said.

I grimaced at the crazy rules and wondered whether Bernadette could trace the rubbish back to us. The answer was sure to be yes.

"We'll just have to keep it until I've learned to drive," I said finally. "Then I can get a car and take it to the tip."

"Will that be anytime soon?" asked Ashbert and dragged the bags into the spare room.

"My driving instructor says I might need forty lessons."

"Might be a while then."

"Nah, he just underestimates me," I said and went to get showered.

Chapter 17

I didn't need to be in work on Tuesday morning so, despite me having a babysitting job that night, it felt like a day off. We spent the day curled up on the sofa together, surrounded by the still-present rubbish of yesterday's decorating, eating biscuits, drinking tea and watching movie after movie on Adam's giant TV. We'd watched *National Lampoon's Vacation*, *Con Air*, *The Cannonball Run*, *Shrek* and were now starting on *Casino Royale*.

I kind of liked James Bond movies. Pierce Brosnan was the Bond of my childhood. There was a certain sexist, sixties charm to the ones starring Indiana Jones' dad and there was an amusing campness in the ones with the guy who did all of his acting with one eyebrow (amusing even though he was old enough to be his leading ladies' granddad!) but Pierce Brosnan was actually James Bond as he should be: handsome, unruffled and super-suave.

Daniel Craig was a good Bond. He didn't have the style or cool or looks of the others but he had a brutal masculinity. On screen, he was chasing a mad bomb maker across the rooftops of some African city, leaping from a high-rise crane to a building site, sliding across table tops, free-running down stairs and off window ledges.

As I polished off a packet of bourbons, I glanced from Ashbert to Daniel Craig and back again. Obviously, I hadn't used anyone as old as Daniel Craig in my scrapbook picture, but I wondered which parts I'd take if I did it again? Not his ears, obviously and definitely not that daft pout that he sometimes wears. Perhaps the eyes that can go from predatory killer to twinkly and blue in a snap? It set me thinking that Bond's appeal isn't so much about his looks (although that coming-out-of-the-sea-in-Speedos scene is one we can all appreciate) but it's more about his confidence and his ability to master manly skills.

"There should be an academy where you can learn to be like Bond," I said to Ashbert, shifting to face him. I wanted to be sure that he properly appreciated the genius of my idea. Bond Academy!

"Isn't that MI6?" asked Ashbert.

"No, no. Not the spy stuff, the other stuff. Like knowing about wine and fighting and being an expert at poker," I said.

His face lit up and I knew I had struck a chord. "I'd love to learn that."

"You ever been a poker person?" I asked.

"No. But I'd give it a go. It would be great to learn."

"I'm sure you're a quick learner," I said with a nod of approval. Ashbert had a lot of boyish charm, but a dash of maturity was something he really needed. If I was going to make the effort to master adulting then it seemed only right that he should haul himself out of permanent adolescence too. A smidgeon of Bondness would do that.

James Bond shot the bomb maker, blew up the embassy compound and was getting a right ticking off by wrinkly old Mrs M when I realised I had indeed eaten the last bourbon.

"I need biscuits," I said.

"We're out," said Ashbert. "I could bake you some."

Then I had my second stroke of genius, because I remembered that I'd scooped up an unopened mini pack of Jaffa cakes from a tray that I'd cleared in the cafe at work. They were in the pocket of my coat. I went to look for them.

"Back in a mo."

I went through the coats that hung near the front door. Mine was underneath, and as I moved things aside a flash of green caught my eye. I pulled out a bright green hoodie and stared at it. Bright green. Pea green. I'd seen this before, peering over the gate at the back of the museum, loitering in the streets here and there. I carried it through and showed it to Ashbert.

"Is this yours?" I asked.

"It's Adam's," he said.

"But you've been wearing it."

He looked at me. "Yeah. Oh, you found biscuits. Well done."

"I saw you – was it you? I saw you wearing this outside Boots the other day, didn't I?"

"Um. Might have done."

"And were you outside the museum as well?"

"I was, yeah," he said. "A couple of times."

"What were you doing?" I asked.

"I was just following you," he said.

I tried to process this. My mind turned over this new nugget of information and tried to file it somewhere under *normal boyfriend behaviour* but it wouldn't fit.

"I need you to explain why you'd want to do that," I said slowly.

"I just want to see you," he said, which made it sound sort of normal. "To watch you," he said, which didn't sound normal at all.

He saw the concern on my face and gave me a goofy grin. A loving goofy grin. "Like when I watch you at night, sometimes."

"Wait, what? That was real? I thought I was having a bloody nightmare. Why on earth would you do that? Regular people don't do that."

He snorted good naturedly. "Sure they do."

"No, they don't."

"What about thingy in *Twilight*?"

Oh no. He was part Robert Pattinson. I despaired to think that teenagers everywhere (me included) had thought it romantic and intense that the vampire who didn't need any sleep would spend the whole night watching over his human love interest.

"Let's get a couple of things straight," I said to Ashbert. "Apart from the fact that it's fiction, it's just wrong on many levels."

"What is?"

"*Twilight* generally, but the creepy watching thing in particular. Edward Cullen is nearly a hundred years old, yeah? And he's spending all night watching a seventeen-year-old girl sleep? It's uber-creepy. Creepier than James Bond's seduction techniques and that's saying something."

"Right," said Ashbert happily. "James Bond is creepy but not as creepy as Edward Cullen. Got it." He turned to watch TV. He hadn't got it.

"And following people is creepy," I said.

"Is it?" he said, confused.

"You need to stop it."

Ashbert was crestfallen. He wore an expression like a kicked puppy. But I had to press on, for his own good. This was surely what Cookie meant about *shaping* a man. Ashbert needed me to be assertive, to tell him what needed to change.

"Right, there's something else that you need to know," I said. "There's no easy way to say this, but I'm really fed up of sausages with onion gravy."

His face took on the expression of utter dejection. The kicked puppy had just been told that there was no Father Christmas, no Tooth Fairy, that it would never get its foot on the property ladder and that its parents had killed off the pandas and polar bears with decades of environmental degradation. "But... but it's your favourite," he said.

"It *was* my favourite, years ago! We all change and grow, and *nobody* has their favourite all the time, or you'd get sick of it. I have got sick of it, I literally have permanent indigestion."

He nodded slowly, got up from our sofa den and walked silently into the kitchen. I hoped I hadn't overdone it; I didn't want the kicked puppy to go stick his head in the oven. I was tempted to follow and watch over him, but would that undo the good I had achieved with my moment of brutal honesty? I had made impressive progress on this brain teaser when Ashbert came back, leafing through the pages of one of Adam's cookbooks.

"What about *sausages in red wine and tomatoes*?" he asked.

I counted to ten. I was ready to put this clueless puppy in the oven myself and turn it up to max. But I didn't. I was proud of myself for not screaming or throwing the book across the room. Instead, I kept my cool composure and left the room.

I went to the bedroom and sat on the floor with my old pals, the much-graffitied rocking horse and Gida the slightly-charred Cretan goat. They were currently better company than my dream boyfriend. I decided it was time to create another Florrie blog about tackling relationship issues like an adult. I showed her setting clear boundaries by pointing sternly at a pack of sausages. As I've honed my style over the years I've come to realise that the power of a great cartoon is being able to convey a tricky concept with just an image, a couple of speech bubbles and maybe a brief caption. I think I nailed this one, I really do.

Ashbert popped his head round the door.

"I have a question," he said. "If you take sausage meat out of the casing and fry it to form a pasta sauce does it still count as a sausage? If we allow that one in then I think I've got a fortnight of non-sausage sausage recipes –"

I screamed and hurled a pencil at him. He managed to get his head out of the way just in time.

I furiously sketched an annoying puppy, slain by a trio of arrow-sharp pencils. Unfortunately, I'd made the dead puppy too bloody cute. I screwed up my drawing, ashamed.

Chapter 18

Evening, babysitting-o'clock, and I was glad to be out of the flat and away from my cute but infuriating dream-boy.

The house was easy enough to find. It was in an area I knew, not that far from my old house. I rang the bell and looked around while I waited. It was in a road of tall detached houses with walled gardens at the front and garages. Quite a nice road, and the garden was all neat borders and razor-sharp edges, like they'd got a proper OCD gardener in to do it.

The door opened. My face fell. I could feel it falling, like the strings in my brain had been cut.

"Hello," I said.

James Reynolds, part-time museum curator, part-time paper boy, part-time something at the university (I still wasn't sure what) stood in the hallway.

I tried really hard to force a smile onto my face.

"You!" he said. I saw his face leap through a series of expressions: confused, angry, frightened, concerned, suspicious... He was doing all the classics; he'd be great to sketch. "What are you doing here?"

"I'm the babysitter," I said.

"No," he said firmly. "I want a proper babysitter."

"I am a proper babysitter."

"Someone responsible."

I bit back the sarcastic reply about an entrance exam that so nearly came out of my mouth and went with a quiet smile instead, trying to ooze responsibility.

"I'm a very responsible babysitter. In all my years of babysitting, I haven't lost one yet."

James exhaled loudly and looked defeated. "If this turns out to be a disaster..."

"It won't," I assured him.

He looked at his watch. "I'm going to be late anyway." He huffed, leading the way inside. He turned and looked at me. "Anyway, I thought your name was Lori?"

"It is," I said.

"I'm sure I spoke to a Melissa," he said.

I nodded. "Yes, it sounds a bit the same, doesn't it? I've had that before. Still, I'm here now."

He gave me a suspicious scowl, but he didn't have time to reply before a mop-haired boy ran down the stairs with a strangely shaped plastic construction in his hand.

"Theo, come here and say hello to the lady who's going to look after you this evening," said James. "Lori, this is Theo."

Theo came and shook my hand solemnly. It was only then that I thought how odd it was that James would have a child. The fusty attitude, the charity shop tweeds – James was hardly dad material.

"Theo," said James, "Lori knows *all* of the rules, so be sure to stick to them."

"How old are you, Theo?" I asked, aware that it made me sound like my mom. I was a bit clueless with kids but I felt I should start with some solid facts.

"Ten," said Theo, "although it will be my birthday in three months, so I get a tolerance built into all of the rules, cos I'm nearly eleven."

"No, you're not and no you don't," said James over his shoulder as he pulled a jacket on. He kissed the top of Theo's head and paused before leaving. "My contact details are on the notepad on the kitchen table, and I've jotted down a few bits and bobs you might need. Uncle Phil's laid up in the other room."

"Uncle Phil?"

"I mentioned on the phone when I booked you. This is his place but he's likely to nap for most of the evening."

"Oh, that Uncle Phil," I said. "Sure."

Uncle Phil must have been the one he was standing in for at the newsagent. He'd mentioned some sort of operation, hadn't he? I needed to double-check and I had a dozen other questions but James closed the door and was gone.

I looked around the room. I was in charge of another human. A whole one. All by myself.

"Shit," I said, suddenly nervous.

Theo stared at me like I'd just pissed on the carpet.

"–zu dogs are my favourite," I added quickly. "What's yours?"

"Cock," he said and wandered into the kitchen. He returned a second later, munching on a Jammie Dodger. "–er spaniels," he finished.

I laughed. He did too. This was easy! And technically neither of us had sworn. Win!

"Okay, so what do I need to know, Theo?" I said.

He answered very promptly. "No telly after eight, no food for me after nine, but you can eat what you want, of course. Can I be in charge of the telly until eight?"

"Yes, of course," I said. There was only half an hour left.

Theo plonked himself on the sofa. I spent a considerable few moments debating whether I should sit next to him or not. Sitting with him on the sofa might seem too chummy. If I took the armchair would I seem distant and aloof? But if I sat next to him would that appear creepy? I decided to risk it and sat down on the sofa.

On screen, Theo scrolled expertly through a maze of digital offerings and selected some vintage cartoons. Always a good choice. I snorted along with Theo to the horrific violence that Wile E Coyote managed to visit upon himself in his efforts to catch the Road Runner.

"If he can afford all those explosives, why doesn't he just spend that money on a pizza?" said Theo.

"Do coyotes eat pizza?"

"All right. A Nando's," said Theo. "He'd like a Nando's."

"I don't know. Maybe they don't have Nando's in the desert."

"Or a Greggs," said Theo.

Wile E Coyote swung on a rope into the path of a truck and squashed into the radiator grill.

"Or if they take him to hospital, he'd get fed there."

I was gripped with a sudden panic. Was it all right for a ten-year-old to watch such things? How old was I when I first saw a cartoon character meet a grisly death? Had the rules changed? I looked at Theo. He didn't look traumatised, but what did I know? This seemed like a good time to go and check the note that James had left in the kitchen.

I walked through into the kitchen and got myself a glass of water. The note was on the table.

Melissa,

Rules for Theo: No TV after 8, no food after 9. Theo is normally very good at sticking to the rules.

Help yourself to snacks from the breadbin. If you want to take a cup of tea to Uncle Phil around 9 he would appreciate it, but don't worry too much. He likes it a deep chestnut-orange colour (think Donald Trump), with one sweetener.

My contact number is below, I expect to be back at 10:30.

Nothing there about violent cartoons, and he did say that Theo was good with the rules. I relaxed a little and looked in the breadbin. There were several boxes of shop-bought cakes and a loaf of bread for toasting. I slid several cakes into my bag for emergencies and made some toast. This was an unexpected benefit of babysitting. I could eat loads of food and save myself a bit more money. I wondered if James would be shocked if I ate all the food? Probably not. I found a carrier bag for the rest of the cakes and left them on the side for later.

I went back through to see Theo already munching on my toast.

"Want some toast?" I offered.

"No, I'll get something in a bit. It's time to turn the telly off," he said.

I checked the glowing digital display. He was right, it was exactly eight o'clock. Wow, this kid was super honest. He picked up the remote control, twiddled with some buttons and the display switched to a game of some sort. He settled back in the chair and picked up a controller.

"Wait," I said. "What are you doing?"

"Playing *Beast Dimensions*," he said, his eyes wide and innocent.

"You were supposed to turn the telly off after eight," I said.

"The telly is off. This is a game. The rules don't mention games."

He was right. There was no mention at all of video games, which was a glaring loophole in the rules. I sighed in defeat.

"So, what's it all about then, this *Dimensions* game?" I asked.

138

He gave me a look as though I was about a hundred years out of date. "It's a toys-to-game third person platformer that uses RFID chips in the avatar units."

I think my face betrayed my complete lack of comprehension. I'm not even sure I knew all of the words he'd just said.

He tried again. "It's an adventure game and your progress data and avatar abilities are stored in the action figure," he said, taking a plastic model of a cartoon fox off the top of the games console below the TV and waggling it at me.

"Nope," I said, shaking my head.

He sighed. "The toy things" – he waggled the fox – "go on the console" – he put the fox back – "and play along with the screen things. And I got through to the fourth world with Incendio. That was until I lost him."

"Lost who?"

"Incendio. The dragon character I was using."

"A toy?"

"Yes. I hid Incendio in Dad's works bag so that it would make him smile when he saw it. It would be pretty funny to see a dragon sitting in your briefcase, right? But it must have fallen out. He never even saw it."

I pushed away the curiosity about why this kid felt the need to cheer his dad up (surely, he knew that some adults were just naturally grumpy; they were happy that way) and picked up my bag.

"And this dragon, it's red, right?" I said, rummaging through.

"Yeah."

"With little stubby wings?"

"Yeah."

Anything like this?" I asked, pulling out the plastic toy I'd picked up while cleaning last week.

"No way!" Theo yelled in delight. He took it from me and turned it over to check. "You found it!"

He went to the console and put the dragon on a little hexagon next to the fox. A triumphant fanfare played through the TV.

"Do you want to play?" he asked.

I grinned. It felt as though this was possibly the nicest thing that Theo had within his power to offer to me. "Yeah!"

He dug around in the cubby hole below the television and pulled out another controller and then grunted with frustration. "The battery's gone!"

"I'm sure we can fix that," I said, confident in my role as adult. I flipped the cover off at the back. Two AA batteries. I went hunting. I pulled out a few drawers in the kitchen but I couldn't find an obvious stash of spare batteries. Time to think laterally, so I cast about for something else that might take similar batteries. I found a small controller near the front door. Something to open the garage door perhaps. I looked inside and found two AA batteries.

"Bingo!" I said and rushed back with my trophy. I would need to remember to mention it to James. He could sort out his door opener later.

Beast Dimensions turned out to the best fun. I was a fennec fox called Reynella and I ran around, jumping over things and picking up coins. And I found the button combination which made me strike a kick-ass pose and flick my ears. Theo kept telling me to stop messing about and keep up with his character, Incendio, but I could tell he was impressed.

"You're just jealous of my furry magnificence," I said.

"Fennecs aren't as furry as red foxes," he snorted.

I couldn't put my finger on exactly why, but this felt like a subtle undermining of my newly-acquired adult expertise. I didn't actually know fennec foxes were real things.

"I think you'll find," I cringed inside at my Adam-like tone, "that a fennec fox is by far the furriest of the foxes."

Theo giggled as he concentrated on the game. "You can't possibly know that," he said.

"Of course, I can!" I said. "I'm an adult!"

He laughed again. "I know you're older than me, but have you ever touched a fennec fox? Or even a red fox?"

How to answer him? The lie was on the tip of my tongue, but I could see that he was expecting it. I needed something better.

"You think we don't get them round here?" I said, casting my hands around as if we might have overlooked a fox in the room.

"We don't get fennec foxes," said Theo. "They live in Africa, don't they? We get normal foxes round here, going through the bins and stuff, but they don't hang around so you can pet them."

I saw it was five past nine by the clock on the wall.

"Is it bedtime soon?" I asked.

"Yup. I'm just gonna get myself something from the kitchen."

"No food after nine," I said.

"I know," he said. "I'm just going to get a drink."

I followed Theo into the kitchen and decided now was the time to take Uncle Phil his cup of tea. As I put the kettle on, Theo poured milk into the liquidizer.

"Making a milkshake?" I asked.

"Yup," he said, pouring golden syrup in and adding an enormous dollop of ice-cream. He followed this with half a packet of chocolate hobnobs and a fistful of marshmallows.

"Um, isn't that food?"

He put the lid on and whizzed the whole lot up. "Not anymore."

I shrugged. Theo was clearly an expert in making the most of the rules, and who was I to stop him?

I poured the tea and pulled my phone out of my pocket to open a browser window. I was nervous of doing things like this in Adam's flat as I was certain that Lexi would somehow monitor everything. I wanted to see whether I could find anything like my pendant. I googled *magic pendant Crete* as a start. There were quite a few results about jewellery that mentioned the word *Minoan*. It wasn't a word I knew. I tried it out. "Minoan."

Theo looked over with interest.

"Minoan?" he said.

"Minoan," I repeated. "I'm researching this pendant of mine. What does Minoan mean?"

"Something to do with the Minotaur," said Theo. He poured out his milkshake. It had the consistency of quicksand. A court of law could probably spend weeks debating whether it was a liquid or a solid. "There was a King Minos. In Greek mythology. It's in my book of Greek myths. The Minotaur was his son. Sort of."

"Which one's the Minotaur?" I asked. I'm only really confident on the ones that are in Harry Potter.

"A man with the head of a bull," said Theo.

I nodded seriously. "Yeah, I've seen him on the market. He runs the fruit and veg stall."

Theo laughed and tried to stick a straw in his milkshake. The milkshake put up a good fight. "The queen gave birth to the minotaur," he said. "She fell in love with a bull and got the craftsmen to build her a big wooden cow that she climbed inside so the bull might –"

"Woah. Cut," I said. "Was this a PG-thirteen rated myth?"

"A lot of them are like that. Zeus, he was at it all the time."

"Okay, I think it's milkshake time. Save the filthy legends for another day."

I finished making Uncle Phil's tea and carried it through towards the back room, along a long hallway lined with packed bookshelves. My phone rang and I put the tea down on a radiator shelf in the hallway to see who it was. Adam.

"Hello Adam," I said cautiously.

"Lori, I think we need a bit of a chat," he said. Was he deliberately trying to sound like our dad?

"It's good to talk," I said, deliberately chirpy.

"I've seen an invoice for three thousand condoms," he said. "They've taken fifteen hundred pounds from my bank."

"Ah, that."

"What on earth are you playing at Lori?"

"Three thousand condoms," I said, playing for time. I couldn't see a way to deny it, so I decided to go on the offensive. "Well I don't really think that was my fault to be honest, Adam."

"What? Are you mad? Did you press the button?"

"I did, yes, but I think that any normal person would have done the same," I said. "You must have seen that television show where the contestants are locked in a room with nothing but a button to press. The average person lasts three seconds before they press the button."

"What button?"

"It's human nature, Adam."

"Are you comparing what you've done to a game show?" he said, his voice going a little squeaky with unrestrained emotion. "This is exactly the sort of immature attitude that's got you into this situation! You need to be responsible for your own actions. I expect you to pay me back for those condoms."

"What?" I said. "You can use them, can't you?"

"Three thousand condoms!"

"It might take you a while, but –"

"Lori, I'm not going to discuss this any further. You've messed up and you will pay me back. Now, I'm going to be out of touch for a while – I've been booked in as a last-minute replacement for a thing filming in Tierra del Fuego – but you really need to get your act together."

"You were going to tell me where Mom and Dad are."

"Not a chance, Lori. You were going to show that you can stand on your own two feet, but from what I can see you need to try *much harder!*"

He ended the call and I stared at my phone with impotent rage. If I hadn't been in someone else's house I would have shouted abuse at Adam, just for the satisfaction of it, but I managed to stop myself from making too much noise. I did blow a big raspberry at the phone before I stuffed it back into my pocket though.

I picked up the cup of tea, took a deep and cleansing breath and went through to find Uncle Phil. I'd expected to find an ancient shell of a man reclining in a hospital bed, but I found a gentle-looking older man sitting in a leather armchair watching a television programme about ant colonies or something. He looked up at me as I set his tea down on a small table beside his chair.

"You don't look like a Melissa," he smiled.

"People say that."

"I must congratulate you."

"On what?"

"Young Theo's not laughed so much in a good while."

I grinned. "He's a lovely boy."

He turned his tea cup round to reach the handle.

"Trump-tastic."

"Pardon?"

He pointed at the tea. "Nice colour that. You get my seal of approval."

I couldn't help but laugh at that. "I don't get a lot of praise."

"Three thousand condoms, eh?" he said with a sly look on his face.

I'd fallen into the trap of assuming that all old people were deaf. I felt my face colour, and quickly replayed the other parts of the conversation in my head. What else had he heard?

"An interesting conundrum," he said. "Assuming that you don't have the energy to use them all for their intended purpose." My face grew hotter and hotter. "You're too young to remember that soldiers in the Gulf war used them to keep sand out of their rifles, I imagine?"

"Yes."

"You could always see if the military will take them off your hands."

"Not the fluorescent ones though," I said.

He nodded sagely. "Balloon animals for those ones, you could make a fortune as a street entertainer. You've got plenty to practise with."

Uncle Phil was teasing me. I resolved to take it like an adult. "Well if you need any yourself, just pass a message to James. Actually, on second thoughts, don't." Sometimes my mouth horrifies my brain.

"Don't worry, I won't say a thing," said Phil, tapping the side of his nose.

"I'd best see how Theo's getting along," I said.

As I headed back to the living room, I saw a huge natural history encyclopaedia on a bookshelf and took it with me. I sat down beside Theo and while his dragon did incomprehensible things in a fantasy land on the TV screen, I flicked through to find the entry on fennec foxes. They did live in Africa (I didn't know that) and, apart from the laser sword and cloak, the one in the game was a surprisingly accurate representation. They really did have giant ears that made their faces look like cute little bats. I showed the picture to Theo.

"Cute," he said. "Still not as furry as a red fox."

I felt things spiralling out of my control. Theo was running rings around me and I was supposed to be the adult. I needed to do something. I glanced down at the book, held my pendant and pointed discreetly at the picture of the fennec fox, then I flipped the page and did the same with the red fox.

Moments later there was a movement in the corner of the room.

"Well, what's this?" I said as innocently as I could.

Theo dropped the controller in surprise as two foxes bolted across the room. The red fox moved very quickly, while the tiny fennec fox trotted daintily on its Bambi legs. Both looked as shocked as Theo at their arrival and, even though both creatures were considerably smaller than I had expected, I realised that I had just unleashed two sharp-toothed carnivores into the house. I had the feeling that perhaps this had been a bad idea. I wished I'd had the feeling before I brought them to life. Oh, well, nothing to do but persevere with the plan.

"All we need to do now is get hold of them and we can see which one's the furriest," I said. "By the way, are we looking for softness of fur, or depth of fur, would you say?"

Theo had recovered from the initial shock enough to consider this.

"I'd say that the depth is the main thing to look for, but we should judge both. Where did they come from though?"

"They were just sort of there," I said.

"No, they weren't."

"Do you have another explanation?"

"No," he said.

"I wonder how we get hold of them?"

The red fox ran round the room, barking sharply. The fennec fox trembled and yipped each time it shot past. The fennec fox grabbed a cushion between its teeth and carried it into a corner where it chewed experimentally on the tassels.

Theo approached the fennec fox cautiously, wanting a closer look, but I guess he looked as though he wanted to take the cushion away, because the tiny fox ripped a huge chunk off the cushion and retreated under a chair, leaving a flurry of feathers in its wake.

Where had the other one got to? I heard the sound of smashing crockery coming from the kitchen and ran through to stop it. The fox was on the worktop, trying to get its jaws into the breadbin. When it saw me, it shot out of the kitchen again. I followed, pulling the kitchen door closed behind me.

"We ought to try and contain them," I said to Theo.

"My dad's going to think I did this on purpose so that I could stay up late," he said, his face serious.

"No, we'll make sure your dad knows that you didn't do this," I said, wondering how exactly I *was* going to explain this to James.

The red fox ran up the bookshelf as if it was a staircase. I had no idea foxes could do manoeuvres like that. It didn't seem to like being at the top though, as it tried to squeeze behind the books, sending everything cascading off the shelf. It moved along the entire shelf in this way, emptying it of its contents: atlases, car owners' manuals, Readers Digest novels and heavy textbooks. Every thump made it hasten along. It must have decided that it felt too exposed when the shelf was empty, so it made a leap for the next highest thing in the room which was a tall standard lamp. Obviously the lamp wasn't the most solid thing perch that it could have chosen, so both the lamp and the fox toppled to the floor with an almighty crash. At that moment, the fennec fox made a brief foray out from its hiding place to retrieve the rest of the cushion and shook it savagely from side to side, filling the room with a snowstorm of feathers.

I would say that things were getting out of hand but, in truth, things had got out of hand some time ago and were now trying to destroy everything, possibly including the hand.

"I think Dad might have a packet of dog treats in the jacket he wears when he does the papers," said Theo.

"That's an inspired idea, Theo," I said.

Theo led the way to an under stairs cupboard that was part pantry, part coat storage room. There was a large coat rack, and the walls were lined with bulky packets and tins that would find their way to the kitchen at some point. The feature that I was most interested in was the fact that this cupboard had a door that closed firmly.

"We could try and get them into here," said Theo.

"Smart thinking, padawan," I said.

We found the dog treats and laid a path of meaty biscuits into the pantry. I grabbed a broom out of the pantry and hid behind the door. Theo flattened himself against the wall on the other side. The red fox was the first to pick up the trail, and followed it greedily into the pantry. The fennec fox still hadn't dropped the cushion, but he trotted over, looking for all the world as if he was judging the red fox's bad table manners. He stood at the doorway of the pantry and I swept him inside with the broom before one of them ran out again. We slammed the door and made sure the catch was in place.

"That was fun," said Theo.

I nodded, breathing a ragged sigh of relief.

"Why don't you go and get ready for bed?" I said. "I'll do a bit of straightening up down here and I'll try to explain to your dad what the situation is when he returns."

Theo nodded and headed upstairs.

I quickly began to tidy, starting with righting the lamp and putting the books back on the shelves. I reckoned I had about twenty minutes to undo at least a little of the damage.

I heard a key in the front door before I even got to the end of that thought.

James walked into the room where feathers were still drifting lazily in the air and stopped with the expression of a man who has returned to find his house has been destroyed by the world's most incompetent babysitter. Because that was what had happened.

"Foxes!" I said.

"You're a maniac," he said.

"Theo's fine," I added quickly.

"I should never have left him."

"He's gone up to get ready for bed, but there's been a bit of an incident."

"You think?"

He shook his head and walked towards the under stairs cupboard to put his coat away.

"Don't go in there," I said.

"Why ever not?" he said. There was a slur in his voice. He'd clearly had a drink or two.

"Foxes," I said.

"Real foxes?" He made a disbelieving 'pfff!'

"Dad! Dad! There are foxes in the house!" said Theo, thundering down the stairs in his pyjamas.

"Foxes? Right." James gave me a stern look. He had the perfect eyebrows for stern looks. It was actually a little bit sexy. Masterful even. "You got Theo to play along with your nonsense?"

"There really are foxes!" said Theo.

"Really? Where did they come from?" asked James.

"It's a mystery," I said. "A complete mystery."

"We trapped them in the pantry with dog treats. They made a right mess," said Theo gleefully.

"You need to get to bed, young man. You need your sleep. Say goodbye to Lori. She's going."

"Da-ad! How can I sleep when there are foxes in the pantry?" complained Theo.

"You'll cope," said James.

Just then, the foxes started to scream. It was the most unearthly, terrifying noise, only slightly muffled by the door. It genuinely sounded like the soundtrack to a horror movie or something. It was accompanied by the crashing of things falling over inside the pantry.

"There's foxes in the pantry!" yelled James.

"We told you," said Theo.

"I'm not a liar," I said.

However squiffy James was, he sobered up instantly.

"Theo, bed. You." He actually prodded me. "We're sorting this thing out."

Chapter 19

"Have you got a plan?" I asked. "Because I get the impression that you're not, you know, one hundred percent sober."

"No, I haven't got a plan at all," he said. "And yes, I am drunk, because I've had a challenging evening. How big are these things?"

I sketched them in the air. "One's normal fox size."

"Like a dog?"

"Like a small dog."

"A Chihuahua?"

"Well, the other's more of a Chihuahua type of thing. The red fox, it's... well, it's a fox. Take a look, just don't let them out."

He approached the door and opened it a crack. The screaming sound faltered slightly, and there was an accelerated scrabbling as well. James peered into the cupboard.

"I can't see anything," he said.

"Is the light on?" I asked. I was sure that Theo had put a light on in there.

"Yes, the light's on. I just can't see any foxes."

"What? You can hear them in there," I said, wondering how you could possibly miss a pair of foxes going bonkers in a small cupboard.

He pulled the door open and we both stared. The cupboard was empty of foxes, but there was a new feature. A hole in the back wall where there hadn't been one previously. The foxes were no longer screaming, but they were making a new set of noises somewhere beyond the wall. I wasn't sure what they were doing exactly, but it sounded as if they were destroying something.

"Does that go outside?" I asked.

"No, it's just a plaster partition with the garage. Come on."

James hurried round to the kitchen. I slammed the cupboard door closed, so that the foxes couldn't come through again. I also picked up the carrier bag full of cakes, with a vague thought of putting some of them back, as James was home so early that he'd never believe I'd eaten them all. I followed James through a door into the garage.

It was an average-sized garage and it was mostly filled with car. I didn't know anyone put cars in their garages these days.

"That's Uncle Phil's Jag," said James, his voice lowered so that he didn't spook the two foxes who were rootling through some boxes at the back.

"So, do you live with your uncle?"

"Theo and I are staying here for a while. It's a temporary thing."

Then there was a noise from behind. It was the click of the door from the kitchen, the sound of a latch falling into place.

"Tell me you have a key for that."

"Inside the house," said James. "Don't worry, I always bring this out here with me." He held up the remote-control device from the kitchen. "We can go out the front of the garage."

"Ah," I said.

"Ah?"

"I took the batteries out of it for the video game controller."

He gave a long sigh and put the remote back in his pocket.

"Not to worry," he said, mostly like he was trying to reassure himself. He thought for a while. "Listen," he said.

"Listening."

"I need to thank you for managing to get these things locked away."

"Oh. Okay."

"They could have bitten Theo or something. I'm very grateful."

I smiled. I was obviously a massive fraud who had caused all of these problems in the first place but I wasn't about to tell him that.

"So, we have two problems," I said. "We need to sort out those foxes and we need to get out of here," I said. "And we need to do both of those with the minimal damage."

"Damage?"

"I think the little one likes tearing up soft furnishings," I said, giving a meaningful nod to the soft-top Jaguar.

James nodded. He went over to the garage door and pointed at some sort of mechanism above his head.

"This here is the manual winder. If the electricity fails or you find yourself stuck like we are now, it's the way that you'd open the door."

"Brilliant!" I said. "We can do that."

"The problem is that Uncle Phil broke the handle off a few weeks before his operation. Getting it fixed was one of the jobs on my list while I'm here."

"Not to worry," I said with a brave smile. "We can sort this out. I've even got some snacks to keep our spirits up."

I lifted the carrier bag full of cakes that I'd cleaned out of his bread bin earlier and held it open. He grinned and reached inside to grab a cake. At that moment, the red fox ran from its position at the back of the garage and as it rocketed past us at top speed, it grabbed the bag of cakes in its fang-filled mouth and hauled it out of our hands. It disappeared over the soft top of the Jaguar and hid in the gap down the other side. We could hear the sounds of it ripping open packaging as it tore into the cakes.

"Right, now it's personal," I said. "I was looking forward to a cake. We need to trap them and now!"

We worked our way around the garage and examined the options that we might use to trap a pair of foxes and operate a broken door winder. James peered at the winder and announced that he could probably operate it manually with a pair of pliers and began sorting through a side drawer in search of one.

Meanwhile, I assembled the basics of a superb fox trap.

"Check this out," I said.

He looked round and checked it out. I generally expect the 'checking it out' facial expression to have a bit less scepticism.

"What's that?" he said.

"It starts as a simple washing basket." I had placed it upside down on the bonnet of the Jaguar and then used a pair of clothes pegs to prop up one end. I had tied the clothes pegs to a piece of string so that any fox that went under the basket would be trapped when I pulled them away.

"These are foxes, not the Road Runner," said James.

"We just need some bait," I said. "Your job is to steal a cake back from the red fox's stash in a minute. First, we need to make

151

something more secure to put them into. This won't hold them for long."

I had a roll of netting, and I was sure that we could create a big bag from it, but it took quite a long time. James reluctantly joined in and helped me use string to fasten two huge loops of netting together into a large bag. More string around the top gave us a handy drawstring that we used to hang the bag up from a ladder that was stored along the roof of the garage. In the meantime, the red fox was steadily eating its way through the bag of cakes and the fennec fox trotted back and forth along the shelf, looking down enviously.

"The little one's going to be our best bet. If we get some cake under the trap it'll be straight down," I said, nudging James.

He went round to see if he could rescue some cake from the red fox. It slunk under the car as he approached and he was able to retrieve a Mr Kipling's French Fancy. We waved it around a bit so the fennec fox wouldn't miss it and then we put it under our trap and stepped back to wait, holding onto the string. We didn't have to wait for very long. It was obviously hungry and it went straight under the washing basket and gobbled up the cake. They probably don't get many French Fancies in the African desert. I pulled the string and the washing basket fell off the pegs, trapping the tiny fox. I let James transfer it to the bag hanging from the ceiling, which he did with a minimum of fuss once he'd donned a pair of gardening gloves. Now we had to repeat the process with the red fox. Unfortunately, it had eaten nearly all of the available bait. James went round to see if there was any more he could salvage.

"Greedy bugger's eaten the lot," he reported. "He looks a lot less perky now though."

I went to see what he meant. The red fox looked back at us from its hiding place underneath the car with a glazed and slightly unfocused expression. We edged closer and it moved away, but in a very half-hearted and lethargic manner.

"It's got bellyache," said James.

"I once ate a whole Viennetta," I said, sympathetically. "With my hands. Like it was a choc ice."

"Maybe we can just grab it," he suggested.

I nodded. It was as good a plan as any. He lunged forward with his gloved hands, but the fox found some last reserve of energy to shoot out of its space and scramble up the shelving. It made it about halfway to the top before sagging and falling backwards onto the car. Unfortunately, it displaced most of the contents of the shelf as it scrabbled for purchase. Rollers, trays and (most significantly) tins of paint clattered down onto Uncle Phil's Jag. A tin of crimson paint burst open and splattered across the soft top and down the paintwork at the sides.

James made a low moaning sound as he saw the state of the car, but all credit to his powers of focus, he grabbed the fox as it bounced onto a paint-free part of the car and wrested it into the bag.

We stood and looked at the mess. It was all over the car, and all over me as well.

I picked up the paint can and read out what it was. "Vinyl matt emulsion. Can be re-coated in thirty minutes."

"What does it say about cleaning the brushes?" asked James.

"After use, clean brushes with plenty of water," I read.

I looked up at James. "We can get it off with water!"

"Only if we can do it in thirty minutes. Maybe we can find a car wash..." His face fell. "But I've been drinking."

"You can't drive."

"I can't drive."

The look of panicked disappointment on his face made me really want to help.

"I can drive," I said. I didn't mention that I'd had my very first lesson ever that very day. It was unhelpful, I thought, given the circumstances.

"Right! Let's do this then," he said. "I'll get the pliers on this winder, we can put the foxes in the back and take them... somewhere after we've washed the car."

"Yeah!" I said. "Although I do have paint all over my clothes. I'll make a mess of the upholstery if I get in like this."

"Not a problem," said James. "See that hanger up at the end of the shelf? Uncle Phil's beekeeping outfit. Get into that and it'll be fine."

I wrestled my way into Uncle Phil's beekeeping suit while James worked on the winder. The suit turned out to be something like an elaborate boilersuit with a complicated hood. James got the garage door up and found the car key on a hook at the side of the garage. We put the bag containing the foxes into the boot, where they screamed pitifully. I prepared myself for my second driving experience of the day.

Chapter 20

I wanted to maintain an aura of calm confidence, so I settled silently into the driver's seat. It felt very different to Terence's tiny car. The seat was low and made of leather and the dashboard featured lots of expensive-looking wood, like an old person's sideboard or a Wetherspoons pub. James sat in the passenger seat and handed me the key. I put it into the ignition, but before I turned it I tried to remember all of the checks that Terence had drilled into me. I fiddled with the mirror and the seat and then turned my attention to the gearbox. It was some ludicrous contraption featuring letters and numbers. I stared at it, as if it was the Countdown Conundrum, in an effort to will those jumbled letters into something meaningful, but there were no vowels, and two D's. I'd just have to work my way through them using trial and error. My feet went to the pedals but something was wrong. There were only two.

"Is your uncle's car definitely driveable?" I asked James.

"Oh yes, he looks after it very carefully. It's in tip-top vintage condition, but he only takes it out on special occasions."

So, it was safe to assume that there wasn't a missing pedal. I turned the key in the ignition, knowing that the only way to find out how to work this car was by experimentation.

"Is it worth a lot of money then, this car?" I asked, keeping my tone casual.

"Not sure to be honest, but Uncle Phil loves it like a baby."

The engine of Uncle Phil's baby purred away and we clearly weren't going to move until I did something, so I tried the pedals. Nothing happened, so I turned my attention to the mysterious gear stick. It went *P R N D D 3 2*. Maybe they were in code and I just had to work through them one at a time. I moved the gear stick tentatively to *R* and we slid straight back into the shelving with a small bang. Luckily, it didn't make any more paint fall onto the car. I tried not to look at James as I quickly discovered which pedal was the brake and then tried *N*. That was no good, so I tried *D* and we crept slowly forward. I was jubilant. The car was moving in the correct direction and I also knew how to stop it if I needed to! I went down the drive at the side of the house and stopped at the kerb. I tried the other pedal. It made the car move again and I turned us safely onto the road. I had complete mastery of the pedals. There was a *go* pedal and there was a *stop* pedal. It was all I needed. The car kept moving. I felt compelled to move the stick to the position 2 and it worked! I was in second gear and I hadn't broken anything yet. I realised that I had no idea where we were going.

"Where is there a car wash?" I asked James.

"I think there's one next to the petrol station near the big traffic lights," he said. I had no idea what he was talking about but he gave me lefts and rights to take, so I followed his directions. We'd been driving for a few minutes, the engine making quite a lot of noise because I was scared to move it to another position, but James simply nodded.

"You're just like Uncle Phil. He likes to hear the engine revving as well."

I smiled as if I was a complete petrolhead and was doing this on purpose.

We got to the petrol station and pulled onto the forecourt.

I went to buy a token from the yellow-haired woman in the cashier's booth. On the way over, I scanned the dark road for green hoodie-wearing stalkers. I'd already decided that if I saw one he was getting a knee in the goolies and an elbow to his position as sort-of-boyfriend.

"If you take a soft-top through it's at your own risk," said the cashier. She frowned. "Can you hear screaming?"

I harkened. It was the foxes.

"No," I said.

"It's coming from your car."

"Oh, that. My boyfriend's into thrash metal. Devil Preacher, Terminal Panda, Thunderquake, um, all the bands. That's the chorus of *Eat My Fruit, Bitch*. It's a classic." I screamed along a bit.

"Thrash metal?" said the cashier.

"Yup. Just come back from a concert in fact."

"In a biohazard suit?" she said.

"It's a beekeeper's suit," I said, "and, yes, there's an interesting story behind why I'm wearing it."

"Oh, yes?"

"Yes," I said and took my token and went back to the car.

"Everything all right?" asked James as I got in.

"Peachy," I said.

I drove the car into the car wash, putting the token into the machine on the way in. I stopped at the bump in the floor as instructed and we waited. After a few moments, the car was sprayed with water and the shaggy blue brush monsters at the sides started to whizz round. They went down the sides of the car and whirred and chunked as they went around the back. But it was the horizontal roller on top that I was worried about. As it came onto the soft top, the fabric of the roof sagged down towards our heads.

"Should be getting a good cleaning," said James. He was working hard on that optimistic tone. He wasn't very good at it.

As the brushes moved along, they dragged the soft top along slightly, pushing it slowly into the down position.

"No!" yelled James. A gap appeared and water started to pour into the car. We both reached up, but with our seat belts on we fell short. We scrambled to release the seat belts and tried to pull the roof back into place, but there was nothing to get a grip on, and water was running down our arms.

"This is terrible!" he shouted over the cascade.

"We need to do it from outside!" I yelled.

I timed my exit for that moment when the side brushes were out of the way. I nipped out, skilfully. Seriously, it was like a scene from *Indiana Jones and the Car Wash of Major Inconvenience*. I climbed onto the bonnet and James was beside me. From here we could reach over the windscreen and pull on the soft roof, shutting it again. I had the left side and James had the right. I turned briefly to grin at our small triumph, but the brushes came over again and I buried my face between my outstretched arms. It wasn't a painful experience, but the menace and noise of the automated machine and the complete soaking that I got made it seem as though the car wash lasted for much longer than it really did.

When the brushes had all retracted and the machinery fell quiet, I dared to open my eyes. James looked as appalled as I did. We both had the imprint of a wiper blade across our face, like a battle scar. We carefully slid off the car, our legs a bit wobbly.

"It's done a good job on the paint," I said, looking at the roof. I pulled open the door and was pleased to see that the interior was not awash with water. I shook myself, in an effort to get the excess water off Uncle Phil's beekeeping suit and slid back inside.

There was a mournful howling coming from the boot and we discussed where we should release the foxes. It was fully dark now, so we drove to the park by the airport and pulled up in the small car park. We wrestled the bag out of the boot and unfastened it to release the foxes. They ran off into the night.

We were both wet through and shivering with cold, so we got back into the car, worked out how to put the heater on and drove Uncle Phil's baby back to its garage. If you've ever wondered how it feels to have stiffened emulsion drying against your skin at the same time as wearing an outer layer that's soaking wet, I can tell you it's a miserable experience, so when James offered me use of the bathroom and produced from somewhere a set of women's clothes I wasn't about to ask questions.

I came downstairs wearing clean clothes and feeling almost normal. James handed me a tumbler with a thin layer of something potent and warming, which I sipped gratefully.

"So?" he said, giving me a strange look. "Uncle Phil says I need to ask you about balloon animals."

Chapter 21

James topped up our glasses when I'd finished my explanation. When he stood, I could see that his brows were knitted. I could have kicked myself. What sort of idiot would come clean about making a giant condom order just because the button was there and their brother was being annoying? The sort of idiot who knew that Uncle Phil was available for easy cross-checking. Maybe I could have woven a plausible lie that made me look less stupid and shallow, but it was too late now.

"Sorry," I said. "I didn't mean to make you angry."

"Oh, I'm not angry," he said, his face softening. "That's my concentrating face. I was trying to think of some practical suggestions. I was wondering if the university could be persuaded to take them off your hands for freshers' week? They've given them away before, although I think they're trying to play down the idea that freshers' week is a giant sex party."

"Oh." I was stunned. "That's actually a great idea."

"I'll have a word with the vice-chancellor, see if I can sell it to her. She can be a bit old-fashioned." I couldn't help a small snuffle of laughter at that. "What?" he said.

"Old-fashioned," I said, nodding towards the dry clothes he had changed into (which included a knitted cardigan for goodness sake!). "That's like the cat calling the pottle black, or whatever the saying is."

He flopped back and rolled his eyes, amused. "Yeah. I know I'm not exactly down with the kids."

"No."

"Elena used to tell me I was trapped in another decade."

"Elena?"

He shook his head and it seemed it was shook at more than just my question.

"Elena is my ex-wife. Theo's mom. Things are..." He pulled a face. "This evening..."

"Were you out with her this evening?" I asked. I had no idea what the situation was, but he clearly hadn't had a fun time.

159

He sighed heavily. "No. God, no. That would have been a different kind of terrible evening. No, we haven't seen Elena since she left. It's been over a year now."

"Oh, okay."

He raised his tumbler. "You need another drink?" he asked. "And that's code for 'I need another drink'."

He took our glasses and filled them at the drinks cabinet.

"This evening, I went out to see a friend of Elena's, Pippa, who said that Elena had been in touch. It turned out that I had been invited out under false pretexts. Pippa had planned the whole thing as a date. Perhaps I should be flattered. Should I be flattered?"

"Do you feel flattered?" I said, taking the fresh glass. James had been a bit liberal with the measures but it was a very pleasant and cosyfying drink so I wasn't going to complain.

"No. I felt cheated," said James. "I was an idiot not to realise what I was walking into. It didn't go well. I couldn't wait to get back here."

A nugget of guilt took hold at this point. "Was that because you were worried about Theo?" I asked. I didn't say the words 'because you'd left him with the babysitter from Hell' but then I probably didn't need to.

He looked thoughtful. "Perhaps it has something to do with Theo," he said. "Not that I thought he was in any immediate danger, but I mean, the stakes are higher when you have a child. There's a feeling that you can't just go round having fun."

I frowned at that. "You can't? Why not?"

"Someone has to take responsibility. A child needs stability. His mother's gone off to travel the world, so I need to make sure that I don't mess things up around here."

"So, what's she doing, exactly?" I asked

"Elena's a doctor. Always been a real high flyer," said James. "She's a great doctor. Great mom. It just wasn't enough for her." He stared into his glass. "She'd done voluntary work overseas before we met, and she'd said lots of times that she wanted to go back to it. I thought she meant small stints, or maybe something more when Theo was older. I was wrong. She'd seen so many things in the world that needed fixing, she was constantly itching to go back out there and fix them."

He sipped his drink thoughtfully.

"No, that's not entirely true," he said. "Elena wanted to see the world. Being a doctor, volunteering, that was a means to an end. What she really wanted, what she wants, is to travel everywhere, see everything. It's like she's got this massive bucket list in her head and it's like she's lost the great game of life if she doesn't manage to swim with the dolphins, climb Everest, swim the Amazon and visit Machu Picchu."

"Gotta catch'em all," I said.

"Exactly. I think it got to the point where she saw me, and maybe even Theo as being like a millstone around her neck, holding her here."

I swigged my drink, remembering halfway through that it was whiskey, not the cheap wine I'm used to quaffing. I coughed and tried to turn it into a thoughtful noise.

"Being abandoned's no fun, is it?" I said.

"Ah. How goes the search for your parents?" he said. "Any word?"

"Nope. The only communication with anyone in my family is with Adam, and I've already told you how that goes. This is Adam. Watch." I affected a voice that was somewhere between Adam and Homer Simpson. "'Lori, you need to act more like a grown up and pretend you're me. Because I'm great! I've been catching dinosaurs and digging up mummies in Fuerteventura and I've got my own TV show and what have you ever done with your life, eh?'"

"Another globetrotter," said James with a wink.

"Another over-achieving globetrotter," I emphasised. "Why does everyone assume I need to match up to his standards? Why can't I just be allowed to get on with my life in my own way?"

"Exactly. Here's to getting on with our lives in our own way." He clinked his glass against mine and smiled at me. Actually at me. Like, he smiled and he looked at me. With his eyes. An entirely improper shiver ran through me.

"Sooooo," I said, "Pippa."

"What about her?"

"Not girlfriend material, huh?" I could imagine that James would have high standards, so it wasn't hard to imagine things going wrong. "What, was she not smart enough? Not pretty enough?" I asked.

"Not pretty enough?" he said. "Really? What kind of man rejects a woman purely because she doesn't match up to some secret list of ideal physical traits?"

Two thoughts jostled in my head. One was that I had known plenty of men who were just like that (one guy had dumped me immediately after taking me to bed, claiming that wearing a push-up bra was false advertising and he should report me to Trading Standards). The other thought was that Ashbert was the walking proof that I was equally capable of such shallowness.

"So, you'd go out with any woman?" I said archly.

"I'd like to say that I would. I know there's some biological hard-wiring within us all that works below the surface. Isn't there an entirely unscientific formula about your ideal partner being half your age plus seven years?"

"Is there?" I said and thought. "Fifty-seven. Wow, I've been totally hitting on the wrong guys."

"Possibly got a bit confused with the maths there," said James. "The age thing is our subconscious trying to find a healthy partner. It's an evolution thing. Same goes for the whole facial symmetry and golden ratio thing."

Uh-oh. James had forgotten that I was a doofus and didn't understand any of this highfaluting talk.

"Golden ratio?"

"Sure," he said. "It's about the relationship between the lengths of the different body parts."

"Oh, that!" I said. "I've known a lot of guys who were fixated with that. More than a couple who would text me pictures. Mind you, you can't really get a sense of proportion from a picture. I texted one guy back to explain that and so he sent me another with a six-inch Darth Vader action figure in shot for scale. Weird picture. I've still got it somewhere. Dick and Darth. It's like the world's worst buddy cop movie. *'One's a Sith Lord, one's a flaccid penis. Together they will bring the city's criminals to just–'* you okay?"

James was staring at me. I think I might have been a bit drunk and gone off on a conversational tangent. It certainly took James a long time to find his voice.

"No, I don't mean that," he said. "I definitely don't mean that. The golden ratio is about how the proportions of the body compare. It's where the ratio between the two measurements is the same as the ratio between the larger measure and the total of the two."

"Um?"

"The ancient Greek sculptor, Phidias, used it to create classically beautiful figures in the frieze of the Parthenon. They're just astonishing."

"Ah, it's a Greek thing."

"It's like this, if I may..." He put his drink down and tentatively reached out to touch my face. "The height of your nose," he said, placing thumb and finger above and below, "versus the width of your nose. The height of your nose and the length of your ears. The distance from your hairline to the bridge of your nose and from the bottom of your nose to your chin." With each statement, his fingers softly touched my skin. He was like an explorer taking a casual stroll across my face. Like that but, you know, nice. And a bit sexy.

"And you put all the numbers into your calculator and if the numbers come up right, you have a perfectly beautiful face."

"And do I?"

"What?"

"Have a perfectly beautiful face?"

He laughed.

"That bad?" I said.

"Lori, you don't need maths to tell you that you're beautiful."

"Sounds liked you're avoiding the question to be nice instead of being honest."

"Not at all." He sighed. "Pippa, tonight's would-be date, is a very beautiful woman. Intelligent and witty too. She's a barrister. But, no, she's not the woman for me. Attractiveness – physical attraction between two people – is not something you can work out with a formula."

Intelligence is though, I thought. I almost certainly fell far short of James' standards.

"At least I don't need your clever golden ratio to tell me that I'm too stupid to be girlfriend material," I said.

James blinked, slightly panicked. "Girlfriend material?"

"I mean hypothetically."

He shook his head. "You have a unique mind, Lori. That much is certain."

"Unique mind? Ha! Now you're definitely being kind instead of honest."

He simply arched an eyebrow at me. The damned man didn't even try to deny it! I picked up a cushion and playfully bashed him. It was unfortunate that I picked one of the cushions that had been savaged by a fox. Whatever was in this glass was potent and fast-acting, because I cared less than I probably should have that we were now surrounded by a haze of floating feathers. James wafted a hand across his face.

"I had a snow globe when I was a child," he mused at the drifting feathers, "and the thing I wanted more than anything was to be inside that charming little world where everything was safe and cosy. I feel as though I am tonight. Thank you, Lori."

He reached out and squeezed my hand briefly, which made my pulse quicken. The moment passed, and he climbed off the sofa.

"Feathers are a terrible allergen for kids. I'd best get the dustpan."

I'm no domestic goddess. I was happy to lift my feet as he cleared up the feathers around me. I half-listened to his chatter about Elena, but truthfully, I was thinking about being inside that cosy snow globe together.

He stopped and looked at me. I felt there was a potential moment between us. I gazed into his dark and expressive eyes."

"Seriously?" he said before continuing with the sweeping. "Dick and Darth? Jeez, I'm going to have nightmares."

Chapter 22

I woke and, for a moment, couldn't work out where I was. It wasn't my home. My home had been sold by my devious parents who had selfishly used the proceeds to follow their dreams in wildest Wales or Guatemala or Norfolk or somewhere.

I was on the sofa in James' living room (he was a bit posh so maybe he called it the drawing room or parlour). I was underneath a rough-woven throw that my mom would have described as 'ethnic'. I was still wearing another woman's clothes; I peeked under the throw and checked.

I stared vacantly at the ceiling and tried to remember what had happened.

We'd gone to the car wash, released two wild animals in the park and come back to the house for a stiff one. Warming spirits were good for a tired body. I'd knocked back a couple, we'd bitched about our estranged loved ones, he'd stuck his fingers in my face, we'd had a 'moment' or maybe half a moment and then, as I sank another drink, he'd swept up and told me more of his woes and...

I'd fallen asleep on him, knocked out by some frantic fox-based exercise, a couple of shots and his dull recollection of his bitch of an ex. That wasn't good. Falling asleep as someone opened their heart to you. Was there a positive spin to be put on this? No. It had almost certainly cemented his view that I was a clueless snowflake with no discernible skills or prospects. His perfect match would be a doctor or an academic or a globe-trotting explorer – super intelligent, cultured and suave like himself. Like James Bond.

"Hmmm."

Putting aside my current social predicament (and if waking up in a strange man's house because he's bored you to sleep isn't a social predicament, I don't know what is), it was interesting to think that James Reynolds possessed a number of the attributes that I suppose I admired in James Bond. He was sort of like James Bond but without the violence and gadgets and over-presumptive bedroom behaviour.

I located my phone (it had got wedged in a crevice) and started typing a document. I entitled it *Making My Ideal Man* then backspaced and renamed it *Making My NEW Ideal Man*. I would fill in some details and thoughts later. It was time to get out of here. I'd not yet been paid but decided I'd rather face poverty than the shame of bumping into James. It was barely seven o'clock. The house was quiet. I just needed to find my shoes and keys and creep out of there before anyone woke.

"Stealthy, Lori," I told myself and sat up.

On the next armchair over, Theo sat, reading on a tablet.

"Morning, stealthy Lori," he said without looking up.

"Ah," I said.

The lad smiled at me. "Stealthy Lori snores, you know."

"Does she?"

"Like a hippo."

"Has our guest woken?" called James from the next room.

"Yep," said Theo.

James came in with a tray bearing a pot of tea and a pair of hot buttery crumpets.

So much for creeping out.

"Morning," he said.

"Last night..." I gave up on a reasonable explanation. "I'm sorry."

James smiled. I realised he didn't do it often and it was a delight to see when he did.

"Ah, my personal troubles are dull enough to send anyone to sleep."

"Still," I said, "I'm sorry."

"I'm glad you're here," said Theo.

"That's nice," I said.

"Because we never did work out which fox was the furriest," he said solemnly.

James gave me a quizzical look. "Yes, Lori. Which one was the furriest?"

"Hmmm," I said. "I did carry out a brief assessment when we'd captured them, and I concluded that while the fennec fox had very soft fur, the red fox had a greater depth of fur. In overall furriness, I would say that the red fox was the winner."

"I knew it," said Theo with a quiet confidence. "I told you."

"You did," I conceded and poured myself a tea.

"I checked over Uncle Phil's car in the cold light of day," said James.

I pulled a face.

"No, it looks good," he said. "I think we did a good job on that."

"We?"

"There's no 'I' in team," he said on his way back to the kitchen.

"Depends how you spell it," I said.

I pulled out my phone. Now was as good a time as any to make the most of James' status as a fully-fledged and mature man for my own personal notes. I had just jotted, *Teamwork, modest, knows wise ancient sayings*, when he returned with a plate of crumpets of his own.

"Theo says you had some questions about a brooch or something," said James.

"Hmm? Oh." I touched the pendant at my neck. "We were just discussing whether it might be Minoan or something."

"Do you mind if I have a look?" he said.

"Of course. You know all about old Greek stuff."

"Old Greek stuff," he said. "That's exactly what it says on my master's degree."

He sat on the sofa beside me. I was suddenly very conscious that I was probably suffering from appalling bed head and morning breath.

"The chances of it actually being Minoan are supremely slim," he said and leaned in to get a better look.

"I bought it in Crete," I said. "Didn't think much about it at the time."

He peered at it intently and then all of a sudden we both seemed to become flustered by the fact that he was fixated on my cleavage. I blushed, he gave a light cough and looked away.

"Let me get a magnifying glass," he said and stood.

"They're not that small," I said. It was an attempt at a joke, to defuse the embarrassment. Unfortunately, I think I sounded like a woman with a complex about her modest-sized boobs. I've got modest boobs like Holland's got modest mountains.

While I took the pendant off, James rummaged red-faced in a sideboard drawer. I marvelled at the fact that he had a magnifying glass. Only old people and experts have magnifying glasses to hand. I added a note to my phone document: *Always has the right tool to hand.*

I held out the pendant, and he inspected it, turning it over to look at the back too.

"It's a lovely piece," he said. "Lovely colour."

"I got it from a little shop just off the market square in Malia. The guy was really old, and maybe a bit deaf because he didn't hear me saying I wasn't looking for jewellery, he just kept lowering the price. I almost thought he'd give it to me if I held out."

"Can you remember the name of the shop? I know Crete quite well."

Imagine knowing Crete quite well! I bet when James knows a place quite well he doesn't mean where you can get two drinks for the price of one in happy hour either... I made a sneaky note: *Knows foreign and exotic locations.*

"I don't know," I said. "I can picture it exactly but I don't know the name."

James straightened up. "I'll need to dig a bit deeper to understand how old it might be. It's not my area of expertise. Cameos have been made the same way for hundreds, maybe thousands of years."

I looked at him. "Really? Plastic and glue haven't been around for that long, surely?"

He gave me an appalled, sideways look. "I never know when you're joking, Lori. The contrast colour isn't plastic, it's where someone has carved away a layer of stone that's a different colour. The skill of making a genuine cameo is in selecting the correct stone as well as the carving."

"Oh. Wow." I peered again at the pendant. I had a renewed respect for it. There was a real delicacy to the carving. The woman on the pedestal was beautiful. It was clear from her confident, perky stance. The man who knelt before her seemed *really* into her. It oozed from every aspect of his body language. James seemed to read my thoughts.

"It's very expressive, isn't it?"

"I wonder who they are?" I said.

"It's possible that it's a depiction of Pygmalion and Galatea," said James.

Pygmalion. The name sounded like something I'd heard but when I searched my memory for a clue, nothing was forthcoming.

"Pygmalion didn't like women," piped up Theo.

"Ah yes," I nodded.

"Not that he was gay," added Theo helpfully, "more that they weren't good enough for him."

I found myself taking against Pygmalion already.

"He carved his ideal woman out of ivory and fell in love with her," said Theo.

"That's right," said his dad.

"The goddess Aphrodite was flattered that the statue looked like her, so she brought the statue, Galatea, to life for Pygmalion."

"A real-life woman as a present, just because the statue looked like her..." I mused, wondering why that felt so uncomfortable.

"Yeah," said Theo. "Nobody knows whether Galatea had free will once she was animated, and whether she really liked Pygmalion either. It's like one of those robot dolls men buy."

"Um," I said.

"I'd buy one," said Theo.

"Really?" said James.

"If she could play Xbox or build Lego."

"The attributes of an ideal woman."

It's not often that I am lost for words, but Theo's casual analysis made me stop and think for a whole variety of reasons. Not only had he managed to put his finger on the exact reason that the story was disturbing but it made me immediately think of the relationship I had with Ashbert, if you could even call it a relationship.

"These myths," I said. "Are they age-appropriate?"

"How so?" said James.

"I mean there's a lot of sex and stuff in them."

"We can learn about every aspect of human interaction from the myths," said James. "They lay out the toughest areas so that we can examine them."

"Like soap operas," I said.

"Yes, exactly. Take that issue there of the sex dolls. It's going to become one of the biggest ethical questions that we face in the coming years. Is it a good and healthy thing to provide a robot that enables someone to have what looks like a sex slave? Or a Lego slave," he added with a sideways glance at his son.

"Surely the market is fairly limited," I said, more ruffled than disbelieving.

"I'm not so sure," said James. "I read about this German survey which found that forty percent of the men asked could imagine themselves buying a sex robot for themselves. We need the next generation to be prepared to look at these issues and make sensible decisions."

A quick note: *Willing to discuss difficult subjects.*

"You are super smart," I said.

"I do try," said James.

It was true. This guy was cultured, well-travelled, intelligent and seemed to have a pretty decent handle on raising his son right.

"Although I should warn you, my knowledge of contemporary music is staggeringly poor," said James. "In case we were thinking of forming a pub quiz team."

I saw an opportunity to add to my list.

"But how did you get to be so clever?" I asked.

"Flattering me now?"

"I mean..." I shrugged. "Tell me about yourself."

"Eat your crumpets," he said, "and I will bore you to sleep again."

I blushed and ate crumpets.

"I'll get the ear plugs," said Theo.

"Heard your dad's stories too often?" said James.

"No, but I've heard Lori's snoring."

"Cheeky," I said.

"So, what do you want to know?" said James.

"How you know all this Greek stuff, for one."

"My first degree was in archaeology."

"Like Indiana Jones."

"Yes, although I don't think he went to Lampeter University. And I don't think he spent his summers doing digs in the Scottish wilderness."

"You camped out in the wilderness?" I asked and made a surreptitious note.

"Camped, yes. Climbed the cliffs around Skara Brae looking for evidence of Neolithic settlements." He smiled to himself. "In truth, I think we spent more time hiding out in local pubs and sampling the local whiskey. Do you know Scotland?"

"Cookie and I went to a Radio One weekend festival in Dundee once."

"Nice," he said politely. "The Scotland I love is a bit further north." He glanced over at his tweed jacket on a chair back. "It's rubbed off on me a little. Not that Harris tweed and a love of the strong stuff is all there is to Scotland. Anyway, I must have got sick of rain and midges because my passion kind of slid sideways into Greek archaeology. Perhaps you might agree that Crete is a mite more enticing than Dundee?"

I nodded in firm agreement. "I got punched in the face in a nightclub and then Cookie ate a dodgy kebab and threw up all over my shoes. I had puke between my toes on the train home."

"Not necessarily Dundee's fault," James said thoughtfully. "I was still a young and carefree man then so I just set off for Greece and explored – Crete eventually, yes, but also Rhodes and then across into Turkey to Ephesus and Hisarlik. I financed myself by working as an usher at the opera amphitheatre in Athens, a barman and, for two awful months, as a water-skiing instructor."

"That doesn't sound awful," I said.

"Really? I had to sleep on the beach and check my shoes for scorpions in the morning. And you try spending all day trying to get fat, drunken tourists to stay upright. I can now say, 'keep your knees bent and feet apart' in German, Russian and French. I can also swear in five languages."

"Impressive."

"Useful at international conferences. But I was happy in Greece. I started work on my master's; a life of academic study beckoned. I was in my early twenties and, for the first time, I could actually see where my life was going."

I grunted softly. I was no longer in my early twenties, not really. Could I say the same about my life?

"Of course," said James, "that was when I ruined everything by falling in love."

"Bleurgh!" said Theo and stuck his tongue out, disgusted.

"Falling in love is wonderful," I told him.

"Love sucks," he said.

"Don't you have a school to go to?"

"It's the holidays," he said, tutting. "Don't you have work to go to?"

"No, I –" I stopped. Shift rotas flashed in front of my mind. "Oh, crap."

I jumped up. James deftly caught a crumpet as it flew from my lap.

"Gotta go," I said.

"I'm sure you'll make it with seconds to spare," said James.

"Doubt it. My shift started half an hour ago."

Chapter 23

Rex noted my lateness and gave me a mini-lecture on the virtues of punctuality, a lecture which for some reason encompassed the film *Brief Encounter*, his failed marriage and the D-Day Normandy landings. Confused, I did my shift and headed home together with the bin bag containing my paint-ruined clothes from last night.

When I got home, Ashbert was in the kitchen. It looked as though he'd used every bowl, pan and utensil he could find, but something smelled good.

"What are you cooking?" I asked.

"Cassoulet," he said. "A French classic. You're going to love it."

"Great," I said and then stopped myself. "Aren't you... aren't you angry?"

"Angry?" he said. "I mean the recipe is a little tricky but nothing I can't handle."

"I mean, angry with me."

"What for?"

"Where do you think I was last night?" I said.

"You were babysitting."

"Yes, but then I didn't come home and I didn't call and you were probably worried."

He gestured helplessly with a wooden spoon. "You told me to stop following you. What could I do?"

I gave an exasperated huff. "Ashbert, there's being a creepy and possessive stalker and then there's being an indifferent doormat and there's a whole range of things in between. You should be angry with me for being out and not keeping you informed."

"I should?"

"You should."

I stomped off, angry. Was I angry with Ashbert for his lack of passion or with myself for treating him so shoddily in the first place? I couldn't tell.

I added my bin bag of fox-ruined clothes to the pile of paint-spattered clothes I had created after my redecorating efforts. I suspected some of these were beyond saving. I picked up a t-shirt that was caked with congealed paint. It wouldn't even open out flat. The jeans were the same. They were never going to be clean again. I divided all the clothes into two piles: those that might be salvageable and those that weren't.

I put the first pile in the washing machine. I briefly considered stuffing the second pile into the bin, but that was never going to work with Bernadette the bin police patrolling the building. I decided to purge them from my life in the most decisive way possible. I gathered up the clothes and grabbed matches and barbecue lighter fluid from under Adam's sink.

"Back in a minute," I told Ashbert.

"Wait up," he said.

"What?"

"I've got to say, I'm very, very angry with you, Lori."

"Are you?"

He waggled his spoon at me. "Very angry." He didn't sound very angry.

"What about?"

"You went out last night and didn't come back and I was left here worrying where you'd gone with strict instructions not to follow you."

I sighed. "Are you actually angry or are you pretending to be angry because that's what you think I want you to be?"

He stared at me and frowned. Sauce dribbled from the end of the spoon.

"Can you repeat the question?" he said.

I growled and hurried out. I went down to the communal garden and put the clothes onto the barbecue. Ashbert had told me that all residents were permitted to use the barbecue (he'd read it in the handbook). It was one of those half oil drums mounted on legs, so it was perfect for an impromptu clothes bonfire. I doused them thoroughly in lighter fluid and threw on a match. It was such fun watching them being completely consumed by the flames that I wondered if anything else needed burning. My mind went to the ruined rug that I'd put in Adam's spare room, but I decided that it was probably too big to burn in the barbecue, however, I had another idea. As I made my way back upstairs I called Terence and booked another driving lesson.

"Tomorrow at ten," I confirmed as I re-entered the flat. "Looking forward to it."

"What are you looking forward to?" asked Ashbert.

"This," I said, sniffing deeply at his cooking. I gave him a suspicious look. "Has it got sausages in it?"

"Well, yes," he said, "but so much more as well."

That was why it smelled so familiar. I wasn't getting through about the sausages, was I? "Just because it takes you all afternoon, doesn't mean it's not still sausages in a different form," I said.

"Oh, I haven't been doing this all afternoon," he said eagerly. "I've been practising my moves, so that I can be the man of your dreams."

"Practising...?" My mind immediately swivelled to *Sizzling Sex Positions for Adventurous Lovers*. Wasn't that just playing with yourself?

"You know, like James Bond," he said.

"Oh. Oh, right." Poker. He meant poker. It was still playing with yourself but in an entirely different way. "That's great," I said. "Was it easy to pick up the basics?"

"Yeah, it was. I mastered the *passement*, the *saut de bras* and the *roulade*."

"Did you?" I knew there was a lot of fancy terminology. I had no idea what any of it meant but it sounded good.

"Apparently, I'm a natural," he said.

"Says who?"

"The guys in the park."

"What guys in the park?"

"Mickey, Trepid, the Jones boys. Great lads."

My heart lurched in my chest. My stupid, stupid naïve Ashbert.

"You've been playing in the park?" I gasped.

"Yeah. They showed me what to do. They're the best fun."

"What? Are you mad?" He was scaring me now. I could picture it: cards in one filthy, scabby hand, bottle of meths or

175

Liquid Lightning cider in the other. "You know those kinds of guys are dangerous."

"They take precautions," said Ashbert and then grinned. "Although one of the Jones boys got his fingers snapped."

"Oh my God."

"It's okay. It's one of those things where you're gonna expect to get hurt. Trepid says I should expect to suffer a broken arm or leg before I'm ready for the big leagues."

I felt faint.

"Do you owe them any money?" I asked, fearing limb-breaking debt collectors coming to the door.

"No, it wasn't like that," he said. "They're my friends."

I could have kicked myself. I'd forgotten that Ashbert was no more worldly-wise than a toddler.

"Aw come here," I said and hugged my stupid, naïve puppy. "Maybe I'll come with you and meet them at some point. I worry about you, that's all."

"That's nice," he said. "I was trying to be the man you want me to be."

"Now I've been thinking today about some other things we'll put on the list of skills you might like to learn. Do you want to see?"

"Definitely."

I fetched some sketch paper and fastened it to the fridge door with Adam's magnets. I copied out the list I'd typed on my phone. I embellished it but only a little with some ideas from James Bond.

Teamwork
Modesty
Knows wise and ancient sayings
Always has the right tool to hand
Knows foreign and exotic locations
Willing to discuss difficult subjects
Camping in the wilderness / survival skills
Climbing
Knows a lot about whiskey
Tweed (wears classic British clothes)
Cultured – opera / theatre
Bar skills – can mix a perfect martini

Water-skiing
Can speak several languages
Can handle scorpions

"What do you think?" I asked him.

"Most of them look fine," he said, "but could we maybe drop the scorpions?"

I put a line through that one. "There. I'm not even sure where we'd get hold of a scorpion anyway, although I saw some big spiders outside in the storage area. So, where do you want to start?"

He considered the list for a few moments. "How about whiskey and culture?"

"Good call," I said. "How about I book us in to see a show at the Hippodrome? We'll go for whatever we can get into in the next day or two. Lexi, can you tell us what's on at the Hippodrome?"

"There is a performance of *Stiff Upper Lip* tomorrow evening," said Lexi. "Tickets are available. Would you like to buy some?"

"Yes," I said. "Will you need some card details?"

"I can use the saved card details if you would like me to?" she replied.

This was excellent news! I could add it onto the list of things I'd need to pay Adam back for. "Yes please, Lexi. Two tickets."

I turned to Ashbert and smiled. "Sorted! It sounds really classy, doesn't it? Maybe one of those comedies from the olden days. That just leaves the whiskey. You might need to find a book and learn some basics before hitting the actual hard stuff."

"I can't wait," he said.

"That's the spirit!" I said, then fell about laughing at my own joke while he gazed at me in mild confusion. I think the fumes from paint-sodden clothes had got to my brain a little.

Chapter 24

In the morning, I hauled the ruined rug down to the street in time for my next driving lesson. Predictably, Bernadette Brampton, head of the residents' association, was beside me in a matter of seconds.

"Don't worry, I'm not leaving it here," I said.

"I didn't say you were," said the snide little so-and-so.

"I'm waiting for a lift so I can dispose of it properly," I added.

"I'm glad to see that you're taking responsibility for your rubbish," she said and made a big show of heading back into the building but I could see her loitering in the communal lobby area, eyeballing me.

When driving instructor Terence turned up a couple of minutes later, she was still there. Terence parked beside me and came round to sit in the passenger side.

"Someone dumped that there? Shocking!" he said, indicating the rubbish.

"No, I brought it down," I said. "Can we put it in the car and take it to the tip on my lesson?"

He put his hands on his hips and gave me a look. "Miss Belkin. I don't know where you got the idea that by booking a driving lesson you would also get a man-in-a-van service, but I'm afraid I must tell you that it simply doesn't work that way. We will not be taking that rubbish in Arabella, no. Why's that woman spying on us through that door?"

"Oh, that? That's Bernadette. She's one of my neighbours. I told her I was going to put my rubbish in your car boot and she said that I'd never fit it into a car this size."

"Did she now?" he said, affronted.

"She did. Said she would wager a fiver on it." I looked at the rubbish and then at the tiny boot of the car. "I'm starting to think she might have been right."

"Hold your horses," said Terence. "I'll not have Arabella's honour impugned."

"Oh, I wouldn't want to impugn," I insisted. "Impugning is not my thing."

179

"Watch and learn. One thing I'll say about Arabella, she's a lot more flexible than people give her credit for. A good girl. Flexible and, if you treat her right, quite accommodating."

While I tried not to picture Terence's idea of a flexible and accommodating girl, he leaned across the back seat, did something with head rests and levers and folded down the seats. The back of the car was instantly transformed into a sizeable space.

"Oh. Interesting," I said peering in. "It *almost* looks as if it would fit."

"Of course, it would fit," said Terence with a small huff.

He loaded the bagged rubbish into the back of the car and slammed the boot down.

"That's great, does that mean we can go to the tip?" I asked.

Terence was giving a knowing and superior look to Bernadette. "Well, yes, I suppose so," he said.

We got to the tip without incident but I should have realised that Terence would switch up a gear with his crazy-ass analysis of society's ills.

"Look at them all," he hissed. "Typical ancient Volvo driver over there. Bought an estate to take the kids up to uni and now he's justifying it by using it to take Aunt Maud's old piano to the dump."

"I think he's recycling his orange juice cartons, actually," I said, but Terence wasn't listening. I left him ranting about cars with a towing ball and how they were all caravaners, not happy unless they could drag their own personal bubble of space around with them. I dragged the bag from the back and hauled it out. I had to ask which was the correct skip for horrible paint-covered rugs as it wasn't very clear. When I got back, I saw Terence sliding something into the back of the car.

"What's that?" I asked. It was a ruined swan, some sort of ancient garden ornament that suffered the double indignity of being incredibly ugly and also having lost most of its paint, exposing whatever it was made from in ugly dark patches.

"Shabby chic," said Terence, tapping the side of his nose. "All the rage. My wife will love it."

I stared doubtfully at the swan. If his wife was casting for a horror film that featured a dead-eyed zombie swan then he'd found just the thing. "When it's painted, you mean?" I asked.

"God no. Just as it is. Wouldn't be shabby chic otherwise."

What sort of relationship did Terence have with his wife? I'd seen films where a gift of a horse's head was considered a threat, and this seemed as if it might fulfil a similar role. I felt for the woman.

I maintained silence on the subject, but as we continued the lesson, the zombie swan rolled noisily in the back to remind me of its presence. As we neared a small run of shops, I remembered something else I needed to do. I indicated to pull in.

"What are you doing?" Terence said.

"Another quick errand, won't be a tick."

I ran into the off-licence and went to the counter. "Can I have some miniatures of whiskey please?"

The assistant took four different brands from a shelf behind him and put them in front of me. I wasn't sure which ones Ashbert might need.

"I'll take them all," I said, reaching into my pocket for the cash.

On the way back to the car, I passed a Polish supermarket. Dad always tells me that they're great places for picking up a bargain and I wondered if they might have some whiskey to add to Ashbert's taste experience. I went in and gazed at the shelves. It would have been handy if they'd included some translations on some of these things. There was the time Dad brought some chickpeas, thinking they were potatoes from the picture on the tin. Mom served them up with fish fingers, now *that* was a peculiar meal. There were some miniatures, very much like the ones I'd just bought from the off-licence. I couldn't discern anything much from what was written on the label, but the liquid inside was very much the colour of whiskey. There was another bottle nearby that looked as if it might be vodka or gin. I grabbed the whiskey coloured one - Migdalowy, it said. Perfect!

I paid and popped it into the bag with the others. When I got back into the car Terence seemed unhappy.

"You do know that this is supposed to be a driving lesson, don't you?" he asked.

"I do," I said.

"Arabella is not your personal runabout."

"I know."

"I'm a human being with feelings, don't forget."

"Of course, I won't."

Terence went on to ensure that I couldn't forget he was a human being by talking incessantly about his feelings on a wide range of issues for the rest of the lesson. But I was almost sorry when the lesson ended and Terence drove off with the awful swan. I would have really enjoyed being a fly on the wall when he presented his wife with such an unforgettable gift.

Ashbert was in a state of high excitement when I got back inside. He'd been shopping. I'd given up asking him how he did this when he had no income as far as I knew.

"Check this out!" he said. "I got some clothes."

He picked up a jacket.

"Tweed!" he declared happily.

It made me smile as I thought of James, but I pushed that thought away. This was about Ashbert. He had some corduroy trousers as well, in a lovely shade of biscuity brown. Certainly, a mature choice in clothing. He pulled out a much smaller garment. My eyebrows shot up.

"Speedos?" I said.

"Speedos," he said.

I looked at the tiny budgie-smugglers. "Not exactly class British clothing."

"Ah, no," he said, "but if I'm going to be more like James Bond then I need to perfect that scene where he comes out of the sea," he said. "Also, there's a load of camping equipment downstairs in the tool shed so I can get back to nature and learn how to survive. And I got a massive knife and a replica pistol so that I can look the part as well. I'm sure they'll come in handy when I'm practising my dangerous animal skills on the trilobites."

I gave him a stern look. "You weren't thinking of using weapons on the trilobites, surely?"

"No, I wasn't. I just think I might get a bit more respect from them if they know I mean business."

I was about to query this idea. Surely it was ridiculous to imagine that the trilobites would be intimidated by guns or knives? Then I remembered something Adam told me ages ago. Apparently, a crow can tell the difference between a man with a gun and a man without a gun. Was it possible that a trilobite had similar skills? Given their only relatively recent contact with mankind it seemed unlikely. (But, then again, I'd seen *Jurassic Park* and those velociraptors could work out how to use door handles so, who knew?)

"You've been very busy," I said.

"That's not all," he declared with a large grin. "I've read an entire book about whiskey and also started to learn a foreign language. *Wyt ti'n dod fan hyn yn aml?*"

The exotic guttural tones made me quite weak at the knees. I took him by the hand and looked him squarely in the eye as I led him towards the bedroom. "I don't know what you just asked me, but to be honest, you had me at Speedos."

I spent the afternoon drawing and blogging. My devoted readers, however few they were, deserved a bit of fresh content.

I decided that I simply had to have Florrie learning to become an expert. Florrie's a can-do girl and she mostly tends to wing it if she's up against a fearsome challenge, but it was so obvious now that she should become an expert in a few things. It would come in handy for future stories as well. I thought carefully about what she should learn. The current series of strips was about adulting, so she must learn a key adult skill. I thought back to Lexi's list and knowing the price of eggs. Money would be a good thing. I had her talking with a friend about how they might stretch their finances, so Lori researches everything that they spend money on and finds cheaper alternatives. From there, she helps some other friends do the same, reads a couple of books and she's an accountant three days later. As an accountant, she helps people invest their savings and she realises that understanding stocks and shares would be useful, so she spends time with a stockbroker (I did this. I don't recommend it; he was very boring) who tells her all she needs to know to begin stockbroking. The final part of the strip showed Lori rolling a wheelbarrow from the doors of the bank with all of the cash she'd got for her friends. I looked it over, pleased with my work and uploaded it to the blog.

I also spent some time getting ready for the evening. We had tickets for a posh theatre show and I wrestled with the question of what I should wear for an evening of culture. As an adult, should I wear something a little bit more formal? I didn't have a posh frock, but I hit upon the idea of creating something like a Grecian goddess look using one of Adam's bedsheets. If I wound it around myself in attractive drapes, then I would look every inch the sophisticated theatre-goer. Securing the sheet proved to be tricky, but I managed it with a selection of bulldog clips from Adam's desk and some button badges he'd picked up on a student protest during a visit to Thailand. A few '*Power to the People*'s and '*Smash the System*'s were enough to keep my sheet in place.

Ashbert had no problem as he dressed in his new tweed and corduroy. He kept pulling at the edges of the jacket, complaining that it was scratchy, but I told him that part of the lesson was to learn to put up with some minor discomfort, a bit like wearing high heels. He looked momentarily terrified at that, but I assured him that I wasn't asking him to wear high heels.

As we walked into the city centre, I couldn't work out if the tweedy look suited Ashbert. On James, it had a certain worldly and reassuring charm. On Ashbert? I couldn't work out if he looked like a geography teacher or some sort of Jeremy Corbyn stripogram. What did it matter? The pair of us were off out for a classy and adult night of culture.

The Hippodrome was a big swanky venue, just on the edge of Chinatown. I think my parents had taken me there to see a couple of pantomimes when we were kids but, in recent years, it was only something I walked by on the way to the retro eighties nightclub in Chinatown or the big music venue up on the dual carriageway. We joined the queue inside. I wondered if there was some other show on, as the audience really didn't look as if they were dressed for a night at the theatre. Black t-shirts and denim jackets seemed to be the favourite outfit for the men, and the women were wearing what my mom would have called 'mutton dressed up as lamb'. I tapped the shoulder of the man in front of me who had a grizzled beard and a beer gut, sort of like Santa's younger, slobbier brother.

"Which show are you queueing for?" I asked him.

"*Stiff Upper Lip,*" he replied, in a far softer voice than the rough and ready look would have suggested. "Seen it twice already."

I nodded. "So, er, what's it about?"

He looked at me then, and took in my Grecian goddess dress and Ashbert's tweed and corduroy. "It's the AC/DC musical."

"Yes?" I said, none the wiser.

"All their greatest hits. I can tell you the plot, but I don't want to spoil it for you. Which is your favourite song and I'll tell you if it's in the show."

I scoured my mind for anything that I might know about AC/DC. The mention of their greatest hits suggested it was a band, which was odd because I thought AC/DC was slang for being bisexual.

I took a chance on the show's title. "*Stiff Upper Lip?*" I said.

He nodded, approving. "A classic, and not one of the mainstream hits either. Good on you. That's cosplay, yeah?" He flicked a finger up and down my sheet dress. "From the asylum scene?"

I nodded dumbly.

"Yeah, yeah, I get it, and your boyfriend's the dorky doctor. Genius!" He turned to explain our outfits to his friends who, like him looked like Hell's Angels but acted more like middle-aged IT managers allowed out for the night by their wives. The group of friends gave our "costumes" a cheesy thumbs up.

Ashbert and I looked at each other as we moved forward into the auditorium. It was a huge space. Plaster cherubs gazed down on us from the heights. There were people in the boxes high up on each side. I wondered if there was any AC/DC-loving royalty in attendance. I felt mature and cultured just being in the place. We had seats midway down a row and we squeezed past several other people to get in.

"There's nobody here under fifty!" hissed Ashbert to me.

"Well, that's because culture is something you embrace as an adult. We might be punching above our weight here, but let's go with it," I said.

We settled down in our chairs while middle-aged rockers and their underdressed partners found their seats. For a classy venue, the seats weren't as big as I'd have expected. You get plumper seats, wider armrests and far more leg room at the local multiplex.

"Did you notice that they didn't have a popcorn and hotdog stand out there?" I whispered to Ashbert.

"Maybe you don't get popcorn at the theatre," he said. "I mean it's a live performance. You don't want to put the actors off with crunching noises."

"But what about hotdogs?" I countered. "That's almost silent food."

"True."

"Cookie does this party trick where she opens up her throat and just swallows a hotdog sausage straight down in one go, no chewing."

"That's impressive."

"It goes down a storm with blokes at parties."

187

"I think we all like food-based talents," he said.

Look at us, I thought. Having an intellectual conversation about food and theatre while on a classy evening out together. I was impressed with us.

"They weren't even selling big cups of coke," I said.

"I like those," Ashbert agreed.

"I like to get a really, really big one," I said. "Then I can pretend I'm a Borrower, drinking from a human cup."

"You're just making me thirsty, thinking about it."

"Well," I said, doing a little rummage in my bag, "I haven't got a tub of coke but I do have..."

I pulled out a bunch of whiskey miniatures.

"Nice," he said. "Time to put my research to the test."

"It'll make the evening more fun, yeah?"

He inspected the labels before cracking the seal on one of the tiny bottles. He sniffed at the bottle gently.

"Hmmm." He wafted it under my nose. "What are you getting?"

"Strong alcohol," I said. "A hint of turps."

"The nose of a good whiskey is a subtle thing," he informed me. God, he sounded knowledgeable and, yes, it was sexy. "You have to let memory and instinct be your guide." He sniffed. "Yes, I'm getting a scent of evening beach."

"Evening beach?"

"Mmmm. Salt, wood smoke, sandy notes." He sniffed again. "Just a hint of old man's pockets."

"Um."

"A dustiness. A mere suggestion of humbug. Copper coins and –"

I elbowed him as the lights went down and the audience fell silent. Ashbert took a swig and coughed at the spirit.

"Yes. Good stuff," he squeaked.

In the darkness, a drum and high hat began beating and then a deep, pounding guitar started up. I was surprised to recognise the riff.

I leaned over to Ashbert. "I know this. It's the music from *Iron Man*."

"Cool," he whispered back. "You reckon Iron Man will be in it?"

"Here's hoping," I said and took a swig of his whiskey. Screw evening beaches and old men's pockets. It tasted of fire and warmed my throat.

It was hard to describe what we saw over the following hour. The steady consumption of whiskey miniatures probably didn't help.

Stiff Upper Lip, it became clear, was a jukebox musical of AC/DC's greatest hits (I recognised bits of about four of them). It had a bizarrely convoluted plot that seemed to exist solely to squeeze in as many of those hits as possible. I could see no other reason for such an exhausting journey for the hero who must become a rock star, visit a sexual health clinic and be in a train crash with a dream sequence involving him paddling a coracle through a river of blood. All that in the first half.

After the interval – during which we joined the massive queue at the bar, failed to get served in time and decided to stick to the whiskeys – the second act just got weirder and more complicated. I gave up on trying to understand any of it – culture is hard! – and decided to just watch it all unfold.

"What do you think?" I asked Ashbert.

He swigged from one of the whiskey miniatures and made a curious lip-smacking sound. "Most of them are way too strong," he said. "They might be better mixed with something else. This one is nice though."

He offered to me the one I'd got from the Polish shop, the Migdalowy. I took a sip. He was right. It was completely different to the others I had sampled. It tasted strongly of marzipan and left my mouth feeling scoured in a different way to the other whiskeys.

Ashbert took several more sips from the Migdalowy. He was coughing a bit and wore a doubtful look on his face.

"Are you all right?" I said, cupping my hand to his ear, as the audience were joining in with a loud song that might have been about a card game, but seemed to be set in the sexual health clinic.

"I don't know," he said. "Maybe I've drunk too many of them. I feel a bit off."

He pulled at the collar of his shirt and tugged at his tweed jacket as though it was too warm.

A niggling, shapeless suspicion crept into my mind.

I texted Cookie. *What tastes like marzipan?*

She texted straight back. *Marzipan.*

I know Cookie. She wasn't even being sarcastic, it's her thought process.

Apart from marzipan? I texted.

Cyanide and Semtex both taste / smell like marzipan, she replied.

I looked at Ashbert in horror. Cyanide poisoning! Was it intended for Ashbert or me? We'd both drunk some. Who could possibly want us dead? The suspects instantly queued up in my mind. Bernadette Brampton, for our flagrant disregard for rubbish disposal etiquette? Driving instructor Terence, for abusing his car and his good nature? Rex at the museum, for unforgiveable lateness? Adam, in far off Turtley Dago or wherever he said he was, for wanton condom buying? Or was it Ashbert's new gambling pals in the park, this being vengeance for some undisclosed gambling debt?

Or maybe this was accidental and all my fault. How was I supposed to know that the Polish shop sold dangerous substances in little bottles? Maybe it was for killing mice or something. Didn't they have laws in Poland to mark it with a skull and crossbones?

I texted Cookie. *What should you do if you swallowed cyanide?*

Die, she replied.

Not helpful, I typed.

She came back with *Induce vomiting. Before you die.*

Right. Induce vomiting.

I turned to Ashbert. "I need to make you sick."

"What?"

"Put your fingers down the back of your throat until you gag."

"What?" The noise from the crowd was louder. There was some sort of chanting about someone called Jack.

"PUT YOUR FINGERS DOWN YOUR THROAT!" I bellowed at the top of my voice.

"What?"

I had no choice. It was a medical emergency, so I grabbed Ashbert by the back of the head and pushed my fingers into his mouth. He immediately bit down hard, and so I brought my other hand round to smack him on the side of his head. I couldn't honestly tell you if it was a pain reflex or if I was genuinely cross with him because he hadn't understood the urgency of what I was doing. The next thing that happened was that he released my fingers from between his teeth, so I pushed them further into his mouth. Still not understanding, he shoved me away, hard. I toppled over the seats behind us where I knocked a ginger woman over and several big men in denim gave me really angry looks.

I had no time for that, I really needed to get the message across to Ashbert about induced vomiting. A flash of inspiration came to me. I would demonstrate what was needed. I waved at him to get his attention and pushed my fingers down my own throat, as far as I could manage. I pushed a bit further and it kicked in properly. I threw up everything that I'd eaten that day, straight on top of the ginger woman who was just getting up from the floor. I signalled to Ashbert that he should do the same and he stared at me, dumbfounded. I jumped up and down and gave him my strictest arm-waving and, with a compliant shrug, he reluctantly put his fingers into his mouth. I didn't see what happened to Ashbert after that because the woman I'd knocked over thumped me violently in the face. She packed quite a punch for a tiny little thing, and I was about to explain and apologise for the mishap that she'd suffered when she drew back her fist and hit me again.

I've heard people talk about red mist descending and I was never really sure what that was all about, but after the second punch connected, some internal mechanism took over and I grabbed her arm and bit down on it heavily. I'm ashamed to say that it felt good, because I heard her screech with pain and it stopped her hitting me. At that point, I thought there might still be a chance to calm things down and explain what had happened, but at the same time as I saw Ashbert vomiting down the back of someone's neck in the row in front of us, a large pair of hands lifted me up from behind and dragged me to the aisle.

The strong hands that held me weren't letting go. Amid the shouts of horror and fury and the stomping, chanting, howling of a thousand rock fans, those hands hauled me out into the empty foyer and dumped me unceremoniously in a chair.

In the distance, there was a shouted "I was only doing what she told me!" and a yelp.

I looked at the security guy.

"We're having a medical emergency," I said.

"What?"

"We've been poisoned."

He spoke into the radio clipped to his lapel for a moment. "We will see," he said. "You've been drinking?"

"That's how we got poisoned. If I die before the police get here, I think it was Bernadette. Probably."

He spoke into the radio again. He seemed awfully calm. Maybe people got poisoned in the theatre all the time. That would explain why it wasn't very popular.

A few minutes later, another theatre heavy came up the stairs. He plonked my bag and our whiskey miniatures down on the table in front of me. "These yours? Your boyfriend's scarpered."

I was too terrified to properly answer him. Terrified that the poisoning or whatever would kick in at any moment. I reached for them. The heavy made to stop me but I found the bottle of Migdalowy.

"This one. It's this one."

The men gave me a blankly uncomprehending look.

"I bought some stuff from the Polish supermarket that I thought was whiskey," I said, "but it tastes like marzipan and makes your mouth feel a bit weird when you drink it."

The guy who'd first nabbed me took the bottle from me and then laughed. I'm a big believer that laughter is the best medicine but laughing at a dying woman is just wrong.

"Cyanide tastes like marzipan!" I said.

"So does almond essence," he said. "Migdalowy. Almond essence. It's for cooking."

I stared at the little bottle. "Are you sure?"

He patted his chest. "It's Polish. I'm from Warsaw."

"I've been to Walsall too," I said. "I took the train. Doesn't make me an expert on Polish."

"Warsaw in Poland," he said, all humour gone.

Really? I thought. I could have sworn I'd got there by train. Admittedly, the bloke did have a bit of an accent.

"Ah," I said. "A bit of a misunderstanding then. No harm done, eh?"

I was overwhelmingly relieved to discover that I wasn't about to kick the bucket and it was disappointing to find that the security guys didn't share my happy sense of relief. Stony-faced, they made me wait until a first aider came to take a look at my twice-punched face. While the first aider was applying a small dressing to a cut next to my eye I heard a familiar voice.

"I thought I made it clear that I didn't want to see you again."

I gave Sergeant Fenton and her sidekick, Constable Stokes, my best smile. My best smile made my face hurt.

"You didn't want any more calls about me," I corrected her. "I told these guys not to bother. It seems it was all a misunderstanding."

The police sergeant, who I was starting to feel had something against me, gave me a steely glare. "Unfortunately, like all of your misunderstandings, it has caused a good deal of inconvenience to those around you. Why are you wrapped up in a bedsheet anyway?"

"Wardrobe crisis?" I tried a different smile on her but that really made my face hurt.

She didn't return the smile, in fact her gaze was firmly fixed on the point where the sheet crossed over in front. I didn't even need to look to know that a 'Smash the system' badge was on show. She wasn't impressed.

"Last time we met, you were wearing a curtain," said Sergeant Fenton.

"It was a rug, sarge," Constable Stokes corrected her.

"A rug. Indeed. I wonder if you own any ordinary clothes at all."

"I don't think having an avant-garde approach to fashion is a criminal offence," I suggested. "And there's been no harm done here."

Her gaze travelled up to my face again. "Really? Well that remains to be seen. We need to see whether the various parties assaulted by you this evening decide to press charges."

"Assaulted *by* me? I was punched."

"And, from what I hear, you deliberately vomited all over a number of theatregoers. Punching or vomit-attack. Can you suggest which might be considered worse?"

"Actually, there was this one time in Dundee where –"

"*And* I think the theatre will be in touch about the cleaning and the damage. Perhaps in your world that counts as a good night's work, but it's my view that you are a menace to the public, Miss Belkin."

"Bit harsh."

Sergeant Fenton looked to the first aider. "Is she okay to go?"

The first aider shrugged. There was only so much a woman with a box of sticking plasters could do.

"Good," said the sergeant and hauled me to my feet.

"I could have concussion."

"Indeed you might," she said. "We'll get a doctor to have a look at you down at the station."

"But I can't go to the police station," I protested. "I'm... I'm underdressed."

"Underdressed for the cop shop but not for the theatre," mused Sergeant Fenton. "Interesting."

"There is a bit of a cold draught in the custody suite," said Constable Stokes.

"Then we shall swing by your apartment," said the sergeant. "Collect some clothes, check to see if your boyfriend is there, maybe see if there are any small house fires or herbal cushions for us to deal with."

This was not good. I tried to look meek and sorry and all of the things that appease power-hungry authority figures, but she didn't let up with the tight-lipped glare. She loaded me into the back of a car and drove me round to Adam's place. She walked me right to the door. They hadn't cuffed me. Maybe she was seeing if I was going to run.

Bernadette Brampton, queen of the residents' association, was in the lobby. Jesus! Didn't she have anywhere else to be? The woman was an incurable busybody.

"Oh dear, what's happened here?" she asked.

"Nothing," I said. "We're off to a fancy dress party. This is my Greek toga. These guys both got coppers' uniforms. Oh, the embarrassment when they realised."

"Excuse me, madam," said Sergeant Fenton, leading me past. "Miss Belkin is just assisting us at this time."

I forced a laugh. "Oh, Tracy here really likes to get into character. Method acting for a fancy dress party. Wow."

Bernadette was having none of it. "Officer, I have some serious concerns about this young woman."

"Do you now?" said Sergeant Fenton, unsurprised.

"So I need to know if something has occurred that could endanger my other clients."

Clients? Did she think she was a solicitor or something?

I groaned inwardly. Actually, I think I might have groaned outwardly but they both ignored me.

Bernadette stepped forward, eager to peddle her malicious gossip.

"This person is living in a flat that is not hers. It belongs to a man called Adam who has always been a delight."

Of course Adam had always been a delight. "Adam's my brother," I said rolling my eyes.

"It's just a bit strange that we haven't seen any sign of him since you turned up," said Bernadette, lips pursed.

"Well of course you haven't seen him," I said. "He's in –" Oh. Where was he? I tried to think of the place that he'd mentioned. Had the place had a Spanishy sort of a name? "He's abroad."

"Well we might need you to give us some more details," said Sergeant Fenton.

"He might be in Spain," I said.

"You could call him then," said Bernadette, her arms folded.

I hated her for the smug challenge, but Sergeant Fenton looked at me expectantly.

I pulled my phone from my bag and called Adam's number. I put it onto speakerphone and we all heard the automated voice announce that he was not available.

"No, I bet he's not available," said Bernadette, "and I bet it's connected with the rolled-up rug that I saw you getting rid of today, isn't it?"

Sergeant Fenton was giving nothing away, but surely, she could see that Bernadette was a dangerous lunatic who obviously watched way too much crappy television? She must have been monitoring everything that I did and she'd built this mad theory around it all.

"That was just a rug," I explained. "I got rid of it because it was covered in mess."

"I bet it was," said Bernadette with a leer.

"Let's take a look at the rug, shall we?" said Sergeant Fenton.

"We can't, she took it away in a car," said Bernadette triumphantly. "Pretty suspicious, wouldn't you say?"

"That's only because you patrol the rubbish area like the mad old baggage that you are!" I said, out of patience now.

"Easy now," said Constable Stokes. "Watch the language."

"What are we supposed to do with rugs we need to throw away?" I said. "We can't put them in the bins and if we take them to the tip you accuse us of murder! Do you know how mad you sound?"

"Miss Belkin," said Sergeant Fenton slowly. "No one's mentioned murder. Only you."

Bernadette's expression hardened further. If my mom had been on hand she might have suggested that if the wind changed she'd stick like it.

Chapter 26

I was arrested. This was a first for me. They put me in the back of the car, in handcuffs this time, and drove me to a police station.

Have you ever tried to send a text when your hands are cuffed behind your back? It's not easy. I wanted to get hold of Cookie, as she'd be able to sort some of this out with the police. I stabbed at my phone, trying to imagine the sequence that I'd need to follow and remember where all the letters were on the keyboard, but after a few minutes the policeman saw me wriggling and took the phone off me.

At the station, I spent several lifetimes sitting in a room with nothing in it apart from a scruffy table and some chairs. I asked a couple of times if I could have a pencil and paper but they said no. Is there anything in the Geneva Convention about inflicting boredom on a person? If there isn't, there seriously should be; it was barbaric. I had to settle for singing the songs of McFly under my breath to check that I still knew all the words to them. I can confirm that I did, and it wasn't as exciting a pastime as I thought it might be.

Eventually, Sergeant Fenton came in with a platinum blonde colleague, who introduced herself as Detective Constable Boyce, and they settled on the other side of the table. It was such a relief to have a break in the boredom that I was almost pleased to see them. No, I was pleased to see them.

They told me they were going to record our chat, which was good, because then I wouldn't have to repeat myself. They asked if I wanted a solicitor but I couldn't think of any use I'd have for one. I asked for pencil and paper instead and they were happy to oblige.

"Let's start with a simple question," said Detective Boyce.

"I'd stick with simple questions throughout with this one," said Sergeant Fenton.

"When did you last see your brother, Adam?" the detective asked me.

I looked to the ceiling.

"A Sunday dinner, I think. Maybe four, five months ago. At our house."

"The flat on Silver Street?"

"No, our house. Where our parents live. Lived."

"But you now live at the Silver Street address."

"Moved in a few weeks ago."

Detective Boyce frowned. "But you've not seen Adam in all that time?"

"No. I got the keys to let myself in. But Adam's cool with that," I explained. "We've spoken on the phone a lot."

"The most recent time being?"

"Two nights ago. I was round at James' house, babysitting."

Sergeant Fenton consulted a notebook.

"That would be James Reynolds."

"Ye-es," I said slowly, bewildered and impressed that they'd know who James was.

"And what did you talk about with him?" said Detective Boyce.

"James?"

"Adam."

"Oh," I said, breaking into an irrepressible smile. "He was very angry with me. I'd bought some things on Amazon that I didn't mean to buy but how was I to know what those buttons did?"

"You argued?"

"Yes."

"Do you and your brother argue often?"

"Do we ever! Wow. I don't think we've had a civil conversation in years."

"Do you and your brother hate each other?"

I recoiled. "Hate is a strong word, detective. I don't think I really hate anyone. Too much effort involved."

"Dislike?" suggested Sergeant Fenton.

I gave it some thought. "He really doesn't seem to like me very much. Always telling me what to do. Never happy. Just because he's got a super-duper job and he's on telly programmes. None you'll have watched. It's usually National Geographic type stuff. But it's telly, you know."

198

"So, jealous?" suggested Detective Boyce.

"I suppose he might take a look at my carefree lifestyle, my artistic integrity and wish he had some of that."

"I meant you of him," said the detective. "Are you jealous?"

Cor. That was a deep one. I'd best give an honest answer though. I was under oath, wasn't I? Hang on, didn't they need a Bible for that? I thought about the question.

"Our parents have nothing but good things to say about him. I'm the one who stayed at home to look after them but it's always 'Adam this...' and 'Adam that...' They're really proud of him." I sighed, a sudden weight on my chest. "I'd like a bit of that."

"Where are your parents at the moment?"

"I don't know," I said sadly.

"Where's your brother?"

I shrugged.

"Where is Adam, Lori?"

I shrugged again.

They left me alone for a long time (taking my pencil and paper with them, which was a low blow). It was dark outside, I didn't have my phone to tell the time, but I guessed it was way, way past midnight when they returned.

"How we doing, Lori?" said Detective Boyce.

"Tired," I said.

"Well, you can go beddy-byes when you've answered a few more questions," said Sergeant Fenton.

Detective Boyce put a laptop on the table and opened it.

"Now, Lori, do you know the difference between direct evidence and circumstantial evidence?"

"No."

"Right. Well, there's a few things I want to show you and maybe you can explain them because, together, they look quite suspicious."

"Okay," I said.

She clicked the mousepad and a picture came up.

"That's the barbecue in the communal garden," I said automatically. Despite my tiredness, it felt like it was a quiz and I was eager to win.

"And you were using it to destroy some clothing."

"They were covered in paint," I said.

"Red paint?"

"Dragon's Blood."

"Pardon?"

"One of the colours. Whispering Wound. Puce Springclean. Plum Barrage. Tudor Intrigue. Lots of colours."

"Why didn't you just bin the clothes?"

"That's easy," I said. "I already told you what Bernadette's like with the bins. There's a whole booklet she's written about the dos and don'ts of living here. I had some clothes with paint all over them and I didn't know how to get rid of them so I burned them. It seemed like the obvious thing to do."

"Obvious?" said Sergeant Fenton.

"Yeah."

"And this painting was at James' house," said Detective Boyce.

"No. In the flat," I said.

The two policewomen exchanged a look. I didn't like the look.

"And the rug?" said Detective Boyce. "Did that have 'paint' on it as well?" She did air-quotes around the word paint. I wasn't sure she knew what air-quotes were for.

"It did have 'paint' on it," I said, giving it some air-quotes of my own, joining in for the hell of it.

"And what happened to the rug?"

"Terence my driving instructor helped me take it to the tip."

"Which tip?"

"Ah."

"You don't know?"

"No, I need to think," I said. I closed my eyes and visualised the journey and Terence's accompanying monologue. "We went down to Summer Row and round via the roadworks which are totally unnecessary. They just do it to use up their annual budgets so they don't have them cut the next year. It's all just cones. No one does a blind bit of work. And then we went down the ring road and through that bit where everyone's got a BMW or Mercedes and the housewives are only using them to pop to the shop but can they park them straight? Can they heck as like."

"Is this necessary?" said Sergeant Fenton.

"Hang on. Nearly there. Then it's right along the high street. Once upon a time that all used to be fields and you could leave your door open at night. And then left near the old train engine works. That was a glorious age of steam, back when Britain was truly great. Coal smoke, good for the lungs. And then we turned in and we were at the tip."

I opened my eyes.

"Seriously?" said Sergeant Fenton.

"Tyseley tip," said Detective Boyce. "Near the railway museum."

"See?" I said.

"We'll check it out," said the detective and clicked on the laptop. "What about this? You and another man – I believe you've referred to him as Ashbert – were also seen digging on the waste ground across the road from the flats. We have a team there now."

"Do you?" I said, surprised. It wasn't a very exciting place. There wouldn't be much there for them to do.

"Why were you digging there?"

"I was getting some earth to make a habitat."

"Habitat?"

"Trilobites," I said, hoping that she wouldn't know that there was no such thing in the modern world. "I have some in Adam's bedroom."

"What would be in the walk-in bathtub?"

That threw me. I'd not shown them Adam's bedroom when we went inside to get some clothes. And the walk-in bath hadn't been there when Sergeant Fenton first visited. Detective Boyce read my expression with ease.

She brought up another picture. My trilobite habitat. Little Dougie was trying to scrabble up the side. He'd be hungry for his tea. Or would it be breakfast now?

"We've had a little poke around," said Detective Boyce. "I'm curious as to why you'd have a tub of flesh-eating arthropods in your brother's bedroom."

"Flesh-eating?" Well, I suppose they were.

"This isn't looking good, is it, Lori?" said the detective.

"Isn't it?"

201

"Let me present a scenario to you," she said. "You can leap in any time you like to correct the minor details."

"Okay."

"You don't like your brother. You've recently been kicked out of your parents' home and maybe you went to stay with him. But you've got a boyfriend – or is it two boyfriends?"

"Two boyfriends?" I said, and then I thought... And the guilty little thought was *oh*.

"– and you want a place of your own. Now, I'm not saying you murdered Adam purely to get a place to live, although it's tough getting on the property ladder these days."

"Murdered?" I said.

"I don't know how you did it. But it was messy, wasn't it? Who knew human bodies produced so much blood, eh? Maybe you considered burying him on the waste ground. Or maybe just his bones, once those little crab things had consumed his flesh. Nice touch that. And then all you had to do was dispose of the forensic evidence. The blood-soaked clothes. The rug. Did Terence know you'd killed him?"

"No!" I said.

"Oh, so you had an innocent man help you destroy criminal evidence?"

"No!"

"Ah, so he was in on it."

"Stop it! You're confusing me!"

"That's not particularly hard to do though, is it?" said Sergeant Fenton.

They put me in a cell. I slept. I cried. I think I cried in my sleep which is a neat trick. Whatever, my pillow was wet when they woke me up again.

They gave me a cup of tea and some toast, which was nice of them. But then I remembered that they were trying to put me in the frame for murder and that wasn't nice.

Sergeant Fenton and Detective Boyce met in the interview room. It didn't look like either of them had slept.

"Where is your brother?" said Detective Boyce. No, good morning, Lori. No cordial greeting. Just straight in there.

"I told you," I said. "I don't know. I think he's in Spain."

"Yes, in Spain. But you didn't sound very sure. Can you remember where exactly he is and what he's doing?"

"He said he was doing some filming."

"Filming. Good."

"He does a lot of that, but I think he said he was a last-minute replacement. I can't quite remember the name of the place. It was one of those something-del-something names, like Costa del Sol but not that, you know?"

"So, he's somewhere, but that place isn't the Costa del Sol," said Sergeant. "Enlightening."

"You last argued with your brother two nights ago, you say," said Detective Boyce.

"That is correct."

"You were at James Reynold's house at the time."

"I was. You can ask him."

"We have," said Detective Boyce in a voice straight out of the Sinister School of Acting.

"What's your relationship with Mr Reynolds?" asked Sergeant Fenton.

"We don't have one. We just work at the same museum."

"You spent the night at his house."

"I did, but that was only because I fell asleep after we.... Well, we had a bit of a mishap with some paint and his uncle's car."

"Did you now?"

"Yes," I said and gave a heavily edited version of the story about a friend's car getting covered with paint.

"Can I be clear on this point?" she said. "You had two entirely separate paint-based accidents in the course of the last thirty-six hours, and the clothes-burning and rug-dumping schemes that you've described for getting rid of the mess were because you're nervous of the rubbish sorting system in your brother's flat?"

"Yes, that is correct," I said, to be sure that the tape recorder captured the neat, but slightly damning summary. Why was she making me sound like such an idiot?

"Since we last spoke, some further evidence has come to light," said Detective Boyce. She started a video clip on her laptop and I saw straightaway that it was CCTV from the garage forecourt.

It showed me pulling up in the Jaguar. The picture quality was really good. The lighting really brought out the red of the paint on the Jaguar body and roof.

"That's some nice protective overalls you've got on there," said Detective Boyce. "Our forensics guys wear them to avoid contaminating a crime scene."

"Actually, it's a beekeeping suit," I said.

"You know, maybe you didn't kill Adam in the flat," said Sergeant Fenton.

"I didn't."

"Or maybe you thought you had but you'd left the job half done."

"I really didn't," I said.

"There's no sound on the CCTV footage," said Detective Boyce, "but the store manager distinctly remembers hearing screams coming from inside your car. The boot."

"I need to explain about the screaming," I said. I was about to say that it was a funny story, but in the short time that I'd known her, I'd come to realise that Sergeant Fenton's sense of humour was not very well developed.

"Yes, you do," said the sergeant. "You should know that we have arrested your accomplice."

"Who? James?"

"Oh, so it was James who assisted you?"

This was terrible news. I couldn't believe that things were getting so out of hand. I pictured the police taking James away while Theo watched, and it felt unbelievably awful.

So," said Detective Boyce, "you – what? – inveigled him into helping you conceal the crime?"

"I don't know."

"You don't know if it was your idea or his?"

"No, I don't know what 'inveigled' means."

"Did he help you?" said Sergeant Fenton. "We have him in another room and he's telling us all manner of interesting things. You'd best give your side of the story before he blames it all on you."

"Blames me for what?" I demanded, more tired and flustered and unhappy than I'd ever been before. "Murdering Adam, who isn't dead? And how was I supposed to have killed him? With my bare hands?"

Sergeant Fenton dipped into a fat wallet, pulled out a pair of plastic bags and put them on the table. I saw that they contained Ashbert's knife and replica gun.

"Ah!" I laughed. "Wow, I can see that this looks bad, but you'll laugh when I tell you what those are for." They both looked at me. "Right, well my boyfriend wants to be more like James Bond. A little bit of a life lesson and little bit of role play." I winked.

"Now, which boyfriend wants to play at being James Bond?" said the sergeant. "Is that Ashbert or James?"

This was so messed up. I took a deep breath.

"Okay, let me tell you about the foxes," I started.

Chapter 27

I learned something interesting about police stations during my time there. I don't know if they're all like this, but the one I spent the night in had a tunnel! It went next door to the magistrates' court, which I thought was a great idea. There should be more tunnels in the world for those times when you can't face the weather or the neighbours or whatever. One moment I was in a cell and a few minutes later I was in a courtroom. James was there too. I looked across at him. He looked awful.

We weren't there as long as I expected. I thought there might be a trial or we might be sentenced or something but it turned out we were only there to establish if we were to be granted bail, and we were released pending further investigation, which sounded ominous, but I was grateful to be away from the place. It took a few more minutes to do paperwork and have our belongings back and then James and I were outside the building, free to go.

We stood, numbly facing the office buildings across the road.

"I'm really sorry," I said.

"What for?" he said, not looking at me.

I struggled to think what it was I was sorry for.

"I think," I said, carefully. "I think I'm an idiot."

He nodded reflectively and licked his lips.

"Do you think I'm an idiot?" I asked.

He thought about it long and hard.

"You're one of the nice ones," he said. He slapped his pockets. "I think I'd best go home and see how my son is."

"Of course," I said. "I could walk with you, if you like."

He pulled a strange grimace – not an unkind expression but a pained one.

"You know," he said, "I think I need to be alone with my own thoughts for a bit."

"Oh. Sure," I said and, thinking that a man who had just spent a night alone in a cell but still needed time alone with his thoughts probably had a lot of thoughts to think, I waved him off.

And that was it. I was alone too.

"Psst!"

I looked behind me.

"Psst!"

I checked my phone to make sure it wasn't on.

"Psst!"

I looked up.

There was a figure in a green hoodie clinging to the outer wall of the police station, two storeys up.

"What are you doing up there?" I hissed.

"I'm stuck!" Ashbert replied.

"But what were you doing?"

He shuffled his feet and adjusted his grip. It looked quite windy up there. I wondered how long he'd been standing there.

"Is this a jailbreak?" I said.

"Surprise!" he said.

Oh, God. Of course, that's what he was doing. He had said many times that he just wanted to make me happy, so it probably seemed like a logical thing to him.

"You could get killed!" I hissed.

"I was only doing what you told me."

"What?"

"Like James Bond."

"But not killing yourself by climbing up buildings and..."

"It's just like we practised down the park."

My mouth formed a question and then I thought.

"Poker," I said, flatly.

"What?"

"Poker. I said you should go learn poker."

"Oh. Not...?"

"No. Not parkour."

I began to turn away. A policeman walking by looked up and saw Ashbert.

"Oi! You! Get down!"

"I was just practising my parkour," said Ashbert.

"I don't ruddy care," said the policeman, producing his handcuffs.

I started to walk away. The policeman called out to me.

"Hey. You know this man?"

I shook my head. "Not as well as I thought."

Chapter 28

On the long walk back to Adam's flat, I too was alone with my thoughts. Unfortunately, I didn't have many thoughts worth thinking and so checked my phone instead.

I saw straight away that Cookie had been busy in the last few days. Apparently, I had managed to get a text successfully sent to her. It said *Police invested thank I cured Adam.* I really don't know what it says about Cookie, but apparently, she understood that I meant to say the police had arrested me and thought that I'd killed Adam. Since then she'd taken to social media in a big way. She'd set up an online petition for my release, and she'd used some pictures from my blog to create what looked like a viral campaign. Using Florrie's face, twisted in anguish, was a stroke of genius. The strip that she'd take it from was one where Florrie was wrestling with a recipe that used a "cup" as a measure, and Florrie is going through her collection of cups, wondering which one is the right size. I sent Cookie a text to let her know that I was out. I also saw that I had an email from someone whose name I didn't recognise. I reckoned I could read that once I was back in the flat, after a long bath and a bit of a nap.

There was crime scene tape across the door to Adam's flat and a policeman inside who told me that I wasn't allowed back in until they'd finished processing the scene, whatever that meant. I gave him instructions about feeding the trilobites, hoping they'd like corned beef. I told him to write the instructions down but he didn't.

As I left the building, Ashbert dropped from a first-floor balcony onto the pavement in front of me and gave me a wide smile.

"Don't let Bernadette catch you doing that," I said, shaking my head. "Or the police. In fact, don't let the police catch you doing anything." I frowned. "How did you get away from that copper at the police station?"

"A little *saut de précision* to a low wall, a *saut de chat* over a bollard and into the gardens behind the courthouse."

"I thought you were stuck."

"A man with handcuffs and a Taser is a great motivator," he said.

"We can't get into the flat," I said.

"I saw."

"God knows where we're going to stay."

"Then that's something he and I have in common," he said smugly.

"Oh?"

He took on what I think was meant to be a bold and manly stance, which was sort of fifty percent Henry VIII and fifty percent knitwear catalogue man. "I, your perfect man, shall take the lead and provide for us. We can have a roof over our heads tonight, no problem."

"Goody."

"Remember me saying I'd got some camping and survival gear?"

"Oh. Yeah!" I was impressed. It was a genuinely brilliant idea.

He went to retrieve his equipment from the tool store at the back of the flats.

"So where are we going?" I asked him as he set off under the considerable weight of the tent and two giant rucksacks.

"We just need somewhere a little bit out of the way with grassy areas," he said. "Any ideas?"

I gave it some thought.

"I do have an idea," I said.

We made our way across town to the park where I'd released the foxes with James a few nights ago. It took a lot longer to get there on the bus, or maybe it only seemed that way because Ashbert was carrying so much luggage that I had to steer him around so that he didn't send pensioners flying like skittles.

As afternoon greyed into evening, we walked into the park. Ashbert immediately approved.

"We need to find somewhere to pitch the tent that is fairly flat, but not at the bottom of a hollow, as it might flood," he said.

"Surely the most important thing is to pitch it somewhere that's out of sight of the local busybodies or muggers," I suggested.

We searched around and identified a couple of potential spots, but Ashbert muttered darkly about possible lightning strikes or insect invasions. After a while he declared that the perfect spot would be the small island in the centre of the park's ornamental lake.

"Don't be daft, how will we get there?" I said.

"I will wade across with all the stuff and then come back for you," he said. "Easy!"

I wasn't convinced, but he removed his trainers and socks, rolled his trousers right up and stepped in. He howled when he stepped on a stone, so he backed up and looked around for something to protect his feet. I tried to use the time to persuade him that we didn't need to camp on the island, but by now he was getting properly carried away with his role as Bear Grylls, so after a few minutes he was wearing bizarre flip-flops made from crushed cans and elastic bands that he'd found in the bin. He went back into the water and this time he made it across. Remarkably, the water didn't come above his mid-thigh at any point, so he got the tent and rucksacks over without incident. This meant that it was my turn.

I tried to view it as a romantic adventure, but I couldn't help feeling like a Disney princess who needed to be carried by the man, like she was some sort of pathetic and useless creature. He tried to scoop me up into his arms in exactly that style, but I told him that wasn't happening so he gave me a piggy back instead. As he waded across I tried to keep my eyes fixed on the island and not on the surrounding murk, but I couldn't help myself. I definitely saw fish in there, and I wondered if Ashbert could feel them brushing his legs or whether they automatically avoided him. I could also see all sorts of obstacles, like car tyres and bits of bike. It crossed my mind that if Ashbert tripped over something we were both in for a soaking. We made it over though, and Ashbert erected the tent within the small cluster of trees and bushes. The tent was green, so it was helpfully camouflaged as well.

I sat on a lump of broken concrete that I'd commandeered for myself.

"I've thought of something that might be a problem," I said. "There's no way the takeaways are going to bring food to this island for us."

"We're not having takeaway, are we?"

"I think a desperate situation like this calls for a curry. With a mountain of poppadoms."

"I was going to forage for food," he said.

"And what are you going to forage for?" I asked him.

"Nuts."

"Nuts?"

"And berries."

"Could you possibly forage for a chicken korma with pilau rice, a keema naan and aloo sag side?"

"Probably not."

"Thought so."

Ashbert wore the pout of a man whose survivalist fantasies were being trampled on. "Fine. Why don't you phone the takeaway and see where in the park they're prepared to deliver to. I can meet them there. I'm going to light the stove now, so we can have a cup of tea."

He fed twigs into a thing that looked like a tiny aluminium jam jar, and then spent some time getting them alight. He knelt over it and poked more twigs in, one at a time. I could tell it wasn't hot because it still rested against his leg, but he put a small can of water on top of it and stepped away, looking satisfied.

Meanwhile, after pacing back and forth to get a mobile signal. I found one and dialled the nearest takeaway. Forty minutes and twelve phone calls later, the stove still hadn't got the water boiling and I was thinking of reporting several Indian and Cantonese restaurants to trading standards for failing to honour their promise to deliver anywhere within a three-mile radius.

"No takeaway for us," I reported back to Ashbert glumly.

"I'll just have to go hunting," he said with glee.

I wanted to ask him what he planned to hunt and what he planned to kill it with, as the police still had his knife, but I nodded wordlessly, preferring not to know.

I took over the twig feeding duty. It was amazingly tedious, because it still wasn't possible to discern any actual heat coming from it, so it felt as if I was a one-woman production line whose sole purpose was to produce burnt twigs. Thoroughly unengaged by the marvel of fire, I turned my attention to the email on my phone I'd been sent earlier:

Dear Miss Belkin,

I hope this email finds you well. I've come across your blog today and I'm fascinated by what you have to say. I'd love to interview you and share your work with the world. I have a column in one of the UK's best selling papers. Let me know when you're available and I'll travel to you.

Regards, Chorley Danglespear

Chorley Danglespear. Sounded posh. And a journalist from a national paper wanted to interview me about my blog! This was, in a day of crappy annoyances, wonderful news. I couldn't wait to tell Ashbert but thoughts of newspaper interviews flew out of my head when he came crashing back through the trees. I heard him before I saw him.

"I only went and did it! Check this out!"

He carried what looked like an exploded pillow in his arms. It was only when he stood in the glow of the stove fire that I saw it was a bird.

"You killed a goose!" I said.

"Better than that!" He turned so I could see its dangling head. "It's a swan!"

"Blimey!"

I'd never seen a swan at such close quarters, and I was immediately struck by how big it was. It was far bigger than the grotty lawn ornament Terence had rescued from the tip.

"Er, well done," I said. "I mean, how...? No, don't tell me."

"It's a tale bards will sing for years to come."

"Good for them. But what shall we do with it?" I asked.

"I thought we might use the stove," he said airily, and then his eyes went from the swan to the stove and back again. "Of course, we might need to cut it up a bit."

He took the swan off a distance and started to rifle through his bag, looking for some utensil with which to carve up a huge bird. I texted Cookie while I fed more twigs into the stove.

How do you cook a swan?

She came straight back on that. *Did you just butt text me?*

I tutted and phoned her.

"No, seriously," I said. "How do you cook a swan?"

"You can't," she said.

"Not with that attitude."

"That's not what I mean, Baby Belkin. You're not allowed to cook them. They all belong to the Queen."

"Oh." This was very bad. I glanced up, half expecting to see the police helicopter swooping down with Sergeant Fenton poised to make an arrest now that we'd gone and committed an actual crime.

"That's the mute swans at least," said Cookie.

"What, the ones that don't talk?"

"It's their name. I think they can make noises."

At that there came a number of noises, including honking, an angry hissing and the screams of a very surprised man. I reached him in time to piece together what had happened. The swan, now looking very much alive (although mightily annoyed) had flapped back into the water, but not before viciously pecking Ashbert's face.

"I thought you killed it!" I said.

"I thought it was dead!" he managed to mumble, through his mutilated lips.

The swan paddled indignantly across the darkening pond.

"I think swan might be off the menu," I said.

We gave up on the idea of eating. We gave up on the idea of a hot drink as well, sipping tepid water and pretending to enjoy it while slapping bugs from our faces and arms.

In the end, we went to bed because there really wasn't anything else to do. I began to wonder if biting insects like their meat pre-tenderised because they were definitely attracted to Ashbert's battered face. By the time we climbed into the sleeping bag, the swelling around his lips had been augmented by inflammation from dozens of itchy insect bites. He was still devoted to making me happy though. He offered to lie underneath me, so it was softer, and then he worried that I didn't have a pillow, so he curled himself around my head, patting my hair in his lap. I even think he might have been singing lullabies at some point, but that might have been a dream.

I was exhausted from a night in the cells and a day of wilderness-living misery and I slept like a log. However, when morning came, I couldn't wait to get out of there. Ashbert said he would carry me back through the water, although when he came to strap his homemade flip-flops onto his feet, he found more clusters of insect bites and I could see him wincing with the pain.

I put it all behind me, and went off to work, leaving Ashbert at the camp. My mind was already turning over various plans to avoid another hateful night in the park.

Cookie found me in the women's toilets, trying to wash my hair in one of the sinks.

"I've never been so glad to come to work," I said. "You'll never guess where I spent the night."

"A skip?"

"No."

"Prison?"

"No. But thanks for the campaign to free me. I'm sure it helped."

I told her the story of my rubbish night on Ashbert Island. Cookie looked shocked at the swan murder; there are certain things that Cookie holds dear, and she does not approve of cruelty to wildlife.

"Just to be clear, which was the most annoying part?" she asked. "Was it being in a tent, or was it Ashbert's constant efforts to make you happy?"

I sighed and thought about the answer. I really was getting very fed up with Ashbert, but why did it make me feel like such a bad person? I had created Ashbert. I had brought him into my life. I owed him my time and my company, didn't I? I resigned myself to another evening of caveman-style hunger and boredom.

And then James phoned me up and invited me out for dinner.

"Dinner?" I said.

"Well, Theo and I are going to grab a burger and fries but, if that's not beneath you..."

215

"Hey. As long as I don't have to catch it and kill it myself, I'm in," I said.

Chapter 29

We went to a fast food drive-through place near that new development where the car factories used to be. James sent Theo to the counter to order for us. I asked for burger and fries and a thick chocolate milkshake. And a side order of nine chicken nuggets. I was hungry.

I had – oh, vain woman I am! – worried that James would scoff at my tired and dishevelled appearance. But he looked just as bad.

"A tough day?" I asked.

He heaved a deep and heartfelt sigh.

"A bit of fallout from the whole, you know, 'murder' thing."

"I'm sorry. Again."

"Don't be," he said. "On the one hand, Theo's been well looked after by Uncle Phil. But this kind of situation can't be good for a boy: an absent mother camping with indigenous peoples halfway up a mountain somewhere, a father in prison..."

"Hey, you're not in prison yet," I said which wasn't half as comforting as I meant it to be.

"Social services will no doubt begin to show an interest. School have already had a 'chat' with me about having to sell our old house because..." He shook his head.

"Because?" I said.

His smile was unintentionally bitter. "Living the simple life of a global traveller is surprisingly expensive. Elena dipped deep into our finances."

"Bitch."

"Well, I wouldn't put it so strongly but thanks. And the salary of a university academic and part-time curator is surprisingly small. But, hey, there's no point complaining. As our good friend, Epicurus, said, 'Do not spoil what you have by desiring what you have not. Remember, what you now have was once among the things you only hoped for.'"

I have no idea who Epicurus was. It might have been one of his work colleagues.

"And what do you have now that you had once only hoped for?" I asked.

"Chips!" said James and pointed.

Theo came back with a tray heaped high with boxed and wrapped food. Burgers! Fries! Nuggets! And not a bloody swan in sight!

I practically inhaled half a dozen nuggets. Seriously, no pausing for breath in between. Theo stared at me.

"Sorry," I said. "Not had a proper meal today."

"Maybe we've all had tough days," said James.

Theo gave a game shrug. "Mine was cool. I spoke to the policeman who came to collect Uncle Phil's car."

"They did what?" I said.

"Forensics want a look, apparently," said James. "I take it they've been round to your place too?"

"Yup. They're still there. It's all sealed up. I'm kind of temporarily homeless."

"And the policeman used to be in the army," said Theo, "and I asked him about where he'd been and he told me all about his time in Afghanistan. It was really interesting."

"See?" said James weakly. "Some good has come from the day."

"Yes," I said with forced cheeriness. "I'm sure we've all got something to be grateful for."

"Yes." James thought. "Oh, I've been asked to give the key address to the potential Ancient History students at the university next week."

"That is good," I said. "Oh. I know. I'm going to be interviewed about my blog."

"Are you?"

"By a national newspaper no less."

I showed James the email. He read it and then pulled a funny face, as if it might not be brilliant news.

"Interesting," he said. It wasn't a good 'interesting'.

"Exciting," I suggested.

"Hmmm."

Couldn't he see that this was going to be great for me? I was thrilled about his university speech or whatever it was.

218

"This, um, Chorley Danglespear doesn't say what his interest is," said James after reading the email again.

"Yeah, he says it right there: he's fascinated by what I have to say," I pointed out. I wondered if James was still a bit sleep-deprived from his time at the police station.

"Tabloid journalists aren't known for writing columns purely about artistic merit," he said. "If I were you, I think I'd be a bit careful with what I said to him, that's all."

"I'm always careful about what I say to –"

James gave me a look before I even finished the sentence and we both burst out laughing.

"You are many things, Lori," he said to me. The intensity of his accompanying stare was enough to send a small shiver of pleasure through me. "But taking care about what you say is not something that I'd put at the top of the list."

I had to acknowledge the truth of this.

"Listen," he said. "I did ask you out for a reason tonight."

"Oh?"

"I had an idea about your pendant. You know we lived in Crete. I was out there for nine months cataloguing a collection for a local museum. Well, when he was much younger, Theo was friends with a boy whose father runs a bar in Malia. They still Skype each other from time to time. I thought we might get his help with finding your stall holder and you could ask him yourself."

"That would be great!" I said.

"But let's kill three birds with one stone. Get back to this Chorley Danglespear and arrange a time to meet and, when you come over to ours to Skype with Hector in Crete, let me coach you through a few hints and tips about dealing with the press."

"Have you had much experience with the press?"

"No, but I might just be able to offer a... worldly perspective on things."

"It can't hurt."

"Exactly."

I nibbled a fry. "What's the third bird?"

"Third bird? Oh. Yes. It's a sofa bed. If you need it."

"You mean tonight?"

I looked at the man who I had caused no end of hassle and heartache over the last forty-eight hours and he was offering me an alternative to the cold, hard groundsheet of Ashbert's island den. I could have cried.

"If you're homeless," he said. "If you need somewhere."

It occurred to me only then that I had left Ashbert on that wretched island to be eaten alive by insects for another night. He was probably wondering where I was. He was probably alone and hungry and needed me more than ever.

"I'd love to stay on your sofa bed," I said.

Chapter 30

I went round to see James, to kill those three birds as we'd arranged. It wasn't a pleasing metaphor, after the swan horror on Ashbert Island.

"I wonder why people don't update some of the daft sayings in English," I said, as he opened the door. "You know, like the one about killing two birds with one stone. It's completely unsuitable for vegetarians."

James nodded. "Perhaps we need a more twenty-first century reference for efficient multitasking." He stood aside so that I could walk in and I could see that he was giving it some serious thought. "No. I have no idea. I don't think efficient multitasking comes naturally to me."

I had little to add. "You sometimes see these lists of things called life hacks," I ventured. "My favourite one is putting ice cream in a Nutella jar that's nearly empty to make a tasty snack, but I'm not sure that it's as punchy as killing birds. Actually, I'm not even sure if vegetarians can eat Nutella either."

We settled on the sofa. Theo was nowhere to be seen. I'd been looking forward to Theo's company, but I realised that I was thrilled to get James to myself. I was conscious of how close we were on the sofa, our legs almost touching as he turned to me with his serious face. I really liked his serious face, it made me want to soften it, with say, a kiss or something.

"Let's have a chat about this interview," he said. "Now, do you think you could practise pausing for a second or two before answering a question?"

I paused for a second or two, pushing thoughts of kissing from my mind so that I could concentrate.

"Yes," I said smugly. I was smug because I was pretty sure I hadn't said *Mississippi* out loud.

"Very good! Try to use that time to think about what you're saying. Imagine that the smallest fragment of your sentence can be printed on its own. Does it make you look stupid? If it does then think of another way of saying it."

"Right. Got it." I detected the faintest scent of aftershave, something subtle and manly that made me want to lean in closer and inhale deeply. I was getting distracted again.

"Another thing you could think about is this. Try not to be drawn into making any statements that might seem extreme in any way. Tone things down a bit." He gave me a look. "Actually, tone things down a lot."

I scowled at him.

"And something that I really want you to think about is photos. If he wants you to pose for a photo, don't let him trick you into pulling a face. If he takes your photo, you want it to be smiley and normal, yes?"

"Of course," I said, wondering who on earth would let themselves be tricked like that.

"That's great news," he said, standing up. "Now, I hope you like tuna? I'm making a Greek salad with some tuna steaks."

"That sounds amazing," I said. I followed him into the kitchen. "No Theo this evening?" I asked.

"Staying over at a friend's," said James, "although I did get him to talk to Hector, his buddy. He's expecting a Skype call from us in thirty minutes."

I helped with the salad, to the extent that I was capable anyway, which mostly meant adding olives to an already attractive, glistening pile of delicious things. I popped one in my mouth and quickly realised that they were the ones with a stone still inside. I needed to find the right moment to discreetly spit it out or he would know that I'd filched one.

"Just pop the stone in the bin over there," said James, even though his back was to me.

I did as he suggested. "How did you know?" I asked.

"My ears are highly attuned to the sounds made by stealth eating," he said. "Theo is a devil for it."

"Wow," I said.

"And there's a mirror on the wall over there," he said. "I just happened to see you pop an olive in your mouth."

I gave him a light punch in the shoulder and laughed. He was doing something clever with the tuna so I went and had another olive just because I could.

"Right, that can marinade while we're on the call to Hector," James said, wiping his hands.

Moments later, and we were both sitting at the table, chatting to a boy of Theo's age with the widest smile.

"Hello to you both from the best place in the world," said Hector.

"I'm not going to argue with that," I said. "I loved Crete."

"You like the beaches?"

"Er, yes." I was thinking of the nightclubs and the two-for-one deals on fishbowl cocktails but, sure, the beaches too. "Thank you for helping with this, Hector."

"Not a problem. My father has always told me to be helpful to the people who love our home and they will cherish it as we do."

"And give you a decent tip," said James. He turned to me to explain. "This young hustler waits tables sometimes, and everyone loves him."

I smiled at Hector. "So, do you know the street where there's a big church with a shoe shop right next door?"

"It is just around the corner," said Hector and trotted off. He held the tablet up so we could see where he was going. It was like being back on holiday and I sighed at the recollection. A short while later he held up the camera to the shoe shop. They'd changed their window display since I was there, but I tried not to be distracted by the shoes. It was definitely the right place.

"Perfect, Hector, that's the place. Now a few paces beyond, there is a window set into the wall; it looks as if it's been there forever. The guy only had a few pieces for sale, and he kind of leaned out to chat with people who walked past."

Hector moved slowly along the ancient wall, showing us the view as he went.

"Here we have the drainage pipe from the roof, and here we have a cat who wants to know if we have some scraps for him. Here we have a painting that is really faded, and here we have a souvenir shop. Is this the one you meant?"

"No, it wasn't modern like that," I said. The shop window on the screen was like hundreds of others in the town, filled with cheap imported plates and trinkets. "I was sure it was just next to the shoe shop, because the man called me over when I was looking in the window."

"Go back, Hector, let's have another look," said James.

Hector backed up and we got the same things in reverse (although the cat had moved on).

"Can we have another look at the painting?" I asked. Hector stepped away from the wall to get a better view. It was a faded mural but it was clear enough to determine what it was supposed to be. The shape of the window set into the wall was right. The man who leaned across the sill was the same man. I peered really closely. He held a pendant in his hand that was only a small dot on the screen, but somehow, I knew it was my pendant.

"Um, it's that shop in the painting," I whispered.

Hector chuckled. "Did you sample the special cigarettes during your visit?" he asked.

"Thank you Hector, we don't need to be quite so cheeky," said James sternly, but Hector laughed again.

"No, he's probably right," I said. "I must have bought the pendant from somewhere else. Do you know anything about that painting, Hector?"

"No. It's been there forever."

"You've helped a great deal. Thank you, Hector," I said.

James ended the call and we went back to the kitchen to cook the tuna.

"A dead end then?" said James, lighting the gas. "Although it's always nice to chat with young Hector."

He seared the tuna in a pan that was so hot I was sure he'd set it on fire, but he somehow made it perfect. I opened a bottle of wine and poured us both a glass. The meal was exactly what I needed after about a million sausages and I had to stop myself from making continuous nom nom noises in appreciation.

"Oh, that was so good!" I said afterwards.

"I'm delighted that you're so easy to please," he said. Now what would you like to do. Watch some TV? Game of Scrabble maybe?"

"Are you, the academic, seriously going to play Scrabble with me, the cleaner?" I said.

His face fell. "I'm sorry I was so rude to you on your first day, it was unforgiveable."

I felt terrible for spoiling the mood like that. If it needed a game of Scrabble to get it back on course then I should just suck it up.

"Scrabble it is," I said, "and I liked that you told me some things I didn't know. I'll make sure everyone knows about Common Era now. Maybe I'll do a blog about it at some point."

Scrabble didn't get played much in our house when I was growing up, mainly because I stole the tiles and added them to artworks as bold captions.

James got me completely on the back foot when he managed to get *vixen* on the board with one of his first moves. I was dying to make the word *fox* with that *x* just to make him laugh, but I didn't get the letters. I stared at my motley collection of letters.

I added *pan* and let James add up the score. He was already in the lead, but I didn't care. He wasted no time in adding *speed*, which meant I could no longer attempt *fox*, which was a weight off my mind, to be honest.

I leaned forward and added *gem* across James' *speed*. I'd put the letters down carelessly and I reached to straighten them at the same time as James, and he brushed my hand with his.

A thrill coursed through me at his touch. He added an *s* to my *pan* to create *span*. Why hadn't I seen that?

I gazed at the board and added a *b* and an *a*. James frowned at the board.

"That's not right," he said. "I mean it's great that you made *sag* across there, but it's not a real word going down now, it says *bae*."

"Bae's a word," I said.

"Of course it's not, it's meaningless."

"No, it means *bae*!" I said. "Like *Babe* with a letter missing. It's what young people call their boyfriend or girlfriend."

He looked at me for a long moment. "If this is a bluff then you're good, *really* good," he said.

"Not a bluff! You can google it," I said.

I believe you, Lori," he said, tenderly, and leaned in. "I love that you just taught me something that I didn't know."

It seemed as if time slowed right down. I was aware of every small detail that surrounded us, from the colour of the curtains to the amount of wine that remained in the bottle, but at the same time my entire being was transfixed by James' gaze. He looked at me so intently, and I saw his lips part slightly as he leaned in towards me. My breath caught in my throat as I anticipated the taste and feel of his mouth on mine. I closed my eyes.

"Who's Ashbert?" he asked me.

My eyes snapped open and I could feel myself blushing right down to my feet with a mixture of lust and weird embarrassment. Had I misread his body language? No! He was definitely about to kiss me, so why on earth had he brought up Ashbert? How did he even know about Ashbert?

"Er," I said, playing for time and trying to organise my face back into talking mode when it had been hell-bent on snogging mode. "Ashbert?"

"Yes, the police mentioned him. They said you were seen digging with him and they made it sound as if you and he are an item."

"Right. Yes. That would be one way to describe the situation. It's complicated though."

He raised his eyebrows. He wanted me to continue. This felt like a terrible idea, but I pressed on.

"So Ashbert was someone I ah, dated, years ago," I said. "He turned up quite unexpectedly, just recently."

How strange that I was already practising the very advice that James had just given me. The less I said on the subject the better, especially given that I had no real clue what was going on myself. All I knew was that Ashbert was somehow dependent on me and it was starting to feel like an uncomfortable burden. I couldn't deny that we were some sort of item though, could I? My lips pressed themselves together, as if they knew that ill-advised words wanted to come tumbling out.

James looked at me as if he could see that I was uncomfortable. He gave a heavy sigh. "Well lucky him," he said. "Listen, there was a favour I wanted to ask you. There's some university open days coming up and I've been roped in with some of the organisation. Anyway, the first one's this weekend and I've hit a bit of a crisis. The admin assistant has gone off work with something called pre-eclampsia."

"What's that?" I asked.

"No idea, and I'm a bit afraid to ask if I'm honest," said James. "So, I'm floundering with some of the stuff that the university likes to call *public engagement*. I think that you have some talent in that area. Did you know that your little speech bubbles were really popular in the museum?"

I grinned. Public engagement! Who knew? "You want my help?" I said, checking that I'd heard correctly. I was a bit incredulous. Scrabble and now this? James seemed prepared to take me much more seriously than anyone else in my life.

"If you can spare some time, that would be wonderful," he said.

"Consider your public engaged!" I said leaping into a superhero pose.

Chapter 31

I slept like a log on the sofa bed. If there's one thing that an uncomfortable night in a hostile outdoors environment teaches you, it's how to make the most of a comfy bed. No insects, no odd rustling from the surrounding trees and most importantly, no Ashbert fussing over me. Of course, while I was lazing around, thinking about how comfy I was, he was still there on that hellish island, which made me feel a bit guilty. I rolled over and tried to push the thought away, but his kicked-puppy face kept appearing in my mind, so I got up and crept out of the house before everyone else was up.

I walked to the park and then wondered how I'd get across to the island to check that he was all right. It turned out to be unnecessary. Ashbert emerged from the water as I approached. He was wearing very little and I could see that he was very cold.

"Are you wearing Speedos? I asked, unsure because of the mottled discoloration that covered him. I once read an article about 'craziest sports' and they had something called bog snorkelling where people swim (or writhe messily) through a trench of mud. I think they come out a bit cleaner than Ashbert, who was draped in pondweed, litter and unidentifiable sludge.

"Sure am!" he grinned. He struck a pose, which was spoiled somewhat by his teeth chattering and the whole smelling-like-a-stagnant-pond-full-of-dead-fish thing.

He stepped forward and made to embrace me. I stepped back. "Hold it right there!" I said. "You will not be touching me while you're in that state."

"But you like it when Daniel Craig does it!" he said mournfully. "I've been practising. I've been back and forth to the island fifteen times this morning. I thought I was getting good at it."

That explained how he'd managed to accumulate the worst of the pollution from the lake. It also explained why he seemed on the edge of collapse. I walked him around the park and rubbed his arms, but that turned out to be a bad idea when I realised that he was covered in painful insect bites. In the end, I made a deal with a homeless guy for his coat. I paid him nearly all of my money for it –

he'd be able to get a new coat *and* a slap-up meal for that, but at least Ashbert could cover himself up and start to get warm again.

"Listen, I need to go over to Norman's before work to make sure he keeps my postcard in the window," I said. "Come with me. I think we need to talk."

When we reached the pavement, Ashbert's squashed can shoes made a clattering sound as he walked. I should have struck a deal for the homeless guy's shoes as well but I only had a pound left and that was to pay for my postcard to be displayed for another week.

"I think it was wrong of me to give you all these tasks to do," I said.

"Oh no, definitely not," said Ashbert. "I've enjoyed doing them. I enjoy making you happy."

"It's not a healthy basis for a relationship though, is it?" I said.

"What? Don't you like to be happy?" he asked with a frown. "I can do something el–"

"No, can't you see what I'm saying?" I said. "You should have your own hopes and dreams. Don't you want to do anything just for yourself?"

"Yes of course! I want –"

I whirled to face him. "Whatever you're about to say better not be about me, or it doesn't count, right?"

He nodded and looked crestfallen. He sighed and walked in silence until we reached the newsagent. We looked at the postcards in the window, mainly so that we didn't need to look at each other.

"We both need to look at ourselves," I said. "I know I've treated you badly. I wanted a knight in shining armour and I ended up trying to make you into someone that you're not. I'm sorry for that. But you need to decide what you want for yourself, and not fixate on making me happy. We all have wants and needs. Look, here's a whole bunch of them in this window. Things people want. Although to be honest, I think you should probably aim higher than *paving slabs (need taking up)* or *window cleaner wanted*. The point is that you need to decide on what yours are. Pick something. Help others. Help yourself. Whatever you do, make yourself happy."

"I'll do that," he said. "Thanks Lori."

"In case you were in any doubt," I said, "you might want to begin your list of needs with somewhere new to live. When I get Adam's flat back I want you to move out of it."

I headed inside the newsagents so that I didn't have to look at his face. As I walked away, I saw a passer-by press a few coins into Ashbert's hand, responding to his dreadful appearance (and smell). An omen? I decided that it was. I knew in my heart of hearts that he was going to be all right.

Chapter 32

I'd arranged to meet Chorley Danglespear after work at a city centre cafe. I found him chewing on an impossibly huge sandwich that seemed to have an entire cooked breakfast wedged between two slices of bread. He clearly recognised me from my picture somewhere and rose to greet me.

He held out a hand that was greasy from the sandwich, caught the look on my face, looked around and then wiped it on the back of his chair before shaking my hand.

"Read all of your blogs," he mumbled through a mouthful of food. "Love what you're doing with the character. Sit. Sit. Please."

I sat. He clicked his fingers for service. A waitress came over.

"What are you having, love?" he asked me. "Coffee? Tea? Three-course meal? On me. Just say it and the girl will fetch it for you."

I paused a second, just as James had taught me. Did that apply to all questions I was asked or only interview ones?

"Just a cup of tea will be fine," I said.

"You sure?" said Chorley, dabbing up a spot of ketchup with his fingertip and sucking it off. "Slice a cake? You could do to put a few pounds on. That's not sexist, is it?"

"Er…"

"Just a cuppa for the little lady," he told the waitress. "We'll shout if we want anything else."

He waved the waitress away and, with elbows planted on the table and fingers steepled together, looked at me for a long time.

"So, Lori. Lori. Florrie. Lori, creator of Florrie. Is your wonderful cartoon character based on anyone you know?"

I waited for a second again, but this question was very straightforward. No danger here.

"Florrie?" I said, pride swelling in me. "She's very much based on me. I'm showing the journey into adulthood that I've made myself."

He looked delighted. "Cracking stuff!" He dipped inside his jacket to produce a notebook. He took another bite of his sandwich.

"So, tell me then. What made you start this series? Am I right in thinking that you've actually been an adult for a number of years?"

He was pretty observant. I guess that comes with being a journalist.

"I was an adult in age, but I hadn't really mastered true adulting, so –"

"'Adulting'," he said as he wrote it down. I could hear the inverted commas.

"So, I set myself a set of challenges," I said, "based on some lists that I found about how to be an adult. That's where it came from."

"Gold. Pure gold," he said with an admiring shake of his head. I felt nothing but relief. James had worried me a little with his warnings, but this man really understood what I was trying to express, and clearly liked it.

"So, you've conquered this adulting thing now, have you, or will Florrie face new challenges in the coming weeks? I bet your life's pretty sorted now, yeah?"

"Florrie will have lots more to do," I said. "I've been arrested this week, so Florrie might have to do that soon."

"Mm, the arrest. I've had my own brushes with the boys in blue. I've got nothing but admiration for the forces of law and order but this nanny state causes all manner of grievances. Want to give me your side of things there?" he asked.

"Well they're worried about my brother, Adam. He's disappeared, but he does that a lot. He's gone off somewhere filming, which is not at all the same thing as being murdered."

"Your brother's Adam Belkin, yeah? Does a lot of documentaries?"

"Yes, that's him," I said, hoping that the interview wasn't going to swerve into Adam adoration, like everything else in my life seemed to. This was about me!

"I met him at a press junket in Qatar a year or so back. God, we got so pissed – sorry! Drunk." He slapped his own wrist. "Pardon my French. This journo I knew from my old Daily Mail days told this hilarious story about a transsexual cripple. I laughed so hard I

234

fell in the Qatari prince's swimming pool. Your brother lent me his towel to dry off."

"Um..."

Chorley sniffed. "Your brother's with One Armed Bandit productions, isn't? Doing that thing in Tierra del Fuego. And he's gone missing, has he?"

"What was that place you just said?" I yelped, recognising the name.

"Tierra del Fuego?"

"Yes! In Spain! Oh, write it down for me, will you?" I asked.

He scribbled it on a scrap of his pad for me, but not before he'd written *Spain* and underlined it and added a smiley face – which was strange.

"There you go. I hope that sorts things out for you now. Anything else you need a hand with? I might need to change me name to Chorley Danglespear, attorney at law at this rate!"

"No," I said, "just get the word out there about my blog and help me leave my stupid cleaning job, will you?"

"Cleaning job? What? Actual cleaning?"

"Yes. Mopping, dusting. That sort of thing."

"Huh," he said. "I thought they only let immigrants do that kind of work these days, not English roses such as yourself."

"No, I had to do an interview and everything. I mean, my parents filled out the application form and sent it off to the university."

"Oh, the university. Even more surprising. Centres of lefty leaning liberalism. They have those affirmative action quotas for all their jobs. If you're not a black lesbian then you might as well throw your application in the bin." He caught sight of my perplexed expression. "You're not, are you?"

I stared. "What? Black?"

He gave me an amused look and spread his hands. "These days, you can be whatever you want to be. That's what they tell us. If you want to call yourself black, say the sky is pink and that up is down then you can. And you can go crying to the bloody Equality Commission if anyone dares to tell you otherwise. No, I've got nothing against the blacks. Or the homosexuals and the lesbians either. What they get up to in their own homes is none of my business."

I was quite concerned and confused about what Chorley Danglespear thought black people were getting up to in their own homes but I was also worried that there might have been an important journalistic question in there somewhere.

"You were asking me about my work?" I said.

"Indeedy-do. You've fought against the odds to get a cleaning job at the university but you don't like it. What's the worst part about it?"

I considered the question. The work was fine, actually, it was the other nonsense that came with it. "My boss Rex is this strange man with a great big bushy beard. He's an idiot too, but I know everyone says that. One thing that was completely crazy was that they made me work this thing called a week in hand. It means that they don't even pay you until you've done loads of work. What are you supposed to do if you've got no money? I couldn't even eat!"

"Tricky that. What did you do?" he asked.

"The only thing I could do. I ate the leftover meals in the cafe. The food there's pretty good, so I had to work quite hard to get people to leave the things I wanted."

"Nice one, Lori!" he said. "You stuck it to the man!"

I had no idea what he was talking about so I smiled at him. After he'd finished his sandwich, he wiped his mouth and struggled to his feet. "Just gonna dig out the camera. Get a couple of shots. You know what would be fun?"

I shook my head.

"It would be fun if we got you to do some of the things in your blog, don't you think?"

"Oh, maybe it would," I said thinking about it. Florrie was a cartoon version of me, so it felt perfectly natural to slip back into that role myself.

"Got a box of eggs back there, love?" he asked the woman at the counter.

She produced a box of eggs from just below the counter, as if they'd been waiting there. He passed them to me.

236

"Right now, do the proud face. You've just learned the price of eggs, and it's like you've won a Nobel prize or summat. Yeah, like that!"

He snapped away for a few seconds.

"Now, let's do the one that went viral where you're looking really confused because you don't know how big a cup is. Yeah, that cup will do."

I picked up a tea cup and contemplated it. It was a mystery that I'd never really got to the bottom of, the cup thing, so it was an easy matter to give it a look of despair and anguish, at the thought of the delicious cake that would elude me.

"Lori, you're a star," he said when he'd finished taking pictures. "So, what's next? Does Florrie discover that milk comes from cows?"

"I think Florrie knows that milk comes from cows," I told him, "although how they turn milk into more milk is a mystery."

Chorley frowned. "How they...? Who?"

"Cows. They drink the milk and then make more milk from it. Round and round it goes."

"Cows drink water, love," said Chorley.

That didn't seem right. Cows always appeared on milk bottles. I'd even seen cartoon cows holding glasses of milk and they looked like they were enjoying it.

"They make milk from water?" I said.

"And grass," said Chorley.

"Oh." I thought about it. I'd always thought they drank milk and ate cheese – an all dairy diet which was why they looked so big and fat. I decided not to tell Chorley this; I didn't want to come across as an idiot.

Chorley was scribbling in his notebook.

"Can't wait to see you in print, my love," he was saying.

He sounded excited so that was good.

I wasted no time at all heading over to the police station after the interview. Sergeant Fenton would be eager to hear my news about Adam's whereabouts. As it turned out, she wasn't all that eager. I waited for forty minutes for her to come out and see me.

"Hi Sergeant, I've got some good news," I said. She raised a cynical eyebrow, as if she didn't believe I was capable of bringing good news. "I know where Adam is. He's in Tierra del Fuego, with the One Armed Bandit production company."

Sergeant Fenton has an amazing poker face. She didn't look at all excited as she made a note of what I'd said.

"Not Spain then," she said.

"Yeah, like I said. Tierra del Fuego," I said. Wasn't she paying attention?

She shook her head. "Don't know why I'm surprised that your grip on geography is as poor as your grip on everything else," she muttered. "Tierra del Fuego is in South America."

"But it sounds –"

"Miss Belkin, I am not here to fill in the gaps in your knowledge. Is that everything that you had to say?" she snapped.

I wondered if she was feeling stressed or something. Her patience seemed even more limited than normal.

"Well, I have a question. Can I get back into the flat now that you know where Adam is?" I asked.

She gave me a long hard look. "I won't know where Adam is until I confirm what you've told me, but as for the flat, we finished processing it a couple of days ago. Of course you can return. We should have left you a phone message. Didn't you get it?"

I shook my head, dumbstruck. For the first time, I saw a small smile play around Sergeant Fenton's lips, as if she was amused by the fact that I'd been homeless for no reason at all. I like to lift a person's spirits as much as anyone, but her attitude was a little bit uncharitable, I thought.

Chapter 33

I caught the train over to the university to catch up with James. I walked across the lovely green campus, round past my museum and art gallery – *my* museum! Ha! – and found the right building. It was one of those buildings that is like a Mr Kipling Fondant Fancy built out of red bricks. Why was I thinking about food? I hadn't had a proper meal all day. Watching Chorley Danglespear messily eat his sandwich had put me right off the thought of eating earlier, and now my stomach was growling. I told myself that I'd help James and then find something to eat afterwards.

I found him in the huge entrance hall. He was opening a cardboard box and was surrounded by loads more. If he'd said that he was organising an open day for cardboard boxes then I would have declared it a huge success.

"What are all these?" I asked.

"Promotional material for the courses on offer here," he said. "We need to unpack the boxes and collate them into packs for the visitors."

I looked across the piles of boxes. The one that James had opened contained densely packed flyers. My brain isn't wired up to do superfast mathematics, but it *is* wired to recognise a humungous task when it sees one. Still, I had volunteered my services so I joined James in opening boxes and making piles of the contents on a nearby table.

The job consisted of inserting lots of pieces of paper into each folder. Some of the pieces of paper looked useful: a train timetable and a map of the campus. A good many of them looked like junk, but they all had to be included.

James went off to do something else, so I decided to make a game out of it or I'd go mad. I set myself a series of challenges. The first one was to fill a folder to the tune of a song. I tried various McFly songs and even some of the AC/DC ones that I half-remembered from my disastrous theatre trip. Some were too slow, and others were way too fast, resulting in a blizzard of flying paper.

What I settled on in the end was that old song from the Shrek film: *I'm on my Way*. It had the right sort of marching rhythm. *Stomp*, a map, *stomp*, a timetable, *stomp* a brochure about summer school.

After I'd done that for a few minutes, I decided to try doing some with my eyes closed. Could I rely on muscle memory to get a full set into a folder? The answer turned out to be *almost*. I tipped a couple of piles onto the floor, but I'd sort them out later if I needed to.

The next challenge? Double handing! Could I do two folders at once holding them in a fan formation and applying a deft flick-flick from each pile? The answer to that one turned out to be *no*. More of the flyers went on the floor than into the folders. I was not discouraged, because this is how we learn and grow, by experimenting. Maybe I'd do a blog where Florrie learns and grows.

"What do you think you're doing?"

The voice cut across my latest fun experiment where I was trying to use my nose to slide each flyer into a folder. I sometimes try to imagine how I'd get by if I lost the use of my hands. It's a skill worth practising, in my view. The question was delivered in the same critical tone frequently employed by Bernadette Brampton, head of the residents' association. I looked up and saw a woman with a clipboard, looking at me with the exact same expression Bernadette Brampton used on me too. The one where I'm supposed to tremble and confess. I was impressed by the similarity. And then I realised it *was* Bernadette Brampton, head of the residents' association.

"Oh, hello, Bernadette."

"I asked you, what do you think you're doing?" she said.

"I think I'm filling these folders with flyers," I said.

"You think?"

"I do. You asked. I think I'm filling folders with flyers. It's also what I'm actually doing. But I'm thinking it too. It's called multi-tasking."

She stalked over and picked up the folder that I'd just filled. She opened it and scrutinised the contents with a sneer. "And why is this timetable upside down?" she asked.

"Because that's the way it went in," I said, slightly incredulous. "Is it any of your business?"

"As the vice-chancellor of this university, I should think so."

"Vice-chancellor?" Oh, went my brain. Does that mean she's my boss too? The museum and gallery belonged to the uni and even I knew that the vice-chancellor was definitely high up. I wasn't sure what the difference between a vice-chancellor and just chancellor was. Maybe the vice-chancellor dealt with all the naughty sexy stuff and... no, probably not that.

"Well, Mrs Vice-Chancellor," I said deferentially, "I did put some of them in upside down but, I figure, you're expecting these students of yours to be pretty clever? They'll be able to turn that round. Just a hunch."

"It's a question of quality," she said. "We need to protect our brand, and ensure that all promotional material reflects the standards that we expect, Miss...?" She looked at me and then, only then, she recognised me. "You! Weren't you arrested for murder?"

"Ms Brampton!" called James, coming over to my aid. "Lori's been kind enough to help out with the open day. On an entirely voluntary basis."

"But... but... the murder?"

"All a misunderstanding," James assured her. "Her brother is fine."

"In Tierra del Fuego," I said.

"Is he?" said James and Bernadette together.

"Yes. Which is in South America, *not* Spain," I said knowledgeably.

"Well," said Bernadette, a little put out by my expert geographical acumen. "Well, Mr Reynolds, might I suggest that you share some of our best practices with the young lady?"

"Indeed," he smiled.

"And measure the standard of her work."

"Nothing will give me more pleasure."

"I'll be back to check on some more of these later on," she said and stomped off.

"She's got it in for me," I said, watching her go.

James shrugged. "It's just her funny little ways."

"I don't find them funny."

"She's got raging OCD and is a control freak. You won't find another university in the land where the actual vice-chancellor personally decides to co-ordinate the activities across the departments. I mean, you'll never catch her actually helping or anything, just straightening edges and criticizing how we do things. I just smile and nod and wait for her to go away."

"She's taken all the fun out of it," I said mournfully.

James looked at me and grinned. "I do have another couple of jobs that need doing."

"Sure."

"The museum has agreed to lend our department some artefacts. I'm very pleased and surprised. After the fuss of the missing Fuseli painting of Zeus, I didn't think the museum would let anything out of their sight again. Anyway, I need to create an exciting display of artefacts. And then afterwards, I have a PowerPoint presentation that's a little bit dull. Can you help enliven it?"

I gave him a look. "Does the queen have a sparkly hat?"

I helped James carry in and position the artefacts. There were some Roman pots, which went on special stands behind a roped-off area, and then in the centre was a large glass display case containing a Roman mosaic.

"A team of us reassembled the mosaic from fifteen thousand pieces. They were recovered from an old midden heap. It took seven weeks," said James.

I peered at it, wondering various things. Like what was a midden heap? "The pieces are all the same shape," I said.

"Yes."

"So how do you know you've done it right? It's not like a jigsaw where it will only fit one way. If you have enough mosaic pieces you could make any picture, so how do you know you've made the right one?"

"Very profound, Lori," said James, "and possibly true, but even though fifteen thousand is a lot, it's still a limited number of tiles, so we were able to deduce what the picture was. It was a painstaking process, but it means that we can all see this gorgeous picture for the first time in nearly two thousand years."

I was blown away at that thought. "So cool," I breathed, "so very cool."

I can confidently say that I completely nailed the PowerPoint presentation. It was dull, but I gave it everything I had. I ran James through the changed version a couple of hours later and he was impressed. He even laughed a few times (in the places he was supposed to).

"Great work Lori. I was hoping you'd add some of your famous speech bubbles. They're great. I wasn't expecting the sound effects, but they're great too. I like that sound of distant cannon fire you have in the background." He clicked the off button and then looked confused. "Wait, I can still hear it," he said, cocking a playful ear.

"It's my stomach rumbling. I haven't eaten all day," I said.

He gave me a look. I couldn't say what it was. Amused? Patronising? Loving? Whatever it was, I liked it.

"How could I keep you here for so long when you're hungry?" he said. "Tell you what, there's a wonderful deli just down the road, I'll pop over there and get us an office picnic."

I liked the sound of an office picnic so much that I even went back to the hateful folder-filling job while James was gone. The tune of the Teddy Bears' Picnic turned out to be very suitable for the job, so I got through half an hour of it without incident.

James came back in and had a sheepish smile on his face.

"It turns out that I had completely lost track of time," he said. "The deli was closed, so I had to get creative." He started to pull things out of a bag, in the manner of a magician whose rabbit has gone on strike. "Someone in our office had a birthday today and they brought cakes in." He plonked down a swiss roll and a box half full of doughnuts. "I raided the vending machines, so we have crisps in every flavour." I was about to point out that he hadn't got any prawn cocktail, but I bit down on my words, because they are revolting anyway. "And then finally, I came across a student carrying a bowl of chips. I don't know where he'd got them from but we agreed a price and here they are."

I fell greedily on the chips as James led me through to a small office, so that we could sit down. He spread the rest of the food across a desk.

"I hope Ashbert won't resent you spending time with me," he said. "I'm really grateful for your help, but I don't want to –"

"I've asked him to move out," I said primly. Actually, it wasn't all that prim, as sugar cascaded from the doughnut that I'd just bitten into.

"Oh?" he said.

"Yes."

"Oh. I'm sorry."

"Don't be," I said. "It was time."

I caught the flicker of delight in his eye, and I smiled to myself.

Chapter 34

On the day of the actual open day, I'd swapped my shift at the museum from morning until evening, so I could be there while it was busy. I had expected to be making tea behind the scenes or something, but James insisted that I'd be a great friendly face to welcome visitors. I wasn't so sure that I was equipped to cope with an influx of young brainiacs and their difficult questions about ancient Greece and Rome, but James teamed me up with Theo, which made me feel better.

I had a clipboard with spare maps, so that I could draw on them and direct people to the correct place. I made sure that I stood in the same direction as the top of the map, so that my lefts and rights would point the correct way.

"Why are you standing like that?" asked Theo.

"I'm facing north," I said. "It's my lucky direction."

He seemed to accept that, and he positioned himself to face east, which was where people were actually coming from.

It turned out that most people who stopped to talk had very simple questions. After an hour, Theo produced some statistics on his tablet about what we'd done:

Pointed out the way to the admin building when people asked for the accommodation tour – 45

Answered questions about local amenities (supermarkets, bus routes etc.) – 27

Answered questions about ancient Greece or Rome – 1

The last one was an easy question too: someone had heard about the reassembled mosaic and wanted to know where it could be viewed. I showed them how to get there on a map (even though it was just across from where we were standing) and told them that it had taken seven weeks to assemble from fifteen thousand pieces that had been found in a midden heap.

"What's a midden heap?" asked a gangly teenager who'd stopped. His father stood next to him and frowned.

"Well, Jordan? If you don't know, perhaps the young lady will tell you?"

I looked at Jordan and saw the same panic in his eyes as was surely showing in mine.

"Think of today as your opportunity to ask the experts, Jordan," I said. "Save your history questions until you see the display. The staff in there are very knowledgeable. There's a buffet in there too. I'm here for any practical questions you might have."

I dodged a bullet there, and Theo was polite enough not to mention it until a few minutes later.

"A midden heap's an old-fashioned word for a rubbish dump," he said.

"You just looked that up," I said.

He turned his tablet to me to show me that he'd done no such thing. He was apparently watching YouTube clips, all with dull titles like "Travels in the Sub-Sahara", "Living with Druids in 21st Century Cornwall" and "Exploring the Giant's Causeway".

"Archaeologists love midden heaps," he said.

"Because...?"

"Because if you look at the things that people throw away, you can tell a lot about them."

I thought for a moment about what a future archaeologist might discover from the things that I threw out. They would have a tough job fathoming the system imposed by Bernadette, so they'd probably deduce (and this wouldn't necessarily be inaccurate) that much of what I spent my time doing was drinking wine.

Gangly Jordan and his dad strolled up again a little later.

"Did you discover what a midden heap was?" I asked.

Jordan was about to answer but the father cut in. "Actually, we want to ask you about how you manage your budget as a student."

Another family had stopped by at that moment. "I'd like to know about that as well," said the mom, a lady with bright red hair.

"Getting a degree seems so expensive these days," said another woman.

"I think you've got to ask yourself whether it's worth them studying a subject like history when it's never going to help you get a job that makes any money," said Jordan's dad to the red-haired mom. "Same as art and all of those impractical subjects."

"I studied art," I said.

Jordan's dad looked me up and down, as though I was evidence of poor academic choices.

"And I'm working as an artist now," I said proudly.

"How unusual to make a living wage from art," said the red-haired mom, looking at me as though I was in a cage at Crufts.

"Oh, I don't," I said. "I work as a cleaner, and I live in my brother's flat."

Jordan gave me an amiable shrug, like he thought that was cool but his dad just rolled his eyes.

"A waste of resources then," he said.

Another mother nodded in agreement. "Education has to serve a purpose."

"Educating people who just fritter their lives away," said Jordan's dad. "That's the problem with this generation."

"You're certainly going to struggle to get your foot on the property ladder," agreed the red-haired mom.

"I don't suppose you've even given that any thought, have you, young lady?"

I looked at him and felt so sorry for Jordan. If Jordan had been in to see James he'd be all fired up about studying history. His dad probably wanted him to be an investment banker or something.

"I think," I said carefully. I had paused for a second or two, thinking of the advice that James had given me, "that it's all about priorities."

"What? That you don't have any?"

"Oh, I do. It's just my priorities in life are *not* the same as your priorities in life."

I smiled at him. I often find that smiling brightly at people will disarm them when they're getting angry with me, and it seemed to work with Jordan's dad. He looked confused and pulled Jordan away. Jordan caught my eye as he went and I winked at him.

The red-haired woman remained, and she propelled her daughter forwards. "Tell me – be honest – do you regret doing that, if you're forced to work as a cleaner and rely on relatives?"

"Gosh, no. I love art. I loved studying my art degree. True, it's left me with a mountain of debt and hasn't helped me get a single job but –"

"It sounds dreadful. Don't you wish that you'd made better use of your time? Maybe tried a little bit harder at the academic subjects?"

"No. No regrets. I love being an artist. Why wouldn't you do what you love if you possibly can?"

The woman made a small noise of dismissal and walked away. I heard her addressing her daughter as she went.

"You can't afford to be a dreamer, Georgia. Honestly, I really don't think that young people know what hard work is!"

I held my head high and tried really hard to look like a role model, but Theo was tugging my arm.

"What's that?" he asked.

I turned to look where he was pointing. I knew straightaway what I was looking at, but the words wouldn't come. I'm not sure whether I didn't trust myself to explain to Theo without a hefty dose of age-inappropriate swearing, or whether the sheer horror of the spectacle had robbed me of speech. If I had been capable of speaking, I might have said something like this:

"That, Theo, is my ex-boyfriend Ashbert, who I stupidly mentioned the phrase 'knight in shining armour' to recently. So obviously, he has taken it into his numbskull brain to pinch a suit of armour from somewhere and get onto a noble steed. Except maybe he had trouble finding an actual horse, because that looks like a big fat donkey to me. Oh, and those people? Yeah, he's herding a crowd of pensioners in front of him. I don't know why."

I didn't say any of that. I made a squeaking sound that represented my indecision.

I defy anyone to do better when their ideal man (brought to life through the power of an ancient Minoan pendant) turns up unexpectedly in shiny plate armour riding a scruffy grey donkey with the probable intention of re-winning their heart. I bet it's the kind of thing that agony aunts have to deal with all the time.

Should I run away and pretend not to have seen Ashbert? Should I yell at him and try to make him go away? The decision was taken out of my hands when Ashbert spotted me and came over with a wave. Theo looked on in astonishment as the donkey trudged over, Ashbert's armour clanking as it moved. I dread to think where he got that armour from. I don't think it came from a fancy dress shop. It looked worryingly... authentic.

The pensioner army milled around, not quite sure where it was supposed to go. There must have been thirty or forty of them! Had he hijacked a coach?

"Lori!" he shouted in a bold and knightly voice.

"Oh, God," I warbled, stunned.

"I am your knight in shining armour!"

"A knight in shining armour," I said quickly for the benefit of any prospective students and their parents who might be passing. "Not mine. Not mine. Nothing to do with me."

"And I've brought some people who might be your parents!" he said and slid off the donkey. The weight of the armour made him over-balance and he toppled to the floor with a noise like the John Lewis saucepan department falling down the stairs. The noise spooked the donkey, which ran off with an excited braying sound.

Now I was really torn. So many things demanded my attention. Should I send Theo to warn his dad about the pensioner invasion? Should I explain to Ashbert how wrong this entire thing really was? I decided that the one thing that I couldn't ignore was the donkey running up the steps into the Fondant Fancy-shaped Arts building.

"Come on Theo, we need to catch that donkey!" I yelled, and gave chase. I should have realised that Theo would be able to run a lot faster than me. What I didn't necessarily expect was that Theo would find the whole donkey-chasing thing enormous fun. He whooped with excitement and yelled "Dad, Dad! Lori's chasing a donkey and it's heading your way!"

I wasn't as speedy as Theo, but I wasted no time getting into the entrance hall. It was crowded, probably because of the buffet, and I think that might have excited the donkey even more. It charged over to the buffet table and knocked it straight over. Maybe that was deliberate, because it carefully sought out the doughnuts and started to eat them from the floor. There were so many people yelling by now that it flicked its ears in annoyance and backed away. It clattered over to the roped-off area.

"No, donkey, not that!" I whispered to myself, but it seemed inevitable. It knocked two of the Roman pots off their stands, and they made such a loud noise as they broke on the floor that the donkey did two things at one. It released copious amounts of poo onto the floor and it backed into the glass case that held the reassembled mosaic. As the entire thing was tipped over in an avalanche of broken glass and tiles, the donkey decided that it had had enough and left the hall.

I was about to give chase but James was in front of me. His face was ashen as he looked at the wreckage. He tore his eyes away to look at me.

"What did you do?" he said.

"Well, I saw the donkey run in here. You see, it's a funny story." His face was stony. "Not a funny story," I corrected myself. "You see, I told Ashbert I thought I needed a knight in shining armour and he took it literally and –"

"Ex-boyfriend Ashbert?"

"Yes. Except he couldn't find a magnificent white stallion or whatever. So, he went and got himself the next best thing. I mean, I've not even got any idea where you'd get a donkey from in a city like this."

"You did this."

"What?" I blinked. "I didn't."

"Ashbert did it to impress you."

"Yes."

He shook his head. He looked like he was going to be sick. "Lori, it's always you at the centre of the wreckage, isn't it?"

I couldn't argue with that. "I – I'm sorry James. I need to go and sort things out."

I ran outside. James would never forgive me for this.

Chapter 35

The donkey had calmed down when it got back outside and was being fussed over by several of the pensioners. One of the women was wearing a hat made out of something that looked like woven grass. The donkey must have thought that it looked tasty because it nibbled the edge while she stood talking to someone, oblivious to the damage. I'd grabbed a section of the rope that had kept crowds away from the display inside. It was clearly not going to be needed any time soon in there, and maybe I could lead the donkey with it. I had no idea of how to use it though. Should I try and make a lasso?

I found Ashbert struggling with the armour, which looked as though it had been made for someone a few sizes smaller. His fall from the donkey had apparently crimped one of the thigh pieces tight onto his leg, so he walked with a very exaggerated limp.

"Ashbert, I want to make something very clear," I said. "This was a terrible idea and I am very angry. I don't want to see you again. Seriously."

He looked at me with the sorrowful eyes, but I wasn't going to be drawn in. "Did you see your parents amongst these people?" he asked, waving an arm across the lawn full of old people.

"No Ashbert! You've brought a whole load of old people over here for no good reason. Why would you even do that?"

"He mentioned a free buffet and a nice cup of tea, dear," said a voice to my side. I turned to look at an old guy with a walking stick who smiled benevolently at me. "He didn't mention the entertainment, though. That was a bonus!"

I scrabbled in my pocket for some money. "Listen Ashbert, I want you to take these people, buy them all a cup of tea and send them home. I'll find something to do with the donkey."

I handed him the money and he went off to speak with some of the oldies. The guy with the walking stick made a thoughtful noise and I looked at him.

"If I might make a suggestion?" he said.

"Go on."

"Well, you can get onto the canal up by the railway station. I'd imagine that you could lead a donkey out of the city to somewhere nice and quiet along the towpath. There were lots of fields there, back in my day. You certainly don't want to expose this poor fellow to traffic, do you?"

He had a point. I sighed and nodded.

Theo appeared at that moment.

"Hi Theo," I said. "Is your dad really cross?"

He nodded. "There are lots of people shouting in there. He sent me outside. Said I'm to keep out of the way while he sorts the mess out."

"Well, do you want to help me with the donkey?" I asked.

"Yeah!" he said, brightening.

"Any idea how to make a lasso?" I asked.

Theo came up with a much better idea than a lasso. He asked the lady with the enticingly grassy hat if we could borrow it, and then, using that, he led the donkey over to me. It stood munching patiently while I tied the rope to its leather-nose-bracelet thing.

"So, the plan is to take a little walk up to the canal and find a field to put it in, somewhere along the towpath," I said.

The owner of the hat had disappeared, along with the other pensioners, so Theo put the hat on the donkey's head. It gave it a rather rakish look, as if it might break into a tap-dancing routine at any moment.

We walked towards the station, and the donkey behaved itself beautifully. Theo walked alongside, making low noises of encouragement, and the donkey really seemed to be listening to him. Up ahead was Jordan and his dad. Jordan smiled at me, but his dad scowled, presumably because I was the face of the useless, sponging layabout that he feared his son might become.

"Is this another attempt to make ends meet?" he asked. "Donkey rides for children?"

I turned to face him. "No, I'm doing a favour for a friend. Listen, why are you so determined that Jordan should be a high earner? Have you even asked him what he wants from his life?"

The father laughed at me. "What an absurd non-sequitur! Jordan and I have had many a conversation about his career, but of course it's a given that he needs a certain level of salary. Only an idiot would think otherwise. How else will he pay back his student loan and afford to buy a house?"

A glance at Jordan told me all I needed to know about the dynamic here. I pushed a little further. "What if Jordan doesn't want to buy a house? Plenty of people don't."

The father rolled his eyes and made an exasperated gasp. "Of course, plenty of people don't. They're called poor people and I want something better for my son than that."

"Well technically I'm a poor person," I said, "but I'm very happy, and I've got my life together rather well, I'd say."

My moment of smug contemplation was cut short as I glanced to my side and saw Theo struggling with the donkey some distance away. It had gone up the ramp of a lorry and didn't seem to want to turn around.

"Must go," I said to Jordan and his father, and ran to help but I was too slow. At that moment, a man appeared behind the lorry. He pushed the ramp back into its slot and slammed the doors shut, somehow failing to notice the boy and the donkey that he'd trapped inside.

I ran as quickly as I could and yelled loudly, but the vehicle pulled away before I could get to it. I looked around. Was there something I could do, something I could throw? Anything to get the attention of the driver? A car pulled into the kerb and a woman got out to greet Jordan and his dad. I didn't hesitate. Theo needed my help. I nipped into the driver's door and slammed it shut. I got the car into gear, checked my mirror and pulled out smoothly. Driving instructor Terence would have been so impressed at my speed as I managed to ignore the distracting shouting as well. I followed the lorry and tooted the horn. As soon as I found out how to operate the lights, I flashed the lights as well, but the driver was completely oblivious, or maybe it happened to him all the time and he was just ignoring me. My initial thought that I would just borrow this car to catch up with the lorry and then return it promptly to Jordan's family went out of the window. It looked as though I'd have to follow the van to wherever it was going.

It took about thirty minutes to get where it was going – thirty minutes of me driving solo for the first time ever, accompanied by the imagined voice of Terence pointing out his views of why replacing the roundabouts with traffic lights was EU bureaucracy gone mad and reminiscing about a mythical time when this whole area resounded to the hammers and drills of good old British manufacturing industry. It felt a lot longer. Not just because even pretend-Terence was deathly dull but because I was worrying about Theo. It wasn't just James' kid in the back of that lorry. It was a good kid, who might have been smarter than Google, but was still a ten-year-old kid trapped in the dark with a donkey.

The lorry pulled into a yard behind a vast building. A warehouse, perhaps? I followed in the car and then got out when I saw the vehicle reverse up towards a door marked *Bay Six*. I walked towards the van as the driver got out and opened the rear doors. The floor of the trailer was level with the warehouse floor, so I had to clamber up to get to the back of it. As I did, I saw the donkey bolt into the warehouse. The driver turned to watch the departing donkey in bewilderment and managed a shout of "Oi!" but completely failed to do anything practical. Evidently, he hadn't noticed Theo, who now emerged from the van behind him.

I hugged him tightly.

"It's okay," I said. "You're safe now."

He pulled away.

"No time for hugs, Lori," he said very seriously. "We need to find Beyoncé."

"Oh, it's got a name now?" I said, following him into the warehouse.

"You can't go in there!" shouted the driver, but we ignored him and continued.

High shelving units rose up around us. Much of the warehouse was dark, but lights came on as we came into their range. We trotted through the aisles until we saw a curtain of opaque plastic ahead of us. It looked like daylight beyond the curtain.

"Do you think Beyoncé's gone through there?" asked Theo.

"How do you know it's even a girl?" I asked.

"I can tell the difference between boys and girls, Lori."

We pushed through the curtain and I was very surprised to see that we were in a shop.

"I've been here," said Theo.

254

"Is this IKEA?" I said.

"I can smell meatballs," he nodded. "Do donkeys like meatballs?"

I hesitated and stared at an array of modernist, eco-friendly, Scandawegian office furniture. This could be one of those situations where I got into trouble for something that was entirely not my fault.

"Are you worried that you let a donkey loose in IKEA?" asked Theo.

"No," I lied. "I think we need to find customer services."

Theo had already connected to the shop Wi-Fi and brought up a map. "This way," he said.

"We're looking for a donkey," I said to the customer services woman, feeling slightly absurd.

The assistant smiled brightly. "I'd be happy to help. What department is that?"

"Um. It's a donkey."

"Is Dünki a light fitting?"

"No."

"Ah. Are you sure?"

"Fairly."

"Perhaps you'd like to check our current range in the catalogue? Page ninety-four."

She handed me a catalogue. My mouth worked as I tried to frame a suitable response. "No. I mean an *actual* donkey. You know, a beast of burden?"

"Oh!" Her face lit up. "That's fine."

Fine?"

"Yes, the Börden range of drawers. You can see those over in storage. Last aisle on the left over there."

I looked at Theo and he shrugged.

"I don't think they understand," he said. "It's too big a concept for them to understand."

We walked away from the desk.

"Maybe she didn't come out here," he said. "She might still be in the warehouse."

We headed back over to the plastic curtain and managed to slip through undetected.

"We need to get up high so we can see," said Theo. "We can use that."

He pointed and we walked over. It was a curious looking apparatus, and it had a sign on it: *Wear hard hat to operate scissor lift.*

"We need hard hats," I said, remembering I was the responsible adult.

We found some hanging nearby so that made it fine. We climbed onto the little fenced-off platform of the scissor lift. There were controls on a small panel, and after some experimentation we hit *platform* and found that the joystick worked for taking us up.

"This is brilliant!" yelled Theo when we were towering above the racks. "There, look!"

He pointed and I could see Beyoncé, her hat clearly visible as she nuzzled a pile of rugs on the shelving.

"Why did you call her Beyoncé?" I asked.

Theo went a little pink and mumbled something.

"What was that?" I said.

"Big fat ass," he said, shamefaced.

I was aghast. "Beyoncé isn't a big fat ass! She's a strong, independent and successful woman."

"No," said Theo, "I'm not saying she *is* a big fat ass. I'm saying she *has* – Down! Down! You're going to miss her."

Theo pressed my hand forward on the joystick and we descended at speed to meet Beyoncé. I jumped out. Moments later, Beyoncé was back under our control. We briefly discussed the best way to get out.

"The loading bay was too high off the ground. Beyoncé can't jump down that far," said Theo.

He was right. "Well, we'll just have to take her out through the shop," I said. "We'll brazen it out."

We passed through the plastic curtain again and stepped out into the shop. We hurried past the lady on customer services, trying not to make eye contact, and then looked to see which was the quickest way out.

Ten minutes later, I was certain we'd done a lap of the entire building, but we were no closer to finding the exit. Everyone had stared at us. A little girl had pointed at the donkey and demanded to know where she could get one.

"Look in the catalogue," I told her. "Page ninety-four."

An employee approached us. He looked about my age, and I could tell he wanted to challenge us, but wasn't quite sure what to say.

"You have a donkey," he went with in the end.

"Yes."

He frowned. "Animals aren't allowed in the shop." He pointed at a sign on an access door with a line through a picture of a dog.

"This isn't a dog," I said.

"Same difference," he said. "Only assistance dogs are allowed in the shop."

"This is an assistance donkey."

He frowned more deeply. "How?"

"She suffers from a complex socio-neurological condition which makes her very gullible," said Theo.

"Does she?" said the man.

"Yes," said Theo.

"Oh, I see."

"We're trying to find our way out," I said. "We've just been going round in circles."

"Ah yes," he said. "Go down there." He pointed at a shadowy gap between fixtures. Surely it wasn't meant to be the way to the exit? We led Beyoncé into the unlikely gap and found that it was some sort of secret passage that brought us out by the tills.

We were trapped behind a bank of tills, but a manager appeared from somewhere and had the presence of mind to open up a barrier to let us out.

"Lori," hissed Theo out of the corner of his mouth.

"Keep walking," I said.

"Beyoncé's just done a poo on the floor."

"Shh. Just keep walking."

Moments later we were back out in the daylight, although grey clouds had appeared, threatening rain.

"Wow, am I glad to be out of there," I breathed. "Now all we have to do is find somewhere to put Beyoncé. We should call your dad."

I pulled out my phone. "No signal," I said. "Actually, that might be a good thing. It means we're out in the sticks, so a nice field can't be all that far away."

I patted Beyoncé's neck and led her on, heading away from the crowds of people. Were they taking video on their phones? Maybe they'd never seen a donkey before.

We walked for a few minutes, and it was still busy. There were roads, people and noise. Everything to make a donkey jumpy. And it was starting to drizzle.

"We need to make sure we can keep her calm," Theo said. "Shall we sing to her?"

I nodded. "What song will we both know though?"

Theo ran through some titles that meant nothing to me. I tried him out with some McFly, but he had no idea who they were. It eventually came down to a choice between *The Wheels on the Bus* or *All Things Bright and Beautiful*. We went with *The Wheels on the Bus*. Theo had some sketchy Wi-Fi on his tablet and we streamed a video to sing along to. We did all the movements as well. I could tell that Beyoncé was enjoying it. I even think that her hat was bobbing in time.

We didn't spot any fields, but we did see a gate that led to a lovely green space. The padlock was unlocked so we opened the gate and led Beyoncé inside. It was allotments, and Beyoncé showed a lively interest in the rows of vegetables. We shut the gate behind us and let her go and explore. The rain started to fall in fat droplets.

"We're going to get wet," said Theo. "And we don't have coats."

There was a shed off to the side. It was gloomy inside – the windows were covered in a century's worth of cobwebs – but there was the faint smell of wood preserver that reminded me of home and the shed that my dad had in our old garden.

"It's fun spending time with you, Lori," observed Theo, settling into a deckchair.

"Thank you," I said.

"You always end up doing stupid things," observed Theo.

Was that a compliment? I think it was. I decided I would take it as one. I took the other deckchair and sat down. This was a cosy shed. There was a table, where someone had been reading the newspaper, and a kettle and mugs.

"Things have been a little bit crazy just lately," I said. "I don't bring trouble into my life on purpose, it just tends to turn up."

He nodded as if he understood. I wished I did.

While we waited for the rain to stop, Theo and I entertained ourselves by playing a game that we made up called *Garden plant as medieval torture*. It was a fun game, fuelled by a plant catalogue that was in the shed. We'd worked our way through the obvious ones like Red Hot Poker and Ladies Fingers.

"Right, you can do Needle Grass," I said to Theo, flicking through the pages.

"Hm. That would be an experiment to see how many needles they need to put under your feet before it supports your weight rather than just piercing your skin."

"Ew," I said. "How many do you think?"

"Loads," he said. "Hundreds. But if they started with just a few then your feet would look like mincemeat after a few goes anyway."

"My turn," I said, handing him the catalogue.

"Balloon flower," said Theo.

"Oh. Easy. That's where they put a bicycle pump up your bottom and inflate your intestines until they –"

"You can't have a bicycle pump, it's medieval remember? You'd have to use bellows."

"Bellows then. Anyway, they inflate your intestines until they explode."

"Gross!" said Theo with a delighted laugh. "Would that make a mess?"

"Oh yes, I reckon so."

I wondered whether this had been the educational diversion that I'd hoped for as Theo mimed the explosive *ka-pow* from his bottom that would shoot him into orbit.

"Are you hungry?" I said.

"Yes."

"Me too."

"When do you think we'll be able to get back home?"

I thought about that. I wasn't terribly sure where we actually were if I was honest.

"When it's stopped raining we'll take a look round. I think Beyoncé will be alright here. Allotment people must be kind people. They'll know what to do with a donkey. We should concentrate on getting you home."

If only I had some food with me, that would make us both feel a lot better. A thought occurred to me. I pushed it away but it popped back again. I picked up the newspaper. It was one of the fat ones with colour supplements to cover every kind of interest. I flicked open the foodie bit and soon found a picture of a pie. It looked mouth-wateringly good. Food porn. I've never understood it. Why show enticing pictures of something that people can't reach into the image and just take?

"Theo," I said slowly, "I'm going to share something unusual with you. Don't be scared because it's –" I ran out of steam on that one. Was it normal or harmless? Who knew? "What I mean to say is, just don't freak out. Watch this."

I held the pendant and pointed at the pie in the magazine. It popped into existence, as I knew it would. Warm chickeny gravy and succulent vegetables dribbled over the pages. The waft of hot golden pastry filled my nostrils. Theo's face was a conflict of shock and delight. I could see that delight (and possibly hunger) had the upper hand as he wasted no time in taking the pie and tucking into it. I repeated the trick on the next page so that I had some pie for myself.

"I don't know how it works," I said to him between mouthfuls, "but I do know that I need to be careful about using it too much. This was an emergency though."

Theo shrugged and carried on eating.

I brushed crumbs and gravy from the colour supplement and turned over the page. My hand froze with the pie halfway to my mouth. There was a picture of me. I looked at the title of the piece. It was *Look out! The Snowflakes are coming!*

"Fucksticks!" I exclaimed.

"Lori!" shouted Theo.

I waved him into silence and stared at the article. It went on for three pages, but my eye was drawn to a quote that had been pulled out into a highlighted box.

"*I hadn't really mastered true adulting*" *says Lori, pictured here wondering how to use a cup.*

Oh. That wasn't fair. I went back and read the opening paragraph.

We all know someone who's a bit hopeless, don't we? Someone who struggles with the basic building blocks of life? Well, we need to look out because there's an entire generation growing up without any of the key skills needed for survival. We're talking about the simplest of tasks including managing money and preparing food. Millennials are so hopelessly ill-equipped that "adulting" is now an accepted verb, used by clueless millennials who master something that previous generations would have taken for granted.

This week I caught up with Lori Belkin, who has muddled through to the ripe old age of twenty-five purely by luck! She has no money, believes that her cartoon blog is her route to success, and in the meantime, is stealing food to survive.

I closed the magazine. That horrible man was not only trying to make me look bad, but he was saying that all young people were as useless as me! It made me sad to realise that I had walked into all of the traps that James had warned me about.

Chapter 36

I pulled out my phone to see if there was any signal here. There wasn't, but there were a lot of missed calls from James.

"Your dad's been trying to get in touch," I said to Theo. "You don't happen to have a phone, do you?"

He shook his head. "I'm connected to a local hotspot though. You can message him."

He passed the tablet over. I went to the home screen and was about to click on the messenger icon when my eye was caught by a folder of links: *Mom's videos*.

I shouldn't have. This was Theo's tablet, his personal tablet. But it was just a tap of the finger and my finger-brain was doing it before my actual brain told it not to. The folder opened.

It was just full of YouTube video links. I recognised a couple of the titles from Theo's video browsing earlier. My fingertip hovered over "Travels in the Sub-Sahara".

"Found it?" said Theo and leaned over, past the donkey's neck. "Oh."

"Sorry," I said automatically. "I didn't mean to. I mean I saw it and..."

"It's okay," he said, but there was a sad tone in his voice. "Look at this one."

He tapped one called "Schools in Sudan". When the app opened it played a promotional video for a worldwide education charity. Theo dragged the timer bar to about halfway through. The video cut from a white-washed concrete school building to a large group of children sitting in the shade of a tree. They were singing a song and clapping along and a white woman with a tan that was fifty percent freckles and fifty percent sunburn was playing along on a guitar, trying to keep time.

"That's one of the good ones," said Theo. "She's in it for quite a bit. Some of them, she's just a face in the background. She looks happy, doesn't she? Do you think she looks happy?"

I couldn't look at Theo's face. I think if I did I would have burst into tears.

"I think she looks happy," said Theo.

"She does," I agreed softly and then, "I didn't mean to pry."

"You're not prying," he said. "They're public videos. Anyone can watch them."

I nodded. "How long has it been since you've actually seen her."

"I don't remember," he said. "It's been a long time. She's very busy and she's helping lots of people. All the things she's achieved."

I felt a sudden anger swell inside me. I think if that woman had appeared in the shed right then, I would have beaten her senseless. The selfishness of it all. To put aside all the good she had in her life – this wonderful boy and his possibly equally wonderful dad – in order to go explore the world, tick a few things of a pointless bucket list, swim with the fucking dolphins or whatever.

"We need to get you back to your dad," I said, minimized the YouTube and went to the messenger app.

Dad was one of half a dozen contacts. James picked up instantly.

"Theo?" he said on speaker.

"Hi Dad," said Theo.

"I'm here too," I said. "It's Lori."

"Lori? Where are you?"

I looked round. "Um, we're in some sort of shed which –"

"But Theo's okay? He's safe?"

"Yes, he's here with me and we're fine," I said, slightly taken aback at James' panicked tone. "What's the matter?"

"What's the matter?! Are you kidding me? I've been frantic!"

I checked the time. It had been about two hours since I'd seen James. Okay, it was a bit of a long time to go without seeing his son, but he knew Theo was with me.

"We've been absolutely fine," I said.

"Are you serious, Lori? You're all over the news and the internet!"

"What?"

"There's a video of a woman, donkey and child running riot in IKEA. I've lost count of the number of people who've sent it to me saying it looks like Theo."

"To be fair, we weren't running riot. We were just trying to find the way out," I said.

"God damn it, Lori! There's CCTV of the two of you joyriding in a scissor lift."

"We weren't joyri–"

"Did you not realise how dangerous that was?"

"But we wore hard hats," I said in a small voice. James sounded properly angry.

"Wearing a hard hat does not excuse doing something so irresponsible!" he yelled down the line.

I was about to say that it was Theo's idea, but that was not the answer that an adult would have given so I kept my mouth shut.

"Where are you now?" he asked.

"Well," I said, looking round for clues. "We're in some allotments, not far from a big IKEA shop. I don't know which one."

"I do! I've seen the bloody videos. I'm on my way to get Theo. Don't go anywhere else," said James and hung up.

I put the tablet down by my bag and we waited like naughty kids outside the head teacher's office until James arrived. I was filled with guilt and shame but I was also angry, with James and myself. James didn't realise that this situation was not my fault. But Theo was right: things always went wrong when I was around.

"Here he comes," said Theo peering out the window.

I stood and opened the door, my heart heavy, like I was stepping up to the gallows. James barely looked at me, almost pushed past me to get to Theo. He grabbed his son and held him tight.

"Are you all right?"

"Yes."

"Did you get hurt?"

"No."

"Did anything... bad happen?"

Theo looked at me and then at the sticky pages of the colour supplement from which I had magicked some pie.

"No?"

"Did it?" demanded James.

"No."

"And you're all right?"

"Yes, Dad. Stop worrying. Lori's looked after me. She really has."

James threw me a look. He might as well have punched me. It was a look that said "This woman? Look after you?" I was lower than an idiot. James' look wasn't a look of hatred but it contained such deep, dark and compounded disappointment that there wasn't much difference.

"We need to go, Theo," he said.

"Is Lori coming as well?" asked Theo.

"I think that Lori can make her own way back," said James. "Don't you?"

I didn't know what to say to that but Theo leapt to my defence, bless him.

"No, Dad. We need to give her a lift. Lori's looked after me really well. She even made me some pie with her magic pendant. It brings things to life!"

Oh no. Of all the conversations that I really didn't want to get into just now... but James just rolled his eyes and looked even more scornful that before, if that was possible.

"Lori's mental health is questionable at the best of times, so don't go believing everything that she tells you Theo."

James steered Theo towards the door.

"James," I said.

"What is it, Lori?" he said in a dead tone.

I didn't know what I could say. I held up the magazine article from the table.

"You were right about the journalist."

"Oh?"

"Everything I said and did looks ridiculous in this article."

James raised an eyebrow and looked as if he was about to say something, but he just shook his head instead, as if nothing was a surprise to him.

He and Theo left the shed and I just sat there for a little while longer, wondering how I could have messed up so badly when I was only trying to help.

Chapter 37

I got back to the museum in time to work my shift. It was a close-run thing. It occurred to me that I could hitch a ride in the back of a lorry again, but it turns out that not all drivers are as oblivious as the one that took Theo and the donkey, so I had a couple of awkward conversations. The second driver (the one who found me hiding behind a fridge in his van) wanted to know why I hadn't just asked him for a lift. I shrugged, as I didn't actually have a good answer for that. He let me get into the cab with him. The fridge was going to the city centre, so after twenty-five minutes of conversation about football transfers, where my contribution was mostly 'oh yes?' and 'how much?' he dropped me off near the museum.

I really wanted to catch up with Cookie and talk through some of the things that had happened in the last day or so, but Rex came in as I was getting my trolley ready.

"A word, Miss Belkin," he said. "My office."

I followed him into his office. I still wasn't sure if this was the place where the oldest office furniture in the world came to die, or whether he deliberately selected these things. Actually, I thought that maybe he'd bought them when they were new, and they were all automatically antiques like him.

He sat at his desk and indicated that I should sit opposite. The electrical cabinet on the wall crackled in greeting as I sat.

"This is just like my interview, isn't it?" I said. "Doesn't it take you back?"

He didn't smile. He pulled something towards him across the desk and with dismay I saw that it was Chorley Danglespear's article.

"We would very much like you to explain this," he said, "specifically, this extract. *'I had no money to buy food when I started work as a cleaner, so I came up with the idea of stealing food in the cafe. I'd wait until someone was eating something that I liked the look of and then I'd try to take it off them before they'd finished or I'd try to persuade them that they didn't really want it.'*"

He looked up at me. It was not a happy look on his beardy face.

"That journalist tricked me," I said. "I didn't even say some of those things. Not in that way, anyway."

"Are you denying that you took food from our customers, Miss Belkin?"

I couldn't deny it. I hesitated briefly, wondering if there was anything I might say that would persuade Rex that what I'd done wasn't as bad as the article made it sound, but I knew that it was beyond my powers. Rex had a naturally unhappy face, but his mouth and jowls drooped so much that he looked like a bloodhound with a mouthful of billiard balls.

"You leave me no choice, Miss Belkin," he said. "We must protect the reputation of the museum, and the welfare of our customers. You will be aware that you're still in your probationary period, so we can dismiss you without notice."

I couldn't believe what I was hearing.

"Am I getting the sack?"

"Yes, you are," said Rex.

"But, wait! Surely, we can talk about this? What if I say sorry? I mean, I *am* sorry."

He shook his head. "No, I'm afraid not. Even if I were inclined to overlook such a thing, and I am not, this article has caught the attention of many people. I even received a phone call from the vice-chancellor demanding to know what I was doing to rectify the situation."

Vice-chancellor! Bernadette Bloody Brampton. This was her doing!

I stopped myself. No. Bernadette might have spoken to Rex but this wasn't her fault. I was being sacked because I made the museum look bad and I made Rex look bad. There was nothing I could do.

"Can I keep my cleaning trolley?" I asked.

"No, of course you can't," said Rex, his brow creasing in confusion.

"Can I just keep one of the cloths then? A microfibre one maybe?"

"No! You are dismissed and you are to leave the premises now, Miss Belkin. You will not be taking anything with you."

"Can I go and see Cookie?" I asked.

"Cookie?"

"Melissa. She works here too."

"And at least she does work," said Rex, "which is clearly more than you ever did. No, she's working. You can cry on her shoulder when her shift's ended. Now, leave. Or do I have to call security?"

The electrical cupboard sparked and rattled as though it too was warning me. Rex opened the door and walked me to the main entrance, making sure I went. I felt like a criminal, which is probably what he intended. It was quite a relief when I left the building and walked away. I'm fairly sure that he stood there for a minute, to make sure I didn't make a last-minute dash back inside for my microfibre cloth. I didn't look back, I walked away, trying to remind myself that I never really wanted his stupid job in the first place.

When I got back to Adam's flat, it was eerily quiet. Ashbert had gone. I had told him to leave and he had done it.

It should have been a relief and, I suppose, it was. But it left me feeling weirdly alone. I had no job, no boyfriend and everyone who'd read that horrible article written by Chorley Danglespear thought that I was a useless snowflake.

"Am I a useless snowflake?" I asked the trilobites as I fed them some worms created by the pendant.

"Using natural language processing to analyse previous speech patterns against the criteria of 'useless' and 'snowflake'," said Lexi.

Oh. I really wasn't sure I wanted to hear this.

"No, Lexi. I wasn't talking to you."

Lexi fell silent. I watched the trilobites eating and tried to find some comfort in their simple pleasure. It was no good.

"Lexi?" I said.

"Yes."

"Am I a useless snowflake?"

"Useless. Having no ability or skill in a specified area," announced Lexi. "Analysis of your previous speech patterns suggests an eighty percent likelihood that you are useless."

"Cheers Lexi," I started.

"Snowflake. The colloquial term for a young generation with a lack of resilience," she said. "Analysis of your previous speech patterns suggests a seventy per cent chance that you are a snowflake. Conclusion: there is a fifty-six percent chance that you are both useless and a snowflake."

"Great."

Chapter 38

How I envied the trilobites their simple lifestyle. In their custom-made environment, with a constant supply of worms, they had a worry-free existence. I wondered what my own version of their ring-fenced idyll might look like. A place where I had everything I needed. Food would appear when I needed it and I'd have a comfy room to relax in. I realised with a jolt that I was picturing my old room in my parents' house. I stopped myself, knowing that I couldn't go back to that, even though it was tempting to daydream.

"What would you do, guys? You know, if you were in my shoes?"

Dougie scuttled away from the others and hid underneath a stone. I could see his legs, so it was a pretty rubbish attempt at hiding, but I knew exactly where he was coming from.

"You have a good point Dougie. If you hide from the world, will it leave you alone? I'm not sure. It's got to be worth a try though. The trouble is, I seem to leave a trail of destruction, so everyone knows where I've been."

The trilobite enclosure was in Adam's spare room which had been spared the more extensive damage, if you overlooked the enormous walk-in bath filled with soil. I walked through into the lounge where sooty stains and scorched soft furnishings were in plentiful supply. Could I fix some of the damage I'd done? It's what an adult would do.

I made a list.

Clean Adam's flat as much as I possibly can
Find Jed the taxi driver and pay him the money that I owe him
Check that Beyoncé is all right

I managed to find some tweets relating to Beyoncé's continued adventures. She was in the care of a sanctuary, and there was even a picture of her munching on some hay. I smiled to see that she still wore the hat.

I called Jed, using Bernadette's name. When he turned up fifteen minutes later, I went out, wearing the pea green hoody. I pulled it over my face and affected a low gravelly voice.

"This money is from Lori Belkin. She owes you the fare from the day that she came back from her holiday."

Jed took the money, and I could feel him staring, so I made the rookie error of peeking.

"Your voice has gone all weird," he said. "Did you eat that dodgy sausage or something?"

So much for my undercover skills.

Back in Adam's flat, it was time to tackle the mess.

"Lexi, I need some help with household cleaning and maintenance. Let's start with the cushions. Can I wash them?"

"You can wash most cushions at a low temperature. Air dry and re-shape by hand. Put the cushion filler into an old pillowcase when you wash it, to prevent a messy leak."

"Oh." That sounded doable. I would make a start on erasing evidence of my stupidity. I gathered up the cushions, releasing new wafts of that appalling kipper-stink and went to find some pillow cases.

An hour later, after making myself a bit seasick watching the cushions going round in the washing machine, I got Adam's cleaning supplies and applied everything I'd learned in my short time as a professional cleaner to making his flat more habitable. Cookie and I had once spent an entire break arguing about whether it was better to sweep then dust or dust then sweep. Cookie said that the universe gave us the gift of gravity and that we should always work with it. Start with the dusting and everything would end up on the floor, ready for sweeping. It's hard to fault Cookie's logic, but I find myself troubled by the cloud of dust that appears when you sweep vigorously. It dirties the surfaces you've just dusted. It remains an unknowable mystery and a subject for future debate.

Adam's flat was so heavily soiled with soot, ash and lumps of unidentifiable grunge, that I decided to compromise with a dust-sweep-dust approach. It would take longer, but the research would be valuable. Cookie was sure to be interested. First, I had to move all of the clutter, so I picked up the shoes, cups and mysterious objects. The concept of the mysterious object belongs to my mom. Whenever she had to clean the house, she would always amass a pile of mysterious objects. We had to go through them as a family and either claim them or figure out what they were.

"Is it the thing that holds the bread bag closed?"

"I think it's the thing for getting the sim card out of your phone."

"It's come off the kitchen cupboard. It's the thing to stop the door slamming."

I moved my bag, so that it wouldn't get in the way when I was dusting, and saw with dismay that Theo's tablet was sticking out of the back pocket. How was I going to get it back to him? I couldn't face going round to see James. I pulled it out and looked at it. He must be distraught to have lost it, so I needed to do something. What about the next open day at the university? There were several, so I was sure that I could catch Theo and, with a bit of luck, avoid James. It seemed like a good plan.

I did the first lot of dusting and took the time to appreciate gravity in action as quite a lot of the gritty stuff fell onto the floor. However, there were flakes of ash that were immune to the lure of gravity, and I watched them float lazily around, waiting until my back was turned before settling back onto the surfaces. I eventually developed a hybrid technique where I pulled the vacuum cleaner around with me. As I dusted a surface, I'd direct the mess into the waiting nozzle of the vacuum. It worked perfectly. I was riding high on a feeling of competence, so I got Adam's brightly coloured feather duster. I guess feather dusters must have been made from feathers in the olden days but this was something like bright pink toy stuffing on a stick. A few cobwebs later it was a nasty grey colour and I was reminded of something from Horrible Histories where they said that the Romans used sticks with a sponge on the end to wipe their bottoms. How on earth did you clean a feather duster? I went back to the vacuum cleaner with a smile. Of course! I switched it on and ran the nozzle over the matted pink and grey mess. Moments later the feather duster was definitely cleaner, but was also very much skinnier. The pink stuff had all disappeared up the nozzle of the vacuum. I put it at the back of the cleaning cupboard with a sigh.

By the time Cookie came round after her shift at work, I had compiled a list of things that I had learned from carrying out a deep clean on Adam's flat. I knew Cookie would be interested, but I used them to illustrate a brand-new Florrie blog as well.

1. A full dustpan can spread mess over an entire room if you drop it.

2. Reshaping a cushion sounds easy but it's something like solving a squishy Rubik's cube inside a sealed bag.

3. It's almost impossible to flush fifteen out-of-date sausages down the toilet. Almost.

Cookie was impressed with what I'd done.

"This place is looking good. You are the Belkinator," she nodded.

I grinned proudly. The multi-coloured chimney breast actually looked stunning against the backdrop of a clean and tidy room.

Cookie indicated that she had food, but I insisted that she took it into the kitchen. There's nothing like a hard day's cleaning to make you house-proud.

"Brought you your favourite thing!" she said.

"Oh, what's that?" I asked, hoping against hope that she didn't mean sausages.

"Leftovers from the cafe at work," she said. "Thought you might be missing them so I did a raid at the end of the day."

"Wait, what? Rex might have caught you!" I said.

Cookie shrugged.

"For a man who looks like a buff Father Christmas, he's a frightening chap," I said.

"Huh! I always thought he looked like Karl Marx."

"He's that singer, right?"

"No, meow-meow. He's the guy that discovered communism. Property is theft and all that. And speaking of theft, it's all a case of knowing your enemy," said Cookie. "Rex is incredibly keen on the rules, I think we can agree on that point, yes?"

I raised my eyebrows in agreement, as I already had my mouth wrapped round a delicious pasty. Cookie was right, I had missed this.

"Well the thing about that is, there is sometimes leftover food. Genuine leftover food. If the cafe doesn't sell all of its pasties, it has to put them in the bin."

I paused and reconsidered the pasty. Only briefly, because it was delicious, but I wondered where it had been.

"Did you go bin-diving?" I asked.

"As far as Rex's concerned, obviously I did. It goes back to the old question about the tree falling in the forest. If nobody was there to hear it, did it make a noise? If Rex wasn't there when this food didn't quite go in the bin then have any rules actually been broken?"

"I'm going to say *yes* and *yes*, but quite honestly I don't care. This pasty should be eaten. It would have been a crime to throw it away."

Cookie nodded. "It's the ethical thing to do. You and I are saving the planet one pasty at a time."

We ate, a silent communion in appreciation of free food. There were doughnuts and flapjacks too.

"Any fun new jobs on the go?" I asked. It's always good to hear what creative new opportunities Cookie has discovered.

"Nah, it's been quiet of late," she said. "No work at all in the small ads, all the cards have gone."

"All of them?" I said, surprised. Maybe Norman had decided that the cards were too much trouble.

"Yeah. So, I've been spending a lot of time fighting your corner on the internet. You know that horrible article has brought all the trolls out against young people? It's just like the summer of '06 all over again."

"Well, no. it's not *exactly* like that," I said, knowing instantly what she meant. "I mean, we had the cause of righteousness on our side in '06, no doubt about it. Having to wear a school tie in the summer heat was cruel and unreasonable. The only reason that nobody took our protest march seriously was that they thought we we'd just got lost on the year ten cross-country run. Pretty sure nobody even knew we were marching."

"Classic distraction technique. Act as if nothing's happening thereby denying the people their right to protest. Well you've got a lot of people on your side this time my friend. It seems that for all the selfish old trolls who think you're a time-waster, there's a bunch of people our age who think you're a hero. You should check your blog stats, I think you might be surprised."

I pulled my laptop towards me and took a look at the visits, comments and followers and found that they had increased a hundredfold since I'd last looked.

"Wow, that is something," I breathed.

Cookie had picked up Theo's tablet. I guessed she was looking at the latest figures as well. She nodded in satisfaction.

"So, tell me what went on with you and James," Cookie said, pulling two cans of cheap cider out of her bag. I thought for a brief moment that maybe adults didn't drink cheap cider. Then I told myself that *no*, an adult must surely be someone who can drink whatever they want, but *crucially*, stop drinking before collapsing face first into a puddle of tears and / or vomit. I took a pull from the can to gather my thoughts.

"I thought there was a spark there. No, I *know* there was a spark there. I'm sure he liked me, but I've messed it all up." Cookie gestured with her can that I needed to tell her all about it. "So, there was a bit of a disaster at the open day I was helping with. A lot of a disaster really. Ashbert turned up with a donkey and a pensioner army and loads of stuff got smashed." Cookie took this very much in her stride. She has heard stories like this before. "Afterwards, James sent Theo, his son, outside to help me sort some stuff out. He's a good lad Theo, and we had it pretty much in hand when he accidentally got shut in the back of a van. That's when things went a bit wrong. There was a chase, a minor rampage through IKEA with a donkey and a little bit of tomfoolery with a fun thing called a scissor lift."

"Tomfoolery?"

"Rex's word. It's handy shorthand. Covers pretty much everything I do," I said miserably. "Anyway. It turns out that the worst bits of it all were captured on video, so James saw them and thought that Theo was in danger."

Cookie nodded, seeing my pain. "Can't you just tell him that you were the victim of circumstances?" she said.

I took another mouthful of toxic cider. "The trouble is, he would say that circumstances like that tend to follow me round. I think he might be right."

"It is true that in the complex interconnectedness of the universe, the parts that you touch, Baby Belkin, do seem prone to unintended ripples."

I nodded at Cookie's ramblings. She understood. She was tapping on Theo's tablet, but then she raised her eyes from the screen and gave me a quizzical look.

"What are these bookmarked videos?" asked Cookie. "And who's this Elena woman who's in all of them?"

"Oh, don't," I said. "That James' ex. Theo's mom. The only contact that poor boy has with her is the videos she posts of her travelling and doing projects. Digging wells in Kenya and teaching schoolchildren on Sodor. She's been all over," I said glumly.

Cookie passed me another can of cider. I opened it and chugged down a couple of mouthfuls, as I imagined how I compared to the selfish superwoman that had dumped James in exchange for the whole wide world.

"She looks like a cross between Helen Skelton and Bear Grylls," said Cookie.

"Huh," I grumped, "I considered it a win when I made it to Crete without somehow making the plane crash, but she's properly travelling and achieving the things she meant to do. Look at her! Saving the world one well at a time."

"There are many ways to save the world, my boon companion," said Cookie.

I didn't respond. Cookie was trying to make me feel better, but it seemed to me that there was little justification for celebrating my ability to turn any situation into a big mess.

One practical thing I could do was to return Theo's tablet so I looked up when the next open day was taking place at the university. It was tomorrow, which was perfect.

"Oh, bugger," I said. Bernadette Brampton, head of residents' association, vice-chancellor of the university, bin fascist and all-round git was giving the keynote speech tomorrow.

There was a video of her on the uni website. She was smiling. I don't know why I clicked on it, probably to see whether the unnatural state of her face was the result of photo manipulation or whether she really was capable of maintaining a smile.

"Hey mate, I've found something you'll want to see," said Cookie, but my attention was on the video.

"Please attend my keynote speech while you're here," Bernadette was saying. "I want you to understand that we do more than just educate our young people. We aim to turn out well rounded individuals who are ready to contribute fully to our society. You will all have seen this article that illustrates exactly what a hopeless case looks like. Let me explain to you how we will make sure you don't end up like this."

The smile had lasted all of a second and Bernadette's customary scowl had replaced it at the end, as she held up a newspaper that clearly showed my picture, next to Chorley Danglespear's article.

"I don't believe that woman!" I howled. I tipped over the can of cider as I jumped up but it was empty, which was slightly surprising, as I was attempting moderation. How could anyone fail to be distracted by this outrageous slur against their character?

"Lori, you need to see this –" said Cookie.

"Look!" I hissed. "Look at what she's saying." I turned the screen towards Cookie and stormed out of the flat, aware that I had perhaps had more cider than I'd intended. I went straight to Bernadette's door and hammered on it, not caring if I was making excessive noise after nine-thirty in the evening. I shouted through her letterbox. "Come here and face me you monster! I've seen what you've done! Come out here and let me murderlise you! Don't worry," I spat. "I'll dispose of the body in the correct bin!"

Several other people came out to the landing. The first one, who I'd seen cycling on the street outside and carrying his expensive-looking bike up the stairs to his flat, frowned at me. "Did you know that you're not supposed to make excessive noise after nine-thirty?"

"Yeah well, it's like trees in the forest. If Bernadette's not here to tell me off then it didn't happen," I said, perhaps a little drunkenly. He pulled a face and retreated into his flat.

"She might be in the laundry room," said a timid-looking woman two doors up.

It didn't sound very likely. I wondered if the woman was just trying to get rid of me. I went to the laundry room and found it empty. I went to all of the other places that she might conceivably have been lurking. No sign of her. Perhaps she was hiding. Perhaps she was just not at home. I'd wasted an hour or so of my life trying to find her and now I was tired. I went back to Adam's flat. Cookie had gone, and mercifully had taken the bag of cider with her. I might have been tempted to down another can in my anger, and that would have been a mistake. Just before I went to bed I saw that she had left me a note. I picked up the piece of paper.

I know where your parents are.

Chapter 39

I woke the next morning and I was in a bad mood as soon as I remembered about Bernadette and her mean swipe at me on her video. I didn't bother going to see her in her flat. I knew where she was going to be later.

As I walked over to the university, Theo's tablet in my bag, I saw a curious sight. There were about eight older people all standing in a line. I thought maybe outdoor bingo was taking off or something, but then they all took turns doing something even more curious. They tottered over to a lamppost, swung round it, some of them waving their walking sticks as they went, some whooping with obvious glee, and tottered back the way they'd come to join the back of the queue again. Ashbert was standing nearby. The shock of seeing him made me forget to question what on earth I'd just witnessed.

"Are you all right?" I asked.

"I am more than all right," he beamed. "I'm happy and I'm busy. Things are coming together for me."

On the one hand this was good news. A tiny gerbil of guilt had been gnawing at the carrot stick of my wellbeing since I last saw Ashbert, and now I knew that I didn't need to worry at all. On the other hand, I was slightly shocked that he was over me so soon. That was a selfish response though, and I told myself sternly that an adult would wish him nothing but happiness.

"So how are things with you, Lori?" he asked.

"I can't say that they're great, if I'm truthful," I said.

"You're not happy?" he said, a look of concern clouding his face. He pulled out a clipboard. It bristled with lists and I could see what looked like a whole load of postcards clipped to the front. "Right, tell me what you need to make you happy," he said, pen poised.

I really needed to think about the next words that came out of my mouth. No flippant remarks, no careless idioms.

"Ashbert, I need to fix my own life and solve my own problems. It's very kind of you to offer your help, but this is for me to do."

I gave him a hug.

"You're buzzing," said Ashbert.

I was. My phone was ringing. I didn't recognise the number. "Hello?"

"Miss Belkin, it's Sergeant Fenton here."

"Oh, hello, Sergeant Fenton. Have you found my brother yet?"

"No. Where are you?"

I hesitated. "Why?"

"Just tell us where you are?"

What was she up to? From her tone, it didn't sound good. "I'm just at home, chilling," I said.

"*I* am at your home," said Sergeant Fenton. "And you are quite clearly not here."

"What are you doing at my flat?" I asked.

"Investigating death threats you made against one Bernadette Brampton."

"What? I didn't." I remembered the angry tirade and the promise to dispose of her in the correct bin. "Oh, yeah. That. I didn't mean it."

There was a pause. Perhaps there was much silent swearing or sighing on the other end of the line.

"Miss Belkin. You need to turn yourself in immediately. Threatening a potential witness to an on-going missing person enquiry is –"

"I told you where Adam is!"

"– a potentially *serious* offence."

A brief shout from the pensioners made me look round. One of them had managed to use the handle of her walking stick to pivot round the lamppost at a surprising turn of speed and the others all hollered in appreciation.

"Look, Sergeant. I've got to go," I said. "People to see. Things to do."

I hung up and hurried on.

When I got to the university, I followed the signs for the open day. I collected an open day goody bag to blend in and munched on the complimentary chocolate muffin as I looked at the programme. Turned out that the keynote speeches were being made in the

282

exhibition hall of the museum. Cruel fate! Would I never be able to escape that place?

My phone binged with a text. It was Cookie.

Where are you? I've been driving all night and you'll never guess where I've been.

I followed various would-be students and their families to the exhibition hall, where a stage and seating for several hundred people had been set up. I sat near the front. I wanted to be able to see Bernadette's face if she mentioned me. The hall filled up soon after I sat down. I had only a minute or two to reflect that my suggestion to Rex, all those weeks ago – that they whitewash the walls and strip out all the fiddly stuff to create a minimalist atmosphere – had been a mite misjudged. It was a beautiful old building, it really was... And then my arch-nemesis, Bernadette Brampton, took to the stage.

She was smiling, but the expression really didn't look as though it belonged on her face and it didn't stay there for long. The crowd shushed as she looked round at them all. I looked round too. Very few of the young people were unaccompanied. Made sense, I couldn't imagine that I would have gone to see a vice-chancellor's keynote speech aged eighteen if someone hadn't made me, or if, potentially it was likely to include a character assassination upon me and everything that I stood for.

"Welcome to our open day," she began. "I would like to welcome all of the young people I can see in the room. Look at you all, the cream of the educational crop: bold young people, ready to don the mantle of tradition, grasp the reins of opportunity and ride the horse of achievement. It's always a delight to see so much interest in our wonderful university, to see wise young heads making the decision to pick this institution as the vehicle for their journey on the road to success."

I was struggling to picture riding both the horse of achievement whilst driving the vehicle that was the university along the road to success. Maybe the horse was pulling the vehicle?

My phone binged. Cookie again.

Are you at the university thing? You didn't guess where I've been. Go on. Guess.

I ignored it and concentrated on hating Bernadette.

"I understand that many people now look at the cost of getting a degree," she was saying, "which can be considerable, and might ask themselves whether it's going to be worth it. I would like you to consider those costs as an investment in your future. You cannot build the house of ambition without the foundation of knowledge. A university education will provide a pathway to opportunities that simply won't exist for you otherwise. You might, of course, consider an alternative future for yourself. You might perhaps choose to ignore all of the benefits that a degree can give you and drop out of society completely."

This last bit was said in an embarrassingly droll manner. She clicked a controller in her hand and the screen behind her changed from a static image of the university's logo to the photo and article featuring me.

It was that darned picture of me looking confused with a box of eggs.

There were stifled giggles from around the room and I felt my face burning. The picture was enormous, more than twice life size. I couldn't imagine hating Bernadette more than I already did, but the sight of my idiotic expression as I gazed at that box of eggs was made so much worse by the sheer scale of the thing.

Bernadette made a patting motion to the room, indicating that everyone should quieten down. "Now I know we were all appalled by this article. It was pointed out to me by a member of university staff."

I felt that comment like a slap to the face. Had James sent the article to Bernadette? I'd made him angry with my thoughtlessness, but would he really be so vindictive? The realisation that he might have done it made me short of breath for a few seconds. I tried to concentrate on what Bernadette was saying. She had made some sort of *but seriously* segue into the next section of her speech.

"This article only highlights that some people are blind to the realities of our world and struggling to cope with modern life. Not all young people are as feckless as this particular individual." I could hear the sound of people around the hall tapping the word *feckless* into their phones to see what it meant. "Part of the role of this university is to shape young people into those who will contribute effectively to society, and not simply fritter away their education."

Movement to my side pulled my attention away. I was stunned to see James sit down in the seat next to me.

"Oh, I bet you're pleased with this, aren't you?" I whispered harshly.

"What are you doing here, Lori?" he whispered back.

I stabbed a finger wordlessly at the huge screen that still held the picture of me having my eggy love-in. "Being the butt of everyone's joke apparently."

"You don't need to hear poison like this. Don't put yourself through it."

"You sent her that article! How could you?"

He looked shocked. "No, I didn't. Why would I do a thing like that? Maybe she's a reader of that horrible rag."

"She just said that a member of staff showed it to her!"

"I'm not the only person who works at this university!"

People around us were starting to make very English noises of disapproval. It started as gentle coughs and moved on to full-blown tutting. Eventually, one woman broke ranks. She leaned over and said, "Do you mind?" (which is as close to a full-blown riot as middle England gets).

James apologised and turned back to me.

"Maybe – just maybe – you've irritated more than one person at this university, eh?" he suggested, not unkindly.

Well, that didn't make sense. I was a ray of sunshine in pretty much everyone's life. And, as that not-entirely-true thought skipped through my mind, I caught sight of someone leaning over the balustrade of the upper level of the hall. Rex McCloud stood there stroking his beard like an evil genius.

"Bastard!" I hissed.

"Well, really!" said the woman who had 'do-you-mind?'-ed us moments before.

I stood involuntarily. I wanted to march up there and give Rex a piece of my mind. But if I served him first, there might not be enough for Bernadette.

As I stood there, I happened to see a uniformed figure entering the hall from the far corner: a police officer. He was moving slowly, cautiously. I turned my head. Two more were coming from another corner. They weren't hurrying. They were making sure they had the exits covered.

I bet Sergeant Fenton was here too. I was tempted to spin round to look but maybe they hadn't seen me yet. I forced myself to sit down.

"Bit of a problem," I said.

"What?" said James.

"I might have publicly threatened to kill Bernadette Brampton."

"The vice-chancellor?"

"Yes, for squealing to the police because we murdered Adam."

"Which we didn't do."

"No. But now I'm here and she's here and the police are here too."

"What?!"

He stood to look. I hauled him down.

"What's happening, Dad?" said Theo, sliding into the space beside James.

"Lori," said James. "Lori is happening."

"Some of us are trying to listen to the speech," said the do-you-mind woman. "Some of us are interested in what she has to say."

I gave an involuntary bark of bitter laughter. It was enough to finally draw Bernadette's attention our way. She stared at me and then, when she recognised me, she did whatever was the next step up from staring, a sort of uber-staring or staring squared.

"Well, ladies and gentlemen," she said to the hall, "we are deeply honoured today to have the young lady from the article with us." She held out a hand towards me. "Perhaps come to take her own first tentative steps on the road to education and success, I give you Lori Belkin!"

Her tone was meant to be withering and condescending but there was a smattering of applause. That was probably just politeness. The British will applaud anything if they're told to. More pressingly, the police knew exactly where I was and I could see them slowly converging on me.

"I'm sure," said Bernadette, fixing me and James with a glare, "Lori has come, as an example to us all, a penitent before this church of learning, ready to *sit* and *listen* to the wisdom of her betters."

Next to me, James looked stunned and confused. You know the phrase *rabbit in the headlights*? Well, James looked more like a rabbit that had been pistol-whipped, hung up by its thumbs and then told that its carrot supply had been napalmed. Not me though. I was the rabbit that wasn't going to take any more of this headlight crap.

I quickly recalled my priorities.

I thrust Theo's tablet into his hand. "You left this in the shed, Theo. I didn't want you to be without it."

I grabbed James' stunned face and gave him a big smushy kiss. "You are a wonderful man and I don't deserve you. I wish I did."

I stood up and made for the stage.

"Sit down, Miss Belkin," commanded Bernadette Brampton.

"Lori!"

The shout was from behind me. I would recognise that world-weary voice anywhere. It was Sergeant Fenton the long and long-suffering arm of the law. I turned.

"Sergeant Fenton," I said. "I'm in the middle of something right now."

The policewoman was halfway down the aisle towards me. She beckoned me towards her.

"Come with us, Lori. No one else has to get hurt."

Hurt?

"I just wanted to put the record straight," I said.

"And we can do that down at the station."

I suddenly saw what this was: speak nicely and calmly and get silly little Lori out of there before she causes a scene (or murders Bernadette Brampton or whatever). No one was actually interested in my view of things. No one actually cared what I had to say.

"But she's saying horrible things about me," I said, shaking my finger at Bernadette on stage.

"Yes," said Sergeant Fenton. "And I'm sure she's sorry. You are sorry, aren't you, Ms Brampton?"

"I am not!" said Bernadette.

Sergeant Fenton cast an exasperated gaze to the heavens and dashed forward to grab me. I ran, leapt onto the stage and turned to face the audience. There was a ripple of gasps in the hall, although I think quite a few people thought this was all an elaborate roleplay to engage prospective students. The encircling police officers – wow! There were at least two dozen of them! – all froze. Their eyes were fixed on my hand, which had involuntarily gone to the pendant at my neck.

Why had my unconscious mind done that? Well, I had nothing to protect myself with but my words and, yes, my pendant. Hadn't I turned to it when life became too challenging? And how small and petty my use of it had been! Magicking up foxes to win an argument, conjuring tasty pies to feed a hungry boy. All the good I could have done with it and what had I done? Nothing of value at all. And now I grasped it because I couldn't cope with a situation blown out of all proportion by a little misunderstanding and some poorly chosen words.

I saw all this clearly and, one might have thought that, in the light of such a revelation, I might have chosen my next words with fresh wisdom and care.

But what I said was: "Don't make me use this."

Now, I liked to think I had grown as a person in recent weeks, that new-Lori was a more mature, thoughtful and worldly individual than old-Lori. Old-Lori, after some hours or days of reflection, might have concluded that "Don't make me use this" was unfortunate phrasing and that those five words had made everyone in the room recategorize Lori from "crazy bitch" to "mad bomber" (everyone apart from a ten year old boy who probably understood exactly what I meant). However, new-Lori – more mature, thoughtful and worldly – had seen the error in her decision in a matter of seconds so she followed it up with: "It's okay. I don't want to hurt anyone."

Oh, Lori!

Towards the back of the room, some people were starting to get out of their seats.

"No, don't leave!" I shouted. "I have to tell you something!"

288

The people stopped. What would you do if a mad bomber with their finger on the pendant – I mean detonator – instructed you not to run away?

"You have something to tell us?" said Sergeant Fenton down in the aisle, trying really hard to maintain her friendly, gentle tone. "We're willing to listen."

I took the microphone from Bernadette, who had frozen in place with a look of terror on her face. Perhaps I looked like a wild-eyed terrorist. When it came to Bernadette, I wasn't even sorry.

I turned to face the audience.

"Hello everybody. I probably don't need to introduce myself. You'll have spotted that I'm Lori, from the article." I pointed to the giant screen behind me, just in case anyone was in any doubt.

"What do you want to tell us?" said Sergeant Fenton.

I thought.

"I suppose I want to talk to the young people in the audience. The teenagers. The sons and daughters." I raised the microphone to my mouth. "Um, it's easy to mock someone when they're presented in a negative way like the newspapers did with me, like Bernadette did with me" – off to the side, Bernadette whimpered and tried to sidle away – "but I thought you might be interested to hear my side of things, just in case it turns out to be something similar to your side of things."

I saw some of the youngsters in the audience sitting up and taking notice, some of them pointing their phones at me.

"Let me start off by saying that most of what was in that article was factually correct. I'm not necessarily proud of everything that I've done." I nodded. It was true. "But," I said, "something that I do want to question is why my generation is constantly being criticised by older people. Millennials – are you happy for me to call us all Millennials? – are measured against criteria that are just no longer valid."

There were some mumblings from around the room and I knew I had their attention. It was time to use some examples that had appeared in the forum discussions that Cookie had orchestrated. I could be a channel for those angry voices.

"I'm going to give you some examples, I've heard from other people, people like you, since that article went live, and they're not happy."

I reached into my pocket to get out my phone.

"Don't do it!" squeaked Bernadette and stuck her fingers in her ears as though I was reaching for a fire cracker, not a smartphone.

"I know that the older people in the audience will be rolling their eyes right now. They can't understand why we're so wedded to our phones. Our lives are on these phones, and it's just not as weird as you think it is. It's just a phone, Bernadette. I'm checking a few facts. Right." I looked at the facts I'd googled. "Let's talk about how wealthy we are compared to our parents. It's not just a small gap we're talking about, it's a vast chasm that is increasing all the time, as the Baby Boomers, who currently hold most positions of power are moving the goal posts to protect their own interests. If you were buying a house in the nineteen-eighties – people like your grandparents or maybe your parents – how much would you need to spend, compared to the average salary?"

I looked around the room.

"Four times. The average house then cost four times the average wage. What about now? What do you think that number has moved to?"

I paused again to check my phone, hoping that the number was correct.

"Ten times?" suggested a voice from the audience.

"Fifteen times," I said. "Fifteen! Who could hope to get on the housing ladder when the increase is so massive? The thing is, it's not just about buying a house, is it? The older generation have failed to preserve all of the benefits that they enjoyed themselves when they were our age. Where is our free university? Where are the good pensions? There is a horrible, pervasive middle-class myth that poverty is simply caused by a poor work ethic." I liked that line. I took it word for word from someone who'd posted a response to Cookie, but I needed all the help I could get. The room seemed to be on my side though.

"We love you, Lori!" I wasn't sure who'd said it, but it gave me the confidence to press ahead. "There are no opportunities. The jobs exist but they don't pay enough for anyone to live on independently. What's left for us? Minimum wage, zero-hour contracts. And, let me tell you, that doesn't mean you get paid for working zero hours. No. Young people can't afford a house, can't afford to have children; and decent pensions have gone the way of unicorns." There was a slight murmuring at that. Damn. Were unicorns the ones that never actually existed? I'd check later. "When Bernadette here tells you that she's preparing you for the jobs market, I think we need to ask her where those jobs are? The opportunities that come up are likely to be snapped up by retired people who fancy a little bit extra pocket money. Let me ask you something now. Given everything that I've just said, why on earth are you still banging on about the goals that kids should be setting themselves? Are you seriously so deluded that you believe that the only thing holding back a young person is the inclination to work hard? If millennials are all useless snowflakes, whose fault is it? It's either bad parenting or bad genes!"

I looked around the hall, determined to look these parents in the eye. At the back of the hall I saw Cookie, she was jumping up and down, waving like a maniac. She pointed at the two people with her. It was my parents. Holy hell! My parents! Where had they come from? I faltered slightly. What was that I'd just been saying about bad parenting? Did my dad have a frown on his face?

I couldn't let myself get distracted now. It dawned on me that the entire hall was rapt. Those who had stood to leave were sitting again.

"What do we think, fellow Snowflakes?" I asked the young people in the room. "Are we going to do what our parents tell us, or are we going to insist that they cut us some slack? The world has changed, and they're not changes that we asked for."

There was a roar of approval, and I saw Bernadette flinch visibly at the change in the mood.

"Right. Enough!" shouted Sergeant Fenton. "You've had your say. It's time to come with us."

"They want me to come quietly," I said to the crowd with a game shrug. "Should I?"

And then, something astonishing occurred. Softly, barely more than a murmur, voices were chanting.

Snowflake!
Sno-o-owflake!
Snowflake!
Snowflake!

It grew louder, slowly, like the approach of a marching band. No, the approach of an army.

Snowflake!
Sno-o-owflake!
Snowflake!
Snowflake!

It sounded like a re-purposed football chant and, sure, the lyrics weren't very complicated but it told me all I needed to know. I wasn't alone. I wasn't wrong. I was giddy with it. I have never in my life felt anything like the rush that comes with a huge crowd of people utterly and completely on my side.

"You're all amazing!" I yelled.

A huge roar erupted and they screamed their allegiance. Revelling in the storm of chanting voices, I looked across at Bernadette Brampton. The vice-chancellor's face was a whole mess of confusion, unable to comprehend what was going on.

"Blind to the realities of our world and struggling to cope with modern life, Bernadette?" I asked her, an uncontrolled grin on my face. "Don't worry. I'd be happy to educate you."

Sergeant Fenton had to cup her hands around her mouth to be heard over the chanting voices.

"You've made your point now! Please! Put the device down!"

"This?" I said, holding up my pendant. "This is just jewellery. Bought it on holiday in Crete."

"What?"

Sergeant Fenton's eyes widened. A split second later I was rugby tackled from the side and I went down to the ground under the uniformed bulk of Constable Stokes. This was apparently the cue for a police officer pile-on and at least three more of them threw themselves on me.

Two separate people grabbed a hand apiece and not gently either. Another, perhaps doubting my honesty regarding cheap holiday jewellery, ripped the pendant from my neck and threw it out of harm's way.

I couldn't see because my vision was obscured by what I feared was policeman moob but I heard Bernadette take the stand.

"Thank you, everyone. The situation's now under control and we can –"

The chanting would not calm down.

"If we can just remember why we're here and –"

I could picture Bernadette flapping her arms for calm but to no effect.

"You shouldn't listen to this woman's dangerous talk. It only –"

The chanting drowned her out. Was that a little sob I could hear?

"She doesn't even know how to sort her rubbish properly!" yelled Bernadette in a near-perfect crazy lady voice.

Strong hands pulled my arms together and I felt the cold steel of handcuffs.

"We need to get her out of here before this turns ugly," said Sergeant Fenton.

As one, the police lifted me up, arms, body and legs to carry me out.

"I didn't mean to cause a fuss," I said.

Judging by her expression, I think Sergeant Fenton would have gladly punched me at that point. I did feel truly sorry for her.

"Don't touch that, sir," called Constable Stokes.

At the edge of the stage, James' hand froze over the pendant.

"It's a valuable Minoan artefact," he said. "Well, possibly."

His eyes flicked from the pendant to the constable and then to me. There was a lot of hurt in those eyes.

"It might be dangerous, sir," said Stokes.

"It's magic," said Theo.

"Not the magic thing again," sighed James.

"She's a nutter!" declared Bernadette, a second before she was struck in the side of the head by a chocolate muffin. It was not the last complimentary goody bag muffin to be thrown at the stage and it was not the last to find its target.

"We'll make sure Lori gets the best care," said Sergeant Fenton and I knew what that meant: straitjackets and electro-shock therapy. Oh, yes.

"She didn't mean any harm," said James.

"Oh, they never do," said the sergeant grimly.

"But it *is* magic!" said Theo and grabbed the pendant from the stage. "Look!"

His dad made to grab him but Theo was already turning and pointing...

Chapter 40

Perhaps Theo picked a painting from the galleries above at random. Perhaps he went for one that he thought was inoffensive and harmless. The painting in question looked as if it had once been an altarpiece and featured a pair of winged cherubs gazing down over a garden. The right-hand cherub erupted from the painting, like a bubble bursting from water, and swooped across the ceiling like a seriously oversized moth.

It turned in the corner and briefly regarded the crowd below, who gasped and shouted in shock (although, you know, I think there was still a proportion of the crowd who thought this was all part of the show and was probably achieved with holograms or something). Anyway, you know that fine line between the face of a healthy, plump baby and a fat, grumpy old man? Well, this cherub definitely came down on the side of the fat grumpy old man. It regarded us with its mean piggy eyes and flew down low, skimming the tops of our heads and making several people shriek in panic. When it reached the opposite wall, a sinister grin crossed its face and it reached behind. It pulled out a bow and arrow. I understood what it was.

"It's Cupid!" I yelled.

"Eros, Lori. It's Eros. See, Dad?"

"What?" said James, turning.

And then Theo swept out his arm to point. I wasn't sure whether it was fear or excitement, but he seemed to have forgotten that he still held the pendant in his hand. As the pointing finger moved across the room, tracking the flight path of Eros, he took in any number of paintings both in the lower hall and the gallery level above.

There was no time to register what else might be coming to life, as Eros had nocked an arrow and now seemed to be selecting a target as he dive-bombed the crowd with his loaded bow, grinning malevolently.

Old-Lori was not a connoisseur of art – not the fusty old oils and watercolours this place held – but clean a frame and an information plaque often enough and something is bound to sink in. That's how I knew that the fine figure dropping out of his painting on winged sandals was Perseus and if he'd stepped out of Burne-Jones' *The Doom Fulfilled* then he was the least of our worries. The vast black coils of a monstrous serpent looped down from the painting and dropped to the floor. Nobody had seen the threat as it looked more like some sort of industrial vacuum cleaner pipe until you saw its face. The head reared up and snapped at the crowd like a demon fish with an attitude problem. Any residual belief that all this was a magnificent, hi-tech, post-modern skit to draw kids to this particular uni vanished at the sight of that fishy monster.

People surged for the door. Brochures were tossed aside. Complimentary muffins were discarded and trodden underfoot. Chairs were tripped over and everyone generally got in everyone else's way. The police weren't much help but, in their defence, I don't suppose they had the training for this. Nonetheless, they had kind of forgotten about me and dropped me like so much trash on the floor.

I found my feet and stumbled, handcuffed, into James.

"Come on, we need to get out of here."

"Serpent..." mumbled James, agog.

"Yes," I said.

"I told you," said Theo, wide-eyed at the destruction he had wrought.

More paintings were coming to life. A giant cabbage plopped out of a still life. Any other time, I would have stopped to stare at a cabbage the size of a small car, but I was distracted by the other things that were bursting into life. Across a mass of confusion, I saw Cookie waving at me as she drew my parents up a flight of stairs to safety. I hoped my parents didn't think this was a regular day in the new life I had forged for myself. I mean, it was kind of par for the course but not exactly regular.

Constable Stokes apparently decided that it would be a good idea to Taser Burne-Jones' serpent. He was wrong. It was a spectacularly bad idea.

As the Taser crackled, the serpent reared high and dove down, massive coils and all, onto the stage.

"Cetus!" yelled Theo (which I assumed was some sort of slang).

James grabbed Theo and ran one way. I grabbed Theo and ran the other. I don't know which of us would have won. The stage flew apart. Something – I think it was the podium – smacked me in the face and something else, possibly a serpent tail, whipped my legs from under me. Giddy, I stumbled away and found myself in a corner by the stairs with Theo and the smashed remains of the podium.

"Where's your dad?" I said.

"Satyrs!" he shouted.

I had no idea what that meant. Then I saw several handsome creatures jumping out of a painting of a forest: from the waist up, they looked like muscular acrobats in Cirque du Soleil but from the waist down they were hairy goats. They swaggered toward us, seemingly not bothered by flying arrows or snapping serpents.

"Oh, Mr Tumble from Narnia," I said.

"Satyrs. Greek fertility spirits," said Theo.

The lead goat-man noticed me staring and winked at me. I rolled my eyes.

"Of course they are," I said.

Some of them turned their lecherous attention on Bernadette – fish-slapped and tossed about, she did look a mess – and seemed very much intent on getting her to dance to their panpipes and drink wine with them. Even I felt sorry for her; no one should ever be forced to hear panpipes. It's like a basic human right.

"Lori!"

I looked across at James' shout. He was on the far side of the smashed stage, at the bottom of the stairs to the first floor galleries.

"*The Return of Neptune!*" he yelled, pointing.

I didn't understand at first – Neptune might be returning; it was clearly a great big artistic character reunion today – but then I saw. The painting above the main entrance was one of the museum's big canvas works, probably by some bloke who had a lot to compensate for. It was like a big still from *The Little Mermaid* but without Flounder and Sebastian and the other cartoon sea creatures. What it did have, apart from Ariel's, was the sea. A lot of sea.

The canvas bulged.

On the ground floor, scores of people had fought their way to the doors and out into the university grounds, but there were still stragglers: police officers, the incurably stunned, a solid knot of loyal but misguided snowflakes who were still chanting.

I grabbed the microphone from the ruined podium and yelled.

"GET TO HIGHER GROUND!"

And then the canvas burst and Theo and I were running up the stairs. Neptune, riding a shell drawn by weird horses surged forward on a huge torrent of water. Chairs, coppers, students, satyrs and giant vegetables were swept together by the sea.

The foamy waters crashed off the stairs and then began to rise.

"This is going to be hell to clean up," I said and then, remembering that I'd been fired and it wouldn't be me doing the cleaning, I cheered up enormously.

"Dad!" Theo shouted.

On the far stairs, across the flooded hall, James was trapped. The hateful Burne-Jones serpent had coiled around his legs in the rising waters.

"Stay here!" I told Theo and ran round the length of the gallery to get to James. On the way, I had to bypass an angry tiger and a band of sword-wangling Arabian warriors. I think the tiger was angry because he'd clearly been painted by someone who'd never seen a tiger before. The tiger and the warriors were keeping each other occupied so all I had to do was run close to the balustrade and I was past them.

James clawed at the stairs and tried to pull himself away from the slippery monster. I came round to the top of the stairs, snatched a sword off a Pre-Raphaelite knight who was looking all moony and lovelorn and inexpertly hacked at the serpent coils. I'm no swordswoman but it was good enough. Hand in hand, we stumbled up the stairs.

I risked one glance back at the serpent to see that it was now distracted by a trio of satyrs arriving on a giant floating cabbage leaf. They were lewdly waggling their man-bits at the beast and would probably soon be regretting that.

From another gallery hall came the sound of explosions. Cannon fire?

"Oh, God. It's all gone a bit wrong, hasn't it?" I said.

"Understatement," said James. "Where's Theo?"

"This way," I said and pulled him along the corridor.

We passed where the tiger and Arabian warriors had been. They had all gone. That wasn't very comforting. There's something decidedly unnerving about being where a wild tiger has been, knowing that it was now somewhere else, anywhere else...

Theo was not where I had left him. Oh, hell! The tiger!

"Psst."

Theo waved at us from a dark side corridor. We hurried over.

"I had to hide," he explained. "There was this tiger..."

"Yes. Clever lad," said James.

"No, Dad. When the tiger came, I brought the lions from the arena to life to fight it."

"Ah."

"And then after the lions killed the tiger, I had to do something else."

"You brought another picture to life?"

He nodded. There was distant roar and a flash of light along a far corridor.

"It was only one dragon," he said.

I clicked my fingers. "Pendant. Now, young man."

He handed it over gladly. I was still handcuffed so could do little with it except hold it tightly in my two hands.

"Don't worry, Lori," said Theo. "I dealt with the dragon."

"Oh?" said James.

He nodded. "There was this big painting of Nelson's fleet at the Battle of Trafalgar."

Cannons boomed, stone cracked and dust drifted down from the ceiling. A great winged shadow passed overhead.

"It's in the process of being dealt with. This way," said Theo and beckoned us along the corridor.

I frowned. "I only left you for two minutes – one minute even. And you did all that?"

"It all escalated kind of quickly," agreed Theo.

To my relief, the chaotic noises faded away behind us as we walked. We didn't speak for a while, aware of the silence, which was in stark contrast to the utter bedlam we'd left behind.

We walked for a while down the tunnel and I could see that the white stone passageway branched up ahead.

Stone passageway?

"Er, I don't recognise this bit of the museum," said James.

"Nor do I," I whispered. I wasn't all that sure why I was whispering. There was something unsettling about this place.

James touched the wall. "It's damp, like an underground tunnel, but that just isn't possible."

I picked up a nub of chalky stone and considered it. Perhaps I was more accustomed to the impossible than he was.

"They remind me of the tunnels in Crete, near Gortyn," he mused.

"Yeah, about that," said Theo.

We both looked at him.

"Oh," said James. He sounded as if he'd had a penny-dropping moment.

"What?"

"We're in a painting, aren't we?" said James.

"Yes," said Theo.

"The labyrinth?"

"Yes."

"Oh, fair enough," I said, looking round. "So we're in a labyrinth."

"No," said Theo. "We're in *the* labyrinth. The one that comes with a minotaur."

I knew this. I did. "Minotaur. Part man? Part, um, something –"

"It's a man with the head of a bull."

"Marvellous."

Chapter 41

We trudged through the labyrinth, looking for an exit and hoping to avoid any cow-men who might be in residence.

"How are we going to fix all this?" said James, not for the first time.

"We bring something else to life to take care of Nelson's fleet and the dragon?" suggested Theo.

"No. No, we're not going to do that."

"Well," I said in maybe a slightly mocking tone, "I remember a certain someone telling me that Greek myths tell us about all human experience or something, lay out the big problems so we can examine them."

"He might have done," said James.

"So, what would Greek myths tell us about this situation?"

Theo had a thoughtful face. "If this was a Greek myth things would just get worse and worse and worse and then Zeus would appear and he would fix everything."

"Ah, yes, the original *Deus Ex Machina*," said James.

"*Sex makky* what?" I said.

"God from the machine," translated James. "It's a plot device, which lazy or inept writers use to wrap up a story when they've made too much of a mess of it. You see it in all the worst books and movies these days but it was good old Aeschylus, or possibly dear Euripides, who invented it. Zeus appears and magics everything back to normal with his thunderbolt."

I tutted. "There's never a Zeus around when you need one."

"Listen," said James as we continued down a longish section of tunnel, "I wanted to apologise properly, Lori. Theo's told me how he came to be in the back of a lorry that drove off, and that it wasn't your fault. I know that everything you did was trying to help."

"I do try," I said.

"I know. Sometimes I don't understand the things you do. If there's a mad choice or a normal choice, you always seem to take the mad one, but you always do it for the very best reasons, and I've treated you badly. I'm sorry."

I kissed him quickly on the lips as a thank you.

"Ew, you two," said Theo, disgusted.

"You've seen worse," said James.

"And read worse in your myth books," I added. "I still can't get over that bit about the Minoan queen who had them build her a wooden cow thing so she could have... intimate relations with a bull."

"Minotaur," said Theo.

"Oh, I thought she did it with a bull and gave birth to –"

"Minotaur."

"That's right. She –"

"Minotaur!"

He was pointing. And he was right. A hairy brute with an ugly misshapen head was coming down the passageway towards us. It was massive, a hulking lump of walking, sweating muscle, approaching with all the menace of a back-alley mugger.

"When you said a man with a bull's head, you never mentioned that it would be a giant man," I said to James as we backed away.

"The classical texts are light on specifics," said James. "Get behind me, Theo."

The minotaur snorted and lowed menacingly.

"Should we run for it?" said Theo.

"Maybe it's bad to run away from a minotaur," I suggested. "Maybe you're supposed to play dead or try to look menacing instead?"

"Again..." whispered James, hoarse with fear. "Classics. Light on specifics."

Wet nostrils flared angrily. Fists clenched, ready to pummel and throttle. Was that dried blood on the tips of his horns? Was I going to be killed by a painting? I'm not sure if I was the kind of person who wanted to die for their art.

"The minotaur was born in darkness," said Theo, in the hollow voice of a boy terrified to his bones. "It's known nothing but the maze and the blood of its victims."

I gazed into the beast's coal-black eyes and wondered what a creature like that wants. And then it hit me.

"Chorley Danglespear!" I shouted.

"Swearing won't help," said James.

I turned to the wall and scratched at it with the chalk in my hand. The minotaur was seconds away but a true artist can create with just a few lines. I stepped back and pointed with the hand holding the pendant.

A fistful of wet luscious grass popped into existence and then into my hand. The minotaur was mentally thrown by this magic. It stopped its approach and sniffed the air. It sniffed the air again and realised that a delicious smell was coming from the clump of grass. I held out my hands and closed my eyes. This would, I thought unhelpfully, be the worst way for an artist to lose her hands, bitten off by a mythical monster.

A wet nose tickled my palms. I opened my eyes a peek. The minotaur nibbled tentatively at a few blades of grass.

"Like it, huh?" I said.

Moments later it was chomping happily and making a small crooning sound.

"Cows eat grass," I told James informatively.

"Yes, they do," agreed James warily.

James and I glanced warily at each other. It felt as though we could afford to breathe again. The minotaur looked up at us, and his face had softened so that it was almost friendly. It nuzzled my arm, its terrifying horns dangerously close to my face.

"You want some more?"

I drew more grass on the wall. It was just some lines but I knew it was grass – artistically, it *was* grass – and so it became grass, a big bundle of it.

"Fill your boots, mate," I said and the minotaur chomped down on it. While the minotaur was eating his fill, I turned to face James and Theo.

"... and breathe! The minotaur is tamed. All we have to do is get out of here now."

"I bet the minotaur knows the way out," said Theo.

He had a point. The minotaur scoffed the last of the grass and even licked my hands clean with its sloppy tongue.

"Good boy!" I said. "Clean plate."

And then I looked at my hands. They were empty. Entirely empty. "Ah."

"Problem?" said James.

"Don't know," I said. "It's eaten the pendant."

"Mr Minotaur," said Theo, "can you show us the way out?"

He didn't seem to understand. He was from ancient Greece and probably didn't understand English. Fortunately, I had recently returned from Crete and knew just what to do.

"Mr Mino-taur," I said in very slow and over-enunciated English and made little finger horns on my head. "Can you." I pointed at him. "Show us." I did a little searching and exploring mime. "The way out." I opened a pretend door. "Por favor s'il vous plait."

The Reynolds boys stared at me.

"Does that ever work?" said James.

The minotaur snorted and set off down the corridor and then turned to make sure we were following.

It took a little while and there were more twists and turns than I would have imagined possible but we eventually came to a rectangle of daylight and the upper gallery of the museum exhibition hall. Looking at it now, it was very obvious that we'd stepped over a border when we came into the painting and now all we had to do to get out was to step back into the world.

I turned and thanked the minotaur but he was already heading off, running towards the life-like (and indeed alive) fields of corn in a large impressionist painting.

"If only we could get everyone back into their paintings," I said.

The sea water was still rising. When it lapped the lower edge of a painting of wolves the whole pack came to life and bounded up the stairs. Magic touching magic. The paintings were bringing each other to life.

"Wolves," said Theo. "They can be dangerous."

"Said the boy who brought a dragon to life to fight some lions," I replied, and we wisely moved in the opposite direction. But the roaring and shrieking of tigers and elephants and whatever else remained downstairs seemed to excite the wolves and they turned toward us.

"In there! Quick!" said James and pointed at a door.

We dashed inside and closed the door. It was only then that I recognised Rex's office. There was a violent thump on the door as a wolf hurled itself against the wood.

"Hold the door!" said James and hauled a filing cabinet over to wedge against it.

Another thump. These were persistent wolves. We dragged dusty furniture across the room to strengthen our barricade. The wolves battered the door, we worked to keep them out and the frankly alarming electrical cabinet on the wall fizzed in time to our efforts. James and Theo pulled a tall cupboard away from the wall, dislodging a large painting that had been standing on the floor behind it.

It was a rubbish picture, just some grey rocks on a hillside.

James shoved the cupboard against the office door. I grabbed the painting to drag it over and saw the title plaque on the frame.

"That picture that went missing..." I said.

"*Zeus wakes on Mount Ida*?" said James.

"Can you show me a picture of it?"

"Now?"

Theo was tapping on his tablet and showed me the image. In a day of surprises, this one hit me like a slap round the chops.

"Is it important?" said James.

I looked at the sparking electrical cabinet on the wall. If a real electrical cabinet did that, someone would have fixed it by now. I rummaged through the top drawer of Rex's desk, found a set of keys and, prepared to have my socks blown off by an electric shock at any moment, opened the cabinet.

"What the –" gasped James.

"Is that?" said Theo.

"Zeus's thunderbolt?" I said. "Reckon so."

Inside was something that you might have thought was a wavy stick to support a houseplant if it wasn't for the fact that it glowed white hot like the business end of a sparkler. I reached out for it.

"Are you sure you should do that?" said James.

"If there's a mad choice or a normal choice" I said, and grasped it.

It vibrated violently in my hand like a, like a... well, like a vibrator. But, importantly, it didn't burn or zap me.

"So, Zeus appears and magics everything back to normal with his thunderbolt, huh?" I said.

"That's the general idea," said Theo.

I looked at it for a moment, wondering how it worked, but then the door exploded inwards. Surely the wolves hadn't done that? No. The foot that trampled through the remains of the wood was that of an elephant.

"What the hell?"

It was a tight fit to get a full-grown elephant through a doorway, but it was having a go.

"Do something!" yelled Theo.

"Bear with me," I said and I held the thunderbolt out on front of me. "Elephantus transformius!" I yelled. The elephant squidged, folded and then expanded and there was a fanged grizzly bear standing before us. This wasn't supposed to happen.

"Forget the Harry Potter stuff!" said James, edging away from the enormous predator. "Just say you want it back in the painting."

"Bear, into the painting!" I commanded.

The bear was sucked from the room with a dull pop. *Zeus wakes on Mount Ida* by Ravioli or whatever his name was now featured a bear prowling around the empty hillside.

I led the way out through the remains of our barricade and into the gallery again, blasting wolves and other random artistic oddities as we went.

"Back to your painting!"

"Back to art world, wolfy boy!"

"Begone, foul creature!"

By the time we were out on the upper level proper, I had cleared all creatures and ne'er-do-wells from the immediate area.

"We have the tools and we have the talent," I said triumphantly.

"Enough tomfoolery!" snapped Rex, storming along the corridor towards us. "Give that back!"

"Careful, Mr McCloud," said James. "You don't know what that is."

"Oh, he does," I said. "Theo, look at that picture on your tablet again."

Theo looked from the grey-bearded museum manager to his tablet and back again.

"Zeus?"

"Zeus?" said James.

"Brought to life from the painting," I said. "It didn't go missing. It was here all along. And, not long after, this weirdy-beardy turns up at the museum. Seriously, Rex, why would the king of the gods want a job in a museum?"

"I came here for some peace and quiet. A well-run museum and art gallery, a touchstone for my world without all the annoyances that come with it. I can balance the books and manage the staff. It's the closest I'm likely to come to a satisfying retirement. And then you came along with your crazed magic to unsettle it all. I wouldn't be surprised if one of the other Olympians sent that pendant to create merry hell for me."

"I bet it was Hera," said Theo.

Rex chuckled humourlessly. "Have you met my bloody wife?"

"But can you fix all this?" I said. "Can't you use your thunderbolt to do one of your *Daily sex Macarenas* and put it all back to normal and restore your peace and quiet?"

Rex crossed his arms and smirked. "As we might have expected, we have here a poorly worded question. The question is not whether I *can*. Of course, I can. It's whether I *will*."

This was classic Rex. Wait until you have an enormous emergency on your hands and then argue about sentence construction. My first, childish, instinct was to kick his shins for being so annoying, but I pushed the temptation aside. What would an adult do?

"Thank you for helping me to improve, Rex," I said with a smile so wide it made my face ache. "*Will* you make everything better with your god powers?"

"No," he said. "I can't expect you to understand the world I came from. Gods, goddesses, heroes and mortals. All so very... needy. None of them were interested in peace and stability. They'd just expect constant rescuing from their –"

"Tomfoolery?" I suggested.

307

"Yes!" he snapped. "Never-ending tomfoolery. I've had enough of helping them and I'm certainly not going to help you. If I make this mess better you will just go and create another one. I refuse to become part of that cycle. I'll make sure that the police know it was all your fault, and they can lock you up out of the way. The museum can rebuild from the insurance. That's my idea of a happy ending."

"I see," I said. "Then you leave me no alternative. I'll have to sort it out myself."

Rex scoffed.

"You? You're not a god. You barely qualify as human."

"Zeus's power is all locked up in his magic thunderbolt," said Theo.

"Pah!" said Rex. "A classic over-simplification. It is the nature of puny mortals to try and understand things that they are simply incapable of grasping. You are young, so it is perhaps to be expected. Children are so much more bearable when –"

A lightning blast caught him in the stomach and sent him sprawling across the floor.

"Seems easy enough," I said and pumped the thunderbolt like it was a shotgun, not because I needed to but because I wanted to.

"Is it wrong of me to say that was really sexy?" James whispered to me.

"Dad!" said Theo.

"Now's not the time," I said, giving James a cheeky grin. "We have work to do."

"But you can't!" bleated Rex from his position on the floor.

"I can. Handcuffs, begone!" The thunderbolt sputtered and my handcuffs exploded into fairy dust.

"But this is magic!" Rex squeaked. "The realm of the gods! You don't understand it!"

"Rex, I barely understand the real world."

"You're an idiot!"

I shrugged. "But I'm always willing to learn. Did you know that cows eat grass?"

"What?"

"I know!"

Chapter 42

"Perseus, come here please!" I shouted.

The wing-footed hunk arrived in less than a second.

"Can you please take Rex for a little fly around the city for half an hour while I decide what to do with him?" I asked.

"But, my lady, it is Zeus, first among the gods."

"I don't have a problem with that if you don't," I said.

Perseus used the hilt of his sword to smash the window, grabbed Rex around the waist and took off above the campus. We all heard a brief fading wail from Rex as he hurtled skywards.

"If he'd said, we could have just opened it," I said and pointed the thunderbolt. "Window, fix yourself, good as new."

It was reassembled in an instant. I grinned at James and Theo. "Let's go and fix everything else!"

Things got a whole lot easier when we found a catalogue of all the artwork. We made a good team. James and Theo would tell me which paintings things were supposed to be in, and I would command them back there. Getting rid of the flood water made our work a lot easier. Once I'd put the French warships back in their painting I decided to put the horrible serpent in there with them, as a thank you present to Perseus. I rather liked the end result. A pair of Napoleonic warships, cannons firing, with a huge sea monster writhing in the storm-tossed sea between them.

The satyrs had come from a painting where some sort of enormous party was going on. When I looked a little more closely at the picture in the catalogue entry, it looked like some ladies out for a nice naked swim who were being ogled by these frisky goat men. I decided to put the flying baby in there with them. He might take their minds off sex with his volleys of arrows. What was I saying? That flying baby was Eros. It looked as though it was going to be a hell of a party.

I found the minotaur still gambolling through the fields of impressionist corn. I don't know if the impressionists went in for minotaurs but I decided to leave him there. He deserved a bit of happiness.

Perseus returned with Rex when we'd nearly finished. I'd already chosen a spot for Rex. The elephant had originally come from a painting of a Victorian menagerie. By modern standards, I'm not sure that the animals were getting the best possible care. They needed organising, and Rex was just the man for the job.

Perseus set him down, and he staggered queasily to a nearby chair.

"Travel sick from your aerial tour of the city, Rex?" I asked.

Before he could answer, I zapped him into the menagerie painting. He didn't look all that thrilled, but he did look like a man who would make sure the monkey's cage got mucked out.

Perseus was very happy to get back to the naked redhead in his painting. I couldn't blame him for that. Perhaps they stood a chance of getting to know each other better now there wasn't a giant sea serpent spoiling their fun.

"She's called Andromeda," said James. "They're destined to get married."

"I do like a happy ending," I said.

We stepped outside into the campus. Some of the art chaos had spilled outside. A few satyrs and miscellaneous mythical mites were on the loose but a couple of thunderbolt spells sent them packing. There were, of course, dozens of sea-soggy, bedraggled and befuddled open day visitors staggering about.

"You think that thing can do a magical mindwipe?" said James.

I considered the thunderbolt, still fizzing in my hand. It was probably up to the job.

"No," I said.

"No?"

"I think everyone deserves a little wonder in their life."

James laughed at that and it almost veered away into hysteria but he managed to bring it under control.

"You are mad, Lori Belkin."

I didn't reply. Such a statement didn't need a reply but, also, my attention was caught by a trio of figures in the shade of a nearby tree. It was my parents with Cookie.

"I've got to talk to them," I said and headed over.

All the times I'd fantasised about tracking down my parents, I'd imagined that I'd easily spot them from afar and run to them in slow motion and they'd run to me and there'd be kisses and apologies all round. But, I was tired, it had been a long day and, I guess, we were going to do this thing like adults.

"Hey, guys," I said.

Dad – my lovely dad in his outdoorsy gear that actually looked like it had had some use recently – mouthed something and pointed in confusion at the museum building.

"CGI interactive presentations," I said. "Quite intense, huh?"

"But I got my boots wet," he said.

"4-D cinema: wind, waves, the lot." I put my hands on my hips and did my best to phrase an angry rebuke at them running off and leaving me homeless – sort of homeless – but I had neither the energy nor the anger. I grabbed the pair of them and hugged them until it hurt. "I've missed you," I said.

"And we you, sunbeam," said Dad.

"You've been so busy sweetheart," said Mom. "Melissa's been telling us about all of the interesting things you've been doing."

It would have been really handy to know what they'd talked about. My parents would have received a highly edited version of recent events, but Cookie's edits wouldn't necessarily match mine.

"Interesting, yes. That's one way of putting it," I said carefully. "And where have you two been hiding?"

"We've been volunteering on farms around Devon, Cornwall and Wales. Building stone walls and so on."

I tried to imagine the scene, but for some reason the picture in my head was of them both wearing slippers and sitting inside, watching television. Now I looked properly and saw that they were toned and brown. They looked incredibly healthy. Mom had stopped dyeing her hair and she looked happier than I ever recalled.

"You've been travelling round then?" I said. "Cookie, how on earth did you find them?"

"'Living with Druids in 21st Century Cornwall'."

"Pardon?"

"The YouTube video. Among all those crusties, new agers and other wonderful folk, I saw two faces I recognised. Hopped in the car and drove down to find them. Been driving all night. I only

311

stayed long enough to make a stirring speech about how parents need to listen to the subtle vibrations of the universe when it tells them to get in touch with their kids."

"The subtle vibrations of the universe being a madwoman who's driven hundreds of miles to make the point?" I ventured.

"Yes. I think Elena might have picked up on the hint as well. I made a few suggestions about the wonders of technology for keeping in contact, even when you're hell-bent on seeing the world."

"That's..." I shook my head and remembered who was with me. I gestured to James and Theo who were standing behind me. "Mom, Dad, this is my friend James and his son, Theo. They've been a great help to me while I've, you know, been sorting things out."

There was a lot of polite handshaking. One minute we'd been wrangling monsters from beyond the dawn of history and the next we were making dinner table small talk.

"Miss Belkin!"

"And this," I said to my parents, "is Sergeant Fenton. She thinks I murdered Adam."

Sergeant Fenton looked as though she'd had a pretty rough day as well. She was soaked with sea water and her hair was plastered wetly against her head.

"Adam's not dead, he's just abroad," said Mom. "We only spoke to him this morning on the satellite phone."

"Well obviously, I'd be delighted to clear this up, if we could prove that he is unharmed," said Sergeant Fenton but Mom was already hitting the buttons on the phone.

"Adam," said Mom. "Adam, dear. Yes. Yes, I know. I've got a police lady here who'd like to talk to you. Yes. No, don't be such a diva darling, we're just trying to sort this out."

Mom passed the phone to Sergeant Fenton with a 'don't mess with my children' glint in her eye. Sergeant Fenton took it politely.

"Mr Belkin? Mr Adam Belkin?"

Sergeant Fenton walked away a distance to take the call.

"So, are you staying long?" I said.

Mom and Dad looked at each other.

"You could stay at Adam's flat," I said. "I could find somewhere else to crash for a few nights," I added with a look at James.

"We wouldn't want to impose," said Dad.

"We could just park the camper van outside," said Mom.

"Camper van?" I said. "You live in a camper van?"

"We love it," said Dad.

"Every day a new vista," said Mom.

"But all that money you'd sunk into the house," I said. "All those things you said about investing in bricks and mortar."

"Ah," said Dad, wistfully, "you see, the thing about the property ladder..."

"Yes?"

"Vastly overrated. We only thought it was important because our parents told us it was."

Chapter 43

We dined at Adam's flat. My parents, Cookie, James and me.

Mom inspected the flat while I tidied away the main course I had cooked: sausages with onion gravy. It was clear the someone had given her a litany of concerns and accusations but she could find no evidence of any damage or wrongdoing. She narrowed her eyes at the new artwork on the chimney breast but that apparently passed muster.

"Well, I'm surprised, Lori," she said. "The place looks wonderful. The policewoman made it sound as though you'd messed the place up quite a bit. The strange painting you've done there on the wall actually looks pretty good."

I grinned proudly.

"'Strange painting,'" said James with an arch expression and a waggle of his sexy eyebrows.

"It's a compliment," I told him.

"It's odd," said Mom.

"Okay, less of a compliment now," I said.

"No, this rug," she said. "It's odd. I'm sure the last time we were here it had a little hole in the edge where it got caught in the vacuum cleaner. And this floor doesn't have a dent in it anymore either. Remember, where Adam dropped a suitcase?"

"Not really, dear," said Dad.

After all of the hard work I'd put into the cleaning, I'd used a tiny bit of thunderbolt magic to fix up the ruined flooring and restore the rug. I made sure that my smile didn't slip and just kept silent.

Despite the offer to camp on the doorstep, I let my parents have use of Adam's flat. After Cookie's intriguing attempts at dessert – polenta and wild apple soufflé – we left them to enjoy a night in a real bed and the rest of us walked home.

As we neared the local community centre by the church, Cookie hitched her thumb down a side road. "I'm heading down this way."

"You don't live in that direction," I said.

She gave me a salacious wink. "You two crazy lovebirds, I know when the universe needs me to travel my own path."

"Yeah, but that street's a dead end," said James.

"Yeah, but is it?" said Cookie.

"It is."

"Yeah, but is it? Or is it your attitude that's a dead end?"

"It's the road. I'm fairly sure."

Cookie stood on one leg, spun round and went her own special way.

We carried on. James linked arms with me and I thrilled at his closeness.

We passed the community centre. A group of pensioners stood outside. They were the same ones that I'd seen spinning around the lamp post yesterday. They all wore purple t-shirts and I squinted, trying to read what it said on the back. They were doing creaky squats and lunges, as though they'd been exercising.

"What does it say on those t-shirts?" I asked James.

He looked. "It says *Ashbert's Golden Years Parkour Academy*," he said.

I let the words sink in. Ashbert's new venture looked popular. More people, old and young, were pressing through the doors of the community hall. As we reached the doors we could hear people talking.

"Such a nice young man. He's done all of the little jobs around my garden that I can't get to anymore."

"He's been a godsend. When he does the shopping, it's bang-on. Gets the bargains, he does."

"Brought him a little present that I've knitted for him."

We stopped and looked through a window. Ashbert, my one-time perfect man, was there with his adoring pensioner army. He was smiling and chatting with them all. On the table behind him was a stack of white cards, many with red ticks over them. White cards, sort of postcard size, the sort you sometimes see in a newsagent's window.

"Help others. Help yourself," I murmured to myself.

"What's that?" said James.

"Something I said." I shook my head, smiling. "Whatever you do, make yourself happy."

"Sounds like a plan," said James. "So, Uncle Phil and Theo are out at the Jaguar owner's club together and won't be back until much later."

"Oh?" I said.

"Maybe we can find something to do to *entertain* ourselves when we get back to my place."

"That would be nice," I said.

"*Nice*?" he asked. "Is that the best word you can come up with?"

I turned to him. "What word would you use?"

He thought for a moment. "Exciting."

"Exciting." I was looking forward to some excitement. I let my fingers drift across the tweedy roughness of his jacket. "Something exciting. Something raunchy."

"Raunchy? I really do hope so," he said. "So, something exciting, something raunchy, something... magical."

I thought briefly of the thunderbolt which was safely shut away in a suitcase under my bed in Adam's flat.

A distant shout came from over the rooftops. "It's a bloody dead end!"

Grinning to ourselves, laughing like secretive teenagers, we hurried on.

317

The Authors

Heide Goody and Iain Grant are married, but not to each other. Heide lives in North Warwickshire with her husband and children. Iain lives in south Birmingham with his wife and children.

Printed in Great Britain
by Amazon